A
THUNDER
OF
WAR

ALSO BY STEVE McHUGH

The Hellequin Chronicles

Crimes Against Magic

Born of Hatred

With Silent Screams

Prison of Hope

Lies Ripped Open

Promise of Wrath

Scorched Shadows

Infamous Reign

The Avalon Chronicles

A Glimmer of Hope

A Flicker of Steel

A
THUNDER
OF
WAR

STEVE McHUGH

47NORTH

Text copyright © 2018 by Steve McHugh
All rights reserved.

Published by 47North, Seattle

www.apub.com

Amazon, the Amazon logo, and 47North are trademarks of Amazon.com, Inc., or its affiliates.

ISBN-13: 9781542047043
ISBN-10: 1542047048

Cover design by @blacksheep-uk.com

Cover illustration by Larry Rostant

Printed in the United States of America

For Elaine

LIST OF CHARACTERS

Layla: Friends and Family

Layla Cassidy – Umbra.

Rosa, Gyda, and Servius – Spirits. Bonded with Layla.

Terhal – Drenik. Bonded with Layla, and the source of her power.

Chloe Range – Umbra. Layla's best friend.

Harry Gao – Human. One of Layla's best friends.

Caleb Cassidy – Umbra. Serial killer. Father of Layla. Husband to Elizabeth.

The Rebellion

Zamek – Dwarf. Warrior commander.

Tarron – Shadow Elf. Possibly the last of his kind.

Dralas – Flame Giant. Friends with Tarron.

Diana – Half-werebear. One-time Roman goddess.

Nabu – Och. Mesopotamian god of wisdom.

Tommy Carpenter – Werewolf. Father of Kase. Husband of Olivia.

Olivia Carpenter – Ice Elemental. Mother of Kase. Wife of Tommy.

Lucifer – Sorcerer. One of the devils created thousands of years ago to be living weapons.

Sky (Mapiya) – Necromancer. Half Native American. Adopted by Hades and Persephone.

Hades – Necromancer. One of the Rebellion leaders. One-time Greek god.

Persephone – Earth Elemental. One of the Rebellion leaders. One-time Greek goddess.

The Rebellion – Mordred's Story

Irkalla – Necromancer. Mesopotamian goddess of the underworld.

Mordred – Sorcerer. Assassin. Warrior. Video-game enthusiast.

Kase Carpenter – Werewolf/Ice Elemental. Daughter of Olivia and Tommy.

Remy Roax – British son of a French aristocrat. Turned into a fox-human hybrid by a witch coven.

Charon – Ferryman for Tartarus. Member of the Titans.

Lorin – Griffin. One of the guards of Tartarus.

Hyperion – Dragon-kin. Member of the Titans.

Shadow Falls

Leonardo – Alchemist. Partner of Antonio. Tinkerer and inventor.

Antonio – Alchemist. Partner of Leonardo. Leonardo's assistant.

Caitlin Moore – Alchemist. Daughter to Galahad. One-time FBI agent.

Hel – Necromancer. Leader of the realm of Helheim.

Avalon

Abaddon – Necromancer. One of the devils created thousands of years ago to be living weapons.

Mammon – Dragon. One of the devils created thousands of years ago to be living weapons.

Elizabeth Cassidy – Umbra. Mother of Layla. Wife of Caleb.

Orcus – Necromancer.

Enyo – Blood magic sorcerer.

Miscellaneous

Vorisbo – Dwarf. Warrior and scientist.

Nidhogg – Dragon.

Cassandra, Grace, Ivy – The three Fates of myth.

Modgud – Giant.

Jomik Rakreas – Dwarf. Warrior and elder.

Bera – Psychic. Soldier. Works for Hel.

1

LAYLA CASSIDY

It was meant to be an easy mission for Layla Cassidy and her team. Get into the realm of Norumbega, move her team to the prison where Mammon's frozen body was being kept, and, after retrieving the body, get out again without any trouble.

The mission had not gone entirely to plan.

"Well, this sucks balls," Remy said as he sat up against a large tree. He was three-and-a-half feet tall, and part man, part red fox. He stood on legs that were more human than animal, but his entire body—from the tip of his bushy tail to his fox muzzle—was covered in fur. Remy had crossed a witch's coven several centuries earlier and they'd decided to kill him by turning him into a fox and handing him over to a hunt master. The spell had gone wrong. It had turned him into a fox, but only partially, and it had also killed all twelve witches and deposited their souls in his body, essentially giving him twelve lives. Last Layla knew, he was on life eight.

Beside him, Layla nodded. "It's not been our best day ever."

The team had gotten into Norumbega without a hitch. Felicia Hales, a powerful vampire who lived in New York, arranged for them all to go through the realm gate and meet up with Mayor Issac Eire. Unfortunately that was where the good news ended. Issac's people turned on him, revealing that they'd been working with Avalon all along. They killed anyone who tried to stop them, and Layla's team were given the choice either to cease fighting, or watch more innocent people in Norumbega die. They chose the former.

The team had been taken to the prison that was their original target and put beneath the trees at the edge of the massive clearing in front of it. The ground was hard and cold with snow still covering large parts of it. Layla was grateful for the warm clothes she'd put on before coming. Her team wore thick jackets over their leather combat armor, with dwarven runes scribed on them. None of them were impervious to the cold, although Remy's fur probably meant he needed fewer clothes than most, but the runes on the armor meant they wouldn't freeze to death.

"At least we're not tied up," Harry said. "You'd think that, considering I'm the only human here, they'd be a little more concerned with the fact that you could actually kill them."

"That's why," Chloe said, pointing to ten townspeople kneeling at the opposite side of the clearing. Each one had an Avalon soldier behind them. If any of Layla's team made a move, they would die.

Harry turned toward the frightened men and women. "I didn't see them. Shit."

Layla looked over at the prison and caught Zamek—one of the last remaining Norse dwarves—staring at it. "What's up?" she asked him.

"They're trying to get inside," Zamek said, pointing to half a dozen people attempting to force the massive metal doors apart. He was shorter than Layla's own five-foot-four height, although not by too much as he was just under five feet tall himself, but he was broad. To Layla's mind he was his own wall. Short, muscular, and unmovable unless he wanted to be moved. He was stronger, faster, and could heal more quickly than a human. Like all dwarves, Zamek was also an alchemist, able to alter the shape of natural matter so long as he had physical contact with whatever he wanted to change. Zamek's long, brown beard was plaited with various colored beads, and, aside from a long, plaited ponytail, his head was shaved.

The prison itself was huge with fifty-foot white columns outside the front entrance and massive glass domes atop several parts of the roof. Built into the side of the mountain, there was no telling how far into the rocks the gray and white stone building went, or how deep it was.

"So, why are we still alive?" Mordred asked.

Everyone turned to Mordred.

"Seriously?" Irkalla replied. "That's your big wonder?"

"Well, they've captured us, and we went quietly to spare more innocent blood from being spilled, but if they can get in there and get Mammon, why are we here still? What purpose do we serve?"

"They can't get in there," Zamek said. "Not unless they happen to have a dwarf working for them. That's dwarven architecture filled with runes. And I placed my own runes on top of those. They manage to get that door open and everyone in a fifty-foot radius is going to be turned to ash."

Layla mentally calculated the distance between the prison and her and found that she was okay. "Not to mention the giant," she said.

"There's a giant?" Harry asked. "Why is this the first time anyone has mentioned a giant?"

The flame giant had been a surprise when, six months ago, Layla and several allies had chased Kristin to Norumbega. They'd stopped her from freeing Mammon, but she'd woken the flame giant before they could get there, and Layla had been forced to drop an avalanche on him. After dropping the avalanche, the group had dragged him back into the prison, and Zamek had reapplied the dwarven runes. It was not a scenario she wished to repeat anytime soon.

"Sorry, there's a flame giant inside," Remy said. "There, now you're caught up."

The team watched as the Avalon soldiers gave up on the door, and two of them grabbed a beaten and bloody Mayor Eire and dragged him over to the group, dropping him on the ground next to Chloe.

"You make me wish that guns could be taken through realm gates," Remy said. "Or tanks."

The man smiled and patted the two custom-made black swords that hung sheathed from his hip. "These are fine weapons, little fox-man. I think I'll use them to skin you with when I'm done here."

"Good luck with that," Remy said, flicking him the middle finger.

"Drako," Mordred said. "What do you want?"

"Kim and I are becoming impatient at our inability to get into the prison. You will help us."

Layla looked between Drako and Kim. Drako was the taller of the two, with a bald head and scarring over his nose that looked like someone had slashed him with a claw. Kim had short, dark hair, and tattoos around her exposed neck. Both wore combat armor and used bladed weapons. Guns and ammunition didn't always survive the travel between realms and had a tendency to explode after making the trip.

"You give me my ax back, and I'll help," Zamek said, pointing to the double-edged battle-ax Kim carried in one hand.

While everyone in the team had been disarmed, only Zamek and Remy had any emotional attachments to the weapons they'd lost. Layla looked down at her metal arm and wondered whether she could turn it into a sword and run Kim through before the innocent people across from them died. No, she decided, there had to be another way.

Drako waved to the soldiers by the hostages, and two innocent people lost their lives.

"No," Irkalla shouted, moving to stand, but she was kicked back down by Kim.

"You want more to die?" Kim asked, a slight sneer to her voice.

"I open that door and a flame giant is going to come out," Zamek said.

4

The concerned glance between Drako and Kim didn't go unnoticed, but Drako shrugged. "We'll deal with that when it happens."

"You have fifteen armed people here," Mordred said. "I'm pretty sure the giant will get a few of you before you stop it. Simple numbers. There's more of you than there were when it last woke up. And it might not be happy to see us again."

"Then you'll have to deal with it," Kim snapped.

Drako tapped his colleague on the shoulder, and she turned as Abaddon entered the clearing. She was of average height with brown skin and long, plaited brown hair that touched her waist. She wore black combat armor that looked more military in design than any of Layla's team. Like everyone else who worked for her, she wore a small wooden bracelet with runes carved into it. Layla had no idea what they were for, but she was certain it wasn't good.

"Devils don't feel the cold, I assume?" Zamek asked as Abaddon reached them.

She looked down at her lack of jacket and smiled. "No, extremes of weather aren't something I'm concerned with. But I think that's a conversation for a time when we're not on the clock."

"We're not getting Mammon for you," Irkalla said. "You might as well just kill us all and be done with it."

"Not quite what I had in mind," Remy said.

Abaddon picked up the mayor by his hair and slit his throat. The white snow quickly turned red as his body was pushed onto the ground. Abaddon put her boot on his back. "Silver dagger," Abaddon said, absentmindedly cleaning the blade on Drako's sleeve. "The mayor is dead. Very sad. I will go back into town and pick every child under the age of eight and butcher them all. Want to rethink your position?"

"As we tried to explain to your friends here, there's a flame giant in there," Layla said.

"How's the hand?" Abaddon asked Layla.

Layla flipped her the middle finger of her metal hand. "Works okay."

Abaddon laughed. "You've gotten harder than last time we met. It wasn't that long ago, was it?"

"Where's Elizabeth?" Layla asked, hoping that the longer she could keep Abaddon talking, the more time they had to come up with a good enough plan to get away without more people being killed.

"Your mother is murdering people who deserve it. She's quite good at her job. I have plans for this realm, and you're getting front-row seats to see them come to life."

Layla knew that Elizabeth was not really her mother. Not anymore. Her mother had died in a car crash years earlier. But Abaddon had forced Elizabeth's spirit back into her broken body, and then forced her to become an umbra, utterly fracturing her mind and allowing the drenik in the spirit scroll to take permanent control. Elizabeth was a killing machine, someone who lived for violence and bloodshed. She reveled in it. It was one of many reasons why Layla wanted to kill Abaddon, even if she wasn't sure it was possible.

"Hey, crazy," Remy said. "How's tricks?"

Kim kicked Remy in the chest, sending him sprawling to the ground. "Disgusting half-breed creature."

"I like her," Remy said, receiving another kick for his trouble.

"If she does that again, I will kill her," Mordred said. His words were spoken very matter-of-factly, and Kim froze mid-strike.

"The great Mordred," Abaddon said with mock applause. "You finally regained your faculties. I did enjoy ripping your mind apart day after day. Baldr, Arthur, even your own brother, Gawain, got involved. It was a lot of fun."

Mordred stared at Abaddon for several seconds. His expression was completely calm, but Layla knew he would have tried to kill Abaddon right there and then if he'd been able to.

"You murdered my friend," Irkalla said.

"Probably lots of them. Which one in particular?"

"Nathan Garrett."

Abaddon almost flinched at the name. "He killed Ares, Helios, and Deimos. He didn't submit to the methods we used to turn him to our side, so he had to die. The funny thing is, I don't even know where his body is. Just in a field somewhere. Did you weep for him, Irkalla? Did you weep for Nergal? He was your husband, after all."

"Ex-husband," Irkalla corrected.

"This little catch-up was nice, but you're going to retrieve my brother now. Drako and Kim will accompany you into the prison."

"All of us go," Layla said. "If that flame giant wakes up, whoever goes in there is going to have to fight. And we don't even know where your brother is."

Abaddon clicked her fingers and a soldier walked over, passing her a scroll, which she gave to Layla. Layla unrolled it, revealing a map of the prison interior.

"How did you get this?" Zamek asked.

"Is this really the time for your questions?" Abaddon asked him. "I've written where Mammon is being kept. Retrieve him. Now."

Layla slipped a tiny hypodermic needle into Zamek's hand, and he nodded. "I'll be back soon. Irkalla is coming with me," he told Abaddon. "Shockingly, I don't trust your people."

"Fine. The rest of you get comfortable," Abaddon said. "Once Mammon is back, I don't want anyone to miss the show."

They were left alone as Drako and Kim escorted Zamek and Irkalla to the prison. Zamek opened the prison doors, and they went inside. Abaddon spoke to her soldiers by the entrance before walking off into the nearby forest.

"What is going on?" Chloe asked.

"You noticed the bracelets?" Mordred asked.

7

"They look like sorcerer's bands," Harry said. "Except they can't be, because they're all wearing them, and I've seen several of them use their powers."

Sorcerer's bands stopped the wearer from accessing their power. Layla had worn one on occasion, although never by choice. She hoped never to wear one again. They essentially turned even the most powerful being into something no more resilient than an ordinary human.

"Let's ask," Remy said. "Hey, numbnuts," he shouted to the nearest guard.

The woman looked confused for a moment, before her expression became irritated and she walked over. "You shout out again and I'll have your tongue," she told Remy.

"Sure. Hey, Abaddon said you guys were all going to do something awful here, and you have to wear those bracelets so it doesn't affect you, but you do know that the runes on them are wrong, yes?"

"What?" the woman asked, slightly concerned.

"Yeah, that's not a dwarven rune," Harry said. "It's just a squiggle. I've noticed it on some but not on others."

The woman looked genuinely concerned and walked over to talk to another soldier. Layla watched the pair look at each other's bracelets. They in turn went on to another one.

"They don't trust Abaddon," Mordred said.

"She's not exactly shy about wasting lives," Chloe said.

Over by the prison, Abaddon had returned from the forest and was giving orders for the remaining hostages to be taken away.

The soldier walked over to Layla's group and hit Remy in the side of the jaw, knocking him to the ground. "Next time you think to sow dissent between us, I'll kill you myself."

"Why don't you trust Abaddon?" Layla asked.

The soldier stepped toward Layla, who got to her feet.

"You punch me, I'll take your hand, and then your life," Layla told her, her voice utterly calm and devoid of anything that suggested she

8

was lying. "Your leverage just walked away, so what are you going to do, exactly?"

The soldier considered her options. Layla was pretty sure that her reputation as a fighter had drifted to Abaddon's soldiers. The last six months had been hard on Layla, and she in turn had become harder. She knew she was still capable of laughing and joking with her friends—when she saw them—but in a fight, she no longer second-guessed herself. She'd had excellent teachers, and she knew without hesitation that she would take the soldier's hand off. There were nearly thirty soldiers in the clearing, and Layla wasn't certain that her group would be able to take them all, but the woman in front of her would die. She would make sure of it.

The soldier took a step back, then turned and walked away, allowing Layla to sit down again.

"You okay?" Layla asked Remy who rubbed his jaw.

"Yeah, you?"

"It's been a long day," Layla said.

"It's about to get longer," Harry said, pointing to the entrance of the prison as Zamek emerged with Irkalla followed by two soldiers carrying an unconscious Mammon.

Mammon was a huge man. At nearly seven feet tall with a short, black beard and long, dark hair that fell freely over his shoulders, he cut an imposing figure. He wore red robes that were emblazoned with dozens of runes.

"I don't think they can remove the robes," Harry said.

Abaddon and Zamek argued, and she motioned for her soldiers to retrieve Layla and the rest of the team.

Zamek walked out in front of them, striding across the clearing toward the group. "Abaddon wants us all together."

"When it all goes to shit, get inside the prison," Mordred said. "Move fast, don't stop."

"What about the prisoners in the realm?" Harry asked.

9

"They're dead," Zamek said softly. "Drako was bragging about how we'll get to see some new weapon they have. Apparently the death of everyone in this realm is just the start. Those bracelets protect them from the effect, or something like that. I've seen similar runes before."

"Hurry the hell up," Drako shouted.

Zamek made a big deal about helping Harry to his feet. "He's only human," he said.

They walked over to Abaddon, where they were forced back to the ground at sword-point.

"My brother," Abaddon said in a loving tone. "Once the others are reunited, we will kill Lucifer for betraying us, and then Asmodeus will be without equal."

"You mean Arthur?" Mordred asked. "I know you used Asmodeus's spirit and power to ensure Arthur was conceived, but you don't really think Arthur and Asmodeus are one and the same, do you?"

Abaddon went to strike Mordred, but stopped. "We will crush you all," she whispered, lips curling in anger. "Arthur and Avalon are, at this exact moment in time, on their way to Greenland to destroy your little rebellion. They'll break your leaders and kill everyone else. You're all done."

Fear filled Layla. Her friends, people she loved and cared for, were still in Greenland. They had to warn them somehow, had to get out of the realm. She forced herself to be calm. Hopefully Avalon hadn't started their attack yet and they still had time. The fact that time moved slower in Norumbega than it did on the Earth realm might work in their favor.

"So, this whole thing was a setup?" Layla asked.

Abaddon nodded. "I was advised not to open the prison while there were dwarven runes on it. No one was sure what they did since it's ancient dwarven we're talking about. I knew that eventually you'd send your expert here to get Mammon out—he's too dangerous to let loose, although I didn't expect him to be so placid."

Layla knew that Zamek had managed to inject Mammon with the syringe she'd given him. It had been made by Persephone and Hades to ensure that Mammon stayed quiet for long enough to get him out of the realm.

"And Felicia?" Mordred asked.

"Felicia's people have worked for me for some time now, so it wasn't hard to make them realize that I am the person they need to back. Felicia is dead, by the way."

The news caused anger to bubble up inside Layla. She'd liked Felicia. Abaddon and her people would pay for what they'd done.

"No one wants to be on the losing side," Remy said. "Especially not people who sell their allegiances."

Drako tried to kick Remy, but he leapt on him and drew one of the blades out of his belt as he scrambled up his torso. Drako screamed as Remy drove the sword into his throat. With one hand still on the hilt of the sword, he vaulted up onto his head, dragging the sword out as he went. Remy dropped to the ground and removed the second blade from Drako's belt.

Blood poured from Drako's wound as Remy kept moving. He ducked Kim's blade and got close enough to drag Zamek's ax free and toss it to the dwarf, who was already running toward them. Zamek caught the ax in midair and changed direction at the last moment, driving it toward Abaddon, who blasted him in the chest with her necromancy power.

Dozens of soldiers attacked the group, and blood magic poured out of Kim's hands, smashing into Harry before he could avoid it. Chloe dragged him away toward the prison entrance as he screamed in pain. Irkalla tackled Kim to the ground, punching her in the face, before rolling off her and running up the steps to the doors.

Mordred blasted Abaddon in the chest with a torrent of air before she could do anything to aid her soldiers. Layla was blocked from getting to the prison by the soldier who had threatened to hit her. The soldier drew a curved knife, and Layla's metal arm instantly changed shape into a broadsword. She drove the blade up toward the soldier's chest, causing the woman to dodge back briefly before darting forward with her dagger. Layla moved to the side and grabbed the silver blade, absorbing the metal into her limb. The silver content in the blade caused her a modicum of irritation as it merged with the titanium and steel of her arm; it felt as though she were holding hot rocks. She swiped her arm-blade across the soldier's chest, bypassing the runes on the armor, cutting through the leather as if it wasn't even there, and killing her.

Layla avoided a blade-swipe from a second soldier as Mordred shouted at her to hurry. He'd created a shield of dense air that he was using to keep people back, but it wouldn't last forever. Magical power was being flung around the clearing with reckless aplomb by those few soldiers who were sorcerers, and while Mordred was one of the strongest sorcerers the world had ever seen, his power was not infinite.

Layla ran up the stairs with Irkalla behind her, and a few seconds later Zamek and Chloe shut the doors. Killing Drako and getting everyone into the prison had taken moments, but to Layla it had felt like a lifetime. And yet they still weren't safe.

2

LAYLA CASSIDY

"You know when I said earlier that this hadn't gone to plan?" Layla said. "Well, this isn't much better."

"Can they get in here?" Mordred asked Zamek.

Zamek was busy placing dwarven runes onto the doors and took a few seconds to answer. "No, but we can't leave this way, either. And not just because of the number of people who want us dead."

There were loud thuds against the door as those outside tried to get at the group, but they didn't last long.

"All of those people in this realm," Harry said. "What'll happen to them?"

"They're due to die," Irkalla said. "I took Drako's spirit as he died. I wanted some information on their plan. Don't know it all, but they have a weapon. Abaddon calls it a realm-killer. Anyone not wearing those bracelet devices loses their abilities. It's why they didn't put any sorcerer's bands on us. The normal band is too close in nature to the new one they've designed. It does funny things to people who wear it while the weapon is active."

"And what does the weapon do?" Chloe asked.

"Drako wasn't really sure. Just that it kills everyone inside the markings, and their deaths create some kind of power-killing mist. I think Elizabeth's job was to round up everyone in the nearby city and use them to create it."

"They're going to kill everyone here as a weapon test?" Chloe asked. Irkalla nodded.

"We can't help them, can we?" Harry asked.

"No," Layla said. "Right now we can't even help ourselves."

"So, Zamek," Remy said. "Any reason why you had us run in here?"

"When Abaddon's people brought me in, I managed to convince them that they should let me go down toward Mammon first, just in case something exploded and killed them all. I had a quick search around and found a realm gate."

That got everyone's attention.

"Why do I sense there's a but coming?" Mordred asked.

"It's not working," Zamek said. "It's not even completed. There are pieces missing, and the dwarven writing doesn't go all the way around."

"Meaning what?" Chloe asked.

"There's no final destination on it," Zamek said.

"So it doesn't work?" Mordred asked.

"No idea," Zamek said. "We need to go take a look."

An almighty boom echoed around the large, empty chamber as something hard hit the doors of the prison.

"You sure those runes will hold?" Irkalla asked.

Zamek looked over at the door. "The last time we were here, Kristin managed to open the door by destroying one of the runes. She'd been told exactly which rune to break, and how to do it, but not how to do it so she could get inside without waking up a flame giant. I've made some modifications. Eventually, with enough power thrown at it, the rune will break and incinerate anyone within a hundred feet of it."

"Even so, let's not be here," Mordred said.

"Can you hear me?" Abaddon's voice asked.

"How is she doing that?" Layla asked, not really aiming the question at anyone in particular.

"The doors have a slight gap between them at the top and bottom. It was hastily done work," Zamek said. "The runes will stop them getting in, but not stop the sound of their voices."

"I'm sorry, we don't want any," Remy shouted. "We rent."

"What?" Abaddon replied.

"Whatever you're selling," Remy said. "Our landlord won't let us renovate the place."

"Do you know who this is?" Abaddon shouted again, seemingly confused by the topic of conversation.

"You're not the loft insulation people?" Remy replied.

"Do you think this is funny?" Abaddon shouted, following up with a noise that sounded like her striking the door.

"Little bit, yes," Remy told her.

"I'm going to head to Greenland and help butcher your friends," Abaddon shouted. "Each of them will die knowing your cleverness is what ensured that their deaths were long and painful. You can't leave, and we can't get in. You're trapped. Enjoy a slow death."

"We need to warn everyone," Chloe said, giving words to Layla's thoughts.

"You all alive in there?" Abaddon called out.

"Are you still there?" Mordred asked. "Do you not have a home to go to?"

"Enjoy the next few thousand years," Abaddon continued as if Mordred hadn't spoken. "Maybe I'll let you all out then, and show you the new world we've created."

"Just piss off and die already," Remy shouted. "You hoofwanking cockwomble."

There was one final bang against the doors and everything went quiet.

"Hoofwanking cockwomble?" Mordred asked. "I like that."

"It's certainly inventive," Irkalla said.

"Dwarves don't have swear words like that," Zamek said. "I've learned so much since being here."

"Let's get out of here," Mordred said, and no one disagreed.

The group headed toward a large archway at the far end of the room. When they reached it, dozens of torches in the room beyond immediately sparked to life. A spiral staircase led up into the glass-domed ceiling and down into the ground, although everyone was watching the giant asleep at the far end of the room. Its skin flickered orange and red.

"That's the giant, yes?" Mordred asked.

"What do you think?" Remy asked, incredulous.

"Just checking," Mordred said. "He's smaller than I expected."

"The eldjötnar, like all Norse giants, can change size," Zamek said. The eight-foot-tall giant looked almost peaceful, and he was considerably smaller than the twenty-foot-tall behemoth that Layla and co. had fought only a few months earlier.

"I've never met one before," Mordred said. "He has runes painted on him." He pointed to the black marks on the giant's arms.

"I didn't notice them last time," Layla said.

"We were a bit busy trying not to be killed by it," Remy pointed out.

"Why hasn't it woken up yet?" Chloe asked.

"Seriously?" Harry asked. "Are you trying to jinx us?"

Chloe shrugged.

Zamek took a step forward and stopped. "The runes in this place, they're made to keep the occupants asleep." He crouched and placed his hand on the smooth floor. "That umbra clone who came here before, she had no regard for the runes and broke them when she entered the prison. I kept them intact. He will not wake. I already looked for runes that might nullify our powers, and there don't appear to be any. I don't think it was designed to nullify anything, because everyone was meant to be essentially in stasis."

"Like Mammon?"

Zamek nodded.

No one asked Zamek if he was sure—no one needed to.

"Okay, so where to now?" Irkalla asked.

"Down below," Zamek said, pointing to the staircase.

Layla took a step forward, and the giant groaned.

Everyone froze. No one made any sound.

The giant groaned again and rolled over, revealing its straw bed. It was facing away from the team, but no one dared do anything that would make a noise. A second later the giant coughed, spluttered, and said something in a language that Layla didn't understand. The group tiptoed behind the archway, making as little sound as possible.

Layla peered around the archway, watching as the giant sat up and scratched its head.

"I don't want to fight that," Mordred whispered. "Giants aren't an easy kill at the best of times."

"Norse giants are immune to magic," Zamek whispered.

Remy put his thumbs up and smiled in the most sarcastic way he could possibly manage.

The giant said something and grew in size until he was over twenty feet tall. He looked over to where the group was hiding and spoke in a voice that echoed around the chamber.

"I think we've been found," Irkalla said, stepping out from behind the archway with Remy, who drew his swords.

The fire giant's body glowed orange and yellow, before he roared a challenge.

The whole team stared as the giant picked up a detached column to use as a club, testing its weight in his massive hands.

"This isn't going to be fun," Mordred said.

"Nothing about today has been fun," Layla pointed out. "But I've got some aggression I wouldn't mind working out."

Chloe cracked her knuckles. "Me too."

A voice echoed from the staircase as someone ran up it. Layla was about to warn them about the danger when a robed figure appeared at the top of the stairs, shouting something unrecognizable to the giant. The giant appeared to understand: its skin stopped glowing, and he placed the column on the ground, before taking a seat.

The newcomer removed a face-covering hood to reveal light-purple skin and a short, black beard.

"Blood elf," Chloe said, her tone a mixture of shock and anger.

"No," Mordred snapped. "Not a blood elf."

The newcomer said something to the group, but Layla didn't understand.

"Shadow elf," Irkalla almost whispered in disbelief.

Remy looked between everyone in the group. "They're extinct," he said. "Right?"

"And yet there one stands," Mordred replied, as the shadow elf stared at them.

The shadow elf said something else in a language that Layla couldn't understand, but the tone was pleasant, almost musical. It was at odds with the elf's walk-into-a bar-and-start-a-fight-with-the-biggest-guy-there appearance.

"Anyone get that?" Remy asked.

"It's shadow elven," Irkalla said. "The elven languages were always weird. I don't know anyone who can speak them." She said something in ancient Mesopotamian.

The elf's expression brightened and he replied.

"What did he say?" Layla asked.

"What year is this?" Irkalla said. She turned to Mordred. "You understand this too?"

Mordred nodded, before also speaking in ancient Mesopotamian. The elf looked confused.

"I asked him why he was here," Mordred said. "He doesn't understand. I do have an idea though." He spoke in a language that almost sounded like what the elf had said, but the elf shook his head.

"Blood elf," Mordred explained. "I spent enough time in their . . . company. I can speak the language. Apparently, it's different enough from elven that he can't understand it."

The elf took a step toward the group and pointed at each of them in turn before pointing to his head.

"He wants to telepathically link with someone," Irkalla said. "It's how elves transferred information."

"That seems like an extraordinarily bad idea," Remy cautioned.

"Do you speak elven?" Irkalla asked. "Because either he learns our language, or we learn his. And apparently, his ancient Mesopotamian is a little rusty."

Irkalla said a few more words to the elf, but he looked confused for a moment as if trying to understand, and then shook his head.

"Not Latin, not Egyptian, not Babylonian, and not ancient Greek," Irkalla said. "He didn't understand any of those languages. Not surprising, considering elves weren't exactly friendly toward the Earth realm."

In the strangeness of seeing a member of a race long thought extinct, Layla had forgotten about Zamek's presence until he started walking toward the shadow elf, who had remained at the top of the stairs.

"Zamek, please don't kill him," Remy said as the team watched Zamek's every move, while a low rumble left the throat of the giant.

"Yes, let's not piss off the giant," Harry said.

Zamek looked over at Remy, and then back to the elf. He spoke softly, his voice barely above a whisper.

The elf smiled and replied, nodding his head. Tears fell from his eyes and he dropped to his knees.

"What did you tell him?" Layla asked.

"I just said hello in dwarven," Zamek said. "He hasn't seen another soul in a very long time. I told him he's been here for thousands of years."

"How many thousands of years?" Layla asked. She looked at the rest of the group. "Do you all understand this?"

Chloe nodded. "We spent some time in the dwarven realms, and while we were there we underwent a procedure to speak dwarven."

"At least four thousand," Zamek said. "The rock doesn't lie. His cell was closed that long ago and it has never opened until just now."

The shadow elf spoke to Zamek, who nodded.

"He wants to telepathically link so he can learn your language, and see what happened to the world beyond," Zamek said. "I think Layla should be the person to do it."

"Why?" Layla asked.

"He can't link with a human, so Harry is out," Zamek started. "I don't think Mordred is a very good idea, just in case the elf sees some unflattering things—no offense."

"None taken," Mordred said.

"Irkalla's older than anyone here, but all of that knowledge at once might do something to his head. Remy is . . . just no one wants to get inside his head."

Remy laughed, and then looked serious for a second. "Hey."

"That leaves Chloe or Layla. Layla has been in our world the shortest time, so there will be less for him to have to digest. You're the only one here who can't speak dwarven, so at least you'll get that knowledge. Also, if this goes wrong, the rest of you can tear the giant and elf into pieces."

Layla took a step forward, hoping there wasn't about to be a fight if either side felt that the other was doing something they shouldn't.

Zamek said something to the shadow elf in dwarven.

The elf got to his feet and held out his hands, which Layla took. The elf looked over at Zamek and said something.

"He wants to know if you're ready," Zamek said.

Layla nodded.

The shadow elf placed his forehead against Layla's and for a second she wondered if this was the stupidest thing she'd ever done. And then the world switched off.

She watched the elf's life through her own eyes. She saw his childhood, the bullying from the sun elves; they were impossibly beautiful creatures with skin the color of porcelain, but the mean eyes of a predator. She saw the shadow elf grow with his people, begin a close friendship with people in a human village in the Earth realm, only to have a group of sun elves kill everyone in the village just to teach the shadow elf a lesson. She saw the shadow elf demand justice from his council, saw them refuse. And then she saw the shadow elf hunt the sun elf and kill the murderer of the people he loved. Four sun elves died at the hands of the shadow elf, and still his rage and grief were not sated. To prevent a war they locked him away, and then he woke.

Layla saw so much more; she saw realms she'd never visited, hundreds of years of life and friendships rolling over and over in her head until she understood their words, their customs, and their lives. And when it was done, and the shadow elf released her hands, she dropped to her knees, her head pounding from the overload of information.

"Tarron Lycor," Layla said softly. "That's his name."

"Layla Cassidy," Tarron said. "It's a . . . pleasure to meet you. Your history is now in my head, although it will take time to unjumble. I have many questions."

"I know why you're here," Layla said. "I saw what you did. I felt their blood splatter against my skin."

Remy was the first to move, his sword drawn.

"No," Layla called out, stopping him. "Tarron killed the sun elf who murdered people he cared for."

Tarron nodded. "I saw you kill the man who betrayed you. His name was Jared."

Layla took Chloe's offered hand and got to her feet, ignoring the comment.

"What are blood elves?" Tarron asked. "What happened to my people?"

21

3

LAYLA CASSIDY

The giant at the end of the room shouted, "Do you plan on making me able to understand?"

Layla blinked. "I understand the giant."

Tarron nodded. "It will be easier if he can understand your language." Tarron got to his feet unaided and walked over to the giant, performing the same power with him that he had with Layla.

"Can we trust him?" Mordred asked.

Layla nodded. "I think so. The sun elves had him imprisoned here because he murdered their prince—the man who killed Tarron's friends. It was meant to stop the civil war. There's still a lot of his memories that are jumbled up. I'm not sure how long it will take before everything stops feeling like my head is in a snow globe."

The giant let out a roar of pain, causing everyone to quickly turn toward him as he dropped to his knees and pounded his fists on the stone floor.

Tarron was kneeling beside him, and placed a hand on the giant's shoulder as if comforting the creature. "He did not deserve this," Tarron said, his voice coarse and full of emotion.

"I think some explanation is in order," Mordred said. "A lot of explanation, to be honest."

"I am a criminal," Tarron said as he walked over to the group. "The sun elves murdered the human village. They wiped them out because I spent time with them and was learning their ways. The sun elves felt it was beneath me to associate with them. They butchered my friends, and their families, just to make a point. When it became apparent that the shadow elf High Council was unwilling to do anything to jeopardize the peace that existed between the two elf people, I murdered everyone responsible. That included a sun elf prince."

"Sounds reasonable," Mordred said.

Tarron smiled. "I thought so at the time. The High Council did not. I was sentenced to a thousand years imprisonment in this place. The prison that the elven races had created with the help of the dwarves. The giant over there is Dralas. He was to ensure no one woke us up, or tried to help us escape. Unfortunately, I was put in here at the same time as one of the devils."

"Mammon," Irkalla said.

"Yes," Tarron confirmed. "And once he was in here, those who put him here didn't want any chance that he might wake up. So they sealed the prison. With Dralas and me inside."

"I'm sorry," Chloe said.

"Me too," Tarron replied.

"Dralas is your jailer?" Layla asked. "But he's more than that. He's your friend. And your bodyguard."

Tarron nodded.

"Who are you? A prince?"

"I was the son of an elder. That brought certain . . . privilege." Tarron sighed. "Essentially, I was a prince in all but title. The children of elders are expected to either follow in their parents' footsteps, or dedicate themselves to a noble goal: science, art, music, that kind of thing.

Bettering the species by bettering yourself. It was something my mother used to say. She was the elder in question."

"What about your dad?"

"He was a guard. Parents weren't required to stay together to raise the child. They would each take the child for an amount of time to teach them their ways, and when the child was old enough they chose which path to follow. It would probably be considered a fairly . . . hippy upbringing."

Layla smiled. "I did not expect that word to come out of the mouth of a several-thousand-year-old person."

"Your human words are confusing. Also, why do you have so many languages? Dwarven. Shadow elvish. Sun elvish. Done. So many languages is something I'm not sure I'll get used to."

"It's just one of the cool things about living in a world with so many different regions and societies, I guess. I never really thought about it before."

Tarron stared at Layla. "The blood elves. What are they? Like I said, your memories are jumbled, and I'm too impatient to wait."

"There was a civil war," Layla said. "Between shadow and sun elves."

"Yes," Tarron said with a sigh. "It happened after I was placed here. We lost."

"You did. And a large number of shadow elves were imprisoned by the Norse dwarves." Layla remembered the rest as it had been explained to her, but trying to tell someone that his entire race of people had been mutated into murderous savages was not something she'd ever wanted to do. She found it hard to get the words out.

Irkalla placed a hand on Layla's shoulder. "Would you like someone else to continue?"

Layla nodded. Her head was still a mass of information, like someone had taken a puzzle, jumbled all of the pieces up into a bag and then told someone to put it together without seeing what it was meant to look like.

"When the shadow elves arrived at the dwarven kingdom of Nidavellir they were given the task of mining the pure magic crystals that were in the bottom of the mountain," Zamek said from the top of the stairwell. "It took centuries, but eventually the magic tainted them, turning them into monsters. They attacked the city, murdering many, forcing most to escape. They're called blood elves. They destroyed my people, and to this day they continue to murder my friends and loved ones. They are a blight on this and every world they touch. There's nothing left of the shadow elves. You are the only shadow elf I've seen since the day they tore apart everything I cared for."

Tarron stared at Zamek for several seconds, his mouth agape. "I do not know what to say."

Zamek shook his head. "I know that some people in my position will look at you and see the monsters your people became, but I don't. I don't blame you. I blame the people who helped twist the shadow elves. I blame Abaddon, and Arthur, and Hera, and every single one of them who wanted a powerful soldier and cared little for who they killed to get it. The sun elves have vanished. I have no idea where, but my guess is they're still arrogant, still impressed with their own intellect, and wherever they are, they can bloody well stay there."

Tarron walked over to Zamek and knelt before him. "I am sorry for what my people have done to yours."

Zamek smiled. "Get up, you fool. You're no more to blame for what happened to my people than your giant friend over there is for us being trapped in here. You want to feel bad, feel bad later when we've managed to get the realm gate working and can get out of here."

Tarron got back to his feet. "There's a realm gate in here?"

"Dwarves made it," Dralas boomed.

"Do you know why?" Remy asked.

"They are . . . odd."

"Well, I'm not disagreeing with him," Remy said. "But they can't have made a partial realm gate just to further their own weirdness."

Tarron looked to Zamek. "He insulted your people. Are you not angry?"

"He's Remy," Zamek said. "He insults everyone. And if you're going to get angry every time someone insults your people, you're going to have a really hard time on the Earth realm."

"And the internet," Mordred said. "Don't go on there. Ever."

"Layla remembers the internet. It's some sort of information center."

"Porn and trolls," Remy said.

Tarron looked confused.

"I assume the information you took from my head will filter through," Layla said.

"It will take time but . . . ah, trolls. Now I understand." He tapped the side of his head. "I remember all of you. Layla's memories of you are mostly fond ones. Except for the pain, blood, fighting, and death."

"Yes, except those bits," Layla said.

"You are warriors of great power," Tarron said. "You are on a quest to warn your friends."

"You don't have to repeat everything you remember," Mordred told him. "Trust me."

Tarron nodded thoughtfully. "I know realm gates. I know the dwarven language. Though I eventually became a teacher, I spent time with the dwarves while serving my time as an emissary for my people."

Everyone looked at Layla.

"If you're going to look for confirmation every time he says something, we're going to be here a while," Layla said as knowledge of Tarron's past began firing in her head. "Yep. Teacher. You taught languages, culture, you tried to get the elves to embrace all other species. You spent time with various other species."

"The shadow elves were keen to integrate," Tarron said. "The sun elves were not. They hated humans, thought they were beneath us. Didn't have much fondness for witches, weres, vampires, or dwarves—not even sorcerers, which is odd considering how powerful elves can be with magic."

"Anyone not elven?" Chloe asked, interrupting him.

"Oddly no," Tarron said. "They liked elementals very much. I think that was because they could tap into something that the sun elves wished to control. The elves can use magic, but not the same magic that elementals use. I think a lot of sun elves were jealous of elementals. They saw it as some sort of affront to their own power. Magic has no effect on elves . . . although considering those magical crystals were responsible for my people becoming blood elves, apparently there is a limit to how long we can be exposed to it."

"So magic just doesn't work on you at all?" Layla asked.

Tarron shook his head.

"Nor on blood elves for the most part," Mordred said. "It's what makes them such a pain in the arse to fight. Although some on the Earth realm seem to be more susceptible to its effects than those we met in Nidavellir. Oddly enough, blood elves can't use magic."

Tarron sighed. "Another part of what we used to be is now nothing more than memories."

"I'm sorry," Layla said.

Tarron sighed again. "I have a lot to learn about my place in the world order that exists today, but right now we have more important problems to deal with."

"I've killed blood elves with my umbra power," Layla said almost to herself, before immediately wondering how Tarron was going to react to the idea that she'd killed people who used to be his kind.

"What's an umbra?" Tarron asked. "Oh, wait, I see now. You were fused with spirits and a drenik inside a spirit scroll. That was something being worked on when I was still free, but it was not something the majority of elves agreed with. A lot of sun elves were all for it, as they considered humans little more than something to experiment on, or to use for cheap slave labor."

"The more I hear about sun elves, the more they sound like the kind of people who deserve to be slapped," Chloe said.

"I won't disagree with that," Dralas said.

"Zamek said you've been in here for over four thousand years," Irkalla said.

"Five thousand years," Layla replied. "And I'm rounding down."

Tarron's mouth dropped open, and he fell to his knees. "I need more information about what happened during my time here," he said, almost pleading. "Layla isn't old enough, doesn't have enough first-hand knowledge."

"Not a chance in hell," Irkalla said with a shake of her head.

"You don't want to be in here," Mordred said, tapping the side of his skull with his finger. "Promise you that."

Tarron nodded. "We get out of here, I get to learn more, yes?"

No one had a problem with that.

"The realm gate is down below," Zamek said.

"I can see if I can help," Tarron said. "I know something about realm gates. Maybe together we can get it to work."

Zamek shrugged. "It's worth a shot."

Zamek and Tarron went down the stairs, with Remy, Harry, and Irkalla following. Layla wondered if the latter wanted to keep an eye on Tarron because they didn't trust him, or Zamek because his calmness was something no one had expected. Either way, she was grateful that the dwarf and shadow elf would have other people in the room with them.

"Tarron is a good elf," Dralas said softly. "I volunteered for this duty to keep Tarron safe from retribution. Some sun elves were unhappy that Tarron was allowed to live."

"Why was Mammon here?" Mordred asked.

"The dwarves and elves helped fight against the devils," Dralas told them. "When it was done, Mammon was placed here because there was nowhere else to put him. Instead of this place being a prison for many, it became a prison for two. Well, three if you count me."

Layla looked at the watch on her wrist. It was black and able to withstand a blow from a hammer, although she wasn't really sure what the point of such a thing was. "We've been here a few hours," she said, feeling a nervous anxiety build up inside of her gut.

"Let's go see if they've figured out how to work the realm gate," Chloe said.

"You staying here?" Mordred asked Dralas, who appeared to be far too large to fit down the stairs.

"I'm okay," he said. "I'll just wait for you all to return."

Mordred, Chloe, and Layla descended the stairs to the floor below, where they found the rest of the group in the room with the realm gate.

"Anyone got good news?" Mordred asked.

"Define good," Zamek said with a slight sigh. "We can't get through the realm gate," he explained. "There aren't enough runes carved into the gate to actually give us the power we'd need to link two realm gates."

"Can we get the power?" Layla asked.

"We can, but it'll take time," Zamek said.

"Is there good news?" Chloe asked.

"We can get picture and sound," Irkalla said. "Zamek identified the missing runes, and he knows the runes on the realm gate he was working on in Greenland."

"You were building a new realm gate?" Tarron asked. "Oh, yes, sorry, I remember now. This is still taking some getting used to. I'll go back to sit with Dralas—I don't think you have time to explain my being here to your friends."

"I'll join you," Irkalla said, making sure it sounded like he had exactly zero choice in the matter.

Remy had found a comfortable chair and waved his hand in their direction. "Scream if anyone needs something."

"I've thought of a problem," Chloe said. "Time here and time in Greenland are different. What happens when we activate the gate and we can't fully link them?"

"The gates link and synch at the same time," Zamek said. "So, what you see here and there are moving at the same time, which will be the time in the Earth realm as that's the center of all the realm gates."

"So, time directly around the realm gates is always the same?" Layla asked. "It's why when we walk from the Earth realm to here, we don't fall over because time moves differently."

"This has been fascinating," Remy said from the corner of the room. "But has the big gate started glowing yet? Because I'm not sure I can stand another conversation without needing to take a piss."

There was a swoosh of power and Zamek scrambled back as the realm gate changed from nothing into a mass of color, and then Zamek's workshop back in Greenland appeared.

Tommy and Diana stepped into view as Nabu hurried to get to his feet. "Damn it, you scared me," Nabu snapped. "I was trying to get this thing to connect to another realm gate."

Nabu had been the Mesopotamian god of wisdom and was an och, a species so rare he might be the only one left. He brushed down his white shirt and black trousers before running a hand over his smooth chin.

"We don't have a lot of time," Layla said.

"What's wrong?" Tommy asked. He'd grown a large beard in the last few months and had been horrified to find it flecked with gray.

"Avalon is on the way to attack the base," Layla said, before going on to explain further.

"I'll go warn the others," Nabu said when Layla had finished.

Diana growled, the werebear beast inside her straining to be released.

"Please be careful," Layla said. "I got the impression that it won't be a small force."

"We'll evacuate who we can," Tommy said as the sounds of an explosion made the walls shake. "Looks like they've started."

Diana transformed into her werebear form. "Be careful," she told everyone. "That means you too, Remy."

"If you die, I'm going to be *really* pissed off," Remy told her, his eyes moist, his jaw firmly set.

"Get to Shadow Falls," Tommy said as the hair on his body grew and he transformed into his werewolf beast form.

"You too," Mordred said as the realm gate flickered before powering down.

Zamek sat still for several seconds as he tried to get the power to restore, and punched the gate when it didn't, breaking off a piece of it.

"So, what's the plan?" Remy asked.

"We get out of here," Layla said. "We get to our friends."

"And we make Abaddon pay," Chloe finished for her.

"My kind of plan," Mordred said.

Everyone left the realm gate room and walked back up the stairs to find Tarron, Irkalla, and Dralas.

"Right, we need to find a way out of this place," Layla said. "Tommy and Nabu mentioned Shadow Falls."

"What is that?" Tarron asked.

Layla shrugged. "A realm, but I've never been there."

Mordred stepped forward. "I have. Looks like there's info in my brain that you need, but I can't tell you that this will be fun."

Tarron stood and placed his hands on Mordred in the same way he had done to Layla a short time earlier. Thirty seconds later, when Tarron had finished, Mordred walked away while Tarron screamed for a good ten seconds, although it felt a lot longer to Layla. Mordred kept his distance, but looked over to see how the shadow elf was doing. When Tarron finished, his face was pale and sweat dripped from his brow.

"You okay?" Mordred called out.

Dralas knelt beside the shadow elf, giving Layla the impression that there was more to their relationship than just jailer and prisoner.

"What did you do?" Dralas demanded.

"Not his fault," Tarron said. "All that pain, and suffering, and hurt, and rage, hate, anger, fury. All of it in your mind and heart for centuries. How are you alive? How are you not a gibbering wreck on the floor? What you underwent at the hands of the blood elves, at the hands of people who called you friend, it broke you."

"I know," Mordred said without emotion. "I was there."

"How'd you come back?" Tarron asked.

"Mario."

"What?" Tarron asked.

"Zelda too. Little bit of *Final Fantasy*. Some *Halo*. Oh, and I got shot in the head which removed the blood curse marks screwing me up. But other than that, video games helped."

Tarron continued to stare at Mordred before speaking. "There's an elven realm gate in this Shadow Falls place. I knew the realm as something else. A shadow elf realm. Whoever named it Shadow Falls presumably knew of its origin."

"We never knew if it was a sun-elf- or shadow-elf-created realm gate," Mordred said.

Tarron laughed, although it seemed bitter and unpleasant to Layla. "Sun elves can't make them. It was always one of the bones of contention between our people. We figured it out and kept the information to ourselves."

"Explains why there haven't been new ones popping up all over the place since the civil war between your peoples," Remy said.

"Can you make one?" Chloe asked.

Tarron nodded. "In theory, yes. It's just some rudimentary elven writings. In fact, working with Zamek, we might be able to combine the dwarven gate that he found with an elven gate. It was something being worked on before I was put in here."

Zamek's eyes lit up. "That would be an exceptionally interesting idea."

"No, it really isn't," Remy said.

"The problem with elven is that it's only readable by elves," Tarron continued, ignoring Remy. "I guess you would call that a weird idea, but it's knowledge that is only passed on by linking minds. And we didn't usually link minds with anyone who wasn't elven."

"Okay, so we link minds," Zamek said. "And then we should both be able to work on this realm gate."

Layla looked over at Mordred. "You okay?" she asked.

Mordred smiled. "I will be."

Layla looked back at Tarron, and a horrible realization dawned. "To activate the gate, we need a death."

No one looked like they were particularly fond of what Layla was suggesting. All except Tarron, who was smiling.

"That's really creepy," Mordred said. "And I know creepy. No one is dying here today."

"I'm happy to see that Layla's memories are still taking on my own," Tarron said. "It is always a longer process with non-elves. You'll probably find that they continue to creep in for several hours or maybe days."

"That's nice and all, but where do we find someone willing to die?" Remy asked. "And don't anyone say from one of us."

"You have a bunch of lives left," Irkalla said with a slight smirk.

"Piss off," Remy said, coughing into his hands. "Sorry, it's a dreadful affliction."

"Technically we only need blood," Tarron said. "No one needs to die here. The death was only ever used to activate a realm gate because it was a way of killing prisoners."

"You used prisoners to activate realm gates?" Chloe asked. "That's more than a little messed up."

"Not five thousand years ago it wasn't," Tarron said. "And we can't get anywhere without leaving this prison to find someone who we can use as a sacrifice."

"I'll say it again for anyone hard of hearing," Mordred said. "No one is being sacrificed today."

"How about if we all bleed a little?" Chloe asked. "How much blood do we need?"

Tarron thought about it. "A few pints," he said eventually.

"Okay, but who's going to get cut that badly?" Layla asked.

"I can draw the blood out," Mordred said. "Blood magic can force something to bleed a lot, more than it usually would. It's not going to be a fun experience though."

"Mordred," Layla said, placing a hand on his arm. "That's a *bad* idea."

"Blood magic is addictive," Tarron said.

"Yes, I know," Mordred almost snapped. "I don't like using blood magic anymore, but needs must and all that. Just get the realm arranged, and then we'll activate it."

"Everyone get comfortable," Zamek said. "I think this could take a little while."

4

Layla Cassidy

It felt like a long time had passed since Zamek, Harry, Irkalla, and Tarron had gone down to the realm gate. Dralas had shrunk to be just seven feet tall and followed the others down after only a short time, leaving Chloe, Layla, Mordred, and Remy up near the entrance to the prison.

Remy took the spiral staircase up a floor to have a look around, and Mordred reluctantly followed him in case, Layla presumed, Remy locked himself in a room or got into some other kind of trouble.

Layla thought about everything that had happened over the last six months since her mother had returned from the dead, and her father had been taken into custody by her allies. It had taken Layla some time to get her head around the idea of realms all being linked to Earth, and that all the mythological places were real and out there somewhere. The fact that it was now second nature to her would probably have shocked the Layla of only a few years ago. But then a lot had happened in those years, and Layla was now a very different person from the one she had been at university. She looked down at her metal arm and thought, *in more ways than one.*

"You okay?" Chloe asked, taking a seat beside her.

Layla smiled. Chloe was one of her closest friends and, like Layla, an umbra of incredible power. Chloe wore a long, dark-blue coat, hiding the multitude of tattoos that she had over her body. Her arms in particular were a homage to pop culture. Chloe had shoulder-length blonde hair and several diamond studs in both ears. Umbra, like most non-humans, healed quickly, and Layla knew that the second the earrings were removed the holes would close. Layla wasn't sure she'd ever seen Chloe without them.

"Eager to help our friends. Eager to leave this realm. Not feeling too good about letting thousands of people possibly die." Layla ran a hand through her hair. She'd had blue hair for as long as she could remember, and over time had changed it so that it was light blue on top and dark blue on the bottom, as if the two colors were fighting one another. She'd changed it again a month ago, and now the light-blue hair reached down to between her shoulders, with the last few inches being dark blue. She sometimes wondered if it should be the other way around, if the darkness should have won out, but the lightness was there to remind her that no matter how dark everything else became, there was light there too. It wasn't subtle, but she hadn't felt particularly subtle when she'd had it done.

"I know," Chloe said. "I am too."

Layla mentally slapped herself. "I'm sorry, I know Piper is there. I should be the one comforting you."

Piper and Chloe had been getting serious for the last few months. Months in which Layla had been too busy to see her friends as much as she should have. She'd told herself that it was better that way, that she'd needed to focus and get stronger, but she knew that it was more than that.

"She wants us to move in together."

Layla raised her fist and Chloe bumped it, grinning. "That's awesome," Layla said.

"She makes me so damn happy, Layla."

"Good, you deserve it."

Chloe's mother had tried to murder both Chloe and her father, trapping them in the realm of Nidavellir. Her father hadn't made it out of the realm alive, and Chloe had been forced to become an umbra to survive. Chloe's mom had been killed a short time later, and precisely zero people mourned her death.

Chloe nodded and smiled, but it didn't reach her eyes. "If they've hurt Piper . . ." Her voice trailed off.

Layla wasn't sure what to say, so she just put her arm around Chloe and hugged her. "I'm sorry I've been less than involved the last few months."

"I get it," Chloe said, rubbing her eyes with the balls of her palms. "Your mum comes back from the dead as basically a kind of demon, all because Abaddon dumps a drenik in her and forces her to reanimate. She cuts off your arm, making you use your metal-shaping powers to create a new one. And your father is a serial killer who will only work with you. That's a whole lot of shit to deal with in a very short space of time."

"I just threw myself into work," Layla said. "My father would give us the names of people who were targeted by Avalon's murder squads, and we'd go get them out of whatever situation they were in. I didn't stop; it was like I couldn't stop. The more I did, the easier it was to convince myself that continuing alone was better than stopping and getting my head into a healthy place. Everyone was so busy that no one really had time to take me aside and point out that I was being an idiot. Tommy tried, but I waved his objections off. Diana tried, but I think I convinced her I was fine. Even Mordred tried, and when that didn't work, he just inserted himself into the work I was doing."

"He cares for you," Chloe said. "We all do. I figured letting you work through it would help long-term. Everyone has been so wrapped up in their own little bubbles that sometimes it feels like we're all

37

drifting apart. It's difficult to go out and fight your enemies, then come home and have a fun old time with your mates. And, on top of that, you had the whole Jared thing to deal with, and I didn't want to rub it in your face that I was happily seeing someone."

"You know I'd never begrudge you your happiness."

"I know," Chloe assured her. "But it still felt shitty of me to be all 'I know your boyfriend was a psychopath, but my girlfriend is awesome.' It didn't exactly feel like something anyone would want to hear."

"Guys, you need to see this," Remy shouted from the top of the staircase.

Layla and Chloe shrugged, but followed him upstairs to a large room that mimicked the one below. Mordred stood at the far end, next to a window that Layla hadn't seen from the outside.

"How did we miss windows in this place?" Chloe asked.

"It's got runes around it," Mordred said without looking back. "I think it's some sort of dwarven thing. We found a bunch of rooms with beds, and what looks like a very old kitchen down the corridor over there." He pointed to an archway that led to a long corridor with torches on each side.

Layla and Chloe reached Mordred and looked down over the realm. "What the hell is that?" Layla asked.

A purple mist rolled through the forest, covering the clearing in front of the prison. It appeared to be only a few feet deep, but was dense enough to hide the ground.

"There was a flash of light," Mordred said, "and then I saw that stuff."

"You think this is the weapon that Irkalla discovered in that soldier's mind?" Chloe asked.

"Yes," Mordred said softly, and Layla picked up on the fear in his voice. "And I *really* don't want to go out there and find out what it does."

"Will the runes that Zamek put up keep us safe?"

"Let's go find out," Remy said, sounding slightly agitated.

They met Harry halfway down the staircase. "I think we've got something ready," he said.

Layla noticed the tension leave Remy's shoulders as he relaxed. Hopefully they wouldn't need to find out how secure the prison was from the mist outside.

Soon after, everyone was gathered in the chamber just outside the unfinished dwarven realm gate room. A large amount of elvish writing was all over the floor and walls, but before he could explain how it worked, Zamek noticed the expression on the others' faces and his smile faltered.

"What's happened?" he asked.

"How good are your runes?" Mordred replied. "I think whatever weapon Abaddon has, they've just used it."

"There's a purple mist floating around out there," Chloe said.

Zamek ran up the stairs as fast as he could, shouting for everyone to wait where they were. He returned a few minutes later. "We're safe. I just wanted to check everything was holding. I don't know what caused that mist, but let's leave and figure it out somewhere else."

"Is the realm gate working?" Remy asked.

"Yes," Tarron said. "We managed to figure out a way to incorporate a dwarven and elven rune into one symbol. It's frankly another level stuff."

"Can we all geek out later?" Irkalla asked from the center of the room. "You ready, Layla?"

Layla nodded and stepped into the center of the room with Tarron standing beside her. "Mordred, we'll need your blood now, please."

Mordred removed a dagger from his belt and cut his hand. An instant later, his eyes turned blood-red as he activated his blood magic. Blood poured out of his wound as tendrils of magic snaked up his arm. "I haven't done this to myself in a long time," Mordred said between clenched teeth as his blood fell onto the stone floor, creating a puddle.

"That's enough," Tarron said.

Mordred stopped his magic and sagged back against the wall. Irkalla stepped up beside him a moment later. "You okay?" she asked.

"The cut has healed," he told her. "It's just the rush of the magic. Using blood magic with someone else's blood is one thing, but doing it to force me to bleed, and then refusing to allow the magic to use that blood to power itself . . . that's a whole different level of control. And not one I enjoyed. Or enjoyed too much. It's hard to tell with blood magic."

Tarron used the blood to draw several lines around the writing he'd already put there, and there was suddenly a low hum of power.

"Realm gate is powering," Zamek said. "This hasn't been done before."

Tarron looked at Layla. "This might feel weird," he said.

He wasn't wrong.

Everything flashed white, and then Layla had the sudden urge to vomit up every organ inside her. An instant later she was on her knees in another room with people shouting all around her. Layla shook her head, trying to clear it, which was difficult with the noise everyone in the room was making.

She took a deep breath. "Will everyone please shut up?" she bellowed as she was helped to her feet by a familiar man she'd never been happier to see.

"You okay?" Tommy asked her.

"That was not fun," Layla said as she left the realm gate, her head no longer feeling like it was full of cotton wool. With Tommy's help, she sat down and was grateful that the room stopped spinning.

Chloe sat beside her and rested her head on Layla's shoulder as Tommy went off to talk to the guards inside the realm gate room. "That sucked donkey ass," Chloe said.

"Let's not do that ever again," Layla agreed, looking around the cavern. "We should move."

"We'll wait for everyone to come through," Chloe said. "Also, I don't want to."

"What happened in Greenland?" Layla shouted to Tommy.

"We haven't heard from everyone," he told her. "But most got away. A lot have scattered and are making their way here. And some didn't make it."

"How many dead?" Chloe asked.

Tommy shook his head. "No idea. Not everyone has arrived. A lot of them fled Greenland and went into hiding. They're taking their time to reach us. It's a good thing we were able to get here as quickly as we did. We let the people who live here know about what's going on, and we managed to prepare the realm for visitors. How bad is it in Norumbega?"

"We don't know," Layla said. "At our guess, thousands died there. Felicia Hale is dead too."

"We heard," Tommy said softly. "She was one of the good ones. She'll be missed."

"Her people who betrayed her won't be," Layla said, allowing the anger to flood her. "They're going to be dealt with."

Tommy stared at Layla for a few seconds. "You sound like Mordred."

"That's because I'm awesome," Mordred said after he came through the realm gate and sat next to Layla. "Did that suck ass for you too?"

Layla and Chloe nodded.

Over the next few minutes everyone came through the realm gate one at a time, each of them sitting next to those who had come before. The sight of Dralas raised a few eyebrows, but no one said or did anything to cause a problem.

"I forgot to tell Tommy about Tarron," Layla said aloud as Dralas sat beside the group. She was about to shout out to him when the realm gate flashed.

"Blood elf," one of the guards shouted. There was a mad rush toward Tarron as Layla tore metal out of the rock around them to put a barrier between him and those who saw him as an enemy.

"Not a blood elf," Layla shouted as Zamek stood in front of Tarron, his battle-ax in hand.

"I'm a shadow elf," Tarron said.

"He's on our side," Zamek said.

"The dwarf is protecting a shadow elf?" Tommy asked, utterly shocked. "I don't think I ever even considered that might happen. Aren't shadow elves extinct?"

"Apparently not," Chloe said, getting to her feet.

Remy walked over to Layla and Chloe. "You both okay?"

They nodded. "You?" Layla asked just before Chloe.

"Not great," he admitted, for once not trying to mask his pain with humor and smart-mouth replies.

The entire group followed Tommy through the cavern and down a tunnel until they reached the exit and stepped out into the sunlight beyond.

"Solomon," Mordred said. "That's the name of the city. Galahad ruled this place, and then Arthur had his people murder him when they attacked."

Layla blinked a few times, getting used to the light, and looked down on the city two hundred feet below. "I'm sorry," she said.

"The attackers were driven off, but only because they got what they came for."

"And that was?" Tarron asked.

"Nate Garrett," Mordred said. "This was the beginning of the end for everything we used to believe in. Magic here works differently than on the Earth realm. It's hard to control, hard to switch off. It's why Arthur didn't want a proper battle here. Too many chances for a few sorcerers to destroy a large part of his army."

Layla remembered Nate from her time when she'd first joined Tommy's group after she'd become an umbra. He'd been one of her trainers, helping her get used to her new powers. She'd liked him and found him to be a fairly easy-going man who knew what he was talking about. But she also recognized the power and darkness that lay inside him, and knew that anyone who crossed him would do best to run as far and fast as they possibly could. He'd died not long after Arthur had declared his true intentions to the world, and a lot of people had mourned his passing.

"Besides, Avalon have bigger problems," Tommy said.

"Like all of the Norse realms," Irkalla finished. "Until they turn their attention to clean-up duty, this is as good a place as any to hide out."

The city of Solomon was gigantic and stretched further than Layla could see. A lot of the houses were nothing but rubble now and she saw no evidence of life in the city. The massive palace at the far end was in ruins, with large parts of it having crumbled onto the grounds surrounding it. An aqueduct circled the entire city, although part of it had also been destroyed at some point. A tram line sat beside it, a hundred feet in the air. The forest was at the far end of the city, which Layla couldn't see the end of, and plains came up to the base of the mountain range she stood on. A huge fort hunkered down next to one of the mountains a short distance away.

Two huge metal elevators had been built next to the large platform everyone found themselves standing on. One was coming back up toward them, while the other reached the bottom.

"How do we get to the city when we reach the bottom of the mountain?" Layla asked.

"There will be carriages waiting below," Tommy said. "It's not a long ride, but we're all stationed at the fort just over there. No one lives in Solomon anymore. Too many people died there, and most of the population was evacuated to another realm, leaving a lot of their things behind. Those who have settled here thought it wrong to move in to their houses, so they live in the forest. Makes it easier to come and go from the fort. Besides, the other realm gate is just inside the mountain there, and it's nice to be close to it in case of emergencies."

"The other realm gate?" Tarron asked. "You have two elven realm gates?"

"Sorry, no," Tommy said. "There were two dwarven gates here, but . . . well, one of them is no longer used. We routinely break it to ensure that no one can use it on the other end. The elven gate is guarded around the clock too. It's been used by Avalon's people before."

"Aren't you worried about the second gate?" Layla asked.

"The second realm gate was a secret," Mordred said. "It goes to a church in Maine. The entire town there is full of people we can trust. It'll be how most of these people came to be here."

The gothic-looking elevator reached the group, and everyone got on with room to spare. Layla noticed that Chloe was looking a bit green and went over to her. "You okay?"

Chloe nodded slowly. "I glanced over the edge of the lift."

Layla took a step to the side, and looked over the metal railing that was all that stood between her and several hundred feet of air. She moved away from the edge, back toward Chloe.

"See?" Chloe asked.

Layla nodded. "This whole thing is made of metal. I promise you it's not going to fall while I'm here."

Chloe nodded again. "I don't think it's going to crash—we're just so high up, I had a little moment of panic."

When Layla had first found herself in the world she now occupied, she was amazed that sorcerers, umbra, werewolves, and the like could still have utterly mundane fears. It was probably the one thing that had made her realize how similar everyone was, despite the power at their disposal.

"Wanna go back to the good old days?" Chloe asked. "Where we would go out for a drink and not have to worry about someone trying to kill us."

Layla smiled. "They were good times. I wanted to try to figure out what I was going to do with my life when I'd finished my degree. Superhero was not on the list of life choices."

"Oh, you're a superhero now?"

"I'm going to start wearing a cape. Not my underwear on the outside of my clothes though—I think that would be a weird look for me."

"I could see you in a cape. Something dark and foreboding. With skulls. The Punisherette."

"The what?"

"I couldn't think of the female version of the Punisher."

"It sounds like I punish people with dance."

Chloe pointed a finger at Layla. "That could be your thing."

Layla laughed. "Anyone seeing me dance has probably had enough punishment."

"If nothing else, that has TV show written all over it."

"A very short-lived TV show."

"Something, something, *Firefly*," Chloe said with a smile that quickly dissolved when the elevator shuddered. "I'm worried about Piper."

"We'll find out," Layla said. "But I'm sure she's fine."

Chloe nodded, but didn't say anything, and Layla knew there was no way of telling if this was actually true. It was just a waiting game. And that worried her.

Thankfully Chloe's concerns about the elevator were short-lived as it softly bumped onto the ground. One side of the elevator lowered, and they walked off.

It was a short distance from the mountain to a large fort that was roughly the size of a football stadium, but without the super-high walls. That's not to say the walls weren't impressive in their own right. The fort's three walls were fifty feet high, and had ramparts occupied with armed patrols. The fourth wall, set back from where they were standing, was a mountain, which rose hundreds of feet above the fort. It meant that any falling rocks wouldn't bury the place, as grooves in the face of the mountain ensured that landslide and avalanche debris would fall away to either side of the fort.

Behind Layla was a huge gate made of metal and wood with runes adorning the inside. Layla guessed that those runes would stop magical attacks. A door opened nearby and a soldier stepped out, the smell of cooking meat following him into the courtyard making Layla's stomach grumble.

A siren rang out across the fort, and the whole place went from calm to busy in an instant.

"What's going on?" Layla asked Mordred and Irkalla, who were moving toward the closest fort gate.

"Realm gate has been activated," Mordred said, pulling open the fort gate and running out onto the plains beyond.

"Probably just more of our people," Tommy said, although his tone suggested that he couldn't be certain of it.

"Let's go make sure," Mordred said, and set off in a jog toward the nearby cavern.

Everyone followed and they were soon in the cave, which had been turned into a base, with even more personnel ready for whomever came through the gate. The realm gate at the end of the cave glowed light blue, before it ignited and Sky, Diana, and two dozen others appeared. Most looked exhausted and were immediately helped by the staff inside the cave. Layla ran over to the newcomers.

"Sky, Diana," Layla said. "Are you okay? What happened? Where's everyone else?"

"We got away," Sky said. "But my parents stayed behind to help us escape."

"Where are Hades and Persephone now?" Mordred asked.

When it became obvious that Sky couldn't say the words, Diana spoke for her. "Avalon took them."

5

LAYLA CASSIDY

Several hours had passed and, after discovering that most of the people in Greenland had managed to escape, Layla had found herself becoming increasingly snappy at the lack of progress, so had left the higher-ups in the Rebellion to their plans. It wouldn't help anyone if she started to get angry. Besides, they were all very keen to talk to Dralas and Tarron, who had received more than one angry glance. Tarron might not have been a blood elf, but he was what they originally were, and that would be enough for some.

Piper had arrived, making Chloe considerably happier, and the pair had gone to find somewhere quiet so they could talk. Layla was glad that her friend's partner was okay. Layla hadn't said much to Piper since she'd started dating Chloe, and she knew that was her own fault. She had been isolating herself from her friends, and after talking to Chloe about it in Norumbega, she hoped that was the first step to making sure it didn't happen again. Layla had also discovered that Kase had managed to escape Greenland, and was in Shadow Falls, so she would need to talk to her and Harry too and apologize for being a thoroughly crappy friend over the last few months, but she had no idea of their exact location inside the city.

So, instead of being around the people of the fort, Layla had gone outside to a nearby tree and tried to relax, although thoughts of her father, Caleb, kept intruding, making it difficult. Tommy had told her that he and Diana had brought him to Shadow Falls from Greenland, and that he was currently being guarded by several soldiers who had orders to shoot him should he become an issue. Layla had been okay with this. He was being kept in a nearby cabin that was adorned with enough runes to stop Odin himself being able to escape, or at least that's what Mordred had told her.

Most of the refugees from Greenland had been moved into the town of Solomon, and several alchemists, who had remained in Shadow Falls after Avalon had first attacked it two years earlier, were busy repairing some of the buildings to house them. She knew that she wanted to go after those who had been taken by Avalon, but she had no idea where they were. She needed to have patience until it was time to act. Unfortunately, being patient was never something she'd been all that good at.

She had her eyes closed, hoping to get a little rest, so hadn't noticed anyone approach until they cleared their throat.

Layla opened her eyes and saw Lucifer standing in front of her. For a long time everyone had known Lucifer as Grayson, the head doctor in Tommy's organization. Since that organization no longer existed, thanks to Avalon, Lucifer had revealed his real identity as one of the seven devils—the same group of ancient warriors that included Abaddon. Thankfully Lucifer and Abaddon were very much opposed when it came to their views on the slaughter of everyone who didn't agree with them.

"Would it be really stupid of me to ask how you are?" Lucifer asked. He was a short man with a long, white beard and long, white hair, which he wore in a ponytail. Harry had taken to calling him Young

Gandalf. Lucifer wore a white shirt, dark jeans, and black boots. He looked like he was going to work on a casual Friday.

"Thought I'd just sit and smell the freshness of this place," Layla said with a slight smile. "This tree smells like orange blossom. It's pleasant."

"I haven't been here in a few years," Lucifer said. "It's a relaxing place to be, but not somewhere I'd want to live. You saw Abaddon again?"

Layla nodded. "She does not like me."

"I can't think of many people she does like. But she got Mammon. That is bad news."

"Yeah, I know. Sorry."

Lucifer waved his hand to dismiss her apology. "We were set up."

"And thousands of people died because of it," Layla said with more than a little anger.

"Not your fault. No one's fault but Abaddon and her people. If you'd have intervened, you'd be dead too. We're going to gather everyone together to discuss how to move forward. Right now, everyone is just helping out the refugees. I assume you'd like to be part of this conversation."

Layla's expression told him that she was going to be involved in those conversations whether or not she was asked.

"Good," Lucifer said. "We need to find Hades, Persephone, and the others who have been taken, but we also need to regroup and prepare for whatever Avalon has planned next. This weapon they used . . . I am unsure what it is, or how it works, but Irkalla says it needs sacrifices. I plan on looking into it and hopefully will discover more information."

"This whole thing never ends, does it?"

Lucifer sat beside her. "Nope. We can't defeat Avalon. We just can't. We don't have the numbers. We're holding our own in various realms, but others have fallen to the Avalon machine, freeing up more people to fight us. We need help. We need a lot of help, and I'm not sure it's coming. We're too fragmented, and without Hades, Persephone, and the like, now we're down on power too."

"Where are all the other members of pantheons that aren't with Avalon, but aren't helping us?"

Lucifer shrugged. "Most are in hiding. Some are the magical equivalent of Switzerland, hoping that if they don't pick a side, they won't be involved. Some are doing both."

Layla chuckled and shook her head. "You are really bad at making me feel better."

Lucifer laughed. "Sorry. How's the hand? I hear you've gotten quite adept at using it."

"Harry called me the Winter Soldier, and then laughed about it for a good few minutes."

"Tommy said something similar. Then started talking about Luke Skywalker, and I sort of zoned out. I think Tommy is just worried about everyone. He's hard to shut up when he's nervous. And everyone is nervous at the moment. We're all on edge. I heard you snapped at a few people."

"I apologized," Layla said sheepishly.

"Don't worry about it. I'm more concerned about you shutting yourself off again."

Layla sighed. "You know about that?"

"I do. I know that a few people tried to talk to you about it, and you pushed them away. I know that Mordred has been keeping an eye on you under the guise of tutelage."

"He's an extraordinarily bad liar considering he was evil for a thousand years."

"Do not change the subject."

"Yeah, I know. I wasn't dealing with everything especially well, and I just thought that staying out of everyone's way was for the best. Should have known better."

"We all do it," Lucifer said. "That's why I suggested it should be me to talk to you now. I kept myself to myself for thousands of years. I was scared that people would discover who I really was, or that I'd feel that need to fight and put myself in a situation where I hurt someone. Solitude seemed like the better idea. It wasn't, by the way. These years with everyone here, before Arthur woke up, were the happiest of my life. And it's been a long life."

Layla watched Tommy and Olivia leave the fort and walk over toward them. "There's nothing good coming from the following conversation, is there?" she asked.

Lucifer shook his head. "Nope."

"Can I ask one thing?"

"Anything."

"They freed Mammon. What happens when he wakes up and goes batshit crazy?"

"Tarron told me about Mammon's cell, which is a little bit like Tartarus, the realm. The prisoner's power level is lowered over time, and when they leave, the power slowly returns. Mammon won't be at full power for a while, but even a weakened Mammon is dangerous. He'll make himself known, and when he does people will die."

Layla got to her feet and brushed blades of grass from her clothes. "Then we better find him before that happens." She turned to Tommy and Olivia. "What horrible thing has befallen us now?"

"Nothing of note," Olivia said. "We wanted to let you know that we finished our talk with Tarron and Dralas. Both appear to be on the level with us, and want to help. We also want to know if you'll ask your father for his help. He took a hell of a whack to the head. And with his band on he might not heal that quickly. He was pretty out of it when he arrived."

"We're going to take him away from the hut and remove his sorcerer's band," Tommy said. "Thought you'd want to know."

Layla gave a slight shake of her head. "Thank you, but I'm not really in the mood to play his games. He never does anything without wanting something in return. In the months since he was taken into custody and kept prisoner in Greenland, I've spent more time with him than is probably healthy to spend with a mass-murdering asshole."

"I can't think any time would be healthy," Tommy said. "But there's something else. We had a communication from an ally in Avalon. Someone who works closely with several high-ranking members. Including Abaddon."

"You have someone in their ranks?" Layla said, surprised at not having heard about this before. She turned to Lucifer. "Did you know?"

Lucifer nodded. "I'm not privy to his reports, but I knew he existed."

"Who is it?" Layla asked, not really caring which one of them answered.

"Atlas," Olivia said.

"Wait, the Titan?" Layla asked. "Don't half of his own people want him dead for betraying them?"

"Betraying them because we needed him to," Olivia said.

Layla had heard about what happened on the realm of Tartarus, a prison realm used by the Titans and those who had gone against Avalon over the centuries. Hades had run the realm, and by all accounts it was a pleasant and good life for everyone there. But then Abaddon and her people had arrived and murdered Cronus and Rhea. Once done, Atlas had helped Abaddon escape from the realm.

"What did he have to say?" Layla asked.

"Prisoners have been taken to the realm of Nidavellir," Tommy said.

"Okay, so I see two problems," Layla began. "One: how do we get there? Last I heard, there are no working realm gates to or from that place. And two: how do we find . . ." She trailed off as the realization dawned on her. "You want me to take my father to Nidavellir, don't you?"

Both Tommy and Olivia nodded.

"To answer your first question, Zamek has a plan," Olivia said. "To answer your second, yes. Your father can track wherever the prisoners are being kept. Also, while you're there, Zamek wants to try to get the aid of the remaining dwarves, and frankly any help at this point is worth going for."

"I'll go talk to my father, shall I?" Layla asked. There was no point in arguing. She knew that something had to be done, and it sounded like the best idea in a big list of really bad ideas.

"Actually, we're going to collect him and take him to the fort," Olivia said. "I was going to ask if you could make yourself scarce for a few hours and help get everyone at the other realm gate over to the palace."

Layla nodded, grateful that she wasn't going to have to be there when they collected her father. She turned back to Lucifer, who was getting to his feet. "Thank you."

Lucifer smiled. "Any time. Just take care of yourself, okay?"

Layla nodded again.

"If you see our daughter, can you send her over too?" Tommy asked. "She went off to Solomon to do something or other, and I don't have time to track her down."

"Will do," Layla said, and set off at a steady jog toward the city.

It took her half an hour to reach the outskirts of Solomon where she saw hundreds of people helping the refugees who had arrived from Greenland. Thankfully, non-humans healed quickly for the most part, but some still needed to see medical staff, and Lucifer had made sure that his people were second-to-none when it came to dealing with emergencies.

Layla made her way through the din of noise and people and into the city proper. She found a guard handing out bottles of water and walked over.

"You seen Kase around anywhere?" Layla asked her.

"Kase was over toward the realm gate," the guard said. "It's a bit of a trek, so use the trams."

Layla looked up at the aqueduct high above her. In the distance, a single tram moved slowly around the track. She followed it around and saw another half dozen moving slowly behind it at regular intervals. "I thought they were broken?" Layla asked.

"Leonardo got busy," the guard said by way of explanation as she handed over a large bottle of water.

"I haven't met him yet."

"He can be hard work, but he's a damned genius. The tram stops up by the palace—if you get on there, you can go to the realm gate temple. Get off before the temple. The temple stop is still probably unsafe."

Layla thanked her and ran through the city to the palace, finding the tram station easily enough. She looked up at the palace and felt a tinge of sadness for the loss of Shadow Falls' king. Galahad had been a good man, by all accounts, and his death had deeply affected a lot of people who knew him.

The tram arrived, taking her away from thoughts of the awful things that had happened to the realm of Shadow Falls. The tram was shaped like a bullet train and at some point it had been painted in blues and greens, although now it was more dirt than anything else. The inside was a shambles and wires hung from the ceiling and panels around the interior, but once she stepped on, the doors closed and it began to move smoothly away.

Layla considered using her power to force it to move quicker, but figured it might screw with something. She didn't want to have to explain why she flung a tram off the track and onto someone's house, or something equally bad.

The journey was an enlightening one as the tramline took Layla across open fields and farmland, as well as over ruined streets and houses. The mountain slowly cast its shadow across the city, and when the tram moved into the darkness the shadow brought with it, the lights inside came on, bathing everything in a purple glow.

The entire trip took half an hour, and Layla got off at the bottom of the hill just before the realm gate temple. She looked up the hill to the huge white stone temple that sat at the top. Two armed soldiers walked around the corner and Layla waved them over.

"Have you seen Kase?" she asked when they were within speaking distance.

"Saw her just over there," one of the soldiers said, a small woman with a kind smile and a scar on her nose.

"How long ago?" Layla asked.

"Ten minutes," the second soldier said. She was the spitting image of her comrade, except without the scar. "She went into the house at the end. Red door."

Layla thanked them and ran to the end of the road, found the red door in question, and pushed it open. She stepped inside and heard nothing from within the house. She considered shouting for Kase, but if she was asleep or trying to rest, she might not want to be yelled at, and Layla would rather not panic her friend if she didn't have to.

The whole place had been cleaned out some time ago, and the lack of furniture or home comforts of any kind made Layla feel a little sad for whoever had once owned the building. She walked around the three downstairs rooms: a living room, eat-in kitchen, and small room that was probably a study, and found nothing of note.

She walked up the stone staircase. "Hey, Kase?" she said as she reached the top of the stairs. She heard a noise from one of the nearby rooms and immediately rushed over, opening the door to reveal Kase and Harry in bed together.

They were under the covers, with Kase's head resting on Harry's naked chest. Layla froze in place as Kase and Harry looked over at her, and all three shared a moment of, "Oh, shit."

"Well . . . we didn't hear you come in," Kase said without moving.

"No, because these houses are pretty well sound-proofed, apparently," Layla said. "Also, you were having sex."

Harry looked between Kase and Layla. "So, on a scale of one to dead, how much will Tommy murder me?"

"I am a grown woman," Kase said firmly.

"I'm going to go now," Layla said, and closed the door. She walked back downstairs, where she burst into laughter. She'd considered mocking the clearly uncomfortable Harry about the situation, but decided that was probably something best done when she wasn't trying not to laugh.

Kase and Harry arrived downstairs a few minutes later, with the latter looking exceptionally nervous about what he'd been discovered doing.

"You going to tell my parents?" Kase asked.

"You know we're the same age, right?" Layla asked. "I don't care who you both have sexy time with. You're twenty-three, Kase, and, Harry, you're older than me. You can both shag anyone you like."

Kase laughed. "I have never heard an American use the word 'shag' before."

"American–British," Layla said with a smile. "So, are you two just having . . ."

"Sexy time?" Kase asked with a sly smirk.

Harry sat on the bottom step of the stairs. "I would like to say something."

Kase motioned for Harry to continue and sat on the floor next to Layla.

"I really like Kase," Harry said. "We've been keeping it a secret because it's all been so shit recently that we just didn't want to be inappropriate and start telling everyone that we're together. Especially after Jared."

"You kept it a secret because my ex-boyfriend was a psychopath who worked for Abaddon, betrayed us all, and tried to murder me? You really shouldn't have. I'm fine."

"Also," Harry continued, "Tommy might actually murder me."

"I keep telling him that my father has mellowed over the years," Kase said. "He's met boyfriends of mine and everything. And I'm pretty sure he's aware that I'm actually an adult and can see who I like."

"Yes, and while that's true, he still might kill me."

"And he knows how to get rid of the bodies," Layla said.

"How is that helping?" Harry almost shouted.

"If Remy were here, he'd have a witty answer to that," Layla said. "Oh god, let me tell Remy."

"No," Harry said. "Not Remy. Remy will take delight in torturing me."

Layla and Kase laughed.

"He's not wrong," Kase said.

"I'm glad you're both happy," Layla said. "But don't think you have to keep it secret from everyone just because we're going through a crappy time. Actually, people might feel better about it all if they see a bit of love blossoming in the world."

Kase raised an eyebrow. "We haven't said the 'L' word."

"You know what I mean," Layla said, getting to her feet. "Also, I need to apologize to you both for being an isolationist over the last few months. I pushed people away, and I'm sorry for that."

"We've all been a bit worried about you," Harry said. "But Mordred assured us he was keeping an eye on you."

"Yes, he's been my fairy godmother of sorts," Layla said. "We could have been killed in Norumbega, and that's made me realize that I shouldn't waste time pushing people away. It doesn't work, and it's unhealthy."

Kase gave Layla a hug. "If it happens again, I'll come slap you around the head."

"Sounds fair," Layla said with a smile.

"Can I do that too?" Harry asked.

"No," Layla and Kase said in unison, before laughing.

"I'm going to the temple," Layla said. "Your parents asked me to gather everyone together so we can decide how we're going to rescue those who were taken in Greenland. Apparently, they're in Nidavellir."

Kase's smile melted away. "That place is evil. I've spent more time than I'd like to think about there. Lots of bad things happened, and I'd rather live my whole life and never go back." She got to her feet. "But whatever is happening there, I'm going. I've seen the kinds of things they do to the prisoners. I've had them done to me. I am more than happy to go back and screw up everyone's shit."

Layla said, "I'm sure there will be plenty of people wanting to help. I'm going up to the temple to get Zamek and a few others."

"I practically had to drag Harry away from them," Kase said. "They all get together to talk about realm gates, and I begin to fall asleep."

"I am here," Harry said.

"What were you trying to do at the realm gate?" Layla asked.

"The gate is damaged," Harry said. "Stops people from trying to use it at the other side, but it repairs itself. Zamek wants to make the realm gate change its designation so it doesn't have to keep being damaged. It's harder than it seems."

"I'll see you both back at the fort," Layla said, wanting to leave before the twinkle in Harry's eye turned into a long-winded explanation of realm gates, their runes, and the dwarven language. She left the lovebirds alone and jogged up the hill to the temple, where she heard Zamek before she saw him. He punched the wall of the temple, which began to break apart before he used his alchemy to fix it.

"Bad day?" she asked him.

Zamek turned to Layla with a smile on his face. "Yes. I'm waiting for Harry to come back from . . . I assume him and Kase are having a relationship."

"You figured that out?"

"I've seen the way they look at each another. You do not look that way at a platonic friend or sparring partner. They actually used that as an excuse once a few months ago. Sparring partner." He shook his head. "I had to stop myself from laughing."

"Who's the guy over there?" Layla asked, pointing to a man in a brick-dust-stained white robe and tanned boots kneeling in front of the realm gate.

"I can hear you," the man said, standing up and turning around. He removed the robe to reveal dark trousers and a blue T-shirt and dropped the robe onto the floor. "This temple's acoustics carry whispers. Took me a while to get it to work properly."

The man appeared to be in his mid-forties—although as so many non-human species aged differently than humans, he could have been thousands of years old—with short, white hair, and a perfectly maintained white beard. He walked over and took Layla's hand. "Leonardo," he said in a strong Italian accent.

"Wait, *the* Leonardo?" Layla asked. "I thought it was just a name."

"Why does everyone always say that when they meet me?" Leonardo asked. "Yes, *the* Leonardo." He waved his hands around theatrically, and a man and woman came out of a side room.

"That's Antonio," Leonardo said, pointing his thumb in the man's direction.

"Great introduction," Antonio said, offering Layla his hand, which she shook. Antonio was several inches taller than Leonardo and had a barrel-like chest. He was bald and clean-shaven, and his smile appeared to be genuine and full of warmth. He wore white-and-gray military fatigues and black boots.

"Are you his military guard?" Layla asked him, which Leonardo appeared to find hysterical.

"His partner," Antonio said, rolling his eyes in Leonardo's direction. "Although his murderer might also be an option in future."

The woman who was with Antonio shook Layla's hand. One side of her head was shaved, while the hair on the other side was left long. She wore jeans, a red shirt, and black trainers. "I'm Caitlin Moore."

"Galahad's daughter," Layla said before she could stop herself. "I'm so sorry."

"It's okay," Caitlin said. "I stayed here after most left. I didn't think it right to just . . . run away is probably the wrong term, but that's how it felt. We're trying to help Leonardo get the realm gate to change direction but, as Zamek's punch told you, it's not going well."

"I think I know the problem," Leonardo said as the realm gate activated.

No one even had time to react as a young woman staggered through the gate and collapsed to the ground. The woman's hair was a mixture of green, blue, and red, and she wore black leather armor with runes inscribed on it. The runes burned bright orange, and the woman didn't move from her collapsed position.

Leonardo was the first to reach her side. "This is Hel," he said.

"Loki's daughter?" Layla asked. "What's she doing here? And how did she get the realm gate to come here?"

"I am still here," Hel said from the floor. "And I can hear you."

"No pun, but what the hell is going on?" Layla asked.

"The realm of Helheim has almost fallen," Hel said. "I came for help. I came to save the lives of my people. Avalon found a way to link Nidavellir and Helheim. They poured hundreds of thousands of blood elves into my realm. If we don't get help soon, we'll lose a key realm in holding off Avalon's advance."

Zamek looked over at Caitlin and Layla. "We need to get back to the others."

"Yes, we do," Hel said, getting to her feet. "Mammon is in Helheim."

Things had just gotten *a lot* worse.

6

MORDRED

Mordred knew that everyone was going to get together at some point to discuss what should happen next, but he needed some time to himself. He hadn't been back to the palace since Galahad had been murdered, and he hadn't wanted to walk inside with everyone else and start openly weeping. Instead, he'd gone to the palace alone, and walked through the empty rooms and hallways until he'd come to the spot where he'd found the body of his friend.

Galahad had been the best of them, Mordred was certain of that. He had been a good man, and his death continued to sting Mordred more than he cared to admit, even years later.

Mordred crouched down in the room where Galahad had died and closed his eyes. "I miss you," he said softly. "I wish you were here to help. I think we could really use it." Mordred sighed and walked through the ruined wall to take a seat at the top of the palace steps.

Pieces of masonry that had at one time made up the rear wall of the palace were scattered across the field. The trees closest to the field hadn't yet recovered from the destruction. Nate Garrett had watched Galahad die, and he'd lost his temper. Mordred wished he'd seen it. Seen Nate finally cut loose on an army of blood elves, seen their fear as a sorcerer of incredible power no longer held himself back.

"We could use you too," Mordred said, thinking of Nate. He was one of the few who knew that Nate wasn't really dead, that he had lost all of his powers and had to go into hiding until they'd returned. It had been hard on Mordred to pretend that Nate was dead, to see people who loved him grieve for his loss, but he'd made a promise to Nate and he planned to keep it.

Mordred wondered if he should go join in the conversation about what to do next. Part of him wanted to, but another part wanted to just do what he felt he needed to do. The last few years had been a strange time for a man who had grown accustomed to having people run in fear from him. People now actively sought out his counsel—they *wanted* to know what he thought. He didn't consider himself a leader, nor much of a follower, but people just went along with his plans. It was quite frustrating. He started to hum the theme tune to *The Legend of Zelda*. It was how he made himself relax, although he'd had to increase the number of songs after people begged him to hum something—anything—other than the themes to Zelda and *Super Mario Bros*. Still, Zelda was the classic of choice.

"I figured I'd find you here," Lucifer said, taking a seat next to Mordred.

"I wanted to say goodbye," Mordred said. "Galahad would know what to do next. He would have stopped Avalon by now."

Lucifer stared at Mordred for several seconds. "You can't possibly believe that."

Mordred sighed. "No, but considering it makes me feel better."

"I was asked to bring you to the meeting. It's happening in the main hall of the palace. Lots of people deciding the next step."

Mordred sighed again. "They really need my help doing that?"

"They *want* your input, Mordred. I'm just an old devil, Hel is the ruler of Helheim, and Olivia and Tommy are ex-Avalon who know how to fight this war. But you, you were meant to be their king."

The mention of Hel's name brought back memories of them together in Helheim. Something close to a relationship had begun between them, but then Mordred had been sent back to the Earth realm to deal with Abaddon and her minions, and he hadn't seen her since.

"No," Mordred almost snapped. "No, no king. Not me. I'm just the unlucky schmuck who happened to have a psychopath for a brother and for a friend. Gawain and Arthur wanted me out of the way so that Arthur could become king. I honestly never wanted the job in the first place. If they'd have asked me to step aside, I probably would have."

Lucifer laughed. "Seriously? All they had to do was ask?"

Mordred nodded. "I know. All this shit, all this trouble, because they never thought to find out if I even wanted the job. Okay, once I'd realized they were murderous assholes, I'd have torn them in half, but at the time I didn't want to be king. I wanted to be drunk in a brothel surrounded by beautiful women."

"You wanted to be Remy?"

Mordred laughed. "Pre-fox Remy, yes, probably. Thinking about it, maybe that kind of lifestyle isn't as pleasant as it sounds." He paused for a second. "You say Hel is here?"

"Came through the realm gate," Lucifer told him. "You two have history."

"You could say that, yes." Mordred got to his feet. "Let's go see what everyone's doing then."

The pair walked through the palace to the main hall, which was roughly the size of a football field. Huge windows lined both sides of the room, and a long table that could easily seat several dozen people around it had been placed in the middle.

The ceiling forty feet above Mordred's head had been painted with murals of various landscapes. The room had once radiated opulence and splendor. The majority of decorations—the pictures on the walls, the thirty-foot-long curtains that covered the massive windows—had all been removed after Galahad's murder, along with anything else that had reminded Caitlin of her father. Mordred understood why she'd done it, why no one came into the palace, but he hoped over time that would change. The throne sat at the far end of the room at the top of a set of steps, and Mordred could make out the single golden crown that had been placed on it. Waiting for a new ruler.

The room was full of everyone who'd either arrived from the realm gate or from the fort. Olivia stood at the end of the table, reading something in front of her. She looked up and motioned for Mordred and Lucifer to take a seat.

"Glad you turned up," Tommy said to Mordred as he sat next to him.

"Well, I couldn't let all of you have the fun," Mordred said. "So has anyone decided anything yet?"

A soldier arrived at the front of the hall and nodded at Lucifer, who made his apologies and left. *Lucky bugger*, Mordred thought to himself.

"Right, the problem we have here is that Abaddon and Mammon are in Helheim, and the people need help," Olivia started.

"And we need to find out more about this weapon," Irkalla said.

"Also, Hades, Persephone, and several others are in Nidavellir," Remy said.

Hel stood. "My realm is under attack. I fear that there aren't enough of us left to hold out against Abaddon's army. My people are dying. I'm only here because there was nowhere else left to go, and Jinayca knew how to get me to Shadow Falls."

"Jinayca is in Helheim?" Zamek said, clearly concerned. "What happened to the dwarves in Nidavellir?"

Hel looked sad. "I'm sorry, Zamek. The blood elves attacked Sanctuary. Most escaped, but a lot died. Jinayca was taken prisoner, and Abaddon had her brought to Helheim to use her knowledge of the realm gates. We managed to rescue many of the hostages in a raid, and she's been fighting with us ever since. She found some ancient dwarven manuscripts and figured out how to change realm gate destinations, so she changed the one in Niflhel to bring me here."

"I'm glad to hear she's okay," Zamek said, relieved. "But that means the last of my people in Nidavellir are still in danger. I need a team to help them, and to rescue any prisoners from Greenland who might've been taken there."

"Okay, so how do we get there?" Layla asked.

"I know the address," Zamek said. "I think I can change the dwarven gate's destinations. So getting the one here to go to Nidavellir shouldn't be a problem. I'll get some help and should be ready to go in a few hours."

"I'll lead a small team into Nidavellir," Layla said. "I'll take Caleb to track down the missing prisoners if we can find something that belongs to one of them."

"I have some things of my mother's," Sky said.

"Excellent," Layla said. "That leaves Helheim, and I assume Mordred has a plan because he's been so unusually quiet."

Before Mordred could say anything, Lucifer returned with a binder and passed it to Olivia. "I did some research," Lucifer said. "I'd heard of this weapon of Abaddon's before. When the devils first fought against the Titans and their allies, they tried to use something similar. Abaddon called it the Devil's Venom, because she's always had a flair for the overly dramatic. This current one looks like a modified version of that, which makes sense since the original never worked properly."

"What does it do?" Olivia asked.

"It siphons life force to power four spikes arranged to cordon off an area. The staffs and a blood magic ritual combine to create a mist that removes the powers of anyone standing inside the perimeter."

"That's horrific," Layla said.

"It gets worse," Lucifer said. "I think Abaddon's in Helheim to go after the Yggdrasil tree. If she controls the tree, she controls the realm gates."

"Why does everyone look very worried all a sudden?" Layla asked.

"All dwarven realm gates have a piece of Yggdrasil inside them," Zamek said. "It's what links them together. The address of the realm gate is pure dwarven knowledge, but the power to actually activate it comes from the tree. You control the tree, and you can go anywhere, at any time."

"And if you used the Devil's Venom inside the tree . . ." Lucifer said.

"No one could use their powers there," Irkalla finished for him. "Those bracelets they wore in Norumbega would allow them to use their powers, but anyone else would be effectively human."

"Unless we just made some of the bracelets," Layla said.

"Yeah, but I would need several to figure out the runes they're using," Zamek told her. "By then the tree could have fallen."

"So this Yggdrasil tree, it's in Helheim?" Layla asked, looking over at Hel.

"The tree itself is in its own realm," Hel said. "There's a temple not far from where we're making our stand. Inside is a permanently active realm gate that takes you to Yggdrasil. It's why I built a giant city so close to it."

"Why not put a huge fort on top of it?" Layla asked.

"It moves," Zamek said. "The temple literally moves around the mountain range next to it. It's why cities were placed all around the mountains, so that it could be defended from anywhere."

"Except Abaddon and her people have taken all of the other cities. So, we have to hope the temple stays put until we can take back the realm."

"Oh," Layla said. "That's irritating."

"Anyway," Lucifer said. "We've had radio contact from the Wolf's Head compound in Germany. Cerberus said that they were under attack. And he described a purple mist after dozens of his people were killed."

"I'm going to Germany," Mordred said. "And not just because of Cerberus. If that compound falls, it won't be long before Avalon's people get into Tartarus, and then we'll have a war there too. Also, I have a plan."

"And that would be?" Layla asked.

"You remember Mara Range?" Mordred asked.

"Who's that?" Hel asked.

"My mum," Chloe said. "She was an evil megalomaniac who wanted to kill everyone who wasn't on her side. Me included. Mordred killed her a few years ago. Did the world a favor."

Mordred hadn't wanted to kill Mara—in his mind the choice of her death should have been given to Chloe first—but allowing Mara to live would have meant the deaths of innocent people, so he shot her in the head. He'd told Chloe the next day and she'd hugged him and cried with relief. Mara Range had been responsible for the deaths of countless innocents. No one was sad about her removal from the world, not even her own daughter, as it turned out.

"Well," Mordred said, bringing the conversation back to the topic. "She made a bunch of those irritating bracelet things. You know what I mean, right? The ones that allowed people to travel from the Earth realm to another realm without the need of a gate? The ones that caused us so much grief a few years back? You remember those, right?"

"We all remember, Mordred," Olivia almost snapped.

"Excellent. Well, I found a stash of them," Mordred explained. "Seeing how we haven't seen anyone from Avalon using them in the last few years, I think we can all assume that the ones I have are the last batch."

"How many is a stash?"

"A few thousand," Mordred said. "They're being kept safe. Means I need to get them back to Shadow Falls so they can be sent through to Tartarus."

"How are we going to get the bracelets into Tartarus?" Irkalla asked.

"That's where it gets complicated," Mordred said. "We all thought that Abaddon and her people bounced into Tartarus with those bracelets and then bounced out again, but that's not what happened. You remember when Hera tried to take over the compound and managed to free Cronus?"

"I was there, so yes," Tommy said.

"Well, I heard that Hera got Avalon to force Hades to allow a small group of her supporters into Tartarus to ensure its . . . security."

"Yeah, Dad wasn't thrilled," Sky said. "It was about four people. They stayed an hour or two and went back. One was Deimos."

"Well, one of them managed to paint a blood curse mark on the home of Cronus and Rhea," Mordred said. "We didn't find it until after the attack, but the bracelets had the exact mark. The same curse mark was found underground during the attack on Shadow Falls. We destroyed the mark in Shadow Falls and Tartarus, but I remember it. I get into Tartarus using one of the bracelets, remake the curse mark." Mordred paused. "I forgot to mention about a dozen of those bracelets go to Tartarus, and the rest have a blank destination. Did I forget that bit?"

"Yes," Irkalla said dryly. "So, we get to Tartarus, draw that mark, and we can get the bracelets into the realm?"

"That's the plan. If Zamek can provide us with what we need to put on those bracelets to take us from Tartarus to Helheim, we can get the Titans straight into the battle and everyone will be happy."

"It's not that simple," Zamek said. "A human has to make those bracelets. Mara could do it because a witch is essentially a human who has forced herself to learn magic—it's why it kills them." He paused. "Harry could do it. I could tell him how, and he could do it."

"Can't you just change the realm gate here to go to Tartarus and save everyone some time?" Hel asked.

"Yes, if I knew the address for the realm gate in Tartarus," Zamek said. "Does anyone here know the realm gate address? Because last

I heard the only people who knew it were Persephone, Hades, and Cerberus."

No one did.

"I get it wrong, everyone who steps through that gate dies," Zamek told them.

"So," Mordred said. "I go through the dwarven realm gate in the cavern here in Shadow Falls, which takes me to Maine. Once there, I make a call and get those bracelets ready for departure. We go to Germany, rescue everyone, become heroes, use the Wolf Head realm gate to get to Tartarus and, after I make the mark in Tartarus, Harry uses one of those bracelets to bring the rest of them to that realm. Then we bring the Titans to Helheim and save the day. Simple."

"Nothing is ever that simple," Tommy said.

"I'm coming with you," Hel told Mordred. "You're going to end up in Helheim anyway."

"Do you have enough bracelets for everyone?" Olivia asked.

"I doubt it," Mordred said. "There are tens of thousands of people in Tartarus."

"May I make a suggestion?" Tarron asked. He'd been silent throughout the entire meeting.

"Of course," Mordred told him.

"Zamek changes the gate's destination to Nidavellir and we all go through," Tarron said. "Zamek then returns here with the prisoners, including Hades and Persephone, who know the realm gate destination. Zamek uses the address to change the realm gate in the temple at Shadow Falls, and goes through to Tartarus. If there are a lot of prisoners, I can also create an elven gate that will help get us back here. Saves a lot of possibly hurt people marching through enemy territory."

"You can create a brand new elven gate?" Layla asked. "Like the one you created in Norumbega?"

Tarron nodded. "It will take time, but yes. I only need to know a destination address, and I know the one here for the elven realm gate in

Shadow Falls, so I can link them. So long as there isn't already a gate in Nidavellir. Can't have two elven gates in the same realm. Except Earth. I have disconnected the gate that goes from Norumbega to Shadow Falls, so the Shadow Falls elven gate is available to reconnect somewhere else. So, to reiterate, we use that gate to all come here. While I'm arranging a realm gate in Nidavellir, Zamek will use the dwarven gate we arrived through to come back here. He'll then change the destination of the gate to take him to Tartarus. He goes to Tartarus and, once there, he changes that gate to go to Helheim and links the dwarven gate in Helheim with the one here. Once we're back here we follow him through the realm gate to Helheim. Simple."

"We have wildly different views on the world simple," Remy said.

"All dwarven realm gates are two-way streets," Zamek said. "You change the destination of one, and it changes the destination of the one linked to it. Technically, following Tarron's idea means that Tartarus would no longer be accessible via the Wolf's Head compound realm gate. So, right now the temple realm gate goes to and from Helheim, but once I change it to take us to Nidavellir, the realm gate on the Helheim side will cease to go anywhere until its destination is changed."

"So, someone could just change it back to here and undo your work?" Irkalla asked.

"Yes," Zamek said. "So, no one should do that."

"I gave orders to change nothing on the Helheim end," Hel said.

Mordred thought for several seconds to try to get his head around what Tarron had said. "I . . . think that works," he said eventually. "Are you sure you can create a new realm gate?"

Tarron nodded. "A hundred percent, yes. It means Zamek can change the realms as needed on his end, and I can on mine. If there's an elven gate in Helheim, we could just use that one instead and all go straight there. Basically, I made your bracelet plan completely redundant, Mordred. Apologies."

Mordred caught Tommy trying not to laugh. "I liked my plan," Mordred said almost wistfully. "It was a good plan."

"His is better," Hel said.

"Yes, it is," Mordred agreed. "We still need to go to Wolf's Head though. If Avalon gets into Tartarus before we can change that realm gate, then we're going to have problems. And if Abaddon is after the tree, then we need to move fast."

"Everyone get your teams ready and prepare to ship out within the hour," Olivia said, and the meeting broke up.

Mordred stood and watched everyone file out of the room, until only Layla was left sitting at the table. "You have something to say?" Mordred asked.

"I want to thank you for keeping an eye on me," Layla said.

"You were heading into a dark place," Mordred told her. "Discounting the time I was no longer in control of my own mind, I've been where you are. I've looked over that precipice and seen nothing wrong with the darkness below. Someone had to drag me back from it. A lot of someones, actually. Everyone needs a hand sometimes."

Layla got up from the table and walked over to give Mordred a hug. "Since I've been here, I've heard a lot of people talk about how Galahad was the best of you all from your days at Camelot."

"He was," Mordred said.

"I'm sorry for your loss."

"Thank you."

"But you should know something, Mordred. You're the best of us."

Mordred smiled and tried to say thank you, but the tears flowed instead and he found himself unable to speak. They continued to hold each other, neither of them saying another word.

7

LAYLA CASSIDY

After the meeting had ended and Layla had left Mordred, she'd felt considerably better about everything. Both of them had needed to talk to people, although Layla had no idea that saying something nice to Mordred would have that effect on him. She supposed he hadn't been told a lot of nice things over the years. But Layla had needed the release too, to cry without questions, without anyone trying to ask her if everything was okay. Just two people who had gone through vast quantities of shit comforting each other. Layla had gone to get ready for her mission. She put on some black leather, rune-scribed armor, and picked out two silver daggers that she hung from her hips. It was always useful to have options when it came to the unknown fight that lay ahead.

When she was ready, Layla went to see her father. Caleb Cassidy was someone whom Layla had tried to put out of her mind for the better part of her teenage and early adult years. He'd been a crappy father and, as it turned out, a monstrous person. His murder toll was in three figures, and he wasn't shy about wanting to add to it. He deemed criminals to be people who had forsaken their right to live. In Caleb's mind, it was up to him to dish out the punishment that they deserved.

Caleb had been placed in a cell beneath the palace. The cells had remained mostly intact and were designed to keep even sorcerers from escaping. Runes had been carved into the brick of the dungeon, and six guards rotating on shifts remained outside Caleb's cell. There was never one guard alone, and no one went into his cell without backup.

No one except for Layla. Caleb was evil, Layla was pretty certain of that, but he'd never shown any aggression toward his own daughter. He told her that he would escape one day and resume his mission, but he never made any move to actually do so. He would happily remain in his cell until he could escape without harming the people he claimed he wanted to protect.

The dungeon was much smaller than Layla had imagined, especially considering the number of people who had lived in Shadow Falls before the attack had effectively turned it into a ghost town.

Layla walked up to the cell door, saying hello to the two large men who guarded it. One was playing some sort of card game on a small table, and the other was reading a book. The card player waved in Layla's direction without looking up, his concentration on something in front of him. The reader looked up from his book, then went right back to it.

Layla removed the keys from a hook on the opposite wall from the cell and opened the door.

Caleb Cassidy was just under six feet tall, bald, with a short blond beard and deep-green eyes. He was broad-shouldered, and being incarcerated had given him the time to increase his already considerable muscle mass. He looked more like a bouncer than someone who had once been a decorated FBI agent.

The cell had a bed, toilet, sink, small table, and a chair. Caleb sat at the table, playing with a set of cards.

Layla watched for a second as her father turned toward her. "Hello, Layla," he said with a warm smile.

"Dad, are you playing poker by yourself?"

Caleb looked down at the four hands of cards that sat around the table. "I got bored of blackjack, and there's only so much solitaire a man can play without wanting to throw the cards away. Can I assume that you're here to take me somewhere more interesting?"

"We're going to Nidavellir."

"I heard that Hades and Persephone had been captured. Genuinely sad about that. They were both kind to me during my stay. Hades often came to talk to me while we were in Greenland. I enjoyed speaking to him. He was a pragmatic man."

Layla actually believed Caleb was sincere about Hades and Persephone. "Not was, *is*."

Caleb nodded as if coming to terms with agreeing. "Yes, is, my apologies. I assume you'll be using my power to track your friends."

"Yes. That's the plan."

Caleb got to his feet. "Excellent. I haven't had much exercise in the last few days—it'll be nice to get outside."

"A word of warning," Layla said. "No one is in the mood for your games. Sky is coming with us, so if you start to play around, I'll be okay with her launching you off the highest mountain we can find."

Caleb held Layla's gaze for several seconds. "I think I can cope with that."

Layla led her father out of the dungeon and up to the palace above, where Chloe and Sky were waiting for them, both dressed like Layla. Chloe had a sword in a scabbard across her back, and Sky carried a huge claymore on hers, which Layla assumed had once belonged to her mom.

"I'm sorry about your parents," Caleb said. "Anything I can do to help, I will."

Sky smiled, although her eyes remained cold and unforgiving. "Yes, you will." She turned to Layla. "Shall we?"

"Do I get armor?" Caleb asked.

"No," Chloe told him. "Should make sure that you don't try running off into the wilderness at the first sign of trouble."

Caleb's smile was broad and full of nothing but happiness, but Layla knew that behind his outward appearance, he was angry at being undervalued.

Layla nodded toward the palace exit, and the four left and took a tram over to the realm gate temple where they were met by Tarron and Dralas. Dralas carried a massive hammer that was easily the size of Layla, while Tarron had opted for a sword and small dagger.

"This is your father?" Tarron asked.

"And what are you meant to be?" Caleb asked.

"You should be more respectful of Tarron," Dralas said, his tone containing a warning.

Caleb looked over at the giant. "Sure thing."

"Everyone is ready for us," Chloe said. "Also, if you could all behave for about five minutes, that would be great."

They walked up to the temple where they found Zamek inside next to the realm gate. They didn't notice that a group of people had entered, and Layla cleared her voice to get their attention.

Zamek turned to the group first. "Ah, you're here. You should know that where we're going used to be the main base for the blood elves. While it appears that a large number of them have gone, I doubt this will be smooth sailing."

"So, how does this work?" Layla asked. "With the realm gates changing destination, I mean?"

"Mordred gave me a list of ancient dwarven runes that apparently Nate had been working on putting together before . . ." Zamek looked down at the ground for a second. "Anyway, it's a revolutionary discovery. We don't need guardians for realm gate activation. We just needed to know how to manipulate the ancient runes that are part of every realm gate. Unfortunately, I can't permanently change them. They will reset to their original gate destination within a few days. Hopefully, that means we'll be able to use the gate we went through to get back here, so long as I can alter the runes on the other end. It could utterly change the way we travel between realms."

"Cool," Layla said, sounding much less excited than Zamek.

"Before you leave, I have a gift for Caleb," Leonardo said, brandishing what looked like a sorcerer's band.

"I already have one of those," Caleb almost snapped.

"Not like this you don't," Leonardo said with no hint that he cared how Caleb spoke to him, although Antonio visibly bristled at Caleb's tone.

"What does it do?" Sky asked, clearly in a hurry to be going.

"Short words would be useful at this point," Chloe said. "Please."

Leonardo smiled in her direction and nodded once. "I find sorcerer's bands to be . . . limiting. Yes, I know that's their point, but when someone has a power such as Caleb here, it might be useful for them to activate it without having access to other aspects of their power, such as a naturally increased speed and strength. Essentially, it means he can use his ability to find people without the risk of him changing into his drenik form."

"How long have you been testing it?" Caleb asked.

"About twenty minutes," Leonardo said. "Give or take."

Caleb turned to Layla. "You want me to wear untested technology that this person created twenty minutes ago?"

"You could always be forced to eat it, if that helps," Sky said, leaving no room for confusion that she most definitely meant that as an alternative.

Layla removed the key for Caleb's sorcerer's band from her pocket and unlocked it, passing both the band and key to Antonio. Leonardo gave the new band—which looked a lot like the old one—to Layla, who placed it on her father's wrist. When the lock clicked shut, the band glowed a deep blue for several seconds, before settling on its normal petrol color.

"Well, he hasn't burst into flames," Chloe said.

Leonardo shrugged. "I did wonder if it would explode, but apparently not."

Caleb glowered at Leonardo, who remained utterly disinterested in his expressions.

"He's joking," Antonio said, taking a step toward Caleb. "But you should stop looking at him like he's prey."

Caleb looked Antonio up and down and laughed, making the other man bristle with anger.

Sky placed a hand on Caleb's shoulder and squeezed slightly, causing him to drop to his knees. "I want you to understand something, Caleb," Sky said, her tone calm. "If you piss me off at any point, I'm going to kill you. No games, no playing, no second chance. I like Layla, and you can be helpful, and those are the only reasons why you're not currently rotting in an unmarked grave. Am I clear?"

Caleb nodded, and Sky released her grip. "Get the gate activated, Zamek," she said. "We need to leave."

Zamek didn't argue, and a few moments later the gate was up and ready, the view through the gate showing the inside of a large room somewhere in the citadel of Nidavellir.

The team started to move through the realm gate with Caleb going between Sky and Zamek.

"Take care," Leonardo said to Layla. "Be quick."

"But mostly take care," Antonio said with a slight shake of his head.

"I will," Layla told them. "Keep safe. All of you."

"We'll do our best," Leonardo assured her. "Just get back to us."

Layla stepped through the realm gate, which stopped working the moment she found herself in a large room with the rest of the team. The walls were made of dark-red brick that put Layla in mind of blood. The floor was covered in gray stone, and there was nothing else in the room except for a single metal door at the far end that looked as though it hadn't been used in a long time.

Sky removed the claymore from her back and gave it to Caleb. "This belonged to my mom. Can you use it to see where she is?"

Caleb closed his eyes as his power ignited. "She's in the citadel. She's a few floors below us, in a cell. She's alone." Caleb passed the claymore back to Sky. "I can track her without it now."

"We'll head down to find Persephone and try to figure out how we can get out of there without bringing however many blood elves are still here down on our heads."

"Sounds like a plan," Chloe said.

Layla touched the door to the room and it dissolved into a puddle of metal before moving aside so that no one had to walk through it to get out.

Layla's team crept down the stairs that were directly outside until they reached a few floors below and, with Layla taking the lead, they headed down a dark corridor to where Caleb said Persephone was located.

"Hey, Layla," Chloe shouted as they were halfway down the corridor.

Layla looked back at her, slightly surprised that Chloe would be shouting during a mission of stealth.

"You need to see this," Chloe told her.

"I really hope there's no one around who can hear us."

Chloe turned and walked off to join the others standing beside a ten-foot high gap in the wall. It appeared as if part of the brick had been torn apart. She peered through the hole and surveyed the camps that littered the open area outside the citadel. There was no one there.

Layla stepped through the opening in the wall and looked up at the citadel that towered hundreds of feet above her. The roof of the mountain twinkled with tiny gems, which made it seem as though the sky was there instead of miles of rock.

"Where is everyone?" Layla asked.

"It's deserted," Tarron said. "Devoid of anything resembling a living being."

"I know that many of their kind have gone to Helheim, but I didn't expect the blood elves to just abandon this citadel," Zamek said. "So many of my kind died to defend this, and then when they lost it, so many died trying to retake it. For the blood elves to just run off and leave it . . ."

Layla walked over to the nearest camp. The smell of blood and death hung in the air. The camp consisted of six tents in a circle around a long-since extinguished fire. A colossal bridge had once run from the main entrance of the citadel to the top of a nearby cliff. A few hundred feet long and twice as high, it had been an impressive structure, but was now in pieces. She remembered Kase telling her that on their last trip here, she'd been abducted by the blood elves and taken to the citadel. To get her back the rescuers had destroyed the bridge, and a large part of the citadel. Layla could still see the damage from where she stood.

Layla found herself stopping by a large pit. It was ten feet deep and thirty feet wide, with wooden boards planed all around it, topped with some sort of barbed wire. Dried blood drenched every inch of the pit.

"Fighting pits," Zamek said as he caught up with Layla and stood beside her. "The elves use them for keeping their people in line."

"My people have fallen so far," Tarron said, kneeling next to the pit and staring down into the horror that had once resided there.

"How many elves would you think lived here?" Layla asked.

"Thousands," Zamek said. "Tens of thousands."

"It was like Mordor," Chloe said. "But without the orcs and big eye."

Sky and Persephone exited the citadel together, followed closely by Caleb and Dralas. Persephone was leaning heavily on her daughter. A sorcerer's band sat on her wrist, and her face was puffy and swollen where she'd been hit.

"They left me here to die," Persephone said. "Elizabeth figured I was worthless while they have my husband and Nabu."

"Anyone else?" Zamek asked.

"Lots of dead," Sky said. "A few dozen. They've only had our people for a few days, but they murdered almost all of them."

"Your mother does not like me a whole lot," Persephone told Layla.

"I'm so sorry," Layla said. "You need some rest, and we need to take that damned thing off."

Steve McHugh

"They've taken Hades and Nabu to the library," Persephone said. "I'll rest when they're safe."

The library was a massive structure deep inside the mountain, where the dwarves kept all of the knowledge. Layla also knew that it was the scene of massive battles between the elves and dwarves, and last she'd heard it had been overrun by vast numbers of blood elves.

"To the library then," Sky said before moving off, her arm around Persephone's shoulders.

"I still have to play nice, I assume," Caleb said.

"Dad, just once, try to act like you aren't waiting for a moment to escape. Please."

Caleb stared at his daughter for several seconds. "I will help your friends, Layla," he said, turning to follow Sky and Persephone.

"Chloe, can you go with them. Just to keep the peace?"

Chloe smiled and hurried after Caleb, just as the sound of drums got everyone's attention. It was soon followed by the sound of footsteps marching toward them on the ridge high above.

"It's a trap," Layla said, motioning for Sky, Persephone, Chloe, and Caleb to run toward the shadow of the bridge. Zamek, Tarron, and Dralas followed suit.

Layla watched as Chloe practically dragged her father away into the shadows of the ruined bridge and out of sight as hundreds of blood elves appeared on the ridge above them.

Amongst all the faces of creatures who wished nothing more than their deaths, Layla made out one in particular. Her mother.

Layla knew that if her team ran into the blood elf army they couldn't win, couldn't even hope to. She also knew that if the blood elves descended en masse, those in her group who were hidden from sight would quickly be found. She raised her hands in the air. "I surrender," she bellowed. "I need to talk to you, Mom."

Her words were followed by a cacophony of laughter from those watching.

8

LAYLA CASSIDY

The blood elf's fist smashed into Layla's mouth, knocking her to the ground. Layla spat blood onto the floor and waited for another punch, but a commanding voice stopped them.

"Hello, Layla," Elizabeth said as she entered the hut Layla had been dragged into. Her mother had descended the ridge alone, smirking the entire time, and taken Layla into custody, demanding to know whether she was alone. On her assurance that she was, the army of several hundred had split apart with the majority going off in one direction while Layla had been taken in another. They'd walked for several hours, until they reached a deserted row of buildings, and then Layla had been shown the blood elf hospitality she'd gotten to know so well since becoming an umbra.

Elizabeth was roughly Layla's size and had shoulder-length blonde hair, streaked with black. She wore dark-gray leather armor etched with runes. It looked similar to Layla's, although the sharp silver knuckles that adorned the back of Elizabeth's gloves were there purely to hurt. In Layla's mind, that pretty much summed up Elizabeth.

"Elizabeth," Layla said, sitting back on the ground. "I'd like to say it's nice to see you, but seeing how you cut off my arm, I'm more inclined to tell you to piss off."

"You don't seem all that concerned about your own well-being," Elizabeth said.

"I'm not afraid of you, and I've killed enough blood elves not to be afraid of them either."

"Oh, these aren't like the blood elves you fought before. These ones have been here for a long time, fighting amongst themselves. They're more vicious than any you've faced, and I don't think you'll like being in their company for long. In fact, I think I'll take you to Sanctuary and show you exactly what these blood elves are capable of."

"And then what? What happens next? You haven't even put a sorcerer's band on me, so is this just theater, or is there a plan? I escape and you hunt me down, is that it?"

Elizabeth glared at Layla for several seconds. "I hate you."

"Feeling is mutual," Layla assured her. "You're running around in my mother's body, desecrating her memory. And you cut off my arm. I think hate might actually be too tame."

"When I took your mother's body and claimed it as my own, I did not realize the undertaking I would have to endure. Her . . . memories. When I sleep, I remember you. I remember her love for you. I felt remorse for hurting you. Do you understand?" Elizabeth punched a hole in the nearby wall. "Why did you allow yourself to be captured?"

"I needed to see if there was truly any of my mother left in you. There isn't. I know you cut my arm off, but I'd hoped that away from Abaddon, my mother might gain some measure of control, but she was never capable of gaining control. Despite you saying her memories are in your head, there's none of her left."

"I want to kill you," Elizabeth said. "But I'm not sure I want to feel the emotional hurt afterwards. It is a new sensation for me. So you're going to come with us to Sanctuary, where you will watch us search for survivors. And then I will hand you over to Abaddon in Helheim, and she will execute you."

"How are we getting out of this realm?" Layla asked, genuinely curious.

"There's an old elven realm gate beneath the library," Elizabeth said, smiling as she noticed the shock on Layla's face. "Yes, the blood elves made the same expression when we found it. It was unexpected, I have to say. A way out of this realm for all those blood elves, and it sat undisturbed for millennia."

Layla watched Elizabeth for several seconds. "You hated my mother, didn't you?"

"I didn't. I actually admired her ability to do whatever she felt she needed to do. But that was before I removed your arm. Before I felt . . . sorry. You have a drenik in your head—how does it feel about you?"

"Terhal and I have an arrangement. She comes out when I need her."

"And you don't feel like this is a dangerous enough situation?" Elizabeth asked.

"You won't hurt me. That's not because there's any of my mother left in you, but because you're terrified there might be just a few more of her memories to remember. A few more nights of human memories in your head."

"Do not mock me, girl," Elizabeth snapped.

"I'm not," Layla said. "I wanted to kill you. More than anything in this world, I want to be able to do it, but I know I can't. I can't kill my own mother, even if you're not really her. But it turns out I don't need to. Your head is your own little torture. I think that might be enough."

"Abaddon will hurt you in very creative ways."

"Probably, but it's a long time between now and then." Layla knew her friends were out there, and that they'd find her. She wouldn't be handed over to Abaddon, she was confident of that, and the fact that her mother's memories were causing the drenik pain gave her some comfort, as though her mom was still fighting for her even from the grave.

A blood elf entered the hut and whispered something to Elizabeth. She nodded and waved it away. "We're good to go. We won't be stopping again until we reach our destination. If you need water, or to use the facilities, I suggest you do so now."

"Water would be good."

Elizabeth barked an order in blood elf and they brought a canteen, dropping it on the floor by Layla's feet.

"Drink," Elizabeth commanded. "You have sixty seconds. It's not poisoned, by the way—it's from a spring that goes past the dwarven library. It's cleaner than anything you've ever had."

Layla took a taste of the water. She was right, it was cool and refreshing. Elizabeth wouldn't admit that hurting Layla had caused her emotional pain and then poison her, so she drank about half the canteen before handing it back to her captor.

"I changed my mind. Keep it," Elizabeth told her. "I don't have time to be getting you more if you're thirsty. We have plenty to go around."

"Thank you."

Elizabeth's eyes narrowed. "Do not mistake my generosity for weakness. I might not like the idea of hurting you again, but my blood elves are less concerned about my emotional well-being."

The entire group set off the second Layla stepped out of the hut, canteen slung over her shoulder. Layla led the way with Elizabeth on one side and two blood elves on the other.

"Twenty-six blood elves and one umbra is quite the number to guard little old me," Layla said after an hour of walking, as the group stepped under an arch of stone and found a small, partially destroyed hut nearby. "Aren't there better things they can be doing?"

"No," Elizabeth said.

"Blood elves must have been thrilled to find something that showed who they were back when they were shadow elves," Layla said. "And before you yell at me or something, I'm just genuinely curious. We both know neither of us is able to kill the other, so this is about as close to cordial as we can get."

Elizabeth continued to stare at Layla for several seconds. "They pray to it."

"Wait, what?" Layla asked, not sure that she heard her right.

"They kneel beside the realm gate and pray to it. I do not know why. Abaddon doesn't know why either, and none of the blood elves have been forthcoming with a reason. We found another elven realm gate in Siberia, but the blood elves were kept away from it until their blood was needed to activate it. They revered it. No amount of . . . questioning has discovered the reason."

"Seeing how we're being so pleasant," Layla said. "I have one question. If you don't want to answer, just say so."

Elizabeth crossed her arms over her chest, but nodded anyway.

"The big blood elf commanders," Layla said, motioning to the one huge blood elf at the rear of the pack. "Why are they so much bigger than the normal blood elves?"

"They are the best of the blood elves," Elizabeth said. "The strongest, the fastest, the most durable. They are not things that you want to fight. And they can only be found here, in Nidavellir. Gives you more of an incentive to behave yourself, doesn't it?"

"Lucky Nidavellir," Layla said.

"Move," Elizabeth commanded.

Layla did as she was told, and continued walking through the increasingly ruined dwarven kingdom, until the smell of smoke reached her. In the distance, fire burned on the walls of the mountain, and as she walked closer, the smell changed to that of burning flesh. Layla coughed and tried to spit the taste out of her mouth, making Elizabeth and the blood elves laugh, and forcing Layla to calm herself and not strike out at one of them.

Elizabeth wafted her hands in front of her face, as if inhaling the aroma as deeply as possible. "Barbecued dwarf is a delicacy for the blood elves."

Layla fought down the urge to vomit and tried to ignore the smell, but the closer she got to the fires, the stronger the smell became.

"Welcome to Sanctuary," Elizabeth said, pointing to the partially destroyed, huge barricade that had once made up the entrance to the city. A number of blood elves sat outside it, and as Layla reached the remains of the barrier, she discovered that the blood elves were roasting what appeared to be the leg of a dwarf over a spit.

Layla vomited onto the ground beside her, much to the entertainment of those with her.

"This used to be a dwarven stronghold," Elizabeth said with a smile, forcing Layla to look up at the entrance, at the dead dwarves nailed to the stone itself and left to rot. "It's now a graveyard. Or fast food outlet, depends on your perspective." Elizabeth forced Layla upright, and pointed her toward the barricade. "Inside, now."

"Why?" Layla asked. "You want to brag? I think you've made your point."

"Inside," Elizabeth paused. "Do not make me ask a commander to carry you in there."

Layla spat onto the ground and walked through the entrance and into what had once been the last city of the dwarves in the realm of Nidavellir. The place was a ruin. Buildings had been burned down, bodies had been dragged into houses and left to rot. Some dwarves had been nailed to the buildings, mimicking those on the barricade. Layla had witnessed the barbaric brutality of the blood elves before, but to see such wholesale slaughter was something she'd never thought possible.

"This is what happens to those who cross Avalon," Elizabeth said.

Layla's mind went to Greenland, and she wondered just how horrific the attack there would have been if so many hadn't managed to escape.

"You brought me here to gloat?" Layla asked.

"Not exactly," Elizabeth said, pushing the younger woman forward. They walked through the city toward a massive gray stone building that loomed over everything around it. It had scorch marks all over it, but was otherwise still in good condition.

"What is it?" Layla asked.

"The buildings of the elders," Elizabeth said. "It was where the plans were decided, and those in charge plotted against Avalon's crusade."

Crusade? Layla thought. *They're all bloody zealots.*

"And I need to go in there because?"

"Because we can't," Elizabeth said. "We believe that the dwarves here had information that would be helpful to our cause. The names of realm gate destinations, runes that could be beneficial. We can't be certain, but it still needs to be checked. And frankly I don't want to risk the lives of my people. I know I said I can't kill you without the concern of emotional trouble, but if you happened to die in the service of Abaddon I'm sure I would be able to get over it. Besides, I don't want to risk anyone on it. Our dwarven helper informed us that they would have put traps inside, and since I don't want to have to try to disarm them, I'm going to have you do it."

Layla laughed. "I can't read dwarven runes. I have no idea how to disarm a trap. Maybe your dwarven helper should come do this?"

"He can't," Elizabeth said. "He's busy helping us track down anyone who might have escaped this place."

Layla made a mental note about the dwarven helper. Zamek would want to have a word with him should they meet. Probably several words. "So, what exactly do you want me to do in there?"

"There's a room at the far end of the elder building. There are runes painted on it, and we want you to open it. And when I say want, I'm not giving you anything like a choice in the matter."

"Can I at least take a weapon with me?"

Elizabeth laughed as if Layla had said the funniest thing she'd ever heard. "You have your umbra powers. Use them. The door we need you to open is black-and-silver metal."

Layla walked over a small bridge with a stream running under it, and up the stairs to the elder building. The front door was already open, and she walked inside, her footsteps echoing around the hall that sat beyond the entrance.

Twenty-foot-high pillars sat every few feet around the hall, each one carved with hundreds of intricate depictions of battles. Doors ran along either side, and a set of circular stairs led to a balcony above, where Layla spotted more doors. Most of the doors were golden in color, and most had dwarven runes etched onto them, although, as Layla had told Elizabeth, she couldn't read them, and therefore had no idea what they said or did.

There were three black-and-silver doors, and Layla sighed as she walked over to the first of them. She saw no runes, although that didn't mean much considering how well they could be hidden, and placed her hand against the door, turning it partly to liquid, and then darting aside to avoid any explosion. When none came, she pushed open the rest of the door and stepped into the large room.

Scrolls littered the floor, the table in the middle of the room, and the desk at the far end. They were stacked, head high, all around the room, and Layla wondered just how dangerous it would be to anyone who was in the room when some of the stacks fell over. She picked up one of the closest scrolls, but it was in dwarven and she couldn't read it.

"This is going to be a complete waste of time," Layla said. She didn't like the idea of being used as a miner's canary. She backed out of the room, careful not to trip over the piles of paper, and walked over to the second of the three doors. This one had a red rune painted on it.

Layla returned to the first room and picked up a blank piece of paper, scrunching it up into a ball. Going back to the hall, she stood behind one of the pillars and threw the paper at the rune-marked door. When nothing happened, she reached out with her power, feeling all around the door, trying to spot a weakness in its structure.

Finding nothing obvious, she pushed out slightly. The door exploded without a sound. One minute it was whole, the next it had ripped apart and flung itself at high speed around the chamber. Layla dove to the ground as a large piece of metal tore through one of the stone columns just inches above her head. She remained still for a few seconds, before risking a roll away from the pillar.

Getting to her feet, she walked over to the hole where the door had once been. Pieces of metal jutted out of the wall, and she carefully stepped through. She wondered how it was even possible, and how much power had been poured into the rune to give it the force that she'd witnessed.

The interior of the room was spotless. A long table sat in the middle of the large chamber surrounded by chairs. She walked to the end of the room, and tried to work out exactly what the rune was meant to be hiding, or protecting. There was nothing there.

"What the hell is the point of all this?" Layla asked, turning a full circle as she tried to figure out what the dwarves who had lived here were trying to protect. Layla moved one of the chairs and sat down. "Okay," she said to herself. "Someone shut the door and drew a really powerful rune on it that would kill anyone trying to open it. Why? Who put the rune there?"

She left the room and went back into the center of the chamber outside. "Misdirection," she decided, walking over to the third black-and-silver door that was also without a rune. She pushed it, but it wouldn't budge, so she crushed it and pulled it out of the doorway, revealing a small room that was empty apart from small mounds of dirt.

They tunneled their way out, she thought to herself. *They made the elves think that the rune-scribed rooms were hiding something, knowing that the elves would be obsessed with getting into a room they couldn't get to. Which means one of the rooms must have a way out.*

She returned to the main chamber, hastily removed a gold door from another room and placed it where the black-and-silver one had been. Checking out the room, she found it similar to the one with all the paper, except for one thing; it contained another door. She went over and gave it a small shove. It opened to reveal a set of stairs leading down to the rear of the building. Relieved at discovering a way out, she quickly repaired the black-and-silver metal door she'd crushed and fixed it into position where the gold door had been. When she was sure that the coast was clear, she ran down the stairs as fast as she could.

9

LAYLA CASSIDY

Layla took the final quarter of the steps three at a time until she reached the stone-covered street at the bottom. A huge iron gate sat between her and an alley beyond, and nearby buildings cast dark shadows over everything around her. She moved the metal aside, creating a hole large enough to climb through, and, once free, ran through Sanctuary's winding alleys, avoiding patrols and staying as far away from the blood elves and Elizabeth as possible.

Layla wondered whether she could use whatever tunnels the dwarves had dug to escape the city, but it looked like the dwarves had collapsed the tunnel the second it was safe to do so. The best option was to keep running.

She reached the end of an alley and had to force herself to stop as she saw another blood elf commander further up the street, although this one had a dark-gray cat with it. A cat that was probably the same height as Layla.

What the hell is that? she asked herself, not sure she actually wanted an answer. She hoped that whatever it was was too far away to be able to smell her. Not wanting to take that risk, she turned and ran back down the alley. She wove in and out of the alleys until she found herself in a large cavern where torches burned along each wall, lighting up the ruins and temple inside. The temple was at least seven stories tall and made from brilliant-white brick.

Her entire plan had been to get as far from Elizabeth and her blood elves as possible, but the maze of roads and alleyways that all looked the same meant she was quickly lost. Hopefully that would make it harder for her enemies to find her, but it also meant she didn't know which way to go next. She turned around as the sound of footsteps alerted her to three blood elves stepping out from the side of the temple.

"You smell tasty," one of the blood elves said. He was the smallest of the three with a nasty cut across one eye and a nose that had been broken so many times it was impossible to know what its original shape had been. "Told not to feast on you, but maybe just a little bit."

Layla watched the three elves as they approached her, until they were only ten feet from her. "I wonder how quickly I could kill you?"

The elves snarled at Layla and one stepped forward. Layla took two steps toward the blood elves, then turned her metal arm into a spear, piercing the nearest blood elf's skull. The metal returned to her arm as the elf dropped dead to the ground.

The other two elves—including the one with the broken nose—charged Layla, who turned her arm into a blade and, dodging the first strike, drove it into the exposed throat of the second blood elf. She darted away from another blow and circled the remaining blood elf. She reached out to take control of the dark-purple sword, but discovered it wasn't made of metal like she'd expected.

"Crystal blade," the blood elf said with a sick chuckle, sounding as if it had phlegm caught in its throat. It darted toward Layla, who had to move quickly to avoid the blade, but the blood elf drew a dagger and twisted itself to stab her in the ribs with it. She jerked away, but it still cut through her leather armor with ease. Layla felt blood trickle down her stomach.

She parried a strike with the sword, and watched in horror as the blood elf's sword cut through her metal arm, severing the blade she'd created. Layla backed away, putting several feet between her and her attacker, who licked the blade with his tongue, cutting it open, but showed no evidence of pain or distress, even as its blood coated part of the weapon.

Layla reattached her metal blade to the rest of her arm, before remaking her hand, and took a deep breath. The blood elf moved forward, swinging the sword in an effort to get her to step back toward a nearby wall, but instead she stepped around the elf, narrowly avoiding being cut, before making her blade twice as long and driving it into its skull.

She withdrew the blade and remade her hand before walking off to the temple where she found a barrel of water. She washed her arms in the cold liquid and splashed some on her face. She wasn't sure whether or not it was sanitary, but it couldn't be any worse than having blood elf splattered all over her.

A low growl from behind her took her attention, and she turned around as a blood elf commander walked toward her, accompanied by one of the cats. Being much closer to the beast gave Layla an unwelcome chance to see just how big it was.

"Saber-tooth panther," the commander said, patting the creature, which was larger than any cat Layla had ever seen. It was as tall as Layla and looked like something you rode into battle. The fur was blacker than she'd assumed earlier and shimmered purple as it moved.

"We introduced some to the crystals," the commander said. "Makes them more trainable."

"Nice for you," Layla said, backing around to the side of the temple and heading down a gentle slope.

"You can't outrun us," the commander said, walking after her as if he had all the time in the world. "She got your scent—she'll track you all over this mountain until she claims her prize."

"Ah, I'm a prize," Layla said sarcastically. "How sweet."

Layla stopped at the bottom of the slope, which opened into a large space surrounded by several small huts. She didn't risk a proper look as taking her eyes off the commander or beast beside him was probably a bad idea.

"So, is it the crystals that make you big then?" Layla asked the commander.

The commander smiled and unslung a black maul from his back, placing the massive steel head on the ground. The head was flat at one end with a spike on the other, and appeared to be made of the same substance as the sword the blood elf had used earlier. Even the shaft of the weapon was made from wood. Her power was useless against it.

"Sit," the commander told the panther, who did as she was told. He turned back to Layla. "I wonder if I can break you like I have the cat. Would you sit on command?"

Layla bristled with anger. "Come find out."

The commander laughed. "Let's make sure you're worth my time."

Layla rolled her shoulders. Her body would ache later, but if she didn't give it everything she had, she'd be dead and last time she checked the dead didn't much care about such things. Better to be alive and ache. She cracked her knuckles as the blood elf put his fists up in a sort of boxing stance as he stalked toward her.

She avoided the first hit and the commander's fist smashed through the wall of the hut behind her. Layla kicked out at his stomach, ducking under his stuck arm and slamming her elbow into his groin before rolling past him, back to her feet. She kicked out at the back of his knee, forcing him down onto one, before he pulled his arm free. She saw the blow coming, and moved to block it in time, but the power of it lifted her off her feet and dumped her ten feet back.

The commander looked pained as he got back to his feet, and picked up his weapon from where it lay.

Layla ran forward, scooped up one of the swords that she was unable to manipulate, and moved toward the blood elf commander, who laughed as he raised the maul to strike. Layla dodged at the last second, avoiding the blow, and drove the blade up toward her adversary's stomach, but he moved quicker than she'd anticipated. The blade only sliced through his side before he backhanded her, sending her spinning. She got to her feet just in time to duck a second swing of the maul.

She changed her arm into a whip as she rolled across the stone covered ground and snapped it up toward the commander, cutting him across his face, which bled profusely. She turned her arm into a blade and sliced the hand holding the maul. The commander roared with rage, dropped his weapon, and threw a punch at Layla, who was already circling around him. He twisted, trying to keep her in sight. She grabbed the sword on the floor with her metal arm, then lengthened it, turning it into a lance, and pierced the commander's chest.

He grabbed the blade and tried to pull it free from his body. Layla let go, stepped toward him, and transformed her arm into a battering ram that smashed into the hilt of the sword, driving it through his chest and out his back. He dropped to his knees, and Layla picked up the maul.

"Shouldn't have thought you weak," the commander said.

Layla said nothing as she drove the spiked end of the maul into the blood elf's skull, releasing the shaft of the weapon and watching as the momentum of the blow knocked him to the ground.

Layla turned to the feline. "You really want to do this?"

The saber-tooth panther growled.

"Can you understand me?" Layla asked in the language of the shadow elves.

Another growl.

"How about now?" Layla repeated in English.

The panther stopped and turned her head to one side, a display that Layla thought was more dog-like than cat.

"You understand this language, don't you?" Layla asked. "Paw the ground once for yes."

The massive animal pawed the ground.

"How is that possible? How can you learn a language?"

The panther turned to look at the temple.

"They put you in there?"

The cat nodded.

She turned toward a commotion behind her to see Chloe, Tarron, and Zamek charge around the corner of a hut, stopping when they saw the body of the commander.

"Layla, step away," Zamek said.

The panther growled, low and menacing.

"No, it's fine," Layla said to the panther, who sat back on her hind legs. She turned to her friends, unsurprised that they'd found her. "This cat understands me. The blood elves forced her to go in the temple." The panther pawed the ground, looking at Layla for acknowledgement.

"It really understands you?" Chloe asked.

The panther pawed the ground again, and Chloe's expression turned from surprise to outright shock.

"It was where languages could be learned," Zamek said, looking over at the temple.

"How did the searching the library go?" Layla asked.

Zamek's expression said that it was not an overwhelming success. "We haven't been there, yet," he said. "We decided to come grab you first while the others scouted for blood elf patrols." He pointed at the temple. "There's a machine in there that used runes on a person to transport information into their minds. I've never heard of it being used on a cat."

"She understands English," Layla said.

Tarron walked up to the panther, stopping a foot away and crouching down. "You're an interesting creature. Why are you wearing a collar?"

"It shocks her." Layla looked at the panther. "Can we try to remove it?"

"She's a juvenile," Zamek said as the panther lay down.

"I'm sorry," Chloe said. "That cat is massive. You're telling me she'll get bigger?"

"No," Zamek said. "Saber-tooth panthers are fully grown in about six months. If you can find them early enough and train them, they're loyal companions. But the level of intelligence this one has shown is beyond anything I've ever seen."

"They forced this one to eat the crystals that turned them into blood elves," Layla said.

"Shit," Chloe whispered. "They tortured this poor animal." She walked over to the panther, who showed no signs of aggression. "Can we get that collar off?"

The panther pawed at the ground and rubbed its head against Chloe's outstretched hand.

"Working on it," Zamek said, placing his hands around the panther's massive neck. "This might hurt. And also, for future reference, I can't believe we're doing this to save an animal that might want to eat us."

"I don't think she does," Tarron said. "She's young. I don't think the programming they tried with her has stuck yet. The fact that she's able to understand a human language is interesting."

Tarron walked off before anyone could stop him, and Zamek shouted in pain as he tried to remove the collar. "Damn thing shocked me," he said, before sucking his finger.

"Need a hand?" Chloe asked, removing a dagger from her belt. She held the panther's gaze. "Do not eat me."

The panther made a huffing noise as if the very idea was offensive.

Layla walked around to the opposite side of the panther. "On three," she said. "We both grab the collar, lift it, and Chloe cuts it."

Zamek and Layla positioned their hands just above the collar. "Three," Layla said, and grabbed hold of the collar, lifting it as the electricity ran through her body. Zamek grabbed hold of his end of the collar, and Chloe sliced through it with her blade.

"Shit, shit, shit, shit, shit," Layla said, hopping from one foot to the other. "That's like holding one of those fences used to keep cows in their field."

"An electric fence?" Chloe asked with a smile.

"Screw you and your grinning, woman," Layla shouted.

The panther rubbed its massive head against Layla's hand, causing her to jump.

"You've made a friend," Chloe said.

"You're free to go," Layla told her. "Free. You can leave now."

The panther sat back, staring at Layla.

"Free," Layla repeated. "You can go."

The cat yawned, showing off its terrifying set of teeth. She licked Layla's hand.

"Congratulations," Chloe said. "You just got the world's most terrifying pet."

Layla shared a look with the predator who was licking her hand. "What the hell am I meant to do with you?"

The cat moved her head so that Layla could scratch her behind the ears as Tarron came out of the temple. "That panther was put in a machine designed for humanoids. That's what allowed them to manipulate her mind, to make her docile. Compared to the wild versions of her kind, anyway. It's a miracle she isn't in constant pain."

A horn blared in the distance.

"We need to leave," Layla said as Zamek began to search the blood elf commander's corpse. "My mom and a lot of blood elves are up there."

"There's a tunnel this way," Chloe said.

"Found it," Zamek proclaimed, showing off a small key. "Let's get moving."

Chloe, Tarron, Zamek, and Layla ran off toward the tunnel with the saber-tooth panther in tow. When they reached the mouth of the tunnel, Layla looked back at the panther. "Just try not to get yourself hurt, okay?"

The panther pawed at the ground.

They ran for twenty minutes before they found Sky, Persephone, and Caleb inside an old house, far enough away from any blood elves that might be patrolling the area.

"What the bloody hell is that?" Sky asked when they arrived with the saber-tooth panther padding behind.

"It's a hippo," Layla said. "What does it look like?"

"It looks like something that once tried to eat me," Sky said. "These things don't give up once they decide you're food."

The cat sat beside Layla, looked up at Sky once, and then ignored her.

"Acts like a normal cat," Layla said. "Except a hundred times bigger. The size of the litter box alone is going to be staggering."

Zamek walked over to a pale-looking Persephone and unlocked the sorcerer's band, tossing it aside as if even touching it might make him ill.

"Thank you," Persephone said, rubbing her wrist. "I feel better already."

"How did the scouting go?" Layla asked.

"I managed to find a key to a sorcerer's band," Zamek said. "Thus ends the good parts of the search."

"My husband is in the dwarven library," Persephone said.

"We found some blood elf patrols and dealt with them," Sky said. "But we need to get into the library, and we thought it better to wait for you all to come back."

Caleb shrugged. "Not in," he corrected. "Beneath. Far, far beneath. Maybe a few miles straight down. Persephone was wearing something of his, so I can track him."

Persephone showed the black ring that adorned her thumb. "He gave it to me before he was taken. Caleb can use this to find him." It was not a suggestion.

"Of course," Layla said. "Where's Dralas?" The giant was conspicuous by his absence.

"He went to search the perimeter," Sky said. "Should be back soon. I don't think he liked being inside a house made for dwarven heights."

"I'll go look for him," Tarron said. "I think we should be moving soon."

"Agreed," Layla said. "I'll come with you—hopefully we'll find him quicker as a pair. When we return, we'll need to get going. Zamek any idea how we get beneath the library?"

"There are a series of tunnels that lead from close to the bridge to the library down below. They might have blood elves in them though, and that might well become a certainty the lower we get."

"We found an elf who was more willing to give up information," Sky said. "It sounds like they've taken the prisoners to where the blood elves lived. The blood elf told us that there are still quite a few of them left in the realm."

"It sounds like it's not going to be a fun journey," Zamek said.

"What's life without a little excitement?" Persephone asked with a smile. She looked considerably healthier than she had when they'd found her. "Go find Dralas. I'll be here."

Layla turned to leave and paused by her father, who sat by himself in the corner of the room. "Thank you for not trying to escape."

"You asked me to help, I'm helping," he told her. "Your mother is here, isn't she?"

Layla nodded. "She's conflicted. Apparently, she didn't realize that hurting me would cause her emotional unpleasantness."

"That beast will turn on you the second you relax your guard," he said, nodding at the cat.

Layla looked at the saber-tooth panther and held her gaze for several seconds. "I don't think she will. The blood elves tortured her, twisted her into something that's no longer one of her kind. I think she understands I saved her life."

The big cat purred and licked the back of Layla's hand.

"Until she gets hungry," Caleb replied.

"There are plenty of blood elves around," Layla said. "You like blood elf, girl?"

The cat made a low growling noise.

"Apparently not. Maybe it's an acquired taste."

"You're really keeping it?" Caleb's voice held his disbelief.

"She's not an it," Layla said, her voice hard, aware that everyone in the room was watching the exchange between her and her father. "And she's not a possession. If she wants to go, she can go. I'm not stopping her."

The cat rubbed her head against Layla's hand, and she scratched her behind the ear. The panther's fur was thick and soft, and she let out a contented noise as Layla continued to scratch.

"And they call me insane," Caleb said, disgusted.

"Keep that up and she might eat you," Sky called out to him, gaining a laugh from several of the others in the room.

Layla and Tarron left the house, the panther following.

"Do you think my dad has a point?" Layla asked. "Will the panther try to eat me? Shadow elves can do, like, low-level empath stuff, yes? Do you sense anything?"

Tarron smiled and shook his head. "No. I sense nothing but a desire to protect you. You saved her life, and she knows that. You've gained a powerful ally today. But you need to name her."

"Yeah, I just don't know what. I don't want to call her something generic, like Shadow or Hunter."

"Maybe pick something from your vast knowledge of pop culture."

Layla laughed. "That's Kase and Chloe's fault. The pair of them opened my eyes to comics, anime, and more geeky stuff than I even knew existed. How about Fluffy?"

The panther made a noise indicating that Fluffy was not an option.

"I will think on it," Layla told her.

"I find it fascinating that your companion is as intelligent as she is."

"Can I ask you something?"

"Of course."

"Why are there big parts of your life that I can't access in my mind?"

Tarron stopped by the end of a row of houses. "Ah, well, shadow elves can limit what someone sees when they link."

"That doesn't seem very fair. And you allowed me to see you murder someone, so why keep the rest from me?"

"I understand that it might not make you think the best of me, but I needed you to trust me for who I am. If you discovered that I'd killed someone once I'd gained your trust, that would have put us at odds. So, yes, I keep things to myself. Just like I can jettison a lot of things about the people I merge with. Shadow elves can't keep more than a few people's memories in their minds. It's only the ingrained, long-term things like language that really stick. A lot of other stuff just sort of floats away. Eventually, you'll start to find that my memories will fade. I don't think anyone in shadow elf society was able to keep them for longer than a few weeks."

Layla expected to be angry about that, but she found that actually she was just disappointed that he hadn't been completely honest. "You didn't tell us that when we agreed to merge with you."

"No, I know. I'm sorry about that. I didn't want an existential conversation when we needed to leave."

The saber-tooth panther let out a low growl, and both Layla and Tarron crouched and made their way to the end of the nearby wall, before looking out at whatever had caught the animal's attention.

"Dralas," Tarron said, standing up and turning back to the panther. "It's okay, he's a friend."

The panther made a dismissive snorting noise.

Layla rubbed the side of the animal's head. "You did good." She hurried after Tarron, who had sprinted over to Dralas. The giant sat on the edge of a cliff, his legs dangling over the side into the abyss below.

"Dralas, you okay?" Tarron asked.

The giant turned back to his friend, his eyes puffy from crying. "I've lost everyone I ever loved. They're dead. All of them. Giants don't live for thousands of years like you do. My family. My friends. They're all gone. The oldest of my kind is two thousand years old. I've missed out on all of that. It hit me all at once. I hadn't realized until I sat and started to think about it."

Tarron placed his arm around the giant's massive shoulder. "I'm sorry, my friend. I did not think."

Dralas smiled. "It's not your fault. A lot happened in a short period of time. To both of us. I just want to be able to see my parents again, and that's not possible. I want to see my brothers and sisters, to hold their children, to watch them grow. That's all gone because the sun elves decided to be dicks."

"It sounds like that's what they're best at," Layla said.

Dralas looked back at her. "That and pompous arrogance. It's their . . . superpower, I guess is the right word."

"You want to come back from the edge of a thousand-foot drop?" Layla asked.

"I'm not going to kill myself," Dralas told her, but even so, he moved back from the edge, taking a seat on a ruined wall.

"Thank you," Layla said.

"You have a large cat with you," Dralas said. "I did not expect that."

"This is . . . I honestly don't know yet," Layla said. "Naming was never my strong point."

"Nice to meet you, nameless one," Dralas said, offering his hand, palm out, for the panther to sniff. She licked his fingers.

"Well, she likes you," Layla said. "I think that's what it means."

The panther swished her in the face with her tail.

The four of them made their way back to the rest of the team, where Chloe was outside looking excited.

Steve McHugh

"I have names," Chloe said as Dralas and Tarron went back into the house.

"For what? The panther?"

Chloe nodded.

"Okay, go," Layla said.

"Binky?"

"No."

"Adora, Selina, Shuri, Jiji, Appa, Hinata, Winry, Angua."

"You're literally just naming characters from anime and comics that you like, aren't you?" Layla asked.

"Technically, it's stuff that Kase has shown me over the years, but there are book characters in there too."

"You like any of those?" Layla asked the panther, who snorted.

"Guess not," Chloe said, slightly downbeat. "I'll keep thinking."

Persephone appeared in the doorway. "We need to go."

"The naming ceremony will have to wait," Layla told Chloe.

10

LAYLA CASSIDY

Zamek led the way through the mountain, and the group came across no blood elves, or even a trace of them. Occasionally, in the distance, they could hear the sounds of horns being blown, but the panther's ears perked up each time and quickly relaxed. Apparently she wasn't a fan of blood elves either, which was something Layla could certainly understand.

Zamek led the group to the mouth of a tunnel that was big enough for a Boeing 747. Crystals twinkled inside, giving light where only darkness would normally be.

"What are they?" Chloe asked, as everyone took a moment to rest.

"We call them sun crystals," Zamek said. "The rays from the sun hit the top of the mountain and heat it up, that heat is passed down through the crystals. We tried not to mine them as the light vanishes the second you remove them from the rock, so this tunnel would have just been for transportation between the dwarven city and the shadow elves below. Back when this place was the working city of Thorem, this entrance would have been heavily guarded."

Tarron looked down the mouth of the tunnel. "Were the dwarves good to the shadow elves who were brought here?"

"To my memory, yes," Zamek said. "We had peace. The shadow elves lived in their own city. They came here as prisoners after the civil war, but we didn't treat them as such. Your people were allowed to roam the realm outside the mountain at their leisure. I'm sure there were dwarves who took liberties with the shadow elves, but I never saw it. But then my position meant I rarely went to the shadow elf city below."

"What was it called?" Chloe asked.

"I don't know," Zamek said. "The elves didn't tell anyone its name. I don't know why."

"Probably because we'd already lost one home and didn't want to have to lose another," Tarron said, his voice containing more than a little anger.

"I am sorry about what happened," Zamek said. "I'm more sorry that my people died because we tried to do the right thing. The sun elves would have destroyed you all if we hadn't agreed to take you. They sent squads of assassins after groups of remaining shadow elves. The rumors I heard . . . if they're true."

"They are," Persephone said. "The sun elves were brutal to their shadow elf prisoners. Trust me when I tell you that whatever awful, evil thing you've heard they did, they more than likely did it."

"And did anyone try to stop them?" Tarron asked.

"The accords were drawn up to deal with the problem," Persephone said. "They were created the moment we learned what the sun elves were doing. They ensured that everyone had the right to trial by one-on-one combat. A large group of sun elves could easily kill shadow elves by the dozen, but one-on-one, the sun elves were no match for the shadow elf warriors."

Tarron took a step into the mouth of the tunnel. "The sun elves butchered my people, butchered humans, took whatever they liked, and there was never any recompense for their actions. And now I'm told no one even knows where they are. When this is all done, I'm going to find them. I will bring to justice those who committed atrocities against my people."

No one else had anything to say after that, so they made their way down the tunnel and found that the lower they went, the fewer crystals lined the walls. Most of the group were able to see in the dark pretty well, although Dralas had to be led by the hand when he kept hitting his head on unseen stalactites.

They didn't see any blood elves, but the group stayed silent for much of the journey. After an hour of walking, the tunnel forked, with one way containing a purple glow, while the other remained in darkness.

"Which way?" Persephone asked Caleb, dropping Hades' ring into his hand. Caleb had been almost silent from the moment he'd been taken from the house where Sky had suggested the panther might eat him.

"Left," he said, pointing to the purple-lit tunnel. "He's about a mile in that direction. I see only darkness around him." He gave the ring back.

"Where does that go?" Sky asked Zamek.

"The purple tunnel goes straight to the heart of the shadow elf city. I assume the other tunnel goes to whatever they found under the library. It certainly wasn't here the last time I was down this far. I suggest we go that way first and find Hades and the others. We might not be able to get back out of the city without causing a commotion."

"Also, I like the idea of being shrouded in darkness," Chloe said.

"I do not," Dralas told everyone, his voice booming all around them.

"It'll be okay," Tarron told him.

Dralas looked down at his friend and nodded firmly. "Let's be going then."

They continued down the darker of the two tunnels with Layla's dad walking beside her. "You know this is folly, yes?" he asked.

"We save Hades and everyone else, we get out of here, and we help defend Helheim," Layla said. "The plan is easy—"

"The execution is not," he interrupted.

"Thank you for your massive amount of help and guidance," Layla said sarcastically. "Now kindly shut up unless you have something useful to add."

Caleb looked angry at having been dismissed in such a manner, but Layla didn't care. She was tired, fed up, and had been through the ringer the last few days. The very last thing she wanted was to be lectured about the survivability of their mission.

After a few minutes the saber-tooth panther began to growl. Everyone stopped walking and moved to the side of the tunnel. Layla, who was next to the panther, whispered, "Blood elves?"

The panther pawed at the ground several times.

"Lots of them?" Layla asked.

More pawing at the dirt.

Layla and Chloe moved up to the mouth of the tunnel, which sat above a twenty-foot drop into a huge empty cavern. Layla dropped down into it and crouched behind a stalagmite. Her father followed with Tarron, Dralas, Chloe, Zamek, Sky, and Persephone just behind them. Persephone gave Caleb Hades' ring again.

"He's over there," Caleb said, pointing to the mouth of a tunnel at the end of the cavern, one of four that led from it. "It's hard to judge though. I think all these crystals are screwing with my tracking."

While everyone discussed what to do next, Layla moved through the cavern with Tarron and Dralas behind her, and the saber-tooth panther next to her. When they reached the end, they entered the tunnel her father had indicated and walked through it until the sounds of voices began to echo all around her. She was grateful for the darkness as she crept to the end, finding herself a hundred feet above thousands upon thousands of blood elves. At the far end of the stadium-sized room was a dais that could have fit hundreds of people at once. Her mother stood upon it as two blood elf commanders did something that Layla couldn't make out.

"We're too far away," Dralas said.

Before Layla could say more, the dais exploded into life.

"It's the elven realm gate," Tarron said. "They're taking the rest of the blood elves out of this mountain."

"We need to hurry," Layla said. "Wherever they're going is about to have a war on its hands."

Layla returned to the others and relayed what she'd seen.

"So, we need to stop them?" Sky asked.

Zamek shook his head. "We're outnumbered ten thousand to one. I say we find the captives and figure out a way to get as far from here as possible. If those blood elves are going to Helheim, our side is going to be screwed."

"I have an idea," Layla said. "If we wait for the elves to go, we can use that gate to leave."

Tarron smiled. "It will have the added benefit of making them unable to return to this realm because I'll link that gate to Shadow Falls."

Layla nodded. "Okay, we find the captives, and we piss off the bad guys. It'll be a productive day all round."

Caleb took the lead as the team moved down one of the tunnels. The occasional blood elf was no match for the nine of them, and they soon found the prison where the blood elves had taken their prisoners. From the darkness of the tunnel, Layla counted two dozen blood elves and many more prisoners as they were moved toward the various huts that littered the area. There were twenty huts in all, all made of wood and stone and looking like they had seen better days. They surrounded a large courtyard that contained nothing but stone and dirt. There were no fences or anything to stop the prisoners from escaping. The only exit was the tunnel the group currently occupied.

Layla sucked down her anger at seeing one blood elf punch a prisoner, knocking him to the floor, then kicking him as he tried to get back to his feet.

"Kill them all," Persephone said, her voice like iron.

Zamek unslung his battle-ax. "My pleasure." He walked toward the two guards at the front of the prison, who reacted to his presence, but died before they could offer any real resistance.

The rest of the group charged after Zamek, who let out a war cry that echoed around the mountain, drawing blood elves to him so that he could cut them down in quick succession.

Layla avoided a blood elf's blade and turned her arm into a spear, skewering a second in the skull before taking its blade and plunging it into the heart of the first. She removed the blade and remade her arm as she moved through the prison, killing the blood elves, who seemed to pour out of the buildings, as she went.

One managed to hit her in the back with a hammer, but the panther quickly tore its head clean off its shoulders and spat it out as if it were rotten food.

The battle took only a few minutes, but by the end there were dozens of dead blood elves, and the rescue party had received only minor wounds.

"Get everyone out," Layla said, looking around for her father. Unable to see him, she turned to the panther. "You find my dad?"

The panther ran off between two huts, and Layla followed, discovering her father crouched over a blood elf, repeatedly stabbing it in the neck and face. A second elf lay on the ground beside the first, its head hacked off. Caleb saw Layla and smiled, his bloodstained face nothing but a horror show.

"I think it's dead," Layla said.

Caleb stood, the smile still on his face, and walked over to a barrel of water nearby, dunked his head inside, and cleaned off the black blood. "It cut me," he said by way of explanation.

Layla sighed. She couldn't begrudge her father killing blood elves—she'd just done the very same thing—but the way he appeared to be genuinely thrilled about it made Layla feel uneasy. She and those she fought alongside took no joy in the lives they were forced to take, but Caleb did. He reveled in it, like an addict getting a fix. He judged who *deserved* it. He'd decided to kill people because he enjoyed it, not because his life was on the line.

"I know you lied to me," she said softly.

Caleb stopped washing his face and looked up at her. "About what?"

"You always said you only killed murderers, rapists, people who hurt others. But that's not entirely true, is it? You killed people who committed financial crimes, who were burglars, people who used no violence but still got away with their crimes, and you couldn't have that. You needed a fix. They're not in the official numbers, are they? I did some research after you came to Greenland and discovered there were, I'm pretty sure, quite a few you never admitted to killing."

Caleb's smile faltered. "Don't know what you're talking about."

"Another lie," Layla snapped. "You make yourself out to be a vigilante who wants to stop bad people, but you tortured people to death. You took your time. And you didn't even only kill people who fell into your safe little Venn diagram of crimes."

"You never said anything."

"No, I didn't. I knew you'd lie again. I knew you'd try to make me feel like I was the one who was seeing things that weren't there. You're a manipulative little bastard. And I'm done with you. When we're out of here, I'm done being the one you work with. I wanted you to know that."

"Then no one will find the people in my head." Caleb winked at her.

"We'll find a way that doesn't involve you," Layla said. "I thought I could bury all I know for the greater good, but I can't. You're a sadist, a murderer, a torturer, and frankly a piece of shit. And we're done."

"Girl, I'm your father." Caleb took a step toward Layla. "You can't honestly think that after all we've been through, rebuilding the bridges, you're just going to cast them all aside. Cast *me* aside."

A low growl emanated from the panther.

"Dad, if you take another step toward me, it'll be your last."

Caleb froze and stared at Layla, who didn't blink.

Layla made her way back to the rest of the team, who were rescuing as many prisoners as they could find, helping them out of huts and settling them in the courtyard. Most of them wore sorcerer's bands, which Layla helped remove after finding several keys in the hut belonging to the commander of the prison. He had been a large blood elf with fearsome scars across his bare chest and arms. He had picked a fight with Sky, who had used her necromancy to rip the creature's spirit in half. The screams of the commander echoed around the prison even after it had died.

They found Nabu in the hut furthest from the entrance. Nabu was barefoot and had been the subject of considerable torture. His bloody face and chest showed a wealth of cuts. Once his band was removed, he sighed with relief as his body set about healing itself.

"Hades isn't here, is he?" Layla asked.

Nabu shook his head. "They took him to Helheim."

"How was he . . . treated?" Persephone asked.

"They didn't hurt him," Nabu said. "Elizabeth said something about needing him uninjured for when they gain access to the Yggdrasil tree, and from what I understand that's not going to happen until they've taken the city where Hel's people are stationed. Hades was treated well, almost like he was guest of honor."

"What was their plan for all of you?" Layla asked.

"They were taking prisoners to sacrifice so they could activate the elven realm gate," Nabu said.

They released fifty-seven prisoners, but at least a dozen more had been taken to the realm gate.

"We need to get to that elven gate," Layla said. "Zamek, take the prisoners and anyone who wants to go with you back to the dwarven realm gate. It's already linked to Shadow Falls so will work fine."

"Sky, I entrust my father into your care," Layla said, looking over at him, but continuing to speak to Sky. "If he does anything you don't like, do whatever you need to."

"Will do," Sky said.

"Dad, you will go to Helheim, and you *will* help them find Hades."

"Anything for my little girl," Caleb said.

"Chloe, Tarron, Dralas, and I," Layla said, ignoring the nausea that sat in her gut, "will go to the elven gate and use that to get through to Shadow Falls."

"Me too," Nabu said. "I'm already healed, and frankly I want to help bring this place to its knees."

"If you are in any way impeded, you leave," Persephone said.

"We'll be fine," Layla promised her. "We'll go save the world together. Okay, that's five of us."

The saber-tooth panther snorted.

"Fine, six," Layla corrected. "Alright, see you in Shadow Falls."

Several of the rescued looked over at Persephone. "You heard her," she said. "She's in charge of this mission—what she says goes. We head back to the citadel and leave." She stood and stretched. "Do not dawdle, Layla. Even without the vast majority of blood elves, this realm is still dangerous."

"We'll wait for you all to leave and cover your journey," Layla said.

"Then we'd best be off," Sky said. "I don't want to stay here longer than necessary." She looked at Layla. "And I don't want you to stay here longer than necessary either."

Within ten minutes, everyone was ready to leave. Zamek, Persephone, and Sky took up the vanguard. The human prisoners were helped by those who had already healed. From the looks on their faces, they were ready to fight anything that came along. Layla hoped they'd get back to Shadow Falls safely, but considering how things could have gone, the fact that they still had a chance of getting there at all was something to be happy about.

Nabu stood beside Layla and watched as the last of the group disappeared up the tunnels to the dwarven city. "I'd really like one day where my life isn't in danger," Nabu said.

"Just one?" Layla asked.

"Well, no, a lot more than one, but right now I'd settle for the one."

"I'd settle for about an hour," Chloe said from behind them.

Layla and Nabu both turned around. "You good to go?" asked Layla.

Everyone said that they were.

"You going to be okay?" Layla asked Nabu.

"They beat my feet," Nabu said. "With a metal bar. Not enough to break anything, just enough to hurt. I'm all for anything that will make me feel better about what happened. Besides, I'm an och, I heal better than any of you, and I'm not very good at sitting things out."

"Let's go then," Layla said, and the group set off toward the elven realm gate they'd seen a few hours earlier.

To begin with, they moved slowly, unwilling to disturb anyone who might be close by, but once it became clear that there were no nearby enemies, they increased their speed and started jogging down the tunnel. They stopped at the mouth and looked down on the cavern where only a short time ago there had been tens of thousands of blood elves. Now it was littered with the bodies of thousands of blood elves.

They walked down the steep slope into the cavern, and Layla's eyes watered as the putrid smell of thousands of blood elves hit her.

"They're all dead," Tarron said, crouching over a decapitated corpse on the ground.

"They fight between one another a lot," Nabu said. "We discovered that the last time we were here. There's a hierarchy, a bit like predator animals, and when there's a challenge it can end with the death of one or more of them. It's quite common, apparently. We don't see the results often because . . ." He turned to Tarron and paused.

"Because what?" Tarron asked. "I think we're beyond trying to spare my feelings."

"They eat the dead," Nabu said. "Blood elves eat corpses. Doesn't matter who the corpse used to be. Dwarven, human, elf. I had an extensive library on the subject back in Greenland. I saw it as a useful way to gain an insight into the enemy. I didn't foresee us being attacked and taken prisoner."

"Speaking of foreseeing," Chloe said. "When you were in Sanctuary, did you see the Fates?"

"The three women?" Layla asked.

"Cassandra, Grace, and Ivy," Chloe replied. "They remained in Sanctuary when we left this realm."

"I didn't see anything but dead dwarves," Nabu told her.

"Hopefully they escaped," Chloe said. "I can't imagine being a prisoner of these people for so many years."

"There are a lot of variables," Nabu said. "Let's deal with one thing at a time."

The team continued on through the cavern until they reached the steps that led up to the dais where the realm gate sat. Blood pooled at the bottom, and there were corpses of humans on the steps, forcing the group to step around them. Layla stopped by each one to see if she knew them, but none were familiar to her.

"Human prisoners," Chloe said. "They have a lot of them here."

"What about the prisoners they took with them?" Dralas asked.

"Good question," Layla said. "Maybe they took them to Helheim."

"Whoever activated this gate didn't know you don't have to drain the people to death, or didn't care," Tarron said.

They reached the top of the dais and saw that the realm gate was partially drawn on the ground and partially on the rock behind it.

"Interesting design choice," Nabu said. He looked over at Tarron. "Have you ever seen anything like this?"

Tarron nodded. "It's so a large number of people can go through while the gate stays open. The marks on the floor provide power to the marks on the wall. It's only the wall that actually activates as a gate. It was a design I knew was being worked on, but I've never actually seen it in practice. This could stay open for hours without the need to recharge."

"How long to change the destination?" Layla asked Tarron.

"Not long to change the writings that are etched here, but longer to use my own power to charge them up. Maybe an hour or two. And we will need someone to bleed on this."

"Two hours out here, exposed?" Chloe said. "That doesn't scream good idea."

Dralas sat on the stairs and looked across the cavern. "At least we'll see anyone coming."

Layla was about to tell Tarron to get started, but he was already kneeling beside one of the pieces of elven writing that made up the realm gate.

"Okay, so you get started, and we'll look for a blood elf corpse that still has some actual blood left," Layla said.

"Check the humans too," Nabu said.

"No," Layla almost snapped. "They suffered enough just being in blood elf captivity for so long." Layla paused and looked over at Tarron. "Sorry, I didn't mean to imply that the shadow elves who were turned here didn't suffer."

"It's fine," Tarron said, looking up from his work. "These are not my people. My people died out a long time ago. Whatever remains of the shadow elves, I assure you I see nothing of it in these . . . creatures that they became. Find one, bring it here. Its blood will help power the realm gate."

Layla turned to the panther. "You stay here, okay?"

The saber-tooth cat lay on the ground and let out a large sigh.

Chloe, Layla, and Dralas descended the steps to look for dead blood elves. It didn't take long to find one. The blood elf commander had been stabbed in the back, and the blade had pierced its heart. Someone had stamped on the back of its head, crushing its face into the stone ground, making it almost totally unrecognizable.

Dralas slung it over his shoulder and headed back to the dais. Layla and Chloe were both grateful that the search was over and made it halfway up the stairs when the sound of laughter echoed through the chamber. They sprinted up to the dais, drawing their weapons as two dozen blood elf commanders flooded out of the tunnel.

"Can we win this?" Dralas asked, getting to his feet.

"No," Layla said looking out over the fifty blood elves. There were several saber-tooth panthers among them.

"This is bad," Nabu said.

"If we die, we die swinging," Chloe said.

Dralas stepped in front of everyone, doubling in height. Layla wondered how his armor grew with him, but quickly decided now wasn't the time for such conversations.

The commanders reached the stairs first, screaming blood-curdling cries as dozens of crossbow bolts fired from all around the dais, taking several of the commanders off their feet and forcing the others to dive aside.

A female dwarf appeared beside Layla, causing her to jump slightly.

"We need to leave," the dwarf said, running a gloved hand over her bald head as more dwarves ran out of a newly created hole in the wall. The advancing blood elves stopped.

Nabu suddenly leapt in front of Layla. An arrow, released by one of the commanders, slammed into his chest with enough force to take him off his feet. He fell back onto Layla, and the pair crumbled to the floor as it gave way beneath them, and the group fell into darkness.

11

Mordred

"You want to tell us how you got this jet to Germany?" Diana asked Mordred, as they flew over Europe.

"Favors," he said. The group had used the dwarven realm gate in Shadow Falls, which took them to Maine, before heading to New York for their flight.

"I'm not saying you should elaborate," Remy said. "But I think Diana might throw you out of this plane if you don't."

"I called in a few favors—turned out Felicia Hales still had a jet in New York. I knew some of the people who scattered after she was killed, and one of them agreed to take us to Germany."

"I'm sorry about Felicia," Hel said, looking up from the seat next to Diana. "I know you liked her."

Mordred nodded. "She was nice. I'm going to kill Abaddon for what she did to her."

"I think you'll need to get in line," Remy said. "I'm quite fond of the idea of going all stabby on her psychotic ass."

"You have a way with words," Hel said.

"It's one of my many talents," Remy said.

"So, Mordred," Hel said. "What happens when we get to Mittenwald? How bad is it going to be to fight our way in?"

"Well, it depends on how much fighting is still going on at the Wolf's Head compound," Mordred said.

He'd wanted to spend some time talking to Hel before they'd left, but it hadn't been possible, and not just because he wasn't really sure how to even start. Every time he looked at her, the urge to tell her what he felt overwhelmed him, and he had forced himself to push it all down, deep inside. It would have to wait until everything was over, or at least until they weren't about to fight an unknown number of enemies. Besides, Hel had been nothing but completely professional when talking to Mordred, which probably meant she wasn't looking to have any kind of personal conversation with him. Hopefully it was something he'd have time to discuss with her later.

"That's not great," Remy said.

"Unfortunately, it gets worse," Mordred said. "The town of Mittenwald is pretty much Avalon territory at this point. It's run by a vicious little asshole named Orcus."

Diana sat bolt upright. "Ah, no, not him."

"I have no idea who that is," Remy said.

"Be grateful," Diana said. "He was a Roman god who thought he could dethrone Hades. He's a necromancer with delusions of grandeur. He likes to hang around with Enyo, who is about as pleasant as scabies."

"Her I've met," Remy said. "She's a bit too fond of blood magic."

"She's utterly addicted to it," Mordred said. "She's also a really good friend of Ares, and apparently hasn't been dealing with his death very well. And by friend, I mean . . . you know. *Friend*."

"Yeah, we get it, Mordred," Hel said.

"I'm talking about sex," Mordred continued.

"Please stop," Remy begged.

"Anyway, apart from having sexy time with Ares and Orcus, Enyo is somewhat deranged," Mordred said. "I assume because of her over-reliance on blood magic, and not because of the sex."

"Why won't he stop saying sex?" Remy asked. "What did we do to deserve this?"

"Okay," Diana said, clearly wanting to stop the conversation from getting any sillier, which was always a concern when Remy and Mordred were involved. "So, we go to Mittenwald and do not engage unless necessary. A fight between us and either of those two is going to be a *really* public fight. And I'd rather not alert the entire Avalon army stationed there."

"My people in Helheim will not last forever," Hel said. "Even with Tommy, Olivia, and the others going there to help. We cannot take long. Besides, if we manage to get the Titans' help, I still fail to see how we combat the combined forces of Abaddon and Mammon."

"I have a plan for that," Mordred said.

"Your plans do not inspire confidence," Diana said.

"This one will," Mordred assured her.

"You feel like telling us what it is?" Hel asked.

"Not really the time," Mordred said. "I promise you'll know once I figure out exactly how I get it all to work. Besides, one problem at a time. Tartarus."

"Are the Titans going to be pleased to see you?" Hel asked.

"Define pleased," Mordred said. "They don't know me for the most part, I imagine. They'll have heard tales and things, but they were locked away well before I was born. They helped Selene and Nate, so I'm hoping that friendship will extend to me, especially considering Selene and I are friends. At the end of the day, we need help. If they don't give it, then it won't be long before Tartarus is an Avalon realm. I think it's safe to say that no one wants that."

No one disagreed with him.

The jet landed at an airfield outside of Mittenwald, and they disembarked. Mordred came out last, and after thanking the pilot, he joined the others, his thick boots crunching on the fresh snow.

"Why is it that wherever we go with you it's always bloody cold?" Diana asked.

"Just once, I'd like to fight Avalon in the Bahamas," Remy said.

"You don't like sand," Mordred said.

"Don't like being shot at either," Remy replied. "And out of the two, I'll take sand over bullets. I'll meet you by the car out front." He set off at a sprint toward the overgrown bushes that lined the fence on one side of the airport.

The rest of the group walked across the airfield to the largest nearby building, excluding the three hangars on the opposite side of the runway. They went inside and gave fake identification showing that they were affiliated with Avalon to a middle-aged woman behind the counter. Mordred had picked this airfield not because it was the closest to the town, because it certainly wasn't, but because the staff were all human. They were aware of Avalon, but none of them gave any indication that they were actively involved with Avalon's war.

The group were waved through with a smile after the woman handed Mordred a set of keys to a Range Rover Discovery. Diana snatched them out of his hand the second they were all outside.

"Hey," Mordred said.

"You are not driving," Diana said.

"Not sure why," he replied, pouting a little.

"You are a danger to everyone on the road. And I'd like to at least feel safe *before* people start trying to kill us."

They all got into the black Range Rover, with Diana driving, and stopped fifty feet up the road to let Remy into the back seat.

"You know, I could have just made myself human," he said, shaking snow from his fur as Diana set off again.

121

"The only problem with that," Mordred said, "is that you have to stay human for a period of time, and no offense, but human Remy isn't the Remy we need right now."

"No offense taken," Remy said. "I'm warmer with fur."

"Besides, you'd also be naked," Diana called from the driver's seat. "I think naked people tend to be something others remember seeing."

"Oh, they'd remember me naked," Remy said with a wink.

"And now I feel nauseous," Mordred said, smiling.

"Is it always like this with you people?" Hel asked from the seat behind the driver.

"No, sometimes it's worse," Diana said.

"Sometimes Mordred starts humming," Remy pointed out.

"I've heard the humming," Hel said. "I find it oddly endearing."

"See," Mordred said. "Someone else likes my humming."

The conversation petered off as the car drove along snowy German roads. Mordred lowered the window in the passenger seat, feeling the cold wind against his face, smelling the freshness in the air.

"You okay, Mordred?" Hel asked him.

"Yeah, I'm good," he told her. "Just been a long few years. Actually a long few centuries is probably more appropriate."

"We're coming up to Mittenwald," Diana said, slowing the car to match the traffic laws of the area, although judging from the complete lack of people, it didn't look necessary.

"Stop the car," Mordred said, opening the door before the car had slowed down to a complete halt and stepping outside, staring off up the street.

"Mordred what's going on?" Hel asked, getting out of the car.

Mordred pointed down the road. "There's no one here. No one. No cars are running, no people. I know it's late, but there are no lights on in the windows either. Just street lamps."

Diana and Remy joined Mordred and Hel.

"Either of you smell anything?" Mordred asked.

Both Diana and Remy took a long sniff.

"No people," Remy said. "Lingering scents, but there's nothing more recent than a few hours ago. Where is everyone?"

They left the car and moved through the deserted town of Mittenwald as quickly as possible, but after running along several streets and finding no semblance of life, they paused at the mouth of an alleyway.

"I have a very bad feeling about this," Remy said.

"You think they powered whatever weapon Abaddon is using at the compound with the people of this town?" Hel asked.

"Yes," Mordred said. "About ten thousand people live here."

"How would they get that many of them up to the compound?"

Mordred didn't have an answer to that question, but he couldn't think of anything good being involved.

The team ran through the deserted town back toward the car and climbed inside, before Diana drove slowly through toward the forest at the far end of Mittenwald. By the time they'd reached the edge of the forest, no one in the car had seen anything to suggest that anyone was left in the town.

They drove carefully down the road that cut through the forest, until they saw a large hotel in the distance, close to Lake Ferchensee. Wolf's Head compound was another twenty-minute drive, so Diana stopped the car outside the hotel, switching off the engine.

"Still no one," Mordred said, looking up at the dark hotel.

They got out of the car again, and Mordred walked toward the hotel. He had to force open the broken automatic doors, and immediately wished he hadn't as the smell of death hit him like a wall. He walked inside the dark foyer and lights flickered to life, revealing a room with pools of blood, and trails that went from the entrance down a nearby hallway. Mordred followed it to a large bar where bodies had been tossed carelessly into a pile.

Remy appeared next to him. "They're a few days old," he said after a sniff.

Mordred stepped around the pools of old blood and picked up a wallet on the floor, opening it to reveal a police ID. "I imagine you'll find that everyone here is law enforcement of some description."

"Enyo did this," Hel said from the entrance to the room. "I've seen her handiwork in the past. These people were killed with blood magic."

"I know," Mordred said. "I've done something similar." Mordred walked out of the hotel without another word, only taking a deep breath when he was away from the death he'd discovered. "We were too late to stop the deaths of all those people," he said softly as Hel walked up behind him and placed her hand on his shoulder. "When Cerberus called us, they must have already been murdered. They used the dead to power that weapon."

"Yes," Hel told him. "I'm sorry."

"You think they got inside the compound?" Remy asked as he rejoined the group.

"We need to go find out," Diana said.

"Not in the car," Mordred told her, his tone purposefully neutral. "We go through on foot. Let's not give them any idea that we're coming."

The four of them ran through the dense forest toward the compound. Mordred felt a mixture of rage at what had been done and sadness for what he'd seen at the hotel.

They were halfway through the forest when the purple mist touched them. Mordred stopped running as his power vanished. He turned around to Hel, Remy, and Diana as they each stepped into the first tendrils of mist.

"What the actual hell?" Remy asked, dropping to his knees. "It's like I'm exhausted."

Mordred had already sat down, and nodded his agreement. "No magic either," he said.

"This stuff is evil," Diana said as she tried to continue walking, but had to drop to one knee after several steps when the mist became more dense.

Hel fell toward Mordred, who did all he could to catch her, but they both ended up lying on the cold earth as the mist flowed over them.

"What is this stuff?" Diana asked.

"Abaddon's weapon," Hel said, placing her hand on Mordred's and squeezing slightly. "We need to either escape this, or find a way to neutralize it."

"It's moving down the hill," Remy said. "Maybe it's thinner up top."

"Any chance you can just use your smoke thing?" Mordred asked.

Remy shook his head. "Need to concentrate to do that. And this just makes me feel sleepy."

"I do not like being made to feel human," Hel said, pushing up from the ground and letting out an enraged cry. "I am not some weak, helpless, meek pet. I am the god of death. The daughter of Loki. The ruler of Helheim. I will not succumb to Abaddon's mist."

Mordred forced himself to sit up and grabbed Remy's hand. "Let's go," he said.

"I'm going to hurt someone for this," Remy said, allowing himself to be pulled upright as Mordred got to his feet.

Mordred half carried Remy for two steps, before he fell to his knees. Diana slung Remy over her shoulder as she stood up straight and started walking up the hill with purposeful strides.

"If I'd known this is what it would take for me to be carried, I'd have found this shit a long time ago," Remy said.

"Shut up," Diana said. "Concentrating."

Mordred half-walked, half-scrambled up the hill, forcing himself to continue as the mist became too thick to see his feet. Hel walked beside him, helping him up when he fell, and let Mordred do the same when she faltered.

Mordred had no way of knowing just how long it took them to walk up a hill that should have taken all of two minutes, but it felt like hours, as though every step was a battle. Eventually, they made it to the top where a giant black staff sat in the middle of a small clearing. It was pumping out more of the purple mist that swirled all around the forest without affecting anything but Mordred and his team.

With no guards nearby, they could try to destroy the staff, or at least figure out a way to stop the toxin. But the closer they got to it, the thicker the mist was, and soon Mordred felt his knees buckle. He dropped to the ground. Hel helped him back to his feet.

If Mordred could just use his magic, he'd be able to breath the gas with no side effects, but having his magic removed made sure that was impossible. Even so, the group eventually made it to the ten-foot-tall staff. It was constructed in black-painted steel and adorned with runes Mordred couldn't identify, which glowed dark red and purple.

"How do we break it?" Diana asked.

Mordred placed his hand on one of the runes and felt the power hum beneath his palm. "I'm not sure there's anything we can do."

Remy removed a blade from his belt, dropped down from Diana's shoulder, and drove the blade into one of the runes. The energy inside the staff exploded outward, throwing Mordred and his team back down the hill they'd just climbed. They tumbled through dirt and leaves as they went, until they finally hit the bottom.

"You all okay?" Mordred asked, but he couldn't lift his head from the ground to see where anyone was. He tried to stay awake, to get his body to move, but exhaustion claimed him as the purple mist rolled over his body, and he slipped into unconsciousness.

12

LAYLA CASSIDY

Nabu was unconscious but breathing as the dwarves recreated the ceiling of the tunnel the team had fallen into.

"My name is Vorisbo," the female dwarf said. "We need to move."

Vorisbo had tattoos all over her bare arms, most of which resembled various creatures—whether they were of myth or lived in the realm, Layla didn't know. A tattoo of a pair of green swords crisscrossed over one eye, and she had multiple earrings in both ears.

Several dwarves appeared out of freshly made holes in the tunnel as Dralas made himself as large as possible within the confines of the tunnel, before picking up Nabu.

"Will he be okay?" Layla asked.

"We'll check once we're out of here," Vorisbo said as she set off down the dimly lit tunnel. "So, let's hurry."

Several dwarves, who were far in front, created new paths in the tunnel with their alchemy powers, and several more closed them as the group moved further and further into the mountain. Tarron remained silent throughout the journey, and Chloe occasionally took hold of Layla's hand, squeezing it to reassure her.

"That's a very dangerous animal you have with you," Vorisbo said.

Layla stroked the saber-tooth panther on the side of the head. "She's become bonded to me, or indebted. Something like that. I saved her from the blood elves."

"My father had one. Treated it like a son. You treat that cat of yours right, and it'll stay by your side for the rest of its life. And they live long lives. About the length of a normal human back on your Earth realm. Not sure how, but people have suggested it's to do with the realm itself."

The cat purred.

"She needs a name."

"It'll come," Vorisbo said. "A name is an important thing. Don't rush it."

Nabu woke up not long after, but he continued to slip in and out of consciousness, so Vorisbo went over to check. "What is he?" she asked.

"An och," Chloe said.

Vorisbo visibly relaxed and drew several runes onto Nabu's forehead. "These will keep him asleep and calm, but we should hurry."

Twenty minutes later the dwarves cracked open the side of the mountain and daylight flooded the tunnel. Layla blinked, shielding her eyes from the bright sunlight with her hand.

"We're not far from our city," Vorisbo explained.

The group descended a long path, where three carriages waited for them. Each of the carriages was pulled by four large horses. A dozen dwarves walked out of the nearby woodlands and climbed onto the horses. Layla wondered how long they'd been there, just watching.

"Put the och in one of those," Vorisbo said to Dralas, pointing to a carriage, before she said something in dwarven to one of the dwarves who climbed up beside Nabu and drove away across the grassland. The rest followed at a quick pace.

Layla looked at the grassland turning into a dense forest on one side and spreading toward another mountain range on the other. She turned back to the gigantic mountain they'd just fled, and looked up at the snow-covered peaks, most of which were enveloped with dark clouds.

"Will he live?" Layla asked Vorisbo.

"We'll know more when we get back to the city. It's a few hours of riding, which is why I sent the carriage ahead. At full speed, a carriage can move faster than the horses alone, but the dwarves who went with your friend will ensure that he's protected."

"So, we'll be going as fast as them?" Tarron asked.

"No," Vorisbo said. "It's one thing to go that quickly with only one person in the back, but with more than one, we'll move slower. Especially with the armor and weapons we're all wearing."

Chloe, Layla, and Vorisbo climbed into the back of one carriage, Dralas and Tarron in the other. The panther ran behind the carriages at Layla's request so it wouldn't spook the horses. They started moving soon after, and Layla had a lot of questions.

"What were the dwarves outside the mountain doing in the woods?" she asked.

"Guarding our belongings," Vorisbo said. "There are creatures in the forests of this realm that would find our horses a pleasant appetizer."

"Where did you all come from?" Chloe asked. "I didn't know there were more dwarves here. Do you know what happened to everyone at the Sanctuary?"

"From what I've been told by the survivors of the attack," Vorisbo began, "it started about three years ago, a few years after several of your kind arrived here from the Earth realm. The blood elves attacked the city of Sanctuary like never before. Thousands of them. The people in the city weathered that storm and used the time to evacuate. They created tunnels that ran away from the city, allowing the majority of inhabitants to leave in relative safety.

"Unfortunately, one of the dwarves in Sanctuary betrayed them by letting the blood elves into the city. They slaughtered many. The survivors moved through the mountains for weeks, until several of them ran into a patrol from our city. We took them home to Hreidmar."

"Hreidmar is your city?" Layla asked.

Vorisbo nodded. "It's the name of an old dwarven king."

"How long has your city been there?" Chloe asked. "I thought all the other dwarves ran from this realm after the blood elf attacks over a thousand years ago."

"Not all dwarves were in the mountain when it fell to the blood elves. Many of us were outside. We searched for survivors for years and years, but were vastly outnumbered by the blood elves and couldn't risk a confrontation with them. We assumed there were no dwarves left inside the mountain, and so the elders decided we should create a new life for ourselves. We've lived in Hreidmar for a thousand years now. But enough about me, what about you? Why do you have a metal arm? Why are you in Nidavellir?"

Chloe ran through the myriad events that had happened to the world since they were last in the realm of Nidavellir. Layla told Vorisbo about her mother and father, along with the metal arm she wore.

"Your mother chopped off your arm?" Vorisbo asked.

"We're not a close family," Layla said. "Anymore, anyway."

"Your mother, this Elizabeth, she relieved the last commander who was here, Baldr." Vorisbo's tone suggested he was not someone she liked. "Elizabeth has been trying to hunt us down. I don't think she likes the idea of a bunch of dwarves just living their lives and occasionally going on hunts to kill blood elves without a chance for them to strike back. If she knew where the city was, we'd probably have had trouble by now."

"She's gone to Helheim, we think," Layla said. "We need to get there and help everyone."

"Maybe the elders at the village can help," Vorisbo said. "I'll be more than happy to organize a war party to go back to the mountain and take that elven gate. I saw your shadow elf friend, by the way— pretty weird to see one of their kind around."

"By weird, you mean it doesn't happen, I assume?" Chloe asked.

"Will there be trouble?" Layla asked.

"He's not a blood elf. He had no part in what they did. He'll be fine. Dwarves aren't humans—we don't hold grudges against people who don't deserve it."

Layla looked out of the carriage window as the conversation flowed between Vorisbo and Chloe. She was worried about Nabu. He was pretty much the closest person she'd ever met to a true immortal, but the wound had looked bad, and she had no idea what the weapons made with fragments of the crystal would do to his body. Och were rare. In fact, Layla wasn't even sure there was another one.

Chloe touched Layla on the hand. "You okay?" she asked.

"Worried about Nabu," Layla admitted. "And my father was unusually calm about being sent back to Shadow Falls. Apart from butchering that blood elf back in the mountain, he was practically normal, whatever that is."

"I for one enjoy his subdued demeanor more than his usual one," Chloe said.

"My father is many things," Layla said, "but subdued is not one of them, unless he's planning something."

After a few hours the group traveled through a tunnel that went under a mountain, and Layla watched the dozens of heavily armed dwarves who were guarding the entrance. They'd created a huge stone hut with a watchtower that was at least fifty feet high—and the hut on top was big enough to house a double-decker bus.

The darkness of the tunnel soon gave way to light as the procession of horse riders and carriages reached the other end. The group continued on down a slope that curved around the side of the mountain. Looking out of the carriage, Layla noticed there was a drop on one side of the path that looked to be incredibly high. Far below them a forest stretched as far as the eye could see, only broken by a huge river that almost cut the entire landscape in half.

"How far down is that?" Chloe asked, sounding a little nervous.

"About two thousand feet at this point," Vorisbo said. "The mountain is about forty thousand feet tall, which is tiny compared to our home mountain, but big enough for our needs."

They continued on the slope for several more minutes, until the city was revealed to them. The city itself would be impossible to see unless you were on the path. Fifty-foot walls sat between the city and the edge of the slopes, and from what Layla could see there appeared to be hundreds of homes inside the walls of Hreidmar.

"How many dwarves live here?" Layla asked.

"About nine thousand," Vorisbo said. "There are probably six or seven thousand humans too. The city stretches into the mountain itself, which is where most of the dwarves live and work. This is just the external part. We dwarves might have left our ancestral home, but we haven't discarded the love of having a mountain over our head."

The group stopped by the main gates, which were opened by the guards, allowing them into the city itself. Shortly after, the carriage stopped, and Layla climbed out expecting freezing cold air to hit her, but she found it to be cool, yet pleasant.

"Anyone else find it weird not to be cold?" Chloe asked. "There's snow on the path coming in."

"Modified runes," Vorisbo said. "They can be changed to buffer against the more extreme weather systems we get here. The humans who live here are mostly farmers, hunters, and the like. They use a lift inside the mountain to get down to the farmland to the north of here. It's all walled off and protected by soldiers there too. We rarely have trouble from anything but the occasional errant blood elf or a panther that gets too close."

Layla looked over at the saber-tooth panther as she padded through the gate, gaining stares from several humans on the stone cobbled streets, as well as from the dwarves who guarded the entrance.

"We usually only see saber-cats like yours when they're trying to eat us," one of the dwarves with Vorisbo said.

"She won't eat you," Layla told him, feeling pretty certain about that. The cat had shown no hint of aggression toward anyone since she'd rescued it. And while that could always change, she got the impression that, once rescued, the cat felt it had gained a new master. She hadn't quite figured out how she was going to take it back to the Earth realm and, once the fighting was done, walk the streets of Hampshire with a saber-tooth panther. She guessed she wouldn't have problems with the neighborhood cats using her garden as a litterbox ever again.

Layla walked away with Vorisbo, Chloe, Tarron, and Dralas just behind her. "Where is Nabu?" Layla asked.

"They'll have taken him to the palace," Vorisbo said. "They have the best medical facilities there."

They walked through the human part of the city, which was sizable. Layla noticed that the houses were between two and five stories in height and built of rock. They were magnificent structures, painted a variety of colors with creatures and runes carved into the very rock.

"Dwarven architecture," Vorisbo said, catching Layla looking up at several buildings. "Dwarves don't really do anything unless they can go as impressive as possible. But these are human homes, and humans don't like having twenty-meter-tall gargoyles looming over them from the tops of their houses. We had to make a few adjustments to the living quarters, make them more plain. Although that didn't stop us playing around with colors and smaller-scale adjustments."

They continued through the city until they reached an entrance to the mountain that reminded Layla of the hangars she'd seen at Heathrow Airport as a kid.

As they entered the mountain, Layla's eyes adjusted to the light beyond, and the magnificence of dwarven architecture was laid bare before her. They were standing fifty feet above the dwarven city that stood inside the mountain, and in the very center was a lift roughly the size of the one in Shadow Falls.

The houses were adorned with creatures of all shapes and sizes, and most of them shone with crystals of every color of which Layla had ever conceived.

"This is the main residential area," Vorisbo said as they descended a large staircase to the street below. Vorisbo and the other dwarves said hello to dozens of their people, who occasionally shook Layla's hand or offered them some food and drink.

"We don't get visitors often," Vorisbo said with a smile. "And dwarves live to entertain newcomers. There might well be a party in your honor tonight. You don't even have to turn up; any excuse."

The group got into the lift and were whisked up several hundred feet to a platform that led to a palace that appeared to be made of pure, black stone, like the citadel. It was roughly twice the size of the palace in Shadow Falls, and there were hundreds of dwarves in armor walking around it.

"We take security seriously," Vorisbo said. "The blood elf attack was centuries ago, but we dwarves live long lives and have long memories."

Layla noticed the occasional strange look or stare from the dwarves at Tarron, but the shadow elf either ignored them or was used to them. Either way, he didn't seem fazed by it.

"Most of my people are working in the mines several miles beneath us, or above us," Vorisbo said, regaining Layla's attention. "We're only about halfway up the mountain at this point."

"This is where your king lives?" Chloe asked.

"No," Vorisbo said. "We have no royal family. The elders live here, along with anyone else who runs the government and city. There's a lift at the side of the palace that goes up to the top of the mountain and down to the bottom, so those who live here can go where they need to as quickly as possible."

The black palace was littered with tiny, sparkling crystals, making the whole thing look to Layla like the night sky.

"Is Nabu in here?" Layla asked.

Vorisbo spoke to one of the dwarves on guard duty, and he replied.

"I really need to learn dwarven," Layla said. "I know I learned it from Tarron, but some of it seems to be vanishing. It seems to take longer to translate words in my head."

"That might actually help," Chloe said. "Vorisbo, any chance you have another one of those machines we learned your language in? I know the one in the mountain is from the ancient dwarves, and you don't have any of those, but do you happen to have something similar?"

Vorisbo nodded. "Of course. As for Nabu, he's undergoing treatment. Once they know more, you'll be contacted." She spoke to another dwarf, who nodded. "Okay, the elders will take a while to get together. In the meantime, I suggest that Layla learn our language."

"How long does it take?" Layla asked.

"I'd like to learn too," Dralas said.

"I already know it," Tarron replied.

Vorisbo took the group through the palace, moving down several flights of stairs to a temple similar to the one back in the city of Sanctuary, although it was about a quarter of the size. The interior of the palace was a mishmash of cold, stone floor that was dark blue or white in color and walls of black rock; various rugs, weapons, and artifacts adorned the walls. Layla wondered if the people who built it were all using the same plan, or if everyone just did whatever they liked. It sort of worked, but it left her with the feeling that the dwarves who lived here were clinging to their old lives.

"What is this?" Layla asked pointing to the chair that sat in the smaller temple. There were three dwarves inside the temple, all wearing robes of deep red, instead of the armor that the others wore. Only Chloe joined Layla in the temple.

"We're scholars," the closest dwarf said in perfect English. She was bald like Vorisbo and also had several piercings on her face, and a tattoo of a dagger over one eye.

"You will need to sit here," the dwarf said. "The runes we draw on you will enable you to learn our language so long as you don't have any memories blocked by blood curse marks." She turned to the rest of the group. "Please tell me she doesn't."

"Not that we know of," Chloe said.

"Nope," Layla told her. "Why?"

"It tends to unlock them," the dwarf said with a cheerful expression. "We had . . . issues."

"Okay, let's go," Layla said, removing her armor and piling it up in the corner.

She climbed onto the chair, sat back, closed her eyes, and allowed the runes to be drawn on her face, neck and arms. And then the world went dark.

13

LAYLA CASSIDY

"Hello, Layla," Terhal said.

Layla opened her eyes and found herself looking up at the sun. She sat up. She was in a field that stretched to the left and right as far as the eye could see. A forest sat behind her, and in front was a large waterfall that cascaded into a river running along the side of the field.

"Why did you bring me to your little part of my brain?" Layla asked. Since Terhal had begun inhabiting her mind, she'd created a small piece of heaven for herself. The deal was that Terhal lived there until Layla needed her, and neither suffered trying to fight for control.

"To talk," Terhal said, her black, tattered wings flicking in the breeze.

"We've spoken a lot over the years," Layla said, getting to her feet and brushing the grass off her leather armor. "Mostly we talk about how you're happy being here, and how you want to know if my ability to control you is wavering so you can leave and create havoc. Which one of those two vastly different conversations are we having this time?"

Terhal smiled, showing her sharp teeth. "It's two things actually."

"Okay, so what are they? And am I still in a chair in a dwarven city?"

"Yes to the latter," Terhal said. "Your brain is currently being bombarded with information. Don't worry, I don't think you being here will have any adverse effect on your mind."

"Thanks for the vote of optimism," Layla said sarcastically.

"The blood elf commanders. I know what they are."

"Assholes?" Layla asked.

"Yes, that, but also, they're not shadow elves." Terhal waved her hand and the view changed to one of a village ablaze. Night had settled in and people screamed as they ran away from a group of attackers who remained in the darkness. The moon cast an eerie glow over everything, and one human ran past Layla, their face a mask of blood.

"What the hell is going on?" Layla asked as everything froze.

"This is the memory of Gyda," Terhal said. "You see, I know you and the spirits can see one another's minds and everything, but turns out Gyda was able to keep things hidden from you. From Rosa and Servius too. Mostly because she doesn't remember any of this happening."

"And you didn't tell me this before because?"

"I didn't know," Terhal said, sounding more than a little upset. "Gyda believes that she accepted me, and then burst into flames as I told her I was going to murder everyone. She ran into the lake close by, and the flames didn't go out. I did tell her I was going to murder everyone. I did try to get her to let me take control. And she did allow it. But only through grief. Her village was already destroyed when I took control. The flames I used were to fight the invaders. I want to make it clear that I didn't fight them because I felt bad over what they'd done to Gyda's family and friends, but simply because it was fun to fight them."

"Okay, what were they?"

Terhal waved her hands and the people began moving again. Hidden shadows cut the humans down as the darkness was slowly lifted, revealing the attackers. There were half a dozen blood elf commanders killing the innocent villagers, but among them were three others, who watched the carnage unfold. They were over six feet tall with golden skin and armor that gleamed, even though they were covered in the blood of those who'd died around them.

"Sun elves," Layla said. "You think the sun elves are the blood elf commanders?"

"A hundred percent certain, yes," Terhal said. "Never been more sure of anything in my life. Except killing people. But apart from that."

"How is that possible? They look like big blood elves, and normal blood elves share a skin tone with shadow elves."

"I don't know. But I've seen both up close and I can tell you they're the same species. These aren't just big blood elves, they're something else."

"Okay, let's say you're right. Why would they attack this place?" Layla asked, walking around one of the elves as it froze in place. "Why would they agree to become commanders?"

"I don't know the answer to either question, but I know I'm not wrong, Layla. The sun elves came to this land of the dwarves, and they butchered humans. I saw it. I fought them. I killed them. I was outnumbered, and so I used the power that Gyda had and set fire to the village. She gained control as I stood over her butchered family. Shockingly enough, she wasn't interested in listening to the truth, and her mind snapped like a twig, so her new reality became *the* reality. One I didn't realize was false until I saw you split that blood elf's head open. Nicely done, by the way."

Layla ignored the praise. "Sun elves." She rubbed her temple. "Why are things always more complicated than I want them to be?"

"Yeah, well, that other thing? I'm vanishing."

"What?"

"I'm going the way of the other spirits. It happened to your friend Chloe, and I imagine your father. I can't stay in your head forever. At least not in the way we cohabit at the moment. So, I'll only be out when we sleep. It's a good thing. For you, anyway. It means I get to stay where I am, and you get all of my power. No need for you to let me out to gain your full power—you already have it at your disposal."

Layla hadn't expected to feel sad at the loss of the drenik. "That's . . . I don't know." She hugged Terhal.

"I'm not dying, you crazy umbra idiot."

Layla smiled. "Still, if I don't get the chance to tell you, thank you."

"Piss off," Terhal said. "I'm not your damn pet."

"Terhal," Layla said with a sigh. "Just once, just this one time, don't try to be an ass. Just accept my words as being sincere."

Terhal smiled. "Layla, I can honestly say that you are the most fun human I've ever inhabited. Now, go save your friends."

"When will you go?"

"When you finally accept all you are." Terhal waved away the incoming complaint. "You've accepted your umbra status, you've accepted me as part of it, but that doesn't mean you're at one with yourself. Chloe certainly isn't—that's why she's never been able to step up to the pinnacle of her umbra power. But once you do, once you're finally at peace with who and what you are, I will vanish and you will gain my power in its total form."

"I don't know what to say," Layla replied.

Terhal shrugged. "Oh, one last thing. Before you go, you're going to want to see this."

The sun and blood elves moved again. The sounds of the humans being murdered echoed all around Layla, who was about to tell Terhal to stop when she saw two dwarves standing next to the blood elves. One wore full plate armor with a helmet, and the other just chainmail and leather. The carnage froze once more.

"The dwarves knew," Layla said.

"The dwarves helped," Terhal said, and the image vanished.

Layla sat bolt upright, almost spilling out of the chair, but catching herself before she fell, as her breathing raced out of control.

Chloe was beside her in an instant, calming and helping her friend to control her erratic breathing.

It took a few minutes, but eventually Layla sat on the cold, stone floor and looked over at the dwarf who had brought her into the temple. The worry on her face made Layla feel bad for scaring her.

"Are you okay?" the dwarf asked.

Layla nodded. "Wait, are you speaking dwarvish?"

The dwarf nodded. "You had quite the reaction to the method we use. We don't get to test it often, so I'm glad you're not a drooling wreck."

"Me too," Layla said. "And ordinarily I'd be pretty angry that you didn't tell me about it being untested, but I think I have bigger problems to relay to your elders."

"What happened?" Vorisbo asked from the door to the temple.

Layla looked at Chloe. "Terhal showed me something. It's real. And I think it's going to cause problems."

Chloe nodded and looked over at Vorisbo. "Can we go to your elders now?"

Vorisbo nodded. "I'll take you. Your giant friend, he decided to have your shadow elf companion teach him the dwarven language. It's not as long-lasting as our way, but honestly I'm not sure Dralas would have fit in here anyway."

Layla got back to her feet and, after taking a tentative step and not falling over, decided that she was good to go. They had reached the entrance to the temple when Zamek appeared.

"What the hell are you doing here?" Layla asked.

"Nice to see you too," Zamek said.

"How the hell did you get here?" Chloe asked.

"I walked mostly," Zamek said. "I got everyone back to the citadel and through the realm gate there before I made sure that it was broken and then made my way to the elven realm gate where I saw a whole lot of angry blood elves. One happened to mention that a bunch of dwarves had turned up and stopped them from killing you. I figured out where the tunnel went and found a few dwarven hunters close to where Nabu was imprisoned and they showed me the way out of the mountain. Took me a few hours to get here. I'd have still been wandering around if they hadn't."

"How long was I in that machine?" Layla asked Vorisbo.

"A little over six hours."

Layla looked at everyone in the room with her. "Six hours? It felt like minutes. How's Nabu?"

"Resting," Chloe said. "We'll know more once he wakes."

Layla felt some relief that her friend hadn't died while she'd been learning the dwarven language.

"On the plus side, the six hours gave me time to get here," Zamek said. "I also brought something with me to move quicker."

"A tank?" Layla asked.

"Actually it's a sort of jeep," Zamek said with a smile. "Leonardo makes these vehicles that use crystals as a power source. It took me a while to put it all back together again once I'd taken it through the gate, but it works well. Much faster than walking and makes almost no noise."

"Wait, why didn't we just take one of those?" Chloe asked.

"Because we didn't know how deserted it all was," Zamek said. "Also, technology going through realm gates tends to . . . break, and Leonardo wasn't sure it would work. I think using the crystals instead of a combustion engine stops it from exploding."

"So, we have a way to get back to the elven realm gate and get out of here," Layla said.

"I only spotted a few blood elves on the way here. Managed to behead one with my ax as I sped past."

"You're smiling," Layla pointed out.

"Yes," Zamek said. "Yes, I am. Anyway, the dwarves I ran into were near the prison where we left you, and they created a nice hole for me to get through the mountain. I think they enjoyed getting a lift more than anything they've done recently. So, you had our language dumped in your head for a second time, although this one is much more permanent. How'd that go?"

"I saw the sun elves work with blood elves to butcher a human village in this realm," Layla said. "I don't understand how it's possible, but Terhal thinks that the sun elves are blood elf commanders."

Zamek blinked.

"There were dwarves with them," Layla continued. "Dwarves and sun elves watching those blood elves slaughter innocent humans. It was like a test or something."

"I have no idea how you saw anything," Vorisbo said slowly.

"My drenik was there. She showed me everything that her first host saw. She blocked it out of her mind and recreated this fantasy where the drenik was responsible for it all. She blamed herself and the drenik for something the dwarves and elves did. This was done just before the elven uprising. Maybe a century before, maybe less—it's hard to gauge without being able to talk to Gyda herself, and I can only do that when I'm asleep, and she doesn't always come because she's . . . not exactly okay with my bond with Terhal."

Zamek stared at Layla for a few seconds, his jaw clenched, his eyes full of anger. "They knew," he said softly, his voice shaking.

"We need to see the dwarven elders," Layla said.

"Those bastards knew," Zamek said, and took a deep breath. "Let's go."

Layla, Chloe, and Vorisbo followed Zamek as he stormed out of the temple. They found Dralas and Tarron sitting outside, eating bread and meat.

"Ah, you're done," Tarron said. "You should try this, it's exquisite."

"We're going to the elders," Layla said. "I think the shit has hit the fan."

"Why is someone throwing shit around?" Dralas asked, looking confused. "Is that a metaphor? Humans have a lot of them. They're weird. Just speak plainly."

"We'll join you," Tarron said, getting to his feet. "You staying, Dralas?"

Dralas stood, picking up a leg of cooked meat and taking a bite. "Coming. Still eating though."

Layla had trouble keeping up with Zamek, who marched through the palace with purpose. People bowed to him as he walked by, and while Layla knew that he normally would have told them to stop it, he had bigger things on his mind.

Zamek stopped in front of a set of ornate wooden doors. The guards in front moved to block Zamek's path with their spears.

"The elders are in conversation," the first dwarf said. He was in full plate armor, with a blue-and-green cape that almost touched the ground.

"Move," Zamek said, leaving no doubt that his words were a command.

"We're sorry, but it doesn't matter who you used to be, you will wait."

Zamek turned to Layla. "We need to get in there."

Layla nodded, moved her hands, and the two dwarves flew across the room, both pinned to the wall, their spears discarded to the ground. Zamek pushed open the double doors and everyone strode into the large chamber where the elders were meeting.

The chamber reminded Layla of a small amphitheater. There was a raised dais in the center of the room and a semi-circle of increasingly higher stone benches that sat against half of the dais. The other half was just bare room. The dais was occupied by two dwarves, who stopped talking as the group strode across the room. Layla quickly counted thirty dwarves on the stone benches. They were a mixture of male and female, and none of them looked too happy at the interruption.

"What is the meaning of this?" one of the two dwarves on the dais asked.

"Shut up," Zamek said, stepping onto the dais as whispers of "*Prince Zamek*" circulated around the room.

The dwarf's mouth dropped open in shock. "You are not a member of the royal family anymore, young man," he snapped. "There is no royal family."

"Did you know about the blood elf commanders?" Zamek demanded.

"What?"

Zamek turned back to Layla. "You saw what the dwarves looked like, yes?"

Layla nodded. She knew where this was going, although she didn't like it much. "Two dwarves. One was male, long black beard, silver dangling earring in his left ear, hair shaved up the middle of his head. Missing two fingers on his right hand. The other might have been male or female, I don't know—they wore black-and-gold plate armor, and their visor was down. They carried a morning star in one hand. It was black, like those weapons the blood elves were using."

"I demand an answer," the dwarf said, putting his hand on Zamek, who grabbed his wrist and swept his feet out from under him, dropping him on his back in the middle of the dais.

"If you touch me again, you lose the hand," Zamek told him, releasing the older dwarf. "You will be quiet."

The dwarf on his back made a noise that sounded as if he wanted Zamek to get on with it.

"Layla, it's all yours," Zamek told her.

"I am an umbra," she said, stepping onto the dais. "I was put through your language-learning machine, and while my brain was absorbing it all, the drenik in my head showed me visions of the first bonding between her and a human who had lived here before the blood elf rebellion. The human's name was Gyda, and she was convinced that the drenik had taken control of her body and killed her loved ones. But it was a lie. It was blood elf commanders who had done it."

A dozen soldiers rushed into the room, but the elder who had been planted on his back a few moments ago put his hands out to stop them, then motioned for Layla to continue.

"This was decades before the blood elves came and took your home," Layla continued. "Terhal, the drenik in my head, believes that these were not shadow elves like my friend, Tarron. These were sun elves. She believes that the blood elf commanders are sun elves. I think she's telling the truth. But I don't understand how it's possible, so we'd like an explanation."

"Now," Zamek said.

"I watched as these commanders murdered innocent people. Did you know? Did you know that the sun elves were involved? Did you know that the commanders are sun elves? Did you know that your own people aided them?"

Everyone in the room started talking the second Layla stopped to take a breath. A man in the front benches stood and stepped up next to Layla, raising his hands in the air. Everyone quieted.

"Clear the room," he said. "The front bench can stay."

No one argued.

"Who is he?" Layla asked Zamek.

"He was my father's advisor," he told her. "He's a good man. His name is Jomik Rakreas."

"I should go," Vorisbo said. "I don't think I should be here."

"You're already here," Jomik said. "You might as well stay."

When the chamber was empty of everyone but Layla, her friends, and the front row of dwarves, Jomik sighed, wrapping his dark-green cloak around himself as if he was suddenly cold.

"Yes, we knew," he told them. "The sun elves came to us and told us that they had a plan to create a soldier that would forever change the face of war. We were pretty happy with our arrangement with them and agreed to see the end results. The results were the commanders, and we were taken aback by how dangerous they were. The perfect soldier. Except then we discovered the truth.

"It turns out that those who first underwent the procedure were not pure sun elves. They were those born of a sun elf and a shadow elf parent, something the sun elves were strictly against. They were prisoners from birth. They had the skin tone of the shadow elves and build of the sun elves. They kept these children in a clandestine prison, training them from birth to be warriors to use against the shadow elves, but then they discovered what the crystals did to them. They turned these assassins into monsters. But they didn't have enough to fill an army, so they turned to blood magic. They took sun elf prisoners—anyone who spoke out against the military dictatorship in charge—and subjected them to blood magic rituals, using the deaths of shadow elf prisoners to twist and change their appearance.

"When we discovered the truth, we demanded they stop, demanded that they destroy the monsters they'd created, but the sun elves refused. We had no idea that they would use the lessons learned then. It's why they had the shadow elves brought here, to work the crystal mines."

"So you knew that these . . . monsters were out there murdering humans as a test?" Tarron asked.

"No, never," Jomik said. "We forbade any contact with the sun elves who were involved in these experimentations. This was thousands of years before the shadow elves became blood elves—no one was even aware of it until after the blood elves had made themselves known. Dwarves live for thousands of years, but to play the long game against our own kind was something none of us had ever considered. Unfortunately, the dwarf in your vision, the one in black-and-silver armor, was my grandfather. To my eternal shame, he helped the sun elves. It's something I've tried to put right for a long time."

"How could you have not known the shadow elves were changing?" Tarron asked.

"Certain numbers of sun elves and dwarves conspired to keep us ignorant until it was too late."

"Who?" Zamek asked.

Jomik looked at Zamek and sighed. "Some wanted to use the blood elves to murder those who stood in their way of the crown. We found evidence of it during the centuries of interrogating blood elf after blood elf, of finding notes about what happened. And . . . we found some of the co-conspirators."

"Who?" Zamek repeated. "Who would betray our own people?"

"For one, my son," Jomik said.

14

LAYLA CASSIDY

No one spoke for several seconds after Jomik's revelation that his son
had been involved in a plot to overthrow the dwarven royal family.

"You were my father's advisor," Zamek said eventually.

"That's why my son decided to try to kill you all," Jomik said. "He
felt that I mattered less to him than you and your family. Unfortunately,
it went horribly wrong. The blood elves were meant to kill as many as
they could before he arrived to save the rest. Unfortunately he didn't
get there in time to save the majority of the royal family. Many fell,
although your parents made it through the realm gate in the citadel."

"Everyone around that gate vanished," Zamek said. "It's been
broken ever since the blood elves attacked. I reactivated it to get here
from Shadow Falls, but I don't think there's any way to find the initial
destination."

"Yes, the elder who arranged it did it wrong. Hundreds of thousands of dwarves vanished. I was outside of the mountain with others,
and it took us several years to even get back inside. When we sent a
small force to the citadel and found it occupied by blood elves, we
believed you all dead, or lost forever. We didn't give up hope, and sent

search parties into the mountain to look anywhere they could, but a few dozen people could never search the whole mountain range. We live long lives, but not long enough."

"Does anyone know where the escaped dwarves went?" Zamek asked.

One of the dwarven elders on the bench shook her head. "No one does."

"The sun elves were behind all of this?" Tarron asked. "The blood elves, the destruction of your kingdom, the murder of my people."

"That's our assumption, yes," Jomik said. "My son has told me that they came to him with a plan to put him on the throne, to make a stronger bond between sun elves and dwarves. They told him that your father didn't understand just how much an alliance would benefit both of our species."

"Where is your son now?" Layla asked.

Jomik looked down at his feet. "He died. He demanded his chance to single combat, and he died fighting. I think maybe the elders agreed just to allow me a small measure of pride. His name will not be spoken of, he is merely my son."

"The sun elves were always traitorous," Tarron said. He placed a hand on Zamek's shoulder. "It appears we have a mutual enemy."

"The sun elves will have to wait," Chloe said. "We need to get to that elven realm gate."

"You want to go *back* to the mountain?" Jomik asked. "I don't advise it."

"The blood elves are mostly gone," Zamek said. "If you commit enough of your warriors to the cause, we could take it back."

"Out of the question," one of the elders snapped, standing.

Zamek said, "You can overthrow the blood elves after a thousand years exiled from our home. Together we can crush those that remain."

"We can't risk our people," the elder said.

"Is it because you're a coward?" Zamek asked, his voice utterly calm.

"Because I will not accept another royal family," the elder snapped, and his expression suggested he regretted it. The other elders gasped in shock; one even unsheathed her ax and raised it threateningly toward the coward.

"Enough," Layla said. "We need to get back to the mountain. We can change the shadow elf realm gate so that the blood elves can't get back. And then we can use it to return to Shadow Falls."

"Why not just use the realm gate in the citadel?" Vorisbo asked.

"It would take too long to get back there," Zamek said. "And if we did use the citadel realm gate, that still leaves the elven gate open for Abaddon's plans."

"Can you help us?" Tarron asked. "Don't you want your home back?"

"More than anything," Jomik said. "What about the humans they used as slaves?"

"They've been taken through to Helheim too," Zamek said. "There may still be a few elves, but we can take the citadel. We can try to find our people and bring them back."

"To rule us," the other elder shouted.

"I don't want to rule you," Zamek snapped. "I want to see my parents again. I want to hold my sisters and tell them I love them. I don't care who is in charge. I never have, and if you suggest otherwise again, I'll lose my temper."

The elder paled.

Layla was about to say something else when another dwarf ran into the room. "It's Nabu," she said to everyone. "He's awake, but it's not good."

Layla followed the dwarf through the palace without a thought of who might be with her, or where she was actually going. All she knew was that a friend of hers was in trouble, and the dwarf was leading her to him.

They entered a room with light-blue stone floors and white walls. Nabu occupied the single bed inside. Dwarven runes had been drawn all around the room, and several were embroidered on the black blanket covering him.

"Hey," Nabu said, lifting his arm to wave.

"They took the arrow out," Layla said.

"Yes, they managed to stop the bleeding," Nabu replied.

"You saved my life."

"And I would do it again. And maybe a third time." Nabu smiled.

"Are you going to be okay?" Chloe asked from beside Layla.

"Not really, no," Nabu said, sitting up with a slight groan of pain. "The crystals apparently do not agree with my physiology. They're poisonous. Having never ingested, injected, or cut myself with a crystal before, I can't say I knew that before today. Even beings who are thousands of years old have their weaknesses. Apparently, this is mine."

"So, you're dying?" Chloe asked.

Nabu nodded. "Yes. I am dying. Not today, but soon. The poison from the crystals has gotten into my bloodstream and is currently in the process of shutting down everything I need to stay alive. My guess is, I have a day. Maybe two. And then I will die."

No one spoke. Layla wasn't sure what to say to being told that a friend was going to die in the next forty-eight hours.

"There has to be a cure," Zamek said. "You're immortal. That's got to mean something."

"Unfortunately, immortal is not impervious," Nabu said. "There's nothing to be done. The dwarves tried numerous things, but nothing is even slowing it down, and I can tell you right now that there's not a single thing to be done back on the Earth realm. Scientific medicine doesn't work on me like on you. And using magic or runes will likely just make it worse. To be honest, I've never needed anything other than my own natural healing ability."

Layla took a deep breath. "So, you're just giving up?"

"Not at all," Nabu said. "Giving up implies that I have something to lose by dying. I am an och. Death is another part of life. And not in that way that religious people say they go to heaven. No, I mean literally. I die. I am reborn."

"Wait, what?" Zamek asked.

"I die. I come back," Nabu said. "I'm not sure I can put those words into an easier context. When we die we become pure energy, which is scattered across the realm we're in. We become part of the landscape itself. Giving power to life all around us. When I was a child, one of my teachers, another och, suggested that the various magical species around the realms come from the death of an exceptionally powerful och. After several centuries as pure energy gifted to so many different forms of life, I will begin the process of rebirth. A human woman and man will have a child, and that child will eventually become me. I will regain my powers and memories, but I will not be Nabu as you know me. But no matter who I am, I will be an och."

"So, it's not really death," Zamek said. "But it'll be centuries before we meet again."

Nabu nodded. "It could be, yes. My one sadness is that I must leave all my friends and loved ones to continue my journey. I have seen and done miraculous things, and it's time to move to the next step."

Layla hugged Nabu. "You'll be missed."

Nabu smiled. "I will miss you too. I will accompany you all to Helheim. I might not be at my peak fitness, but I'd at least like to help defeat Abaddon."

Zamek hugged Nabu with all his strength. "You are a good friend," he said. "And let's go give Abaddon a kicking before you have to leave this world for a while."

Jomik led the group to an armory that was so large it required three floors, where they were all told to take what they needed. Layla picked up a silver-bladed sword, with a blue-and-silver hilt and grip. She was already wearing armor, and declined to change it for anything heavier.

Everyone grabbed a few weapons, while Zamek took black plate-like armor, although it weighed next to nothing when Layla picked it up.

An hour later, several thousand heavily armed dwarves gathered just outside the human part of the city.

"No humans?" Layla asked Jomik, who wore black-and-silver plate armor, and carried a huge war hammer.

"They wanted to come," Jomik said. "But they're used to fighting animals or the occasional blood elf. Everyone here today fought the blood elves when we lost the mountain."

Layla wished Jomik good luck, and found Zamek and Chloe by Leonardo's creation. It had no roof, just roll bars, and both doors were gone. The back seats had seen better days, and blood was splashed around the front of the vehicle, which also happened to be smashed in. The saber-tooth panther lay beside the car. Several dwarves eyed her suspiciously. Someone had placed armor on her body, reminding Layla of the kind of armor she'd seen dogs wear when they went on missions with military teams. It looked like leather etched with dark-blue and gray runes and was the same color as the cat.

"You used this to drive over blood elves. Did you also drive through a wall?" Layla asked.

Zamek patted the beat-up vehicle affectionately on the side. "She's done me proud."

"You drove through a wall, didn't you?"

"Technically it was not a wall, but there were rocks involved, yes. She might need some work when we get back to Shadow Falls."

"We're driving your car into the mountain?" Layla asked.

"Well, I can't leave her here."

Chloe and Layla shared an expression of humor as Nabu walked through the crowd of dwarves and climbed up onto the truck, sitting in the shotgun position. He wore deep-red plate armor and carried a sword at his hip that was in a black-and-gold sheath. The hilt of the sword was in the shape of a white dragon. He turned to Zamek, Chloe, and Layla. "We going, or what?"

Layla climbed into the back of the jeep and looked at the dwarves gathered around her. Vorisbo stood in full armor, hopping from foot to foot as if she were eager for what was coming next. Dralas and Tarron were in the crowd. The giant had grown to massive proportions and towered over everyone around him.

"For the dwarves," Jomik shouted, raising his double-edged battle-ax high in the air.

The dwarves all around him did the same with their weapons, their shouts echoing all around them. Jomik motioned for Layla to say something.

"Thank you," Layla said, unsure what someone in her position was meant to say. "Thank you for helping us. We will take back your home. We will take back your land. And we will make those who took it pay for every drop of blood they spilled as they stole it from you."

The dwarves let out a war cry that forced Layla to hold on to the roll bars. She looked down at Zamek, who was in the driver's seat. "Let's get your home back."

They'd driven only a few feet down the hill when they spotted a dozen dwarves running toward them from the entrance to the city of Hreidmar. Several soldiers ran to meet them and then hurried over to the jeep looking anxious.

"They were scouting inside the mountain," he told them. "One of the scouts got captured and they couldn't get to him before he revealed the location of Hreidmar. A woman, who looks human but isn't, tortured then killed him, and now they're mobilizing, probably on their way here."

"What did this woman look like?" Layla asked.

The soldier shouted over to one of the dwarves who'd just arrived, who described Abaddon perfectly. "They're carrying some kind of metal poles," another dwarf scout added.

"This just got a lot shitter," Zamek said.

"Okay," Layla said, her mind racing. "There are innocents here—people who can't fight. We can't let Abaddon and those elves attack the city."

"We can defend Hreidmar if we need to," Jomik said.

"I don't think that will work," Layla said. "Those poles might be the weapon that Abaddon used in Norumbega. If they get it to work, a lot of people could die."

"How does it work?" Jomik asked.

"It absorbs life energy and puts out some kind of purple mist."

Jomik paled. "The Devil's Venom? That's a myth. My grandfather used to tell us a scary story about the devils and how they tried to take over all of the realms."

"I've seen it," Layla said. "It certainly isn't a myth, and if she gets it to work then we're all screwed."

"Do you know more about it?" Zamek asked.

Jomik shook his head. "No, just that it puts out a mist that removes powers, makes non-humans weak. Humans weren't exactly much of a concern when the devils were first created. They were barely able to keep fire going without burning themselves."

"We need to stop them," Chloe said.

"Agreed," Tarron said. "We take the fight to Abaddon. How long to get a lot more of your dwarves ready to fight?"

"You sure they know where we are?" Jomik asked the scout.

"Not exactly, no," he said. "We shadowed those elves for some time. They certainly sounded like they know we exist, but they didn't mention the city by name. When you escaped, one of the elves activated the realm gate. It went through and then came back with Abaddon and several dozen more elves."

"Which means they have a way in and out of the mountain," Jomik said.

"There's a north passage," Vorisbo said. "We never use it because there are tens of thousands of blood elves between the entrance and the mountain itself. It's the closest way out of the mountain to here, but it takes you up to the top of the forest."

"I have a plan," Layla said.

Everyone turned toward her.

"Right now the elves are inside the mountain," Layla said. "Any idea how long before they're planning on leaving?"

"Nightfall," the dwarven scout said.

"How long until nightfall?" Layla asked Vorisbo.

"Eight hours or so," she said.

"Abaddon is stuck here if that gate goes," Zamek said.

"And I don't think she wants to be stuck here," Chloe said. "She's got a war in Helheim to win."

"How do you know she'll run after us instead of coming to the city?" Jomik asked.

"We're going to have to piss her off," Layla said.

Chloe smiled. "Shame Remy isn't here—he'd be great at that."

"We'll just have to channel our inner Remy," Layla said, "and make a devil want to kill us. So, I want you to get your dwarves to the mountain and make a lot of noise. A lot. We need Abaddon to think you're coming back to take that realm gate and are bringing reinforcements."

"And what will you do?" Jomik asked.

"We're going to go to the mouth of the tunnel Vorisbo was talking about and check that not one of those staffs have made it out. And then we're going to collapse it on as many blood elves as possible."

"I like your plan," Vorisbo said.

"You're welcome to join us," Layla said. She turned to Jomik. "How long before you're ready to get your forces to the mountain?"

"We'll be good to go within the hour," he told her. "We dwarves don't need much time to get ready for a fight."

"True story," Zamek said to no one in particular.

"How long to drive around to the pathway into the mountain?" Layla asked Zamek.

"There's no way to drive the whole distance. I can get us to the mountain and then we've got a few hours walk through the forest to the plains where the entrance is. We should be able to spot any elves walking out with staffs."

"I'm going to need your dwarves to do something else," Layla said. "How long would it take half a dozen dwarves to make a tunnel big enough for all of us that will go from outside the mountain where we're going to be to just beyond where the tunnel collapses?"

Jomik brought over six dwarves and asked them for estimates on time.

"Twenty minutes per hundred feet," Jomik said.

Layla thought about it for a second. "I need this tunnel to go about five hundred feet around the side of the current one. When Abaddon and her elves spot us inside the main tunnel, we're going to lure them out and collapse it on top of them. Then we'll use the new tunnel you've dug to get behind them and fight there. You'll have about an hour to dig this tunnel. Can you do it?"

The dwarves huddled together for several seconds. "Point us to where you want it," one of them said.

Zamek couldn't hide his smile.

"Let's get going then," Layla said. "I don't want to keep Abaddon and her elves waiting."

15

LAYLA CASSIDY

Zamek drove the six dwarves to the clearing before coming back for Vorisbo, Chloe, Tarron, Nabu, and Layla. Dralas and the panther followed them. The giant increased his size to keep up with Zamek's driving, which could have been described as haphazard. Layla soon began to wish there were seatbelts, airbags, and on one particularly unpleasant two-wheeled incident, she just wanted to walk the rest of the way.

It didn't take long for Zamek to reach the clearing outside the mountain. He parked the vehicle and everyone disembarked. Layla hoped she never had to get back into the death machine ever again.

"Zamek, you suck at driving," Chloe said, looking a little green.

"It's my first time," Zamek told her with a smile. "I'm quite impressed by the speed I got up to."

"I'm quite impressed I didn't throw up," Layla told him.

"Will the dwarves you dropped off have enough time to do what they need to?" Layla asked.

"You made it a question of pride," Zamek told her. "They will get that tunnel made, trust me."

"How long now?" Tarron asked, looking like he wanted to get a move on after the panther and Dralas arrived.

"Follow me," Vorisbo said.

The group moved through the forest at high speed. Vorisbo occasionally motioned for everyone to stop while she pointed out one predator or another that lived there. It turned out that Vorisbo was an exceptional guide, as none of them had to defend themselves against anything more dangerous than low-hanging branches. Layla was sure that having the panther with them probably deterred other predators from attack.

Even so, Layla caught the occasional glimpse through the forest of other saber-tooth panthers, or a bear that was twice the size of a grizzly back on the Earth realm. And, at one particular moment, a spider that was about the same size as an SUV. Zamek and Chloe both shuddered at the sight of the spider as it scuttled up an enormous tree into the darkness of the forest canopy high above them.

Eventually, the group made it to the edge of the forest, which looked out at an expansive plain filled with two-foot-tall green and yellow grass. They all crouched down and scanned for enemies.

"Any chance there's anything in there that won't be happy to see us?" Tarron asked.

"No," Vorisbo said. "The predators stick to the forests because the blood elves are so close." She pointed across the plain. "There are dozens of small camps dotted around the plains, but it appears that the blood elves have all gone. Normally you can smell the fires and cooking, you can hear the din of elves. With them gone, it's actually quite peaceful."

"Where's the tunnel?" Dralas asked.

Vorisbo pointed off to the left. "It's down a hill over there. There's a bridge and then the tunnel. You can't miss it."

Layla looked over at the mountain looming high above them, and then across the plains to check for movement. A shriek to the right caught her attention.

"What was that?" Chloe asked.

"Blood elf scream," Nabu said. Layla was impressed that, despite being poisoned, Nabu had kept up with the pace of the group with ease. Not once had he asked to slow or rest, and Layla wondered how much he was running on empty. She hoped he wasn't trying to push himself too much to keep up, but he knew his own body better than anyone, so she trusted him to let them know if he had any problems.

"Let's go find out," Vorisbo said, removing the battle-ax that was hung from a holster on her back and moving through the tree line toward the noise.

The shriek happened twice more as the group moved toward it. The panther growled low.

"She doesn't like whatever it is," Layla said, keeping her voice to a whisper.

Zamek went ahead a little way, then slowly returned to the group. "Blood elves," he said. "Don't worry about whispering. Looks like six of them, and they walked into a web. The screams are them being attacked by exceptionally large spiders."

Layla had a very real desire to walk the other way.

"I saw a large, black staff-shaped thing too," Zamek said. "I think they were meant for the Devil's Venom. If anyone wants to go into that nest and retrieve the staff, they're more than welcome to, but I'd really rather not."

"Can it work without being properly set up?" Layla asked.

"The runes would need to be activated," Vorisbo said. "They won't work if they're just left in there."

"Do you think it would work with fewer staffs?" Zamek asked Nabu.

"The Devil's Venom was a weapon I never actually saw used. I heard about it, but that was thousands of years ago before the Titan Wars. I don't recall anyone mentioning the number of pillars or staffs, or whatever it is they're using."

A blood elf burst out of the tree line not far from where the group sat and ran into the grass, before tripping and falling as two large spider's legs came out of the darkness of the forest, followed slowly by the rest of it.

Vorisbo motioned for everyone to move back into the trees. "They have really bad vision," she said. "If you don't move, and don't disturb the web, they can't see you."

"I'm getting some serious Jurassic Park vibes here," Chloe said.

"I don't know what that is," Vorisbo said.

"Just nod," Zamek whispered as the spider crept slowly toward a scrambling blood elf.

"We could really use that elf to help us get information on the weapon," Layla said.

Before anyone could act, the huge black spider pounced and sank its fangs into the back of the blood elf. The elf dropped to the ground and the team crept away, having no desire to watch what happened next.

They followed the tree line for several minutes, then headed down a hill toward a fast-flowing river with a stone-and-wooden bridge crossing it.

"We could just drop the bridge," Dralas said.

"They'd rebuild it," Layla said. "And it wouldn't force Abaddon back into the mountain."

The ground on the other side of the bridge was dark and littered with the remains of a huge camp.

"It still smells of burning," Layla said as they crossed the bridge.

"And death," Dralas said.

The entrance to the mountain was large enough for a passenger jet with room to spare. Crystals flickered inside. One of the dwarves who had arrived before them stood outside the mouth of the tunnel. Zamek and Vorisbo went over to talk to him, and the dwarf ran off around a large boulder a short while later.

"They're almost done," Zamek said as everyone else joined him. "They're not exactly proud of their work, and they asked for more time to make it smoother inside, but I told him it wasn't necessary."

"I guarantee you that every single one of those dwarves will come back and beautify that tunnel," Vorisbo said. "There will be murals in there before the winter comes around."

"Excellent," Layla said. "How long do you need to get the main tunnel rigged to collapse?"

"We can put runes along the inside," Vorisbo said. "You put enough power in the first one that it triggers the rest."

"Like explosive charges?" Zamek asked.

"Put the power in the last one," Layla said. "We'll get as many as we can with them."

"Someone is coming," Tarron said as voices could be heard echoing somewhere inside the tunnel.

"Doesn't sound like a lot of people," Chloe said.

"I'll check," he said, running off, returning only a few seconds later.

"How many?" Dralas asked, his tone suggesting he was eager for them to arrive.

"Six," Tarron said. "Carrying a staff. It's dark in there, so easy to hide, but they'll be here shortly."

The group moved out of view and waited for the blood elves. One of the six came out of the tunnel carrying a large, black, iron staff, while the other five appeared to be there as bodyguards.

Layla's team descended upon them with ruthless efficiency, killing five of the six in seconds. Tarron stood above the remaining bloody and bruised blood elf. It viewed Tarron with open hostility.

"None of you left," the blood elf hissed.

"Apparently not," Tarron said sadly. "How many of you are there with Abaddon?"

"Millions," the blood elf snapped.

Zamek removed some rope from the staff and tied the blood elf's hands together behind its back, forcing it onto its knees.

"I will die for Abaddon's cause," the blood elf sneered.

"Zamek, Vorisbo, you want to go get those runes done?" Layla asked. "Dralas, can you throw that staff into the river?"

"With pleasure," the giant said, picking up the large staff with one hand and carrying it over to the water's edge.

"No," the blood elf snapped. "No, you must not. Abaddon will punish me."

"Does it work without all four staffs?" Layla asked.

"No," the elf snapped again, before realizing it had said too much.

"Wait," Nabu said, drawing a knife from his belt and cutting across the dwarven runes drawn onto the staff. When Nabu was done, Dralas heaved the weapon into the river. The blood elf cried out as if wounded.

"Where are the other two?" Layla asked the elf.

"Two?" the blood elf asked.

"One of your group's been eaten by spiders," Chloe told it. "You probably don't want to find that particular staff."

"No," the blood elf almost screamed. "No, no, no, no."

"How many are with Abaddon?" Layla asked.

"Thousands," the blood elf said, seemingly deflated. "There are other staffs. They were meant to surround the dwarven village. We have failed Abaddon. Failed our goddess." The elf stood and stared at Layla. "You will die at her hands."

Dralas placed a hand on the elf's shoulder and pushed it down to a kneeling position again. "Where is Abaddon?" Layla asked.

"Coming," the blood elf said. "Right behind us. So many, right behind us. She will kill you, and then me. When you're dead, then I die. I die for failing her." It cackled and then sprinted toward the river and threw itself in. The moment it hit the surface, it was caught by the rushing current and smashed against one of the many jutting rocks that stuck out of the water.

"Holy shit," Chloe said. "That was messed up. Why would it kill itself?"

"Because it's better to die by its own hand than by Abaddon's," Nabu said.

Vorisbo and Zamek both ran out of the tunnel. "Abaddon is coming," they said simultaneously.

"Lots of blood elves too," Zamek said.

"We need time to finish the runes here," Vorisbo said. "Can you stall her for maybe ten minutes?"

"How?" Chloe asked.

"I have an idea," Layla said. "When I run out of here, get ready to drop the tunnel."

"Layla, this seems like a very bad plan," Tarron said. "Abaddon is not someone you want to fight."

"Not going to fight her," Layla said. "Just wind her up a bit. I think I can do that." Layla ran down the tunnel. The sound of marching blood elves grew louder the closer she got. She slowed to a walk and eventually stopped at a part of the tunnel with a long, straight section ahead.

The saber-tooth panther licked Layla's hand, and she scratched the cat behind the ears. "Glad you're here," she said.

Abaddon led the blood elves at the front of the procession. She wore the exact same leather armor that Layla had seen her in before, and her expression was a mixture of hate and amusement. To Abaddon, Layla was nothing more than a slightly humorous diversion.

Abaddon held up a hand and the blood elves behind her stopped marching, although they still banged drums and hit their swords against their shields. The noise was almost deafening inside the confines of the tunnel.

Abaddon raised her other hand and silence fell. "You are most persistent," Abaddon said. There was maybe a hundred feet between her and Layla, although the tunnel made them seem closer. "And you have acquired a pet."

"And killed a lot of your elves, don't forget that," Layla said.

The smile on Abaddon's face faltered for just a moment. "I have come from Helheim to end your hope of adding allies to your pathetic resistance."

"Now say that in Darth Vader's voice," Layla shouted. "I wonder, does your neck hurt always looking up for falling houses?"

Abaddon looked confused.

"Damn it, I thought that was a good one," Layla said. "Not a *Wizard of Oz* fan, I assume?"

"Did you come here to taunt me?" Abaddon asked.

"Pretty much, yeah."

"Because that seems foolish."

"I also thought I'd come see the size of your army," Layla said. "I've seen bigger. Oh, you're expecting your Devil's Venom to incapacitate everyone. Yeah, spiders ate your elves."

Abaddon's eyes narrowed in anger. "You think I need my weapon to kill you all?"

"Yes," Layla said. "I think that's exactly what you need. You came from Helheim to have a great victory over a city of dwarves you presumably didn't even know existed until a few hours ago. I can see that you didn't bring too many blood elves with you."

"You thought you could bring your dwarves here to fight me outside the tunnel? Is that why you're here, to give them time to organize?"

"Not really," Layla said. "I'm here to call you a few names, make you feel bad about yourself. I'll be honest, I'm not the best at it, but you've got to learn at some point."

"I could end your existence with a wave of my hand."

"Go on then," Layla said. "Or do you need that power for whatever you have planned in Helheim?"

Abaddon laughed. "Do you really think I'm just going to tell you everything?"

Layla shrugged. "I'd kind of hoped so, yes. Nice army you got with you. I'm guessing that's most of the blood elves you have left in this realm. That means your realm gate is defenseless. Why, anyone could just go and make sure you couldn't use it. That would really mess with your plans, wouldn't it? If you were stuck here. Forever."

Abaddon's eyes narrowed, and Layla knew she'd hit a sore spot.

Vorisbo walked up next to Layla and rested the head of her ax on the ground. "You must be that haggard wench that everyone keeps talking about," she said.

"See, she's great at pissing you off," Layla said, pointing to Vorisbo.

Abaddon took a step forward, followed by her entire army of blood elves.

"We ready to go?" Layla asked. Vorisbo nodded.

They turned and sprinted out of the tunnel at full speed. Vorisbo stopped and turned at the mouth of the tunnel as the sound of the blood elf horde got closer. She cut her hand and placed it against the tunnel wall, causing the runes to flash white with power.

Vorisbo and Layla, with the panther at their side, ran to the bottom of the bridge as the first lot of blood elves got near the mouth of the tunnel.

"Abaddon isn't there," Layla said, noticing that the sun was beginning to set.

"She's letting the elves go first," Vorisbo replied. "I guess it was too much to hope that she got buried with her troops."

They ran over the bridge as the first elves reached the runes, which exploded. The sound of the tunnel collapsing on hundreds of elves was deafening. Dust and debris shot out of the tunnel, covering the old blood elf camp in muck.

"How many do you think we got?" Dralas asked as Vorisbo and Layla joined the rest of the team on the opposite side of the river.

"A lot," Layla said. "Not all, but a lot. I think Abaddon was at the rear of their little army. You think any of them survived?"

"No," Tarron said. "And I am glad that whatever became of my people is being removed from this world. The blood elves are a disease I plan to eradicate however I can."

"It's going to take those elves hours to get back to the realm gate," Zamek said.

"Sounds like a good idea to me," Layla said as an explosion tore through the collapsed tunnel, throwing rock all over the opposite bank of the river.

"That can't be good," Chloe said.

"Anyone else realize that we've just given Abaddon, a necromancer, hundreds of blood elf souls to use?" Layla said.

They stared at one another. "Well, shit," Chloe said with a resigned tone.

Layla drew her sword, ready to fight whatever came out of the tunnel. More rock and elven body parts flew out, and then Abaddon appeared, followed by dozens of baying blood elves.

"I guess my plan for the side tunnel is screwed," Layla said.

"It was a good plan," Tarron said, drawing the claymore he'd taken from the dwarven armory. "Maybe we can ask her to go back inside and wait."

"Was that sarcasm?" Chloe asked. She'd opted for a claw-like weapon that sat over one of her fists, while she carried a dagger in the other hand.

Abaddon and Layla locked eyes. Abaddon smiled as more and more elves flooded out of the tunnel. All of a sudden the elves tried to get as far away from the mouth of the tunnel as possible as the dwarven army, roaring a challenge, smashed into them at full speed.

Layla and her friends ran over the bridge into the fray, colliding with the nearest blood elves, who were still trying to scatter from the attack inside the tunnel. Layla tore the sword from the hand of a blood elf and flung it through the skull of another, who had raised its own sword to strike. She spotted Jomik in the middle of the fight at the mouth of the tunnel, swinging a huge maul at anything that moved near him.

The elvish army had been devastated by the fall of the tunnel, but there were still thousands of elves alive, and a large number of them were the commanders. Abaddon, who had clearly thought this would be an easy fight, killed any dwarf who tried to take her down. She used the spirits of the dead near her to continuously power her own abilities. The tunnel was quickly emptying as the fight moved further and further up the bank of the river.

Layla had been in fights more times than she could count. She'd been in battles where magic and powers destroyed the surrounding area with ease, but she'd never been in a fight like this. This was close-quarters fighting. She had to force herself to ignore the screams of pain as the smells of sweat, blood, and fear filled the cavern. She didn't even have a moment to focus her power, and couldn't risk just blindly flinging it around in case she took the metal from a weapon being used by an ally.

Layla ducked a sword swipe, driving her own blade into the belly of a blood elf, only to be kicked by a commander into the dwarves behind her. The commander went for another attack, but Chloe blasted him in the chest with her umbra power, throwing him back into a group of blood elves, who all fell to the ground. The nearby dwarves made short work of them. The ground was becoming slick with blood, and despite the dwarves' numbers advantage, the elves were making it hard work for them.

Layla rolled to her feet, stabbing a blood elf in the back and pushing it away from a fallen dwarf, who nodded thanks in response.

"Accept who you are," Terhal said to Layla.

"Now is not a good time," Layla snapped, stopping an elf's blade in midair and driving her sword into his chest. Tarron drove his own sword through the elf's neck.

"Thanks for the assist," Layla said.

"It didn't look like you needed one," Tarron replied with a smile. "But I had nothing better to do."

There was a roar behind her and she turned to see a troll run toward them over the bridge. "What the hell?" Layla asked.

"Must have disturbed it," Vorisbo said from beside her. "We need to take it down, and fast."

The troll covered the fifty feet to Layla in seconds, but she remained calm, and when it had raised its hammer to deliver a killing blow, metal spikes erupted from the earth beneath its feet. They punched through the cracks in the leg armor and pinned it to the ground. The troll dropped its hammer to the ground and swiped at Layla, who easily dodged it. She ran around to the back of the giant creature and discovered that the armor between its lower back and its tailbone was missing.

Layla placed her hand on the troll's lower back, skin to skin, and concentrated with everything she had as Zamek and Nabu kept the blood elves away from her. The troll screamed and clawed at the metal keeping it in place, but Layla ignored it as best she could until she found what she was looking for.

Layla took control of the trace amounts of metal inside the troll's body and ripped them out of the creature with such explosive force that, instead of thousands of tiny holes, several exceptionally large ones tore the troll apart.

When the fighting was over, the dwarves were victorious, although they'd paid a price for that victory. Zamek stood in the center of a group of dead blood elves, his black armor literally dripping with their blood. Jomik walked over to Layla. "Abaddon escaped back into the tunnel. We couldn't stop her. She had a few elves with her."

The army of dwarves and Layla's team ran into the mountain after Abaddon. After twenty minutes of running, they discovered a hole in the side of the tunnel that led directly to the elven realm gate. There was no one inside the cavern.

"She escaped," Chloe said as they reached the dais and found the fresh remains of a blood elf.

"Damn it," Layla said.

"We stopped her," Jomik said with pride. "We took back our mountain."

"Our home," Vorisbo said.

"We lost a few hundred dwarves today," Jomik said. "We will honor their memory."

Tarron climbed the stairs to the dais and began to work on changing the destination, calling out that he was finished a few minutes later.

"We will continue on to the citadel," Jomik said. "We will take this mountain back."

A huge cheer went up from the dwarves, who were continuing to pour into the cavern.

"Thank you for your help," Layla said.

"And for yours," Jomik told her.

Cries of "Prince Zamek" rang out around the chamber, making Zamek look incredibly uncomfortable.

Layla's team said their goodbyes and made their way to the dais. The panther had killed several elves and would certainly need a wash. She licked Layla's hand as she was stroked. "It's good to see you're okay," Layla told her, and the panther let out a slight purr. "We go to Shadow Falls," Layla said. "Then, Zamek, you need to use the dwarven gate to get to Tartarus. I'm sure by now Mordred and team will be getting impatient."

"And then we all head to Helheim," Zamek said. "I've left instructions with Vorisbo on how to activate the dwarven gate in the citadel. I'm hopeful that once they're done liberating it, we will have a powerful ally in this realm."

Layla looked down on the dwarven army who had managed to free themselves from elvish cruelty. Abaddon was running now—she'd lost the battle and would certainly not want to lose the war—but Layla and her allies had proved she was beatable. And she hoped that knowledge would bolster them for the battles ahead.

16

MORDRED

Mordred opened his eyes and blinked at the darkness above him. For a brief moment, he wondered if he had died and gone to some afterlife he'd previously given no thought to. He sat up and remembered the staff, the explosion, and being thrown back down a large hill. The mist had gone, so he stood and brushed the debris off, noticing that Diana, Remy, and Hel were all in similar states.

"That was not fun," Hel said, sitting up and rubbing her head.

"Whatever you did to that rune, Remy, I think it worked," Diana said, getting to her feet.

"Let's go check," Remy said, and he began to walk up the hill. Remy was the only one of the four of them who didn't have a powerful healing ability, and Mordred was concerned that he might be pushing himself too far.

"Wait up," Diana said to Remy, the look on her face telling Mordred that she'd had the same thought.

"I'm fine," Remy said, before sitting down. "Maybe a little tired, but the actual blast didn't seem to do me any harm."

"Yeah, but being thrown down a hill wasn't my idea of a good time," Hel said, now back on her feet.

The four of them made their way up the hill and found the staff in several dozen pieces scattered around the clearing.

Mordred heard shouting in the distance. "I think we should see if we can get into the compound. I think breaking the weapon may have caused them to notice us."

They headed through the forest until they reached a large rocky overhang surrounded by bare tree branches. Fortunately, it was far enough from the wire fencing that their dark clothing helped hide them despite the lack of concealing leaves. They climbed the rocks and looked down over the compound exterior.

Several small buildings had been turned to rubble and evidence of magic was scorched all around the concrete remains. The front doors to the main compound were closed, as were several other entrances, and all had runes blazed on them. Mordred knew the word "hellfire" when he saw it, and wondered exactly how many had died trying to get those doors open. The burn marks outside several of them suggested that more than a few deaths had occurred.

Large green tents had been erected at the far end of the compound, near the main entrance, and several military vehicles—including one jeep with a machine gun mounted on the rear—were parked beside them. Mordred knew they would need to ensure that machine gun played no part in whatever they did to get inside.

"Those are Avalon people," Remy whispered, pointing at the armed soldiers walking around what used to be the entrance to Hades' compound.

"I smell just over a dozen," Diana said. "None are weres. Eight are human actually, which is a little weird."

"And the others?" Hel asked.

Diana shrugged. "Not weres. Magic's a possibility—it depends how long ago they used it. I can only smell fresh magic. Humans are doing a lot of the dirty work since Avalon created the Inter-species Task Force. The ITF has been responsible for a lot of murders. They're essentially the new secret police. Except, not so secret, obviously."

"How far into this part of the compound can you smell?" Hel asked Diana.

"About a quarter of the way, so, yes, there could be a lot more people down there waiting for a fight."

"Okay, so anyone have any good ideas about how we get into a compound that Hades and Persephone designed?" Hel asked.

"Umm," Remy said. "They have tanks."

Mordred looked over toward the entrance to the compound and sure enough there were three gray tanks. "What make are they?" Mordred asked.

"I don't think it matters," Remy said. "They're tanks, that's enough."

"If I can get us inside that fence, leave the tanks to me," Mordred said.

"Do you have a new tank-busting power I'm unaware of?" Remy asked.

"Just trust me," Mordred told him with a smile.

Remy picked up a rock and threw it at the rune-scribed fence. The rock bounced off and hit the ground. "Thankfully, I don't think they're going to design a fence that kills hapless idiots who touch it. We'd see a lot of charred squirrels around here if that was the case."

"What do the runes do then?" Mordred asked.

Remy shrugged. "No idea. Go read them and find out."

"Does it scare anyone else that Remy is the voice of reason here?" Diana asked.

Remy showed Diana his middle finger and she smiled.

Mordred left the others and dropped down onto the grass twenty feet below him. Hel dropped beside him and together they walked to the fence.

"You see the spotlights over there?" Hel asked, pointing to the massive lights at the entrance of the compound. "They haven't looked over here. I assume they're not expecting company coming in over the fence."

Mordred had been reading the runes that were inscribed on the concrete posts separating segments of twenty-foot chain-link fence, and pointed to the nearest one. "They're new."

Hel walked over to it and placed a hand over the rune. "Lots of power in this. *Lots* of power. A few days old at most. It's based on weight. My guess is they have an enchanter on staff."

"That's bad news for us," Mordred said. Enchanters could make complex rune patterns and pour large amounts of power into them, essentially creating powerful, magical mines that could only be changed or disarmed by another enchanter, or someone with intricate rune knowledge.

"How good is your rune work?" Hel asked Mordred. "I'm pretty good, but I know that your friend, Zamek, taught you a few things."

"He knows the original ancient dwarf runes," Mordred said.

Hel raised an eyebrow in question. "I thought they were lost to the annals of time?"

"Yeah, well, turns out that Nate Garrett had them buried in his head. He taught Zamek and me a few, although Zamek got them easier. I only picked up one or two."

"Any that disarm runes?"

Mordred had been channeling pure magical power into his hands and they glowed a faint white color. "Yes, actually, but I think you might want to step back. When this happens, all of you get in, and make sure I have a clear shot at that machine gun. I'd rather not be cut to shreds."

Hel did as Mordred suggested, moving over to the nearest large tree and standing behind it.

Pure magical force wasn't like elemental magic—air, earth, fire, and water—nor omega magic—mind, matter, shadow, and light—which sorcerers couldn't even use until they were several hundred years old. It was not even like when a sorcerer combines his two elemental magics to create something new—in Mordred's case, combining his air and water magics gave him the ability to breathe anywhere. Pure magic was just destructive. It had no other use. It was wild, untamed, and something Mordred didn't like to use an awful lot. It made him think of past transgressions, it made him feel like someone who could do *anything* he wanted. It was not a nice feeling.

He drew the rune he'd memorized from Nate's teachings onto the concrete pillar and poured pure magic inside. The effect was . . . spectacular. Fifty feet of fence on either side of Mordred exploded. Thousands of tiny shrapnel-like pieces flew into the exterior compound like deadly bullets, hitting anything and everything in sight. Mordred saw soldiers drop to the ground in pain, and heard the shrapnel hit buildings and vehicles in turn.

He stepped over the remains of the fence and continued to build up the pure magic inside his body as his companions rushed in ahead of him. He had to ignore the fighting, hoping his friends would be able to keep themselves safe. One of the soldiers ran toward the jeep and climbed into the back. Mordred was fifty feet away when the machine gun fired at him, and he unleashed the power he'd been building up. He heard no sound as the pure white magic ripped everything apart, turning the jeep, machine gun, and bullets that had been fired into white-hot, molten metal. The soldier operating the gun was vaporized as he took the brunt of the force.

A second jeep behind the first exploded along with several fuel canisters that were nearby, ripping one of the buildings apart and utterly destroying the tents that had been there. Mordred turned toward the tanks at the sound of their engines starting and unleashed every ounce of pure magic he had inside of him.

It hit the first of the three tanks and punched a hole through it that expanded the further it went. The shells inside detonated from the force, tearing the tank in two. Mordred sprinted toward the second tank as it turned its turret toward him. He drove a blade of pure magic into the front of the tank and poured more magic into the hole, ripping it apart from the inside out. Fragments of metal pinged off his hastily created shield harmlessly.

The third tank fired a shell, but Mordred used his magic once again. The force and power of the pure magic hit the shell and turret of the tank, obliterating both. When he was done, three tanks were nothing more than scrap, the soldiers operating them dead.

Mordred had used his magic for less than two minutes, and once he was done, his body sagged with exhaustion. Hel ran to him, helping him stay upright.

"Holy shit, Mordred," Hel said.

"Don't do that often," Mordred said. "Can't do that again for some time." That was the main problem with pure magic, Mordred had found. Using it quickly was like holding his finger on the fire button until the guns ran dry in a First Person Shooter.

"Tell me again why we didn't just come through the main entrance?" Remy asked, joining the others in the middle of the yard.

"We were being stealthy," Mordred said.

Remy looked around. "Yeah, this looks stealthy to me."

"We have wildly different meanings for that word," Hel said with a shake of her head as she walked off toward the main gate of the compound.

"Quick question, where are the rest of the soldiers?" Remy asked. "I was sort of expecting something a bit more . . . ferocious."

"You all need to see this," Hel shouted out.

The rest of the group gathered beside her and looked down the steep road that headed toward Mittenwald. Buses sat in the middle of the road. The bodies of the Mittenwald residents lay in ditches on either side.

"There are thousands of people in those ditches," Hel said. "I can feel their spirits when I reach out. They shipped an entire village here and executed them."

"I see one of those staffs down there," Remy said. "Can't smell the bodies though. The mist must do something to them."

"Another staff," Diana said, pointing to a staff that was just outside the compound, surrounded by trees. Hel blasted it with her necromancy, destroying it.

"They break easily enough," Hel said.

"So will the people who did this," Mordred told her, his voice cold and hard.

The four of them went to the entrance of the compound. Remy pushed the door open and stepped inside before the others could get there.

The lights were dimmed in the foyer, which was a stark contrast from the last time Mordred had been here. The floor was marked with bullet holes, and there were old bloodstains on the walls.

"There was a fight here," Mordred said. "A big one."

"Someone threw a grenade," Remy said, pointing to the shrapnel blast against a nearby door. "I'm guessing Cerberus lost the compound."

"Which means that either these assholes haven't gotten into the realm gate, or they have and are currently in Tartarus," Diana said.

"That also leaves us with a problem," Hel said. "If these people have breached the realm gate, how do we get through it?"

Mordred had to admit it was a valid point and one he didn't have an answer to. "Let's check that when we get to it. Hopefully the invaders will have a guardian here to open the gate."

"Someone who will need convincing?" Remy asked with a smile that showed his sharp teeth.

They followed the hallway leading to the lifts that would take the team down to the realm gate rooms far underground. There were more signs of fighting along the hallway: bullet holes, burn marks, and cuts in the floor, ceiling, and walls showed that someone with magic had thrown around blades of air, but there were no enemies in their way.

They reached the lifts and found them destroyed, the doors torn off, the cable inside sliced through.

"Someone didn't want anyone else to go down," Remy said.

"There are stairs," Diana said. "But they don't go all the way to the bottom. There's a second elevator further down inside the compound—we'll have to use it to get to the realm gate, but with this one out of order, it's going to be a long stair climb down."

"Hopefully that elevator won't be broken," Hel said.

"Anyone else getting a serious *Resident Evil* vibe from this place?" Mordred asked as they continued on. "The flickering lights, the creepiness, the bloodstains. I swear if we need to find a key with a shield on it and a matching lock, I'm going to be *really* upset."

"You play too many video games," Diana said.

"Or not enough," Mordred countered. "Video games relax me. I don't think anyone wants to deal with a stressed-out Mordred."

"That's a valid point," Remy said.

The group reached the stairwell and began to descend. Dozens of bodies littered the stairs as they went down.

"Shit," Diana said, stepping over a dead ITF soldier, who had been almost torn in half.

"Hades' people are not known as pushovers," Mordred said.

It took nearly half an hour to reach the bottom of the stairs. They discovered more bodies of ITF soldiers, and those who had worked for Hades along the way. Once at the bottom, they spent a few minutes moving a large barricade from the hallway. The barricade was makeshift and consisted mostly of tables, chairs, and anything else lying around that could be used to keep the enemy busy. A lot more bodies littered the bottom of the stairwell, most dressed in ITF uniform. There were also several that Mordred recognized from his time coming to the compound over the last few years.

"Cerberus and his people put up quite the fight," Hel said.

The hallway beyond looked similar and dozens of dead filled the rooms that led off the main hallway. Parts of the walls were missing and the rooms were a mixture of bullets, blood, and crackling magical energy that Mordred could still feel.

Diana picked up an MP5 and ejected the magazine. "Silver. The ITF came to slaughter."

"Looks like they were given everything back in spades," Hel said. "I count dozens of dead bodies in the ten rooms off this hallway. I can feel them. I'd like to be out of here as quickly as possible. There are a lot of enraged spirits I'd rather not have to deal with."

The lift was around a corner at the end of the hallway and was still working.

"Is this a good idea?" Remy asked.

"They might have people waiting for us," Diana said. "But there's no other way to get to the realm gate room."

Everyone stepped into the lift, and Mordred created a shield of air and ice in front of the doors once they closed. Hel pressed the only button on the panel next to the door and the lift began to move down.

During the thirty seconds they descended into the unknown, they readied themselves for a fight. But when the lift doors separated and nothing happened, Mordred removed the ice and air shield. He stepped out into the hallway and immediately wished he hadn't.

Nailed to the wall with foot-long silver spikes was Cerberus.

"Oh no," Remy said.

Diana ran over to her friend and tried to pull the spikes out, but the silver burned her hands and she had to stop, screaming in incandescent rage at what had happened.

Mordred, Hel, and Remy removed the spikes, lowering the were-wolf's body to the ground. He'd been killed in his human form, and his hands and feet had been removed with a single stroke of a blade.

Kneeling beside the body, Mordred sighed. He'd liked Cerberus. He'd been no-nonsense and loyal to Hades and his family without question. He was someone who Mordred had fought several times over the centuries, and he'd maintained a healthy respect for him. After Mordred's mind had been restored, he'd found Cerberus willing to forgive so long as Mordred joined him for a glass of vodka. The pair had drunk several bottles that night, and whatever their past had been, they'd started anew as friends. Mordred was going to hurt someone for what they'd done to him.

He stood and walked along the ramp down toward the realm gate room. Someone fired a bullet at him that Mordred deflected with air magic. He wrapped tendrils of air around a second soldier, crushing him in his own armor, before flinging him at the first, just as a werebeast Diana charged into the soldier, who lived only long enough to scream one last time. Remy ran past Mordred, throwing a grenade into the doors opening at the far end of the room, then leaping aside as the explosion cut through the area.

"Where did you get a grenade?" Mordred asked.

"Found it," Remy told him, stepping inside the room. He drew his sword and dispatched anyone who lived.

Hel absorbed the spirits of the dead, eyes flickering up into her skull. A smile crossed her face as she used her necromancy to tear the room doors in half, flinging them into the room beyond with incredible force.

Inside the room were Orcus and Enyo, and two people who cowered behind the deactivated realm gate. Enyo finished stabbing one of Hades' guards, pushing his dead body to the ground. "You're interrupting my fun," she said as a snake of blood magic uncoiled itself from around the guard's throat, wrapping back around her arm, making her shiver.

"Enyo," Hel shouted. "We would have words with you."

17

MORDRED

Hel rushed toward Enyo, but was thrown across the room into the wall by Enyo's blood magic.

"You know about blood magic, Mordred," Enyo said as she punched a guard he hadn't seen when Hel had torn the doors off their hinges.

Snake-like tendrils of blood magic from Enyo's palms grabbed hold of Hel's wrists, causing her to scream as pain wracked her body.

Mordred hit Enyo in the chest with a blast of air magic, sending the sorcerer flying over a nearby table.

"You okay?" Mordred asked Hel as she got to her feet.

"I really hate blood magic," she said.

The realm gate activated, and Mordred paused, thinking that Enyo was going to try to make a run to Tartarus, but instead two minotaurs sprinted into the room, roaring as they barreled into the desks that stood in their way. One of the minotaurs charged Diana, sending her through the far wall.

Orcus had been trying to keep his head down once the fighting started, and took that moment to flee, Remy hot on his heels. The second minotaur ran toward Hel, who blasted it in the chest with her necromancy power, turning the spirits inside her into pure force. The minotaur almost shrugged off the blast and hit Hel hard enough to send her flying back out of the room and into the corridor.

The minotaur stomped over to Mordred. Enyo stepped up to it and stroked its massive arm. It was nearly eight feet tall and probably weighed the same as a large car. One of the two horns on its huge bull-like head was broken, leaving only jagged edges. Its hooves scratched against the floor as it removed a long chain with a hook on the end from over its shoulder, swinging the chain around in a menacing fashion.

Mordred didn't see Hel until she leapt onto the nearby table and punched the minotaur in the face with everything she had. The minotaur staggered back, and Mordred hoped that Hel had enough spirits inside her to keep up the level of speed and strength that she would need for a toe-to-toe fight with a minotaur.

Enyo stared at Mordred and smiled. "Just me and you left? The last time we met we were on the same side."

"That was a long time ago," Mordred said. "You get one chance to end this. Or I end it for you."

Enyo flung a tendril of blood magic at Mordred, who froze it in place. Enyo's eyes widened in shock.

"Yeah, you're not going to win this," Mordred told her, running forward and freezing two more tendrils before hitting her in the chest with a blast of light that sent her careening over the nearby table.

The smell of burnt flesh touched Mordred's nose. He couldn't use his light magic in quite the same way as another sorcerer would be able to use fire, but it still had its uses in a fight.

Enyo shot a plume of flame at Mordred, who wrapped himself in a shield of air and continued walking slowly toward her. She poured more and more magic into the plume, until it engulfed Mordred, who put more magic into his shield.

After a few seconds the fire stopped, and Mordred took no small amount of joy in the expression of utter disbelief on Enyo's face. He wrapped air around her and squeezed it tight, but snakes of blood magic cut through the air and took hold of Mordred's wrist.

Mordred dropped to one knee and cried out in pain as the blood magic slowly moved up his arm, wrapping itself around his chest and making him feel as though his entire body was on fire. A second blood magic snake took hold of Mordred's other hand, and soon both were wrapped around his arms and chest, pinning his limbs to his side and causing him more pain than he could ever remember.

"Blood magic is so delicious, isn't it?" Enyo asked, her face inches from Mordred's. "My minotaurs are killing your friends, and then you'll feed my power with your own. You shouldn't have come here."

"Cerberus," Mordred managed to say.

"He should have given me what I needed. He was punished for it."

Mordred dropped to all fours, his hands in the blood of the guard who had died as he'd entered the room with his team. He felt it slick on his hands, sliding between his fingers as the pain in his body became more and more distant. Mordred looked up at Enyo's smiling face, took hold of one of the snakes, and cut it in half with a blade of blood magic that he'd created.

Enyo's screams filled Mordred's ears as she felt the feedback of the blood magic being stopped. The snakes dropped from around Enyo, who scrambled to get away as Mordred got back to his feet, albeit shakily.

"I don't like using blood magic," Mordred said. "I certainly don't like using so much that I could break your hold, but if you think that my use of it isn't considerably more powerful than yours, you must not have been paying attention to the kind of person I was."

Enyo got back to her feet and charged Mordred, a blade of fire extending from her arm. Mordred created a sphere of light between his hands and poured power into it. When she raised the blade to strike, he detonated the magic sphere, aiming every bit of it at Enyo, who was thrown forty feet toward the rear of the room.

Mordred walked toward her, where she was partially stuck into the wall, and ignored the sounds of the others fighting. He needed his focus to be on her: she was too powerful, too devious, to allow her even a second out of his sight. The moment he saw her trying to claw her way out of the wall, he ran toward her, reaching her just as she detonated a wall of flame. He wasn't quick enough with a shield of air and inhaled some of the super-heated air that Enyo's magic had created.

Coughing, he staggered back just in time to avoid a swipe at his heart with a silver dagger.

"If I can't overpower you," Enyo said. "I'll just make you bleed."

Mordred wrapped air around Enyo's arm, holding it back as he drove a blade of light into her chest. She dropped the silver dagger, which Mordred grabbed before it fell to the ground and plunged into her head. "You first," he said, removing the dagger and cutting her throat in one movement.

Mordred watched Enyo die, before turning to find Hel taking a defeated minotaur's spirit into herself. Diana's minotaur was missing an arm and looked like it had been fed through a combine harvester. Diana was drenched in blood and one arm hung uselessly at her side, while she used her other hand to press against a horn wound in her ribs, but she would live.

Hel walked over to Mordred. She had a bruised face and looked pained, but like everyone else seemed to be okay.

"He broke my ribs," Hel said. "Still healing."

"I'm glad you'll be okay. Where's Remy?" Mordred asked her.

Remy walked through the entrance they'd come through only a short time ago. "Orcus tried to escape," Remy said. "He didn't make it very far."

"He dead?" Diana asked.

"Very," Remy said.

Hel stopped by the realm gate guardian, who was still cowering on the floor, holding on to the gate. He looked like he'd not enjoyed being in Enyo's company.

"Activate the gate," Hel said. "We're not done here."

"Take me with you," the man said.

"Did you work with Enyo? Or were you here because you were forced?" Remy asked.

"Forced," the man said.

"He's lying," Hel said. "I can tell. He worked for Hades and betrayed him to Avalon."

"She offered me money to come here," the man managed to splutter. "But I didn't expect this."

"Open the gate, then run like hell," Mordred told him. "The way is clear. Leave. Don't come back."

The man nodded enthusiastically and opened the realm gate without another word. All four members of the team stepped through, leaving the carnage behind them. Mordred took a deep breath as he found himself on Tartarus, exhaling when the realm gate closed behind him.

Just beyond the realm gate, Tartarus was a place of fog. To Mordred's mind it was exactly what he'd expected the place to be, but he knew that the fog eventually ended. They walked down to the shore and found several wooden boats moored there. Each one had oars and room for half a dozen people to sit comfortably. Remy and Diana got in one, with Diana taking up the oars.

"We'll take this one," Mordred said. "Don't drink the water, it ages you."

"Yeah, I've been here before," Remy said.

"We all have," Hel told him.

Diana shrugged and pushed the boat away, beginning to row.

Hel and Mordred climbed into the second boat, and Mordred picked up the oars, settling into a comfortable position as he began to row.

"So, I assume you wanted to talk," Hel said after Mordred had been rowing for twenty minutes. "We've got a little while to ourselves, so let's get this done."

Mordred had prepared himself for this moment for some time, but now that it came to it, he couldn't quite figure out how to start.

"We were having fun together," Hel said, starting the conversation for him. "And then out of the blue you tell me you need to leave, and I ask you to wait until I return from a mission. I return, and you're gone. No word from you, nothing. You just upped and ran away."

"I did," Mordred said, continuing to row.

"If you wanted to call things off, I'd have been okay with that. I would have found it odd, considering you appeared to be enjoying yourself, but things don't always work out. Instead, you didn't even do me the courtesy of actually talking to me."

"True."

"You're an asshole."

"Also not disagreeing."

"You know, I thought I'd tell you that I don't care what you have to say, but actually, I'm kind of curious."

Mordred took a deep breath before exhaling slowly. "I lived over a thousand years with essentially no moral compass whatsoever. I hurt, I killed, I did whatever I liked. And when I wasn't doing that, I was in a prison cell trying to figure out how to escape, so I could go and hurt, kill, and terrorize all over again.

"And after centuries of that, I was free. And I didn't really know what that meant. I threw myself body and soul into defeating Arthur, Avalon, Abaddon, my father, my brother, and any number of assholes who joined them. And then you came along and I felt something else.

"I was having a good time with you. I enjoyed your company. But after a few months, I started feeling something else. I started wanting to go along on missions with you, not because I thought you needed my help, but because the idea of you being taken or killed, those thoughts hurt.

"I'd found someone else to fight for. And that scared me. And I didn't handle it very well."

"You were a dick."

"Yes, that's a fairly good way of putting it. At the end of the day, I love you, Hel. I've loved you for a while now, and I don't really know how to tell you that. I don't really know how to express what I'm feeling because I spent so long just stabbing and hurting things that I didn't have *feelings* for anything that didn't involve rage and hate. Feeling afraid for you utterly freaked me out. Like, utterly."

"You love me?" Hel asked.

Mordred opened his mouth to speak, and then ran through what he'd just said. "Yes," he eventually replied. "I wasn't sure what it was I was feeling, but just seeing you makes me happy. Even angry you who would like nothing better than to tear off my testicles. *You* make me happy."

"You should have told me."

"Yes, probably, but I was terrified that if I unloaded my feelings for you, you'd reject me, or tell me that I was getting too close too soon, or anything that involved my heart being ripped out and used for keepy-uppy."

"Keepy-uppy?"

"It's a football thing," Mordred said. "When we're back on the Earth realm, you need to find an internet connection and search it."

"You like football?"

"Oh, my word no, I'm not really a sports person. The last sport I played had people throwing axes at one another. It was not something they'd show on the BBC."

Hel nodded. "That's a lot to take in."

"It's a lot to say," Mordred told her.

"You love me?"

Mordred nodded. "I do. And if you hate me, or just don't feel the same, then that's fine, but I couldn't go around pretending everything was fine because it clearly wasn't considering I had no idea how to deal with those emotions."

"Because you love me," Hel said with a smirk.

Mordred nodded and sighed. "That was harder than killing a troll," he said.

"That doesn't make it okay for you to run off and not tell me, you get that, right?"

Mordred nodded. "Yeah, I do. I didn't know how to deal with it, and I screwed up. I'm sorry. And I get it if you decide that we can't go anywhere from here. But I wanted to try to explain what's going on in my head, even if *I* don't always understand what's going on in my head."

Hel stared at Mordred for some time. "You seem to be under the impression that I didn't know what I was getting into when we started whatever it was we started. I knew full well. I expected some . . . issues, which is why I didn't want to push you. I didn't expect the response I got, to be honest, but we live and learn. I'm not just going to jump into a relationship with you, Mordred."

While Mordred felt hurt by that, he also understood where Hel was coming from. "I get that," he told her. "I'm sorry I screwed it up."

"When we're done here, and by here I mean with trying to save my realm, me and you are going to have a long talk about this some more. And once I'm satisfied that you're going to act like an actual grown-up, we'll move forward from there."

Mordred smiled. He hadn't been expecting anything even close to a second chance, and he was certain he wasn't going to blow it. "Thank you," he said.

Hel leaned toward Mordred, until she was inches from his face. "You hurt me when you ran. I don't usually give second chances, but I think we could be something special. In other words, get your shit together, and we'll put this in the past and just look forward." Hel kissed Mordred on the lips, pulling away after a second. "Now, get rowing."

Mordred did as he was told and they reached the bank soon after, where the glory of Tartarus revealed itself. It was a beautiful place with rolling hills, and while it was currently overcast and drizzly, it was usually bright and warm. The Titans had been placed there thousands of years ago and had made a city their home. Over time, more and more people had come to the realm to live, away from Avalon's influence, and the population exploded as a result. Last Mordred heard, over twenty thousand people lived in Tartarus, and most of them hadn't left the realm for centuries. The only residents who were not allowed to leave were the original Titans because of a binding agreement with the Olympians that Mordred had every intention of breaking.

Mordred climbed up onto the pier, where Charon stood with Remy and Diana. Charon had the appearance of an elderly man because he'd drunk the water of the lake, and it had irreversibly aged him.

"Mordred," Charon said, walking over and shaking his hand. "It's been a few years."

Mordred smiled; he liked the old ferryman. He was grumpy and took no shit from anyone, which was sort of how Mordred hoped he would be when he was grown up.

"The fox tells me that you've come to piss everyone off," Charon said.

"I didn't quite say that," Remy shouted. "I said 'mostly' everyone. Get it right."

Charon flipped Remy his middle finger, making the fox-man laugh in response.

"If you keep doing that at your age, the digit might seize up," Remy called back.

"Good, then I can just do it to everyone who's a smart-ass little bastard like you," Charon retorted.

A Thunder of War

"As fun as this is," Hel said, "it's not getting us into Tartarus. We need to talk to Hyperion and the others."

Several griffins landed close by the group and stood wordlessly, their normally gleaming sliver-and-golden armor splattered with blood. "I'm coming with you," Charon said. "We had a few . . . *issues* with interlopers. A bunch of blood elves and minotaurs turned up a short while ago, although Hyperion and the others in town managed to kill them all. The bastards used my boats to row over. They deserved to die just for that. You know anything about them?"

"Avalon wants control over this realm—they sent Enyo and Orcus to do the job," Hel said.

"Really?" Charon asked. "They were the best they had? I assume they're not currently a problem."

"They're pretty dead," Mordred said.

Mordred looked over at the four griffins and was impressed by the power and elegance they exuded. The griffins walked around on two legs, their top half an eagle with massive wings that were easily the width of two adult men standing on top of each other. The bottom half of the griffin was a lion, complete with massive paws and a long tail, although their paws had huge, retractable talons instead of claws. They were the jailers, protectors, and guardians of the inhabitants of Tartarus, and they were not a species that anyone in their right mind would want to fight. Not only because of their razor-sharp beaks and the talons on their hands and feet, but also because each of them carried a spear and sword, and they were—in Mordred's eyes—some of the most dangerous users of those weapons he'd ever seen.

"We will fly you," one of the griffins said. It looked at Mordred. "You can use pure magic?"

Mordred nodded.

"Your presence will be tolerated, but if you use it, you will die." There was no suggestion in the griffin's tone that there was another option.

191

"Sounds fair," Mordred said.

"My name is Lorin," the griffin told everyone. "I was guarding the realm gate when several of the creatures came through. I held them off as best I could and raised the alarm. Unfortunately for the invaders, they assumed that swimming here was the best way forward. They aged terribly and were easy prey."

"They didn't die in the lake?" Diana asked.

"No, we took them to the killing grounds to the south," he told her. "They will be dispatched there and left for the creatures that roam those lands. Each of you will be carried by a griffin. One of us will take the fox and a second passenger. Charon will make his own way."

"I have a horse," Charon said. "Also, I don't like being carried a hundred feet in the air."

"We have never dropped anyone," Lorin said. He paused. "I don't think."

"Is that a joke?" Mordred asked Charon.

The four griffins made a weird noise in their throats.

"Yep," Charon said. "Goddamned hysterical, aren't they?"

The griffins took one person each in their talons and lifted them off the ground by their shoulders. Mordred had to admit, it wasn't as uncomfortable as he'd imagined it would be—he didn't feel like he would lose an arm with one wrong move.

The griffins flew over the ancient-Greek-inspired houses with white stone walls and bright orange-and-red-tiled roofs. People looked up and several children waved, which made Mordred feel better about asking them to leave. When Avalon eventually broke through to this realm, they were unlikely to spare anyone, children or not.

The griffins landed and they were met by Hyperion, who was, the last Mordred had heard, now in charge of the Titans. Hyperion looked to be in his mid-fifties with a short, gray beard that matched his hair. Everything about him screamed power and danger, and Mordred knew that the dragon-kin could do a lot of damage to the team before they'd be able to stop him.

"I am all for visitors," Hyperion said. He wore a long, purple cape over deep-red leather armor. He looked like he was going to war. "But we've already had some issues with guests today, and I'd rather not add to them."

"We need your help," Hel said.

"Why?" Hyperion asked.

"Abaddon and her troops are going to take Helheim," Remy told him. "We want you and your people to help stop them."

Hyperion laughed. "You think *we* can do that? Look around you. We are not warriors anymore. We fought the Olympians and we lost. Now we live here, until someone comes along to try to kill us all. We have hundreds of children here—you want them to go to war?"

"They're already at war," Hel snapped. "Avalon came for you today. You stopped them, but they will be back. And in greater numbers."

"Like Tusken Raiders," Mordred said before he could stop himself. "And, as I say that, I realize you have no idea what *Star Wars* is, so I should shut up now."

Remy patted Mordred on the hand. "Good job."

"My point stands," Hel said. "They will find a way in, and they will kill you all. Children, women, men, griffins, they don't care. You join them, or you die."

"Cronus and Rhea were murdered by Abaddon. Most of the other Titans haven't fought in centuries. Atlas was only here because he sided with us when we went to war, and he's proven himself to be a traitorous dog. We don't have the power to end a war."

"No," Diana said. "You don't. But you do have the power to help us end one."

"My son Helios is dead," Hyperion said. "He joined Avalon and murdered innocent people. Selene is still in mourning for the loss of her love and lives her life going from battle to battle, trying to stop herself from feeling. Eos is who knows where. My family here on Tartarus is all I have left. All any of us have left. And you want us to risk that to fight Avalon?"

"Yes," Mordred said. "Because otherwise we might as well bow our heads, drop to our knees, and beg that our deaths are swift. And I don't know about you, but I'm far too old to beg for a goddamned thing. I'm going to fight until I can't breathe, because anything else is just inviting Avalon to do what they wish."

Hyperion looked between the members of the team, before turning to Lorin as Charon entered the square on his horse. He wore armor identical to Hyperion's.

"And you?" Hyperion asked Lorin.

"The griffins will fight," he said. "Abaddon and her people invaded our lands, killed our people. We will repay that act in their blood."

"I'm coming too," Charon said. "Anyone who argues gets punched."

Mordred noticed hundreds of people walking toward the square, all of them wearing the same style of armor, but in different colors, carrying different weapons.

"I recognize the armor," Hel said. "You wore it when you fought the Olympians. My grandfather told me about it."

Hyperion sighed and looked up at the sky, rubbing his eyes with the palm of his hands. "I did not want to get involved in this war, but I guess it was inevitable that Avalon wouldn't just leave us be. Stopping them before they turn their full attention to us is probably the most sensible thing we can do at this point."

"You're going to fight with us?" Mordred asked.

"Do you have somewhere safe for the children and those who can't fight?" Hyperion asked.

"Zamek is coming here to change the destination of the realm gate to Shadow Falls so that we can all go there," Mordred said. "We just need to figure out how we're going to actually get everyone from here to the realm gate."

18

LAYLA CASSIDY

When Layla stepped through the realm gate in Nidavellir and into Shadow Falls, she was greeted by several guards who relaxed the second they realized who it was. Zamek, Tarron, Nabu, Dralas, Chloe, and the saber-tooth panther followed through a moment later. Several of the guards looked at the giant cat with a mixture of awe and terror.

Tarron made sure only he could activate the realm gate, then jogged after the others to where they waited for the lift.

"You okay?" Layla asked Zamek. They all stepped into the lift, which started to descend.

"My people might be free," he said. "Most of my people are who knows where, but those in Nidavellir have a chance to take back their homes. That is a momentous thing to see. But my place is with all of you. Freeing the realm of Nidavellir is only the beginning of what we hope to achieve here. I want to find the rest of the dwarves, just like Tarron wants to find the shadow elves."

"My place is with Tarron. I do not care much for going home. Those I loved are dead, and the vast majority of fire giants were not people I wished to spend time with," Dralas said. "They were never people who understood me. They are about war and carnage, and I just wanted to protect my friend."

Tarron patted Dralas on the arm. "You can come with me to find the elves," he said.

"That would be nice," Dralas told him.

Once the lift reached the bottom of the mountain, they were met by Tommy and several guards.

"That's a massive bloody cat," Tommy said, pointing to the panther. "What did you feed it?"

"I think they're always big," Layla said. "You get used to it."

"Is it friendly?" Tommy asked. "To weres, I mean? Some animals get funny around us."

"It's been around me all day and hasn't tried to eat me once," Chloe said, gaining a playful nudge in the ribs from the panther.

Nabu winced as he took a step, and Layla and Chloe were both there to ensure he didn't collapse.

"What happened?" Tommy asked, concerned.

"Dying," Nabu said. "It's complicated."

"The crystals in Nidavellir poisoned him, and soon he'll die," Chloe said. "Not complicated at all."

"Can we save you?" Tommy asked, his voice full of emotion.

"No," Nabu said. "It's part of my cycle. I die, I am reborn in time. But I refuse to go before I've helped you keep Helheim safe from Avalon."

"We have to get to the dwarven realm gate," Zamek said. "I need to change the destination to Tartarus and then help Mordred get back here with everyone in that realm."

"What if we worked together?" Tarron asked. "If we could modify this dwarven realm gate like we did in Norumbega, we could create a rudimentary elven gate. One powerful enough to stay open for a long time, using the dwarven realm gate as a power source."

"Do I need to hit anything?" Dralas interrupted.

"Not just yet," Tarron said.

"Sounds like a good idea," Zamek said. "Tarron, you get to the mountain and start going through what we'll need, and I'll be back as soon as possible."

"I will go with Layla, Chloe, Nabu, and the big cat that really does need a name to Helheim," Dralas said.

The team made their way through the city of Solomon to the temple where Kase, Harry, Antonio, and Leonardo were waiting for them outside the realm gate, along with a huge congregation of people.

"I assume they're here to go help Helheim?" Layla asked.

"We've just been waiting on you all to get back," Tommy told her.

Zamek changed the realm gate destination to Helheim and activated it. "It'll stay open for as long as you like now," he told everyone. "I need to get back to the others, but you can start feeding people through. It won't stay open indefinitely, but if you keep redrawing this rune every ten minutes or so, it should stay open a few hours. Long enough for me to work on the other realm gate before getting back here."

Zamek ran off, leaving Harry and Leonardo to reapply the rune in question as hundreds of people started to march through the realm gate. Tommy, Olivia, Persephone, and several other high-ranked people went through first, presumably to get set up with what needed to be done. Layla and her team waited for about an hour until Caleb and Sky arrived. She'd been keeping an eye on him in Shadow Falls ever since Layla had left him with her, and her expression suggested it hadn't been a fun time.

It took a few hours before Layla followed everyone else into Helheim. She'd wanted to make sure that there were enough people in Shadow Falls just in case anything bad happened.

The smell and sounds of battle hit Layla as soon as she walked through the gate into a courtyard where a dozen soldiers were sparring. Layla noticed the glances from the soldiers as she turned her arm into a blade, and she quickly remade it, looking around at the large, green-and-blue-tiled floor, and the gray stone walls. There was a large gap in the wall, showing the city below, the spires of dark and light wood reaching up toward the orange-and-red sky.

"That is ominous," Kase said from beside her as they moved away from the realm gate to make way for the continuous stream of people.

"This place gets its reputation because of the sky," Nabu said. "People came here and said it was as if the sky were on fire."

Tommy led them out of the courtyard and into the gigantic city that was surrounded by hundred-foot-high walls. "That's not exactly inviting," Layla said, pointing to the guard towers that sat higher than the walls. There were a dozen that she could see around the front of the wall.

"It encircles the whole place," Tommy said as they walked through the city. "Hel made this city almost impenetrable. The river Gjöll isn't far from here, and anyone wanting to fight us has to cross it first. The only way over it is across the bridge Gjallarbrú, which is guarded by Modgud and her giants. When Abaddon's people come, we're going to know about it. We can see them building their forces in the pass through the mountains to the north."

"What's this city called?" Layla asked.

"Niflhel," Dralas said quietly. "I have been here before. It was not a fun experience."

"How many enemies are there?" Chloe asked.

"From what I was told by Hel, a lot," Tommy said.

Layla's team separated; Tarron and Dralas walked off into the city, and Chloe told Layla that she would go check on Caleb.

"He's been taken to the library," Tommy said. "No idea why."

Tommy ducked under a doorway and into a large room where several people Layla had seen in Shadow Falls or Nidavellir were gathered around a long table that could have seated fifty. There was a large map on the table dotted with several flags of various colors. As Layla got closer she saw Helheim written in the top corner. The city they were in—Niflhel—was marked on the bottom along with the realm gate that Layla and her team had come through. A blue flag sat on top while several other strongholds were marked with black flags.

"We lost all of those?" Layla asked.

Olivia looked up. "Yes, most of the realm is now in the hands of Abaddon."

"Where's the gate to the Yggdrasil tree?" Layla asked.

Persephone pointed to a spot near the far side of the mountain. Thankfully there were no strongholds there. Niflhel was the last populated place before the dwarven realm gate.

"Most of the population of this city are soldiers," Sky said. "The civilians fled through the realm gate several weeks ago."

"Where are they now?" Layla asked.

"Asgard, Midgard, and a few other places," Persephone told her. "Places with a greater chance of holding out. Hel has been evacuating them for a few years now, so we don't have to worry."

"How many blood elves?" Dralas asked.

"Approximately two hundred thousand," Tommy said.

"That is not in any way a good thing," Kase said.

"How long have they been there?" Nabu asked, sitting on a chair nearby. "I'll explain my predicament shortly, I just need information at the moment."

"A few days," Olivia said, raising an eyebrow in question toward Layla.

"They're just there watching," Persephone said. "Modgud is less than thrilled. She has several hundred giants who really want a fight."

"They'll get one," Nabu said, getting up to look at the map.

"Tommy said my father was taken to the library?" Layla asked. "Any ideas why?"

"He thinks he knows how Avalon found us," Persephone said. "All he told me was that we weren't betrayed, and then he asked to see the library and off he went."

"I'll go see him," Layla said. "Just point me there."

"I'll take you," Sky said. "I don't need to know troop movements and plans, and it'll give us time to catch up."

They left the building, with the panther walking beside Layla, occasionally bumping her hand so that she'd stroke it.

"So, you thought about getting her a saddle?" Sky asked.

"I don't think she would like that very much," Layla said, receiving a lick in response. She looked across the city and saw that part of the large wall was missing. "That where Mammon attacked?"

Sky nodded. "So I've been told. It happened just before Hel arrived in Shadow Falls. Mammon didn't do much damage to anything but the wall. Some of the soldiers here think he was just testing out his power. It's being repaired at the moment."

"What about the civilians in the city?"

"Most have been sent under the mountain to the south."

Layla turned around and looked at the reddish mountain range, the color making her think of NASA's pictures of Mars. The pair set off walking down a cobbled street toward a large white building in the distance. "How many soldiers do we have here?"

"Just over twenty thousand in the city."

"Hel and her people have been fighting here for two years. She's lost over thirty thousand soldiers in those two years. Avalon lost five times that many though, so I'm going to assume that's why Abaddon was brought in with all the blood elves. Abaddon and her people are ruthless and well organized. Hel's generals told us that they've lost two forts in the time she's been fighting here. They said that there are patches of soldiers still active in the mountains and forests to the north, but they probably only total a few thousand in number, and there's no way to get them all here. Hel's scouts are still in the mountains. They sent a thousand troops to guard the Yggdrasil tree temple, and we have more ready to head there."

"What about Mammon? He still there?"

"I did a walk of the walls yesterday, and yes, he's still there. He flies between the two highest peaks over there." Sky pointed in the direction of the mountain range where the blood elf forces were amassing.

Layla squinted, but couldn't see anything. "He's still not at full power, I assume."

"I'm assured he won't be for several days, maybe longer. Jinayca told me about some books in the library here that detail what was done to him. He had most of his body covered in blood curse marks. I don't even know how he was able to turn into his dragon shape. I assume he's sacrificing people to cure the marks, but that's something I don't really want to spend too much time thinking about. It just makes me angry."

"And Hades?"

"We don't know," Sky said, clearly upset about it. "Abaddon brought him here for a reason, we just can't figure out what that reason is."

They stopped outside the large building, and Layla looked up at the majesty of the blue and gold domes that sat on the left and right wings of the building. It was a hundred feet high, and reminded Layla of the library in the dwarven kingdom.

"I know what you're thinking, but that's not the library," Sky said.

"But . . . pretty building," Layla said, pointing. "What is it?"

"Courthouse of sorts," Sky told her. "It's where prisoners would be sentenced. The library is over there." Sky pointed to a small red-stone dwelling that didn't look big enough to house anything more than a few rats, let alone a library.

Sky pushed opened the door and motioned at the lantern-lit interior, which appeared empty except for a wooden door.

Layla stepped inside and pushed it open, revealing a set of similarly lit stairs leading down beneath the city streets. The smell of old paper and books hit her instantly.

"Down there is the library," Sky told her. "When you're done, get some rest. There are some rooms in the courthouse that we've taken as our own while we're here. Anyone committing a crime is liable to be punished by being on the front lines in the next battle."

The panther took one sniff, lay down on the floor, and looked very much like she had no intention of moving again.

Sky laughed. "I assume she'll start standing on your desk while you're trying to work next."

Layla scratched the cat behind one of her ears. "I'll be back soon," she told her.

The cat lowered her head to the ground and closed her eyes.

She began the descent to the library, wondering how long it must take for books to be taken up and down the stairs. About halfway down, she started to hear voices, and when she finally reached the bottom she found Harry and Chloe at a table next to the staircase playing a game of cards. Suddenly, Layla's powers vanished, and her arm fell to the floor as pieces of metal.

"Hey," Harry said, putting his cards on the table face up and giving Layla a hug. "Yeah, no powers down here."

"That sucks," Layla said. "When did you get here? I thought you were helping Leonardo."

"Leonardo thought I'd be more help here, so he sent me through a little while ago," Harry said. "Good to see you're okay; you look knackered though."

"It's been a long few days," Layla told him. "But thanks for making me feel better," she added sarcastically.

Harry gave her the thumbs up.

Chloe got up and hugged Layla. "Good timing. Harry cheats at cards."

"I do not cheat," Harry said. "You're just not very good."

"My dad here?" Layla asked.

"Five stacks back," Chloe told her. "He's been reading."

Layla took in the majesty of the library. She couldn't see the end of it, as it just kept going and going, and somewhere in the distance the lights all blurred into one. The library had stacks of shelves on either side of a pathway. Each stack was fifty feet long, and as far as Layla could tell contained a mixture of scrolls and books.

"There are tens of millions of pieces of work here," Harry said. "We had someone from the city who usually works here come down and show your dad where he needed to look."

"Is all of this just from Helheim?" Layla asked.

"All of the Norse realms," Chloe told her. "And the Greek, and essentially there's a copy of everything here somewhere. They have a . . . scribe, I guess you could call her—she's not exactly chatty."

"Who is she?" Layla asked.

"Seshat," Harry said. "Egyptian god of writing, wisdom, that sort of thing. In reality she spends twenty-three hours a day in a sort of functioning coma, where she takes the words from anywhere she feels like and deposits them into a book. It's like nothing I've ever seen. She just sits there, places her hands on a blank book, and after a short time, there are words there. This library has nineteen floors, all underground, each one apparently full of books about the world, history, and things like that. About a third of them are books she wrote. She seems to flicker around to different parts of history, but she can only do a few books a day, according to the soldier who brought us here."

"He's been geeking out," Chloe said.

"There are rooms back there that I don't think have ever been opened."

"How do you find anything?" Layla asked.

"This whole place is rune-scribed," Chloe said. "You use that thing on the wall there, and it starts to ping when you find the book you need."

Layla turned to see a black crystal on a plinth next to the entrance.

"The same marks are on Seshat, so I'm told," Chloe said.

"How did an Egyptian god end up here?" Layla asked.

"Quite a few of them were murdered," Caleb Cassidy said, stepping out from behind a nearby bookcase. "Thousands of years ago, the Egyptians were given a choice: join Avalon or die. Most joined Hera, or one of the groups who were trying to take control of Avalon, figuring that was the best way to stay alive, but a lot of them fled, went into hiding. Seshat came to the Norse realms for sanctuary, and this place seems to screw with her head. I think she's an och, like Nabu, although no one seems to know exactly why she's the way she is, and no one seems to want to find out. She tends to leave people jabbering wrecks if they examine her."

"How do you know this?" Layla asked.

Caleb placed a book on the table. "It directed me to this before I found the book I needed. I think she can partially control that crystal ball thing."

"Okay, leave the incredibly powerful god alone, not a problem," Layla said.

Caleb showed them a leather-bound book. The red cover was old and cracked, but the pages looked new. "This belonged to Cassandra of Troy," Caleb continued. "She was kidnapped by Agamemnon after the war and he tried to turn her into one of the Fates. It's all in here. It's the original diary. Not sure why it's here, but it looks like a lot of the books here are things brought through from other realms. I think Abaddon would like to get her hands on these."

"What's your point about the diary?" Layla asked.

He showed her a second book. "It's from a Doctor Welkin, who frankly is about as close to an inhuman monster as anything I've ever seen. He was trying to recreate the Fates, but never managed it. He did, however, have Cassandra, her daughter, Grace, and her granddaughter, Ivy, in his care. They are the Fates."

"Okay," Harry said. "So?"

Caleb took a deep breath. "Reading all three, I understand how the Fates work. They don't tell the future, rather they give a collection of *possible* futures. Several are in these books, here. Stuff that has happened, and stuff that happened differently. There was no atomic bomb dropped on Russia in 1946, or conquest of America by Mexico, these are all things that *could* have happened, but obviously didn't. Occasionally they keep seeing the same thing over and over, and if they're asked a question and they give the same answer more than a few times, it's likely that they're on to something."

"Okay, I think I see where this is going," Layla said. "Elizabeth took the Fates when they attacked Sanctuary, and they used them to track our movements. Eventually, they pinpointed Greenland?"

"That's the theory I'm working on, yes," Caleb said. "I need to do more, but I think we need to get the Fates away from Abaddon."

"They could be anywhere," Chloe said.

"They're in Helheim," Caleb told her. "Like I said, this diary of Cassandra's is the real thing. I can see her when I use my power. She's being taken to a fortress north of here, just after the mountains—you can see it if you go on the walls."

"You want to go attack a fortress that contains an army of blood elves, and who knows what else?" Harry asked.

"Not attack, just get in, get the Fates, and leave," Caleb said.

"And kill Elizabeth," Layla added. "That's why, isn't it?"

"If the chance is there, then yes, I would take it. You'd do well to do the same."

Layla wanted to argue, but found that she agreed with her father for the first time in many years. "She can't be allowed to run around, I agree. And if she has access to people who can pinpoint us, then we need to get them out of there."

"Glad you see it my way," Caleb said. "I'll go speak to Sky and arrange . . ."

"No way," Layla said. "We'll arrange; you're staying here."

Caleb placed the diary on the table. "Fine. I'll stay here like the good little prisoner." He walked off, clearly angry.

Layla yawned.

"When did you last sleep?" Chloe asked.

"Not sure, it's been a bit of a blur," Layla said.

"Last we heard, the opposing army still wasn't all there, so that'll give you time to rest before they attack," Harry said.

Caleb stepped out from behind the bookshelves, his hands behind his back. "I want you to know that I understand your reluctance to let me be involved in this." He drew a gun and shot Harry and Chloe in the neck, and as Layla turned to stop him, Caleb shot her in the neck too.

Harry blinked, before falling unconscious. Chloe jumped to her feet and fell forward toward Layla, who felt her legs give out. The pair collapsed to the floor.

Caleb showed Layla the gun. "I didn't want it to be this way," he told her. "But you just wouldn't let it go. They're just tranquilizers, but they're used by Avalon on sorcerers, so you'll be out for a while."

"Gonna find you," Layla said, her eyes too heavy to stay open.

"You will, but by then your mother will be dead. As will the Fates. They're too dangerous to live and should be eliminated. Stay out of my way, Layla. I don't want to hurt you, but I will. This is too important."

Layla reached out to grab her dad, but sleep took her instead and she fell back to the floor.

19

LAYLA CASSIDY

"Your dad is a real arsehole," Rosa said to Layla.

She sat on a patch of the greenest grass that Layla had ever seen. Rosa, Gyda, and Servius stood over her, looking down.

Servius offered his hand, which Layla took, allowing herself to be pulled to her feet.

"You have no idea," Layla said. "I'm asleep, yes?"

"Your dad shot you," Gyda said. "I know I have issues with trust and the like, but I honestly didn't see that coming."

Layla stretched. She was angry that her father had knocked her out, all for his own vengeance. The Fates were innocent victims who, short of suicide, couldn't have done anything to prevent Elizabeth's use of their abilities. "We have to stop him."

"That's true, but seeing how you're here, I figured we may as well talk," Rosa said. "How are things?"

"I'm tired, fed up, pissed off, and have generally had a really shit few days," Layla said. "And I don't think it's going to stop anytime soon, so there's that too."

"I have something I need to say," Gyda said with a deep breath. "I'm sorry. I blamed the drenik for what happened to my village. I assumed it was her, and only her, and I hadn't taken into consideration that the elves and dwarves had been behind it. I created a memory based on what I thought happened and blamed Terhal for something she didn't do."

There was the sound of clapping from behind Layla, who turned and watched Terhal walk toward them. "My good woman," she said. "I accept. Considering your screwed-up brain caused me to have a screwed-up memory, I think we both failed ourselves. The sun elves started this. They set it in motion, and now we have no idea where they are to receive the justice we need to deliver."

"First we have to defeat Abaddon," Layla said.

Terhal laughed. "You can't believe that you can kill her? She's one of the most powerful creatures on any realm. She'd crush you. Even without her full power, you couldn't win in Texas when your mother cut off your arm, and you can't win now."

"Slow her down then," Servius said. "You can't win. You need to think of another option, because if you don't, Helheim falls and you die."

"Thanks for the pep talk," Layla said. "I know what happens. There are people better than me who are in charge of this operation. There are people with more power, more experience running it all. I'm just told what to do and when to do it, and I try not to die. Abaddon is somewhat above my pay grade."

"So, why do you want to go after her?" Rosa asked. "I can feel it."

"Because she took my mother and made her a monster. She takes and takes, ruins life after life, and there's no recompense. There's just destruction and horror, and no one can stop it." Layla paused.

"The weapon she used in Norumbega and in Nidavellir, this Devil's Venom," Terhal said. "Why hasn't she used it here?"

"Maybe she can't," Rosa said. "Maybe the realm is too big?"

"She needs Hades for something too," Layla said, her mind working overtime. "Hades is the key. That's why they still have him. They need him for something. Otherwise, why not just kill him and be done with it? Why risk him escaping? I need to talk to Zamek or Nabu."

"Good luck," Rosa said with a smile as the three spirits vanished from view.

"You still haven't accepted who you are," Terhal said.

"Not now," Layla told him.

"Your father is a serial killer and your mother is a monster. You are their child."

"My mother wasn't always a monster," Layla snapped.

"She helped your father commit several of his crimes," Terhal said. "What would you call her?"

Layla was about to speak, but she opened her eyes and found herself on a bed in a white-walled room. She threw the pale-green sheets off her and got out of bed. She was still fully clothed, but someone had removed her boots. She found them under the table in the sparsely furnished room. Apart from the table and bed, there was a small chair and that was it. A window looked down over the city.

She opened the door and stepped outside to find the saber-tooth panther lying across the threshold. Kase sat opposite it.

"She wouldn't leave," Kase said, nodding toward the cat, who got back to her feet. "I think she feels bad that your dad escaped."

"How are Chloe and Harry?"

"Chloe is fine," Kase said. "Harry is . . . your dad took him."

Layla was suddenly terrified for her friend. "How did he get out of the city with him? Last I saw, he was unconscious."

"A pathway at the bottom of the library was mentioned in a book he'd been looking at. No one even knew it existed. It leads outside the city walls and is currently being destroyed so that Abaddon doesn't use it."

"My dad must need Harry for something."

"Runes, we think," Kase said. "He's been working with Zamek for two years, Nabu too. A lot's rubbed off on him." Layla could hear the slight strain in Kase's voice when she spoke about Harry.

"Are you okay?" Layla asked as the pair set off down the long hallway to the staircase.

"If your dad has hurt Harry, I'm going to kill him," Kase said. "No messing about, I'm going to tear his fucking head clean off."

"I don't disagree with the idea," Layla told her. "I really don't think he'll hurt Harry though. He needs his knowledge." She placed her hand on Kase's shoulder. "Harry will be fine. He's tougher than I give him credit for, and he's smart."

"And if the blood elves get him before Caleb finishes whatever insanity he has planned?"

"It won't come to that," Layla said as they reached the bottom of the stairs. "We'll get Harry back."

Kase pointed Layla toward a set of large gold-and-silver double doors. Three guards stood watch. Kase nodded to them and pushed open one of the doors. The sound of voices washed over Layla like a giant wave.

There were several dozen people inside, including a few she'd never seen before. Mordred, Persephone, Hel, and Olivia stood at the far end of a circular wooden table in the middle of the room. Tommy was seated at the table, next to Nabu, who looked paler than the last time Layla had seen him.

Chloe, Irkalla, Diana, and Remy walked over to Layla, each one hugging her in turn as the panther padded over to one of the large windows and lay down in a beam of sunlight.

"We'll find Harry," Diana said. "We have a plan."

"It's Mordred's," Remy said. "Should tell you all you need to know about it."

"Goddamn it, Mordred!" Hel shouted. "You will die."

Everyone in the room fell silent as Hel swore in a language that Layla didn't know.

"What's going on?" Layla asked, loud enough that everyone could hear.

"We're having a disagreement," Persephone said. "Mordred has a plan to deal with your father, get Harry back, and hopefully find the Fates, but it's . . . not exactly something I'd advise."

"What does he want me to do?" Layla asked.

Mordred looked over at her. "Nothing this time. You're not going."

"Screw you I'm not," Layla snapped.

Mordred walked around the table, and Layla's anger at being told what she could and couldn't do started bubbling to the surface.

"You can't stop me," Layla said.

"Probably true," Mordred told her. "We've come to know one another well over the last six months or so, and I know you're a smart woman, and I also know you can take care of yourself, but on this occasion, you're wrong. You can't do this."

Layla took a breath.

"Before you swear at me," Mordred said. "Just listen. Please."

Layla locked eyes with Mordred and, after several seconds, she nodded. "Go on."

"Your father took Harry out of the city and toward a fortress, here," he said, pointing to the map of the realm that Layla had seen the last time she'd been in the room. Niflhel was clearly marked, and the point Mordred had indicated was a small fort to the west of the mountains where the blood elf army was currently amassing their strength.

"I plan on infiltrating this fortress, finding everyone I need to and getting them out," Mordred said.

"And I can't come because?" Layla asked.

"They're your parents, Layla," Mordred said with genuine warmth. "No child should have to kill their own parents."

"That's the plan?" Layla asked. "You're going to kill them?"

Mordred nodded. "I wanted to talk to you about it first, but yes. Your mother died years ago, and it's just a monster walking around in her skin, and your father . . . we all know what he did. I can't ask you to do it, because, frankly, that's all kinds of messed up."

"They're *my* responsibility," Layla said.

"No, they're not," Chloe told her. "Just like Mara wasn't *my* responsibility, just like Merlin isn't Mordred's, or Demeter Persephone's. We're not responsible for our parents' actions, good or bad. They're adults, and they have to take their own responsibility. Between us, I think we have enough dysfunctional parents to fill a sizable support group, but none of us wants to be the one with the finger on the trigger when it comes right down to it. I know I couldn't have killed Mara. And I doubt you can kill your parents, even if it's not really your mum."

"Besides, you go after them, and Harry and the Fates could suffer if you can't do it at the last minute," Mordred said. "This can't be you."

"It shouldn't be you either," Hel snapped from across the table. "It's suicide."

"It's not," Mordred told her. "That fortress doubles as a large prison. And the Hel I know has never built a prison she didn't already have a way out of. So, you tell me the secret entrance, and then I go stop our friends from dying."

"Why would my father need Harry to help with runes?" Layla asked, thinking about what she'd learned from Kase.

"He'd been reading a book about the fortress," Sky said. "He tore several of the pages out that Hel says are directions to a secret entrance, but she won't say where because she doesn't want Mordred to get killed. I for one have seen Mordred defy death about a million times, so I'm pretty sure he'll be fine."

"At this point, I'm certain Mordred is being kept alive just so he can't ruin the afterlife for anyone else," Remy said.

"I'm not sure how to take that," Mordred said.

"However you like," Remy told him with a slight chuckle.

"That fortress is full of exceptionally bad people," Hel said. "The second you get in there, if any of them get out . . ."

"I get it," Mordred said. "But I still need to try. Also, I have a second part to my plan."

"Oh, this should be good," Remy said.

"Shut up, Remy, you're coming with me."

Irkalla laughed.

"You too," Mordred told her, making Remy giggle until Irkalla playfully cuffed the back of his head.

"What's the second part?" Hel asked.

"Before we get to it, I need to know how to get into the fortress," Mordred said.

"Actually, before *that*," Layla interrupted, "I still haven't said I'm okay with not going."

Mordred looked at Layla.

Layla sighed. "Fine, you're right, I can't do it. Doesn't matter how much I think about it, how much it needs doing, I can't kill my own parents. You're right. I would be screwed up if I could. Doesn't mean I want to just sit around and wait for an army to attack us."

"I was going to talk to you about that," Persephone said as a man Layla didn't know walked over to her.

"Hyperion," he said, offering his hand.

"A Titan?" Layla said, shaking it. "Why are you here?"

"Mordred asked nicely," Hyperion said. "Also, I'd really like to kill Abaddon. I brought several thousand people with me who all feel the same too."

"Thousands?" Layla asked, feeling a little like someone who was being given a lot of information all at once. "Okay. I think we need to start again. What am *I* going to be doing?"

"We want you to head to the temple and help secure it from Abaddon's forces," Persephone said.

"I think that's where Abaddon has taken Hades," Layla said, before turning to Zamek, who had apparently arrived in the realm while she was out cold. "I think she wants to use his power to activate the Devil's Venom, and essentially make sure only her allies have full access to the Yggdrasil tree."

"If she uses Hades to power the weapon, there's no telling how bad it's going to get," Zamek said. "That much power all at once."

"We ran into this mist in Germany," Mordred said. "They killed thousands of people there, humans mostly, I'd guess, and I couldn't move through that mist without collapsing. Doing it with the power of Hades would kill everyone not wearing one of those bracelets."

"Right, how do we get there?" Layla asked.

"You'll have to go across the lake," Hel said, coming around to the opposite side of the table and pointing to it on the map.

Layla looked at the map. The only way to get to the temple was by the river. "A boat?" Layla asked.

"I can help with that," Zamek said. "Give me a few hours and I'll have something ready. Apparently boatbuilding is my new superpower."

Layla looked confused.

"He built a very large boat earlier," Mordred said. "It's how we all got from the mainland to the realm gate in Tartarus. He's very proud of it."

"Weirdly proud of it," Remy said.

Zamek made a humph noise and crossed his arms over his chest, but his smile gave away his true feelings.

"Right," Layla said. "Now, what's Mordred's second part of the plan?"

"When did you take control of this meeting?" Mordred asked.

"The second I walked in and you were all arguing," Layla told him. A year ago she'd been concerned about taking control of meetings and leading teams, but Tommy had taken her aside and explained that while she was only in her early twenties in physical age, she had three highly trained spirits in her head, not to mention a drenik that was probably thousands of years old. What she lacked in physical age, she more than made up for in mental experience. Since then, Layla hadn't worried about voicing her opinions.

Diana offered Layla a fist bump, which she returned in kind.

"I prefer the term discussing," Persephone said, "but your point is well made. Mordred, what's your plan? Hel, please try not to yell at him if it's dangerously idiotic."

All eyes in the room turned toward Mordred. "We can't win this fight," Mordred said.

"That's a really shit way to start," Remy said. "Might want to work on your delivery."

"We can't win," Mordred repeated. "Not against Abaddon and a bloody great dragon that's currently flying around the mountain. Layla won't get across the river or reach the top of the mountain. She'll be a sitting duck just climbing up."

"You have a plan?" Tarron asked. He'd been sitting against the far wall with his eyes closed, but had moved over to stroke the panther. He smiled at Layla, who returned the expression.

"Yeah," Mordred said. He looked at Hel, who shook her head.

"This is a *bad* idea," Hel said. "Of all your ideas, this one is the worst."

"Holy shit," Diana said. "How bad does this need to be for it to be Mordred's worst idea? He once had the idea to walk into a nightclub full of werewolves that wanted to kill him, just to piss them off."

"Worked out okay, didn't it?" Mordred said. "And we need a distraction and an equalizer against Mammon and the army of elves."

Persephone sighed. "Oh shit," she almost whispered. "Nidhogg. That prison fortress is Nastrond, isn't it?"

"What are either of those things?" Layla asked.

"Nastrond is where all of the evil pieces of shit end up," Sky said. "They have no allegiance to anyone but themselves, can't be trusted,

215

and generally just like to hurt everyone and anyone. They're not just from the Norse realms, but any realm. My father sent more than a few there himself."

"Why hasn't Abaddon set them free?" Kase asked.

"Because of Nidhogg," Hel said. "The great dragon that lives under the prison. Nidhogg is going to know if you release the prisoners. And he won't be happy. He made a deal with me to eat the corpses. If they stop coming, then living food will make a pleasant substitute. Mordred wants to release one of the most powerful dragons who ever lived, aim it at Abaddon's army, and say, 'Happy lunch.'"

"And two dragons in the same space?" Persephone said. "Well, the results will be catastrophic for anyone nearby."

"An army for example," Mordred said.

"Mordred wants to unleash hell in Helheim," Remy said. "It sounds like a plan to me. I'm just surprised it took you this long."

"See, Remy likes it," Mordred said.

"Didn't we have this conversation before the aforementioned night-club incident?" Diana said. "Remy likes to make things go boom."

"That's not an indication of my inability to spot a good plan," Remy said.

"So, once we unleash another dragon," Mordred said. "We hope-fully make this war a little bit more even."

"Okay, so if we're in agreement, let's get ready to go," Persephone said.

"I want to be ready to go in two hours," Layla said. "We have a long way to travel, and not long to do it. If Abaddon has found a way over the mountain, we need to stop her."

"You thought of who to take with you?" Sky asked.

"Chloe, Lucifer, Diana, and anyone else who wants to come," Layla said. "As many soldiers as you can manage too. If Abaddon gets to that temple, she's going to do it with as few people as possible to ensure it's inconspicuous. Mammon and Abaddon's blood elf army is going to attack us to keep us distracted."

"I'm coming," Zamek said.

"Me too," Nabu said, getting to his feet. "Or at least, I'll be heading directly to the Yggdrasil tree. If Abaddon is there, I can try to hold her up."

"I want to know more about the tree and realm," Layla said. "Is the temple just part of the tree, or is the realm gate inside part of the tree? I'm not sure how this works."

"The temple houses the realm gate that takes you inside the Yggdrasil tree," Nabu said.

"But the temple itself is also part of the tree," Zamek continued.

"From what we know and understand, the tree's roots are in Helheim," Hel said. "The temple is technically just part of the tree, but we call it a temple because . . . well, it looks like a temple. Made of wood and stone."

"And you currently have a thousand people outside it waiting for battle."

Hel nodded. "The only way to the temple is through this city and up the river. They could go over the mountain, but there are all kinds of magical anomalies up there—such as magical power just cutting out for no reason, or becoming exponentially more powerful and uncontrollable—and it would be an unpleasant climb. And if the temple moves while you're climbing, parts of the mountain start to change, and if you're on it when that happens, you'll have no way to get off."

"Why can't Mammon fly them?"

"The magical anomalies screw around with the flight of animals," Hel said. "Birds don't fly over it, they can't. Looks like we caught a break, because Mammon has tried to get close to it a few times and been forced to turn back. We tried putting a fort on top of it a few centuries ago and the constant barrage of the elements and power tore it apart after a few weeks. It's why we don't leave people up there."

"So, Abaddon and a group could climb over the mountain, but it would be a hard climb?" Layla asked.

Several people around the table nodded.

"Has anyone seen Abaddon since she fled back here from Nidavellir?"

"No," several people said at once.

"So, she could have already started the climb?" Layla asked.

"It's possible," Hel said.

"You said you have a thousand people at that temple, yes?" Layla asked. "Why only a thousand?"

"We were going to send more, but then Mammon arrived."

"Abaddon played everyone," Layla said. "She's going for that temple, and she's going over the mountain to get it."

"But a thousand well-trained soldiers waiting at the temple is a big fight, even for her," Tommy said. "And the march over the mountain is hard, so how many people can she have brought with her? She can't do it alone."

"The weapon?" Sky asked. "She uses it outside the temple and she's going to have an easy ride to get inside."

Before anyone else could make a suggestion, the doors to the room opened and Lucifer entered the room. "You're going to want to stop what you're doing and come with me," he said. "We just got some visitors."

20

LAYLA CASSIDY

It turned out that the visitors in question were an endless stream of dwarves. After stepping through the gate, they followed the path out of the building down toward the ruined part of the fort and started to work.

Layla watched for several minutes as hundreds upon hundreds of heavily armed dwarves walked by. She spotted Vorisbo, who gave her a wave, which Layla returned, and then Jomik stopped next to her.

"Good to see you again," she said with a smile.

"We got bored hunting blood elves," he said. "There are only two thousand of us, but hopefully it'll be enough. The rest are still hunting the elves in Nidavellir, making sure no one tries to claim our land back."

Shadows flickered overhead and Layla looked up at the sight of the griffins flying to the walls of Niflhel.

"Haven't been to war in a long time," Jomik said. "I sharpened my ax for it specially."

"I think you'll get your chance to use it," Layla told him as the final dwarves walked past.

"We were told to build the walls," Jomik said. "But we're just going to make the city bigger instead. Lots to build, but that mountain there is ripe as an extension, and it'll be nice to keep my people busy. Might take us a few days to get it finished though—you think the elves will just keep coming until then?"

"No," Kase said from beside Layla. "I very much doubt it."

Jomik shrugged. "Shame. It would be nice to work with the rock here—I've heard it's a wonderful thing. Beautiful color, very easy for alchemists to work with." He looked toward the main entrance to the city. "Surprised the people in the city haven't gone out to fight. I heard Modgud and her giants are out there patrolling the bridge. She's a vicious bugger, make no mistake."

"Mammon keeps everyone in check," Kase said. "He's just flying around up there."

"Mammon's a cruel tyrant," Jomik said, spitting on the floor after mentioning his name. "My grandfather told me tales about when his grandfather fought the devils. Mammon's sadism was legendary. I don't even know how we're going to defeat it without a large loss of life."

"Mordred's going to fire a dragon at it," Remy said, appearing between Kase and Layla.

Jomik blinked.

"Yes, I am a talking fox-man," Remy said.

"I've seen weirder," Jomik said with a slight shrug. "But I'm more interested in Mordred's plan."

"Not so much a plan," Remy told him. "More a collection of stupid that's going to drag along the rest of us. Personally, I'm looking forward to it."

"At some point in time, you could have been a god of chaos," Jomik said.

"I can live with that," Remy replied. "God of awesome would be better."

Layla shook her head and walked away while Remy regaled Jomik with tales of his exploits. She found Mordred and Hel sitting side-by-side beneath a tree, next to a stream running through the grove to a large, nearby well at the rear of the city close to the mountain. She turned to leave.

"It's okay," Hel called after her, standing up. "You can stay. I was just telling Mordred not to die. I don't want to have to drag his spirit back here so I can kick its ass."

She left the grove and Mordred got up and walked over to Layla.

"Can we do this?" Layla asked him.

"Do what?" Mordred asked, looking around.

"Win?"

"Sure, why the hell not? No pun intended."

"They have a dragon, and Abaddon."

"We're going to have a bigger dragon. Well, not bigger, but, you know, *a* dragon. A big dragon. Remy says it'll be fun, and frankly I have no reason not to believe him."

"Zamek went off to start building his boat. We need to set off soon. We can't wait for you to get to the prison and cause a distraction."

"I know," Mordred said. "I tried to think of a way to make it work, but it just won't. You need to go as soon as you can, and so do I. It's all feeling very much like I'm about to go fight the last boss."

Layla laughed. "That's one way of putting it. We don't have checkpoints though."

Mordred thought about that for a second. "No, they would come in handy."

"I just wanted to thank you for your help. It means a lot."

"You remind me of my daughter. She was taken from me a long time ago. I like to think she was too good for any of the realms, or us, or for what we've done to them all. She was too good to have had a father like me. Evil me, not me me."

Layla smiled a little. "I get you."

221

"Don't die. I don't want to lose anyone else I care about. I know it will happen at some point, but, like I said, you remind me of Isabel. I've been told reliably that you're not her, and I know this, but you have her tenacity and her capacity for goodness. Don't lose those things. You'll need them."

"You're coming back too," Layla said, feeling like this was the last speech of a dying man.

"I have every intention of returning. Hel really would drag my spirit back here," Mordred said with a laugh. "What we're going to do today is dangerous, like nothing we've ever faced before. And if we falter, people die. It's a lot to deal with."

Layla nodded. "I know. I plan on making it back here in one piece too." She stepped forward and hugged him. "Thank you for your help these past months."

There was a cough from behind her, and she turned to see Tommy at the entrance to the grove. "You need to go," he told her. "Zamek had the dwarves help—they made two large boats."

"Zamek must be so elated, he's probably having difficulty standing upright with all the blood rushing to his genitals," Mordred said.

"And there's an image I was happy not having," Tommy told him. "Seriously, why would you say that?"

"Because it's funny," Mordred said, bumping Layla's fist. "I'll get my team ready to go. Good luck to you both." He patted Tommy on the shoulder as he left the grove.

Tommy placed a bag on the floor beside Layla. "New armor. Leather, like the stuff you're wearing, but the dwarves redid the runes. Should mean that it'll take more than a few hits now, and it should also stop magic from getting through—at least a few blasts more than the last set."

"Every little bit helps, right?" Layla said, opening the white cloth bag, and removing the dark leather. She picked up a sheathed sword that was inside the bag.

"It's dwarven made," Tommy said. "The dwarves brought it with them. It'll cut through rock."

Layla pulled out the blade and stared at the shining blue and silver runes moving across its surface. She sheathed it. "Thank you."

The sound of a horn blared over the city, followed by another in a different part, and then a third. "That can't be good," Tommy said.

Tommy and Layla set off through the city, running past soldiers who were also trying to find out what was going on. After several minutes, they reached the front gates and found Diana, Hyperion, and Irkalla along with dozens of soldiers.

"What's happening?" Tommy asked Diana.

"Modgud and her people were attacked," she told them.

Layla ran over to the nearby lift and used it to take her the hundred feet up to the top of the wall, which was teeming with a mixture of griffins and native soldiers.

"My name is Lorin," one of the griffins told Layla.

"Layla," she said. "What am I looking at?"

Lorin pointed over to a nearby twenty-foot-high raised platform with a telescope attached. Persephone and Lucifer were already there, so Layla climbed the wooden ladder to join them.

"The timeframe has moved up," Lucifer said, pointing across the landscape to the mountain.

Layla looked through the telescope, scanning over the massive bridge where several hundred giants stood, and saw the marching blood elf army. A noise from high above the bridge took her attention, and she looked up to see a massive dark dragon soaring through the sky.

"Mammon," Lucifer said, his voice full of hatred.

"I want you with me," Layla told him.

The anger in his eyes vanished as he looked over at Layla. "Why?"

"I could say because you're incredibly powerful and would be a great asset, but, honestly, I know you can stand up against Abaddon, and I know she hates you with the fire of a thousand suns."

"You wish to use me as a way to get under her skin?" Lucifer asked.

"If she's focused on you, she's not focused on Hades or us. Frankly, any advantage we can get is a bonus at this point," Layla said, already moving toward the ladder to get down from the platform.

Persephone stopped her. "Find my husband," she said. "Please."

Back on the ground, Layla and Lucifer found Tommy and the others. She explained what they'd seen, and there were several gasps from some of the less experienced soldiers. Others looked angry and shouted for vengeance.

Lucifer, Tommy, and Diana went with Layla through the city at a run, only stopping when they reached the broken wall, which was almost repaired, complete with a new door that was the exact size and shape for a dwarf.

"Why?" Tommy asked Jomik.

"We figured there's going to be some overspill when they come to the front," one of the dwarves said as Jomik sighed. "Wanted to lull them into a false sense of security. They see the door, and think, 'What the bloody hell is a door doing here?'"

"And then you open the door?" Tommy asked.

"No, then we drop the wall on them," the dwarf said.

"It'll be gone soon enough," Jomik promised. "They're just excited to be doing something that doesn't involve mining or farming."

"I think you're going to have all the excitement you can handle," Lucifer said.

The four of them left through the door, which was removed as soon as they'd walked a few steps toward the two fifty-foot boats moored on a stretch of river that couldn't be seen from where Elizabeth and her elves were on the bridge. Chloe, Zamek, and Nabu stood by one massive boat and several dozen dwarves stood by another. The saber-tooth panther, atop one of the wooden boats, let out a roar.

"You okay?" Layla asked Tommy as they watched the dwarves board the boats.

"Kase told me she was going with Mordred," he told her. "I said I'd expect nothing less considering Harry was there."

Layla was surprised to hear that Tommy knew.

"I literally used to be a spy," Tommy said by way of explanation. "As clever as two twenty-somethings are, they're not exactly a match for the Spanish Inquisition. I feel bad that she didn't think to come tell me. I used to joke that boys had to be stopped at all costs, but she's grown into a smart, capable woman. She gets to decide what she does with her own body, no one else. It was shitty that she didn't think she could tell me though."

"I think it was Harry who was scared," Layla said, trying to cheer him up.

"I like Harry," Tommy said. "I like that they both found one another."

"But?" Layla asked.

"No buts. I'm happy for them. Mordred will get him back—if there's one thing Mordred is good at . . . it's confusing the hell out of everyone around him, but the second thing is following through on his promises. He'll come back with Harry—doesn't matter how much of that fortress he tears apart in the process. Be safe you guys. All of you need to come back."

Layla and the others boarded the boat, and they were soon off on the foggy river. The boat's large black sails just needed a skull-and-crossbones to make convincing Jolly Rogers.

Zamek walked over and passed Layla a helm. It was made of black leather marked with runes that looked similar to the ones on her armor. A faceguard, dark red with brighter red-and-orange swirls around the piece that covered the mouth and chin, pulled down from the top of the helm. It looked demonic.

"A gift," he told her.

She put it on, trying not to look surprised that it fit. She pulled the guard down, and there was a flash around her eyes. "What did you do?" Layla asked, impressed that her voice wasn't muffled.

"It's so no one can sneak up on you. You'll be able to hear just like you can without a helm, and it'll make sure you survive a crack to the skull. Probably more than one."

"Thank you," Layla said as Zamek placed a metal helm on his own head that matched the dark-blue-and-silver plate armor he wore.

"We made some for your panther friend too," Zamek said. "It replaces what she's currently wearing, and should make sure she isn't easily wounded. She . . . took some persuading. She's currently down below getting fitted. She hasn't bitten anyone yet."

"A good sign," Layla said.

"Yet . . ." Nabu said with a thumbs up. "When this is over, you really do need to name her. Or, considering how smart she is, at least find a name she likes."

"It's on my to-do list," Layla told him. "Right after, don't die horribly."

Zamek laughed, and Nabu shook his head. She took the short set of steps to the cabin and found two dwarves, Lucifer, and the panther. The dwarves were trying to put armor on the cat, while Lucifer spoke soothingly to her.

"How's that working out for you?" Layla asked.

The panther snorted derisively.

Layla took the massive helm from the dwarves and stepped up to the panther's face. "This will keep you safe," she told her. "I don't want anything happening to you."

The panther opened her mouth, showing the razor-sharp teeth inside.

"Teeth can't stop an arrow, or sword, or bullet," Layla said. "Please."

The panther looked over at Lucifer and back to Layla, bowing her head so that Layla could fix it in place.

"Thank you," Layla said when done, and there was a sound above that made Layla's blood run cold. She ran back on deck. "What the hell was that?"

"That was the battle cry of a hundred thousand blood elves," Zamek said. "I think they just decided to start the fight."

Layla looked over the bow of the ship as their landing site came into view. "We need to be ready," she said, mostly to herself.

A few minutes later, the ships ran aground and everyone piled out onto the red-sand beach.

"Which way?" Layla asked, the sound of the lapping water considerably more relaxing than the noise the blood elves had made only a short time earlier.

"Hel said due west," Nabu said.

"It's over there," Lucifer told them.

"The smell is unpleasant," Diana said. She wore a mixture of chain mail and leather armor, which was laced up the front. Easy to remove when she needed to change shape.

"The river smells okay," Layla said.

"Blood," Diana said with a low growl. "A lot of it."

The dwarves ran up the beach, their axes, swords, and spears ready for a battle that didn't happen. When they reached the beach ridge, one of them turned around and waved everyone on.

Layla reached them shortly after; the steep incline and soft sand made running difficult. She looked down on the dead bodies that littered the ground between her and the entrance to the Yggdrasil tree realm gate, which was inside a gray stone temple a hundred feet from where she stood.

Everyone moved slowly toward the temple, but Diana stopped them. "Lots of death, but a familiar scent too." She walked over to a set of large rocks and moved around it, jumping back when Harry appeared wielding a sword. He dropped the sword when he recognized her.

"Harry," Layla said, running over. "Why are you here?"

"The soldier here, she needs help," Harry said, raising his hands to show that they were covered in blood.

"Medic," Diana bellowed, and Layla moved aside to let Lucifer and a dwarf through.

Harry said, "She just kept saying over and over that she's the psychic. I don't even know her name."

"How did you get here?"

"Caleb found a map in the library," he said. "It shows that there's a tunnel that goes under the river and joins a warren of tunnels under the mountain. It's like an ants' nest under there. No one knows about them, not even Hel. We arrived as Abaddon and a lot of blood elves ran out of one of the tunnels and attacked the soldiers here. The battle was short—the soldiers hadn't expected it. They dragged the bodies back into the entrance of the tunnel behind the temple. It looks like a small cave, but it opens up after a hundred feet or so."

"Where is Caleb now?" Layla asked. "Is my mother here?"

"He's not tracking Elizabeth," Harry said. "He's tracking the Fates, and Abaddon brought them here. When the fighting was done, Caleb just left me and ran off. I found a soldier still alive and dragged her into that little cave when I heard more blood elves coming. We've been there ever since. I tried to stop the bleeding, but I couldn't. I can't actually make runes, I can only understand them."

"You did more than most would have," Layla told him. "You kept her alive, you stayed alive yourself. You couldn't have done more."

"If I wasn't human, I could have," he whispered.

"You never wanted to be anything else before. We've had this conversation once or twice."

Harry nodded. "Maybe now I *need* to be something more." He shook his head. "I don't know."

"I can't do anything here," the medic dwarf said, coming out of the small space where Harry had dragged the injured soldier.

"The silver is too far along," Lucifer said as he appeared. "I'm amazed she's still alive, to be honest."

"I drew an energy rune on her wrists," the dwarf told her. "It'll give her a few minutes without pain, but that's the best I can do."

"Thank you," Layla said to them both. She crouched down and crawled under the overhang into the small cave. "Hi," she said to the soldier.

"My name is Bera," she said, weakly. "Tell Harry he did all he could."

"I will, I promise," Layla said, taking Bera's hand in her own. "I'm sorry. Can you contact Hel and tell her that Harry and my father are here?" Layla asked, and immediately felt shitty for doing so.

"Don't look sad," Bera said. "It's my job to be a soldier. And if my last act as a soldier is to contact my ruler and tell her what happened then it's my honor and my duty to do so."

Bera's eyes rolled back into her head, and her lips moved, but no sound came out. Layla stayed beside her, holding her hand for the few seconds it took for Bera to send her telepathic message.

"Thank you," Bera said. "For letting me finish what I started." Her hand slipped from Layla's and she died.

Layla crossed Bera's arms over her chest, then placed her sword in her hands. "No, Bera, thank you." She left the cave, and everyone immediately knew what had happened. "She will not have died for nothing. None of these people will have died for nothing." She looked over at the temple.

"Someone get this man a weapon and some armor," Diana shouted, pointing at Harry. "You good with that?"

Harry nodded. "You're damn right I am."

"Good," Layla said. "Let's end this."

21

MORDRED

The sounds of the enemy baying for blood reverberated through Mordred's chest as he stood atop Niflhel's wall. He'd been ready to go when Hel had suddenly run off, and Mordred had followed, wanting to see what all of the fuss was about.

Hel stood beside him and sighed. "Hundreds of thousands of blood elves," she said. "This is going to be a long day."

Mordred was about to reply when Hel sagged forward, clutching the top of the stone ramparts. She waved Mordred off as he took a step toward her, and a second later she was upright again. "My psychic. She's dead. She got me a message before she died."

"I'm sorry, Hel," Mordred said. "What's the message?"

"Harry and Caleb are at the entrance to the tree. She said that Layla wants you to know you don't have to do your plan. I believe Layla thinks it's as stupid as I do."

"They still have the Fates," Mordred said. "And we still need an equalizer for Mammon."

"Nidhogg and Tiamet had a complicated relationship," she said. "He might not take kindly to the man who helped kill her."

Tiamet was a name that brought back less than pleasant memories for Mordred. One of the most powerful dragons who'd ever lived, she'd been trapped in another realm thousands of years previously, but a few years ago she was released right into the heart of London. She caused untold damage until she was eventually killed with the combined might of Mordred, Nate, and several of their allies. If Nidhogg had any fond memories for Tiamet, he might not be thrilled to have Mordred standing before him.

"I wasn't planning on telling him," Mordred admitted. "I figured that was more of a second or third-date revelation."

"Dragons have a natural psychic ability—you know he'll be able to tell."

"It came up in my plan, yes," Mordred said. "So, I either don't think about it, or I show him Mammon before he can try to eat me. I think you'll find they're both excellent choices."

"I think you'll find you're a blasted idiot."

"Part of my charm."

"I never said you had any charm."

"Now, we both know that's bollocks," Mordred said with a smile. "You're going to need to speak to the troops." He pointed to the courtyard below, which was crammed with several hundred soldiers.

Hel turned to two nearby soldiers standing next to a gleaming golden griffin, who had eyes only for the army rapidly approaching. "Open the gates."

Mordred waited for Hel to turn back to him. "Be safe," he said.

She stepped forward and kissed him on the lips. "Don't get dead."

"I'll do my best," Mordred said. He left the wall and walked through the crowd of people, stopping when he heard a cheer. He turned around to see Hel on top of the wall looking down on her people.

"These blood elves have come here," she bellowed, silencing the increasingly large crowd, as people climbed onto the roofs of nearby buildings to listen, "to murder and destroy. To take our homes, our loved ones, and our lives. They want to eradicate our way of life. They want us eradicated. I say we stand here today in defiance of Avalon, of Abaddon, of the blood elves she brought to exterminate us. We stand united against this force of evil. We will show these invaders what it means to try to fight Helheim's finest. We will show them what happens to those who try to hurt us. By the end of today, they will have bled and died on our land, and we will stand victorious." She raised a sword in the air and a huge cheer broke out all around the courtyard.

Mordred continued heading toward the tunnel that would lead out of Niflhel. A metal grate in the floor had been lifted up, and Dralas, Tarron, Irkalla, Remy, and Kase stood waiting. All wore leather armor, and all were armed with a blade of some description, although Dralas opted for plate armor that was the size of a siege weapon, and a silver-lined war hammer that probably took four normal men to lift.

"Are you going to be able to fit down there?" Mordred asked Dralas, who answered by shrinking. He adjusted the straps on his armor, but kept hold of the war hammer, before dropping into the grate causing a splash as he landed in the water below.

"So, what's the plan?" Kase asked.

"They found Harry and Caleb," Mordred said. "Harry is fine."

The relief on Kase's face told Mordred all he needed to know about her feelings for Harry. It made Mordred happy to see people finding such connections, even during times of great hardship. Nate would call him an old romantic. He sighed. He wished a fully powered Nate was here—it would certainly make things more interesting. But if wishes meant shit, everyone would be happy all the damn time.

"I'm still coming," Kase said. "Still got to unleash a dragon. How many times do you get to say that?"

"Twice at most," Remy said, jumping down into the tunnel with Kase and Irkalla directly after.

Tarron was last and he looked down the grate and then back at Mordred. "It has been a strange few days."

"No shit," Mordred said. "And I guarantee you it'll get weirder before the day is out. We're lucky like that."

"I'm not sure I've ever met anyone like you before," Tarron said, following the others.

"No shit," Mordred repeated, jumping through the grate after him. He dropped the fifteen feet into two feet of water. Runes had been etched on the interior of the waterway, and white crystals led the way.

"How old is this city?" Kase asked. "We saw these in Nidavellir."

"Thousands of years," Irkalla said. "Back when the ancient dwarves were still around."

The discussion ended when a loud boom was heard from above, and the walls around them shook.

"What was that?" Kase asked, leaning against the wall.

"I don't know," Mordred said. "Sounded like artillery fire, but I've never heard of tanks or anything with artillery being able to get through a realm gate without blowing up."

"I imagine the same is true of the elven gates," Tarron said.

"With enough raw materials, they could bring something here and make it in this realm," Irkalla said. "That sounds like what Zamek did with Leonardo's . . . car thing."

Mordred looked up at the dark ceiling as another boom shook the walls. "That sounds like a distinct possibility. I doubt it would be anything but simple though—technology and blood elves do not appear to mix well."

The group hurried through the waterway until, after several hundred feet in the gloom and damp, they came to a set of stairs. A metal grate sat at the top of the stairs, putting them ten feet over the water below.

"Where does it go?" Kase asked.

Remy shrugged. "We'll discuss the plumbing situation when we get back, if you like."

"Just curious," Kase said.

Mordred started to hum the *Super Mario Bros.* theme tune, gaining a glare from Irkalla. "He said plumbing," Mordred told her.

"I notice you're not apologizing," Irkalla said.

"Why?" Mordred asked. "Super Mario is great. You should really give it a try. Although not with my controller. I don't want it broken."

"You two done?" Remy asked as he picked the large lock on the grate and swung it open. "I'm good at my job."

"Modest too," Kase said as she looked out of the waterway and into a dark tunnel. "It's not exactly inviting in there."

"Smells like mildew," Mordred said, igniting a ball of light between his hands and tossing it into the darkness.

The sound of something fluttering around in the darkness beyond troubled Mordred, and he stood to the side of the grate motioning for the others to do the same. Dralas sighed and didn't move until Tarron motioned for him to do so, just before hundreds of large flying creatures escaped the confines of the tunnel.

"Bats?" Remy asked.

"I don't know their exact name, but I do know they're big bats," Mordred said. "They're not shy about attacking anyone who enters their territory. They really don't like light, and we *really* don't want to go in there without light."

"Why?" Kase asked. "What aren't you telling us?"

"The tunnels beyond link to the fortress," Mordred said as the last of the bats flew toward the entrance, the sounds of their wings echoing after them. "But they go quite far down, and there might be a few . . . inhabitants there."

"Define inhabitants," Tarron said.

"Drakes," Mordred said. "Smaller dragons, about the size of Komodo dragons. They look more like snakes though. They hunt rats and the like, and from what Hel tells me, they'll leave you alone if you leave them alone. But they hunt in the dark. So I'd rather not take the chance."

"Are they Nordic?" Remy asked. "Because I've never heard of them."

"Mesopotamian," Irkalla said, her tone suggesting that she wasn't happy. "Although I thought they were all dead."

Mordred opened his arms wide and, palm out, jiggled his hands. "Surprise. Hel said they breed too quickly. Apparently one of the Mesopotamians brought them here as a gift to someone or other. She forgot that bit."

"You gave dangerous snake-dragons as gifts?" Remy asked Irkalla.

"Sure, why not?" Irkalla said. "Perfectly normal gift between friends."

"I don't want to be your friend," Dralas said with a smile. "Friends don't usually bring gifts that can eat the other person."

"The giant speaks true," Remy said.

"They don't hunt people," Irkalla said. "Usually. Also, they're not able to breathe fire much, and they don't like light, so we'll be fine." She disappeared into the tunnel.

"Much?" Remy shouted after her, as Mordred motioned for him to follow after everyone else had already gone. "Define much."

"Well, you're about the right size for a good meal," Irkalla told Remy, failing to hold back a smile.

Remy's eyes narrowed. "I'm beginning to regret coming on this mission."

"Why?" Mordred said. "Is it the threat of being eaten? Because if it helps, the dragon is *a lot* more likely to eat you."

"How does that help?" Remy asked.

"I said, *if*," Mordred told him, tossing another ball of light into the distance.

Things in the darkness slithered and scurried down paths, and more than once Mordred had to ignite a second ball of light, just to ensure that nothing attacked them from behind.

"That is a massive rat," Kase said as a black rodent ran down a dark offshoot of the main path. "It's the size of a pig."

The scream of an animal being attacked made everyone stop.

"Drakes?" Tarron asked.

"I *really* hope so," Mordred said. "I don't really want to get into a fight with a bunch of animals in an enclosed space like this. I don't think it would work out well for us."

"But mostly me," Remy said. "Seeing how I'm snack-sized, apparently."

"Would you like to get on my shoulders?" Dralas asked Remy.

Remy looked between everyone. "Yes, that's very kind of you, Dralas. I would feel safer up there."

"You have a sword," Kase said. "Probably more than one, knowing you."

"Doesn't hurt to be prudent," Remy told her.

"Or lazy," Irkalla said as Dralas picked up Remy and placed him on his shoulder.

"I wish I had a camera," Kase said. "And an internet connection."

"You're all jealous because Dralas cares about my well-being," Remy called back.

"I just wanted you to shut up for five minutes," Dralas said, making everyone laugh. Even Remy grinned, playfully swiping the back of the giant's head.

"You all suck," Remy declared, which did little to stop anyone laughing.

The laughter ended the second there was another scream from the darkness.

"Not to agree with Remy or anything," Kase said. "But this place sucks."

A large snake-like creature slithered out of a nearby hole in the wall only ten feet from where the group stood. It had a long red-and-green body with the head of a dragon. A black forked tongue shot out of its mouth, the large teeth glistening with red from a recent kill.

"No one move," Irkalla said.

The drake turned its head, seemingly looking from one member of the group to the other. It hissed slightly, before a low growl escaped its maw.

"That is not snake-like," Remy whispered. "That is definitely not snake-like."

The drake struck quickly, darting toward Tarron, who was closest to it. The shadow elf slid to the side, drew his sword, and decapitated it in one smooth movement. The headless corpse dropped to the floor with an unpleasant noise, which was quickly replaced by growls filling the tunnel.

"Run," Mordred said, throwing massive amounts of light in front and behind the group as they all sprinted off.

Mordred risked a look behind and saw over a dozen drakes coming toward them, one of them much larger than the rest. He formed a shield of ice that covered the entire tunnel and then rejoined the group. "It won't keep them long," he said over the sounds of sizzling.

"Why did they have to have fire breath?" Remy asked.

"Because they're dragons," Irkalla said as a drake twice the size of the one they'd seen earlier burst out of a pathway, narrowly missing Kase, who punched it in the head hard enough to send it flying back down the tunnel.

The group continued running until they reached a thick, metal door. Irkalla tried to blast it apart with her necromancy, but it didn't have any effect.

"Rune-scribed," Remy said, dropping down from Dralas's shoulder and drawing his sword. "And it's made of silver. Hel *really* didn't want this opened. I hope you have a key."

Mordred removed the key from his pocket as Remy frantically pointed toward the mass of slithering drakes that was approaching.

"I think we pissed them off," Kase said.

"You punched it, not me," Remy said.

"Now is not the time for arguing," Kase said sternly.

The door swung open and they ran inside. The noises from the other side of the door as it locked shut made Mordred exceptionally glad he wasn't out there.

"I doubt they would have killed us," Dralas said.

"Yeah, but I don't fancy fighting dozens of the things," Mordred replied.

"Valid point," Dralas told him, looking around the large room the group found themselves in. "Where are we?"

"Under the fortress," Mordred said, removing a piece of paper from one of the pockets on his leather armor. "Hel drew me a map of how to get upstairs and release the prisoners."

"Wait," Irkalla said. "I thought releasing the prisoners was bad. That they'll try to attack us."

"They'll attack anyone, and I plan on making sure that the closest thing they see to attack is a very large army that could use thinning."

"Why would they do that?" Kase asked. "Just who are these prisoners?"

"You know about Abaddon, Mammon, Lucifer, and the other four?" Mordred asked. "About them being created through incredibly powerful blood magic. Conceived with the darkest of powers you can imagine, which imbued them with dangerous abilities?"

Kase nodded.

"Well, you know that it was tried again? Me, Nate, a few others?"

Kase nodded again.

"The prisoners in here are what happens when those children born to blood magic are not capable of rational thought. They are animals. Exceptionally powerful animals. They can't use magic or anything like that, but they're really strong, fast, and are hard to kill. They were created in a large experiment that I'm pretty sure Ares had a hand in, about a thousand years ago. Hel and her people discovered it, put a stop to it and brought those they could find here, but a lot of the messed-up stuff put in their heads stayed. Some got out, went on a murder spree, but eventually all one hundred and nineteen were brought here. Which is where they've stayed for a thousand years. They age slowly—though not like sorcerers, much faster than that—and most have died off over the centuries."

"How many are left?"

"Last count, forty-three. The dragon ate the corpses of the others."

"And we have to let those forty-three out?" Remy asked. "Because that sounds . . . what's the word? Stupid."

"Idiotic?" Kase suggested.

"It's not like we're inundated with good plans," Irkalla pointed out. "Let's go unleash the horde of evil."

"Horde of Evil would make an awesome band name," Remy said.

Everyone glared at him.

"Just saying, is all," he almost muttered.

The group moved through the maze of stone corridors, ignoring the opened doors that revealed empty rooms that had long since fallen into disuse. Most seemed to have structural floor problems, and Mordred didn't even want to consider where he might fall if he stepped inside, so they continued on instead.

A set of stone stairs led up to the main part of the fort where all of the prisoners were kept. Each door was silver in color and marked with several runes, and Mordred found it eerie that there were no sounds from any of the prisoners inside the cells. Several skeletons lay on the ground around the fort, many of them wearing parts of the armor they'd died in.

"What happened here?"

"The prisoners last got out a few hundred years ago, but Hel managed to get them all back inside," Mordred said. "These prisoners are almost pure blood magic—their touch causes pain in others. Since Hel couldn't take the chance the injured would spread the contamination, they left them to die where they lay."

"They turn into zombies?" Kase asked.

"What? No," Mordred said. "Not zombies. Just zombie-like symptoms. These people can think and act, it's just that they only want to think about hurting people."

Mordred pointed down toward the thirty-foot-high barred wooden doors. "We need to open them: they lead to the courtyard at the front of the fortress, and therefore toward the army we'd like to make smaller."

"I'll do it," Dralas said.

"Where is the dragon?" Irkalla asked.

Mordred pointed off toward the rear of the fortress, a place that partially sat inside the mountain. "Over there."

"How did the dragon get the dead over there?" Tarron asked.

"Drakes drag the dead to it," Mordred said.

"Oh, not more of them," Irkalla said with a sigh.

"They're too small to be a problem," Mordred said. "When they get bigger they go below, but they hatch up here, where it's warmer. They drag the dead to the dragon, and presumably feed on scraps. One of these people, with all the power they have inside them, probably sustains the dragon for a long time."

"That's really disgusting," Kase said.

"How do we open the cells?" Tarron asked.

"There's a control release rune on each door that reads life signs. Someone dies, the rune activates and opens the door. The main release is upstairs from here."

Mordred pointed over to one of two sets of stone stairs that led up to the floors above. The stairs sat opposite one another further down the main corridor, slightly back from the silver cell doors.

"Dralas, take those up two floors to a wooden door. Inside are the releases to the main doors here, and the doors of the courtyard beyond. Once you've released them both, you're going to have to get your arse back down here and up those stairs there. Don't dally," Mordred said.

Dralas nodded and jogged off toward the door, while everyone else ascended the second set of stone stairs that spiraled up to a large room.

There was nothing in the room, just dust, the occasional cobweb that was large enough to make Mordred reconsider his role in this mission, and four doors. Three doors were open, their runes long since faded, or damaged, but the one in the center of the room had a bright-blue rune that blazed.

Mordred drew a sign over the rune, disabling it. "Hel had me show her I remembered that fifty times," Mordred said.

"I'd have made you do it more," Remy said as they all entered the room.

At one point it had been the epicenter of the fort, but it had fallen into disrepair. A large hole in the roof dripped water, and the wooden tables and chairs, having at least partially rotted, gave the place an unpleasant smell.

Dozens of runes, all the same blue as the one on the door, shone brightly on the far wall next to a large window. Mordred looked out at the battle in the distance. "Trebuchets," he said. "The sounds we heard earlier were trebuchets."

"What are they using as ammo?" Kase asked.

"Giant balls of flaming metal," Irkalla said.

"I kind of wish Layla was here," Remy said.

"I hope she's okay," Irkalla said.

"She's fine," Mordred and Kase said in unison.

Mordred looked down below as the double doors slowly opened. Dralas could be heard running up the spiral stairs that the rest of the team had just taken. Once he was inside the room and had closed the door, Mordred deactivated the runes to open all of the cell doors.

Nothing happened for several seconds. The runes blinked a few times, and then a wail cut through Mordred like fingernails on a blackboard. The remaining prisoners ran into the courtyard, and Mordred motioned for everyone to step back from the window. He walked over to the side of the wall, and from the cover it afforded continued to watch as the prisoners searched the courtyard, before one of them punched the fortress's metal-and-wood doors, disintegrating them.

"Holy shit," Remy said from beside Mordred.

The prisoners fled out into the battlefield, and Mordred made sure to count every one before he nodded that it was clear.

"You sure there's no one else down there?" Tarron asked.

Mordred nodded again, although a glimmer of discomfort stayed with him.

The group returned to the floor below and found no one waiting for them, evil or otherwise. They made their way to the rear of the fortress, moving out of the main building and into a large open area that was big enough to fit a second fortress. They passed beneath a massive black-brick archway, then stopped at the entrance to the cavern.

The inside of the cavern was in darkness, and while Mordred considered illuminating it, he didn't want to piss off the dragon inside.

He took one step into the darkness and waited.

Something inside took a long sniff of the air. "Sorcerer," it said.

"I have second thoughts about talking to Smaug," Kase said.

"You brought friends," the darkness said.

"We need your help," Mordred told him.

"You released my food," the darkness replied.

Mordred took another step forward and really hoped he didn't have to fight a dragon on top of fighting everyone else today. "Mammon is here."

The darkness laughed and two bright-red eyes, each one the size of a man, glowed from the inside. There was a low, threatening growl that made Mordred want to take a step back, but he stood firm.

"Now," the darkness said, its voice harder than before, "you have my interest."

22

LAYLA CASSIDY

The dwarves were the first to enter the large wooden-and-stone temple that housed the realm gate to the Yggdrasil tree. The temple itself looked like the roots of the tree had merged with the stone around the mountain, although there was no tree in sight. It was strange to look up and see nothing but sky. The rest of the team entered the temple, one large room with a realm gate at one end. There were no guardians to operate the gate.

"This is weird," Harry said.

"You know, you can always stay with the boat," Zamek said.

"I need to do something to help," Harry said.

"Getting killed won't help," Diana told him.

Layla looked down at the smooth red-and-gold floor. Two grooves cut on both sides of the temple ran the full length of the hundred-foot-long building. Fire burned in the grooves, low flames lacking ferociousness. "The grooves have some kind of oil in them that's burning."

A scent of flowers filled the air, although Layla couldn't name the flowers.

"Tulips," Chloe said.

Layla raised an eyebrow in her direction. "I like tulips," she said.

"Blood," one of the dwarves called out from closer to the realm gate.

Everyone ran over, and Layla noticed that the blood appeared to vanish behind part of the wall. She ran her hand along the wall until her power picked up a hidden mechanism, a switch that was made to look like one of the many carvings around the temple. Layla pushed the carving, and the wall slid open, revealing a room full of incense jars and several chests of gems and coins.

"Offerings," Zamek said. "When the temple is further north, it's close to several villages, and the inhabitants used to bring items here to offer to the tree."

Layla looked over at the realm gate at the end of the temple. It was four or five times larger than the ones she'd seen before, and almost covered the entire rear of the temple. The gate wasn't activated and, as she got closer, Layla could see that, unlike most gates, this one was made entirely from wood. The wood changed color several times around the realm gate, moving from different shades of brown, to yellows, reds, and black.

"It's beautiful," Lucifer said from beside her. "So, how do we get it to work?"

Layla turned to Zamek. "You think you can get this working?"

Zamek cracked his knuckles and ran his hand over the wood, igniting the dozens of runes that sat dormant around it.

"Give me five minutes," he said.

Less than two minutes later, a lush green field from the Yggdrasil Tree realm came into view. With the dwarves going last, they walked through the realm gate, each of them clearly aware of what they might face.

Nabu stumbled, dropping to one knee on the dirt once through the gate. Layla went to his side, and he waved her away. "I'm not dead yet," he said.

"You're still stubborn though," Layla said, her tone holding a hard edge.

Nabu smiled. "Sorry, the realm gate took it out of me. I'll be fine."

Harry tapped Layla on the shoulder. "You need to turn around," he said.

"What is it?" Layla asked, turning to see what Harry saw. Her mouth dropped open.

"That's a really big tree," Chloe said, her neck craning upward as she tried to see the top of the tree, which vanished in the clouds above.

"Jack's beanstalk has nothing on that," Diana said. "It's the size of the city we just left, and who knows how many miles tall."

The Yggdrasil tree was gargantuan. "It's, what, a mile away?" Harry asked.

"I don't even understand how it got that big," Layla said, mostly to herself. The surrounding land was mostly green and yellow fields. Rolling hills could be seen in the distance to the north, and a large waterfall to the west.

Layla turned to the saber-tooth panther. "Help Nabu."

"I don't need help," Nabu said as the panther picked him up in her powerful jaws, like a cat would a kitten.

"She can hold you like that, or you can ride on her back," Layla said.

"Back," Nabu said, crossing his arms and exhaling. The panther released him, licking the side of his face as he stood up. "Your cat is enjoying herself."

Layla smiled as Nabu climbed onto the cat's back and took hold of the edge of the armor around her neck.

"Well, that's a first," Zamek said. "Let's get going then."

They started running toward the tree. The panther sprinted ahead, paused to let them get closer, then took off again. Layla swore she saw Nabu smile at least once.

They stopped a few hundred feet from the tree and looked around. Huge roots arched dozens of feet above the grass before plunging back into the ground. They pulsed different colors every few seconds.

"I guess we go in there," Chloe said, pointing to the large opening at the base of the tree.

"It looks like a hole made by a lightning strike," Nabu said. "But there aren't any signs of burning or damage."

The dwarves hurried forward as the ground rumbled and three huge giants came out of the hole and stood before the tree, bellowing. They were thirty feet tall but soon they grew to nearly fifty feet, their skin glowing yellow and orange.

"Abaddon was prepared," Lucifer said.

Each of the giants wielded a different, but no less deadly-looking, weapon. "A maul, an ax, and a spear," Harry said. "None of those options sounds wonderful."

"Harry, stay here," Layla said. "Do. Not. Argue."

Harry nodded and took a step back as a dozen blood elves walked out of the hole and began to beat their weapons against their shields.

"Just once," Diana said, growing in size, dark-gray fur spreading over her body, as her armor adjusted itself to contain her new werebeast form, "just once, I'd like a day where I didn't have to fight something. Layla, Zamek, and Lucifer, we'll make a path for you to get through. You three go stop whatever Abaddon is doing in there."

Layla nodded and removed the silver sword from her hip, taking the metal and wrapping it around her arm and hand. She felt the heat of the silver as she manipulated it, but the discomfort was something she could deal with.

The three flame giants collided with the front line of dwarves in a cacophony of sound as Diana, Chloe, and Nabu charged into the fray.

Layla, Lucifer, and Zamek ran through the throng of blood elves, but came to a halt when several blood elf commanders forced a confrontation. One of them tackled Layla, knocking her face down into the dirt. Layla tried to buck the elf off her back, but the weight suddenly vanished. She looked up to see the saber-tooth panther's jaw clamped onto the back of the blood elf commander's head. A second later there was a horrific crunch and the commander went limp.

Layla scrambled to her feet, narrowly avoiding a flame giant's punch, which scorched the earth where it landed. She turned and ran after Zamek and Lucifer, who had both successfully dealt with the other blood elf commanders and hurried toward the tree. The panther ran beside Layla, knocking aside anyone who came within striking distance.

They entered the Yggdrasil tree and found three large tunnels inside it; one on either side of them and one in front. Runes resembling the ones on the realm gates framed each one. Layla looked up and saw hundreds of tiny flickering lights high above, as if she were looking into the night sky.

"Which tunnel?" Layla asked.

"They all go to the same place," Zamek said.

"Middle it is," Lucifer said, and the four of them ran down the tunnel, which eventually opened into a huge circular cavern lined with dozens of realm gates. Each gate was identical to the Helheim gate they'd used to get to this realm. The centers of these gates constantly flickered black, hiding their destinations.

Just as Zamek had said, the tunnels on the left and right both led to the central hub. A fourth tunnel sat ahead of them at the far end of the cavern.

"The wooden realm gate we saw back in Helheim," Lucifer said, "was made from the roots of the Yggdrasil tree."

"Those look familiar," Layla said, pointing to the four tall, black staffs that had been driven into the ground to form a small circle in the center of the cavern. Purple crystals glowed in the tops of them. She tore one of the staffs out of the ground and tossed it to Zamek, who examined it briefly before snapping it in two.

"Good thing these aren't active yet," Lucifer said.

A noise from the tunnel at the end of the cavern got everyone's attention. Layla ran over and found a young woman on the floor. She wore a long, blue dress that was covered in muck and mud, and had bruises around her eyes and mouth.

"Grace," Lucifer said, hurrying up. He immediately checked the woman for more serious injuries and found the remains of an arrow shaft between her shoulder blades.

"One of the Fates?" Layla asked.

"Abaddon has the others," Grace said, her voice weak. "I escaped. Barely."

Lucifer looked up at Layla. "Go on, I'll catch you up."

"There's a gate at the end of the tunnel. It looks like a normal realm gate, but it only goes further up the tree." Grace coughed up blood, and Layla thanked her before running on with Zamek and the panther.

They sprinted through the gate that Grace had mentioned right into six blood elves standing on the other side. The panther threw two elves against the wooden walls of the tunnel as Layla parried a sword slash from one elf, then kicked it away. She spun on her heel and drove her sword-arm into the nearest blood elf's chest, then turned and sliced through the first blood elf's leg armor, crippling it, then neatly impaling it through the neck as it fell forward.

Zamek, having taken care of the last two, raised his ax to his shoulder, from where it dripped fresh blood onto the dark-brown floor. The three of them continued on into a cavern that was identical to the one below, although there was a hole in the tree trunk wall that showed they were above the clouds. More staffs sat in the center of the cavern and the floor was covered in runes that Layla didn't know, several of them glowing a deep red.

Hades hung on a cross in the middle of the cavern, both wrists adorned with sorcerer's bands, his neck, forearms, and legs bound to the wood. He wore only trousers, and dwarven runes had been carved onto his flesh, covering his entire torso.

Abaddon stood at the far end of the cavern holding Caleb Cassidy by the throat, his feet dangling off the ground.

"I waited for you," Abaddon said as a low growl escaped the panther's maw. Abaddon walked toward Layla, still holding Caleb aloft.

"He thought to kill me," Abaddon said. "He actually thought he could." She looked at Caleb. "I see your daughter has inherited your incredible ability to think that you're better than you are."

Caleb kicked Abaddon in the face, and the devil punched him in the stomach hard enough to cause him to spit blood.

Layla took a step forward.

"You don't think I'll kill him?" Abaddon asked.

"She knows you will," Caleb said. He looked at Layla. "Take her."

Layla rushed forward, and Abaddon punched her fist through Caleb's chest, tearing out his heart, but Layla was still moving, not even pausing to see the surprise on Abaddon's face as she crashed into her and drove her arm-blade up toward Abaddon's throat. Abaddon, too fast, caught Layla by the arm and threw the umbra over her shoulder to the hard floor behind her.

With an energy blast, Abaddon sent the charging panther flying across the cavern where she slammed into Zamek before he could get out of the way. They both hit the side of one of the realm gates, landing in a painful heap.

Abaddon drove the silver dagger that Caleb had brought with him into his skull. She looked back over at Layla. "Just to make sure." She removed the dagger and wiped the blade on Caleb's clothes.

Layla stared at her father's body. She had hated what he'd done, and on more than one occasion hated him enough that she just wished he was dead, but seeing him lying there, and knowing he was never going to get back up, left her feeling more emotion than she'd expected. She looked up at Abaddon and felt nothing but rage and hate. Layla got back to her feet and, trying not to look at her dead father, concentrated on getting in close to Abaddon. The devil threw her power at Layla, but it hit the rune-scribed armor, doing no damage. Layla slashed Abaddon's midriff, cutting a long, thin line across her stomach.

Abaddon made no noise, and with a blade she'd yanked from a sheath on her hip, parried Layla's next strike. A punch to Layla's stomach and a knee to her head sent Layla to the floor. Abaddon looked down on her with a smile.

"You see this dagger? This is the very dagger your father thought to kill me with, and the very dagger I just used on him. It'll be almost poetic that I use it to skin you alive. I've longed for this moment. You've caused me far too many problems."

"What's one more?" Layla asked as Hades dropped from the cross onto the back of the panther, who carried him away.

"What?" Abaddon screamed, allowing Layla to move away.

"You forgot about the dwarf," Zamek said, picking up the two axes he'd thrown at the leather bindings that held Hades in place.

Abaddon rushed over to Zamek, who tried to avoid her, but a spirit weapon in the shape of a scythe slammed into his chest. He fell to his knees as Layla tackled Abaddon.

Layla smashed her metal forearm twice into Abaddon's face before changing it into a blade and driving it into her chest.

Abaddon laughed. "The silver feels so good against my flesh," Abaddon said, forcing Layla's metal arm out of her body, then throwing her across the cavern.

Layla got back to her feet in time to see the wound on Abaddon's chest heal.

"I've taken so many souls," Abaddon said. "They sustain me. They heal me. I'm going to kill you all, and use your deaths to activate these staffs. It won't be as powerful as Hades, but it will have to do. This tree will be mine and mine alone."

Layla noticed the bracelet on Abaddon's wrist. "You'll be the only one with power? That the idea?"

Abaddon lifted her arm and gazed at the bronze-colored bracelet. "Not really. You see, once I ignite these staffs, the power they contain will be monumental as it spreads out all across this tree and the realm around it. We will control Yggdrasil, and the realm gates it contains. We could go anywhere, at any time, to any realm, and there's nothing you can do to stop us. Anyone trying to launch an attack against us here will lose their powers—it'll be like humans flinging rocks at gods. We can move entire armies through this realm to anywhere we choose."

Zamek got to his knees, only to be kicked in the ribs as Abaddon walked by. She threw a huge amount of power at Layla, knocking the wind out of her as the runes on her armor faded to nothing.

Layla rolled away, the pain in her sternum causing her to try to catch her breath.

"Stay down, little girl," Abaddon said, mocking her. "You can't win here."

The blast of light-blue, pure magic hit Abaddon in the chest, throwing her fifty feet across the cavern.

"Abaddon, I think it's time for you to shut up," Lucifer said as he came into view.

Abaddon screamed in fury and threw pure necromancy energy at Lucifer, who dodged aside, creating a shield of air and fire that deflected much of the attack. Some got through, and he was forced to roll aside, almost into Abaddon's path, who struck him in the chest with her scythe.

Lucifer cried out in pain and dropped to his knees, but detonated a ball of pure magic in her face. Her scythe vanished as she was temporarily blinded despite using her necromancy as a shield.

Lucifer crawled away, pain etched on his face. "Damn, I forgot how much that hurts," he said.

Layla, now back on her feet, ran toward Abaddon, who noticed her just in time to duck her blade, then send her flying through the air with another blast of pure energy. Layla collided with one of the realm gates and fell to the floor awkwardly, her body burning from the impact.

"Why won't you idiots understand? You. Can't. Win." Abaddon drove her scythe into Lucifer as he tried to get back to his feet, stabbing him over and over, until he dropped to his knees. "If I can't use Hades, I can use this traitorous piece of shit."

Abaddon blasted Zamek as he moved toward her, before turning back to Lucifer. She removed a sorcerer's band from her wrist and put it on Lucifer's. "It's my last one, so it's fitting I use it for someone important. You can't win," Abaddon repeated, dropping Lucifer to the floor and retrieving her dagger from the ground beside him. She dipped her fingers in Lucifer's blood and drew a symbol on the floor, which caused all four of the staffs to glow a dark purple color. "I want you all to witness what I'm about to achieve."

Layla saw Zamek crawl toward one of the realm gates. She tried to get up, but her body protested at the act, and pain roared through her torso.

Abaddon pulled Lucifer's head back and his eyes opened ever so slightly.

"Good," Abaddon said. "I want you awake when you die."

Layla was shocked to see Nabu sprint out of the tunnel, his armor covered in grime. He collided with Abaddon, knocking the dagger aside as they both fell to the ground. Zamek rushed to Lucifer, pulling him away from the center of the cavern, although still not out of danger.

Layla rolled over and forced herself to her feet. She exhaled one long breath, and created a blade from her arm as she took one step at a time toward Abaddon, who was struggling with Nabu over the dagger.

Layla tried to reach out with her power, but she found no metal to control, and before she could reach Abaddon and Nabu, Abaddon drove the dagger into Nabu's stomach. After a second and third stab, Nabu sagged against the floor, his hands trying to stop the flow of blood from his body. As Abaddon raised the dagger to plunge down one final time, Layla screamed in defiance and turned her blade into a spear that sliced through Abaddon's arm just above the wrist, almost severing it.

With rage pumping through her, Layla reformed the spear back to a sword and stalked Abaddon as she backed away from Nabu. Abaddon pulled herself up against one of the realm gates with her one good hand, the other beginning to repair itself as Layla changed her sword into a fist and drove it into Abaddon's jaw, knocking her back to the ground.

Layla recreated the silver blade and went to stab Abaddon in the back, but the devil moved at the last second, and the blade landed in her shoulder instead. Layla kicked Abaddon onto her back, noticing that she looked considerably weaker than she had when they'd first entered the cavern.

"You keep using your souls too much," Layla said, punching her in the face.

"You can't kill me," Abaddon said, hitting Layla in the stomach with her palm, sending her flying. Abaddon stood up, but Layla tackled her back to the ground, only to receive a backhand to the face, knocking her away.

Abaddon got to her feet again, and Layla saw Zamek behind her leaning against the realm gate. The darkness it had been showing changed to hundreds of different realm images, flickering between each of them in an instant.

"You won't win," Abaddon screamed.

Zamek made a noise, distracting her, while Layla grabbed the dagger from the floor and drove it into Abaddon's stomach, much to her surprise.

"Die somewhere else," Layla said, kicking her in the stomach and sending her back into the realm gate where she vanished from view.

Zamek stopped the realm gate and dropped back to his knees. "That spirit weapon shit *really* takes it out of you," he said.

"Where is she?" Layla asked.

"No idea," Zamek said. "I didn't have time to select a realm, I just activated the gate to roll through whatever was there. I didn't recognize the one she landed in, so it could literally be anywhere in a thousand realms."

"Hopefully somewhere alone and awful," Nabu said from the ground beside them. "You need to help me up."

"No, you'll die," Layla said. "You need to stay there."

"Dying anyway," Nabu said. "You can't remove the runes that will activate the Devil's Venom before I die. They'll wipe out the tree and the realm gates. You don't have time." His body began to glow a brilliant silver.

"What do we do?" asked Lucifer, who was still sitting on the floor.

Nabu tossed Lucifer the key to the sorcerer's bands. "I stole it from Abaddon," he said with a smile.

Lucifer unlocked his sorcerer's band and sighed as his power returned to him. "Old friend," Lucifer said, his voice harsh and filled with pain.

"I will see you again, one day," Nabu said. "Now help me up."

Layla and Zamek helped Nabu to his feet, although the expression on his face and the occasional word in a language Layla didn't know made everyone aware of his pain.

"Push me into a realm gate," Nabu said. "I'll die there, I won't trigger the runes, and everyone will get to go home with a win."

"Except you," Layla said.

"You need to find the Fates," Nabu said.

"On it," Lucifer said, now recovered. He walked over to Nabu and embraced him. "Safe travels."

Nabu stood before the realm gate that Zamek had earlier activated and leaned against the wooden structure. "Pick a nice realm. Something with a beach."

Zamek smiled. "I'll see what I can do." He touched the realm gate and it began to slow down, showing each realm for a few seconds at a time. After a minute it showed one realm, and stayed there.

"Where is it?" Nabu asked.

"Look," Zamek said.

Nabu turned and tears began to fall down his face as he gazed upon the beautiful flowers that littered the realm beyond. "Nippur," he whispered. "The paradise of the Mesopotamian gods. My home. How did you know?"

"I started looking into it," Zamek said. "I wanted to surprise you when I got the realm gate done in Greenland. I know the realm to this world vanished a long time ago, and you never got to go back there. They named a city after this place, so I figured it was important."

"Thank you so much," Nabu said, kissing Zamek on the forehead. "You have no idea how much this means to me."

Layla helped Nabu toward the realm gate. "Take care, Layla," he said. "I hope to see you again one day."

Layla wiped the tears from her eyes. "It's been a pleasure," she said. "Thank you."

Nabu began to glow brighter and brighter as he stepped through the realm gate and onto the grass of Nippur. He turned around to see them all and vanished before the realm gate could close.

Layla stood motionless for several seconds, before turning to see the body of her father.

"We will ensure the rites are performed," Zamek said.

"He was a monster in life and he knew Abaddon would kill him, but he fought her anyway."

"Your father died bravely," Zamek said. "No matter how he lived, there is always that."

Layla nodded, not sure that she could find the words to express how she truly felt. She was relieved that he was dead, that he was no longer a threat, but she was also sad that her father, no matter what he had been, was gone.

"Any chance any of these gates go back to Helheim?" Layla asked.

Zamek nodded and tried to activate one of the realm gates nearby, but it didn't work and the realm gate remained off. He tried it with two more gates and got the same result. "Apparently the tree is done," he said. "I think having all of this power flung around inside it wasn't something it liked. We're going to have to take the long way back."

"We need to find the Fates," Layla said. "And then we need to leave this realm and help Hel."

23

MORDRED

Nidhogg the dragon stepped out of the shadow, towering over everyone in the group, except for Dralas, who had made himself grow to over twenty-five feet in height. The dragon's yellow-and-red wings beat once, before folding over the orange and yellow shimmering scales of his back and sides. Nidhogg's chest—the only part without scales—was a deep red color. His massive, black talons clicked as he walked over the stone.

"You say that Mammon is here." It was the first thing Nidhogg had said since coming out of the shadows.

"He's trying to destroy us," Mordred said.

Nidhogg lowered his head toward Mordred. "I do not like his kind. He is not a true dragon. He is an interloper, born of human parents and given power he does not deserve."

Mordred watched as Nidhogg's tail flicked around, the razor-sharp barbs on the end gouging a large hole in the wall; he didn't even appear to notice.

"Well, he certainly likes flying around like a true dragon," Irkalla said.

"Irkalla," Nidhogg said. "It has been a long time. How is Tiamet?"

"Dead," Irkalla said.

"Excellent," Nidhogg replied, and laughed.

Mordred let out a slight sigh of relief. Tiamet's death had been something that he was hoping wasn't going to come up, but he was glad that Nidhogg didn't seem too bothered about it.

"I assume she continued to believe she was better than she was," said Nidhogg. "An infuriating dragon. I never lorded my power over humans—it's barely worth getting up in the morning for them."

"Do you know where the Fates are?" Remy asked.

"The Fates?" Nidhogg asked.

"Nidhogg," Irkalla said sternly.

"They are not here," Nidhogg said. "Why would they be?"

Mordred sighed. "Damn it, I'm an idiot."

"He said it this time," Remy said, pointing to Mordred.

"Caleb took Harry after the Fates," Mordred said. "That's who he was tracking. And he tracked them to Abaddon."

"Abaddon took the Fates," Kase said. "I guess she doesn't want them out of her sight."

Nidhogg sighed. "You people talk too much."

"Are you going to help, or not?" Dralas asked, his voice booming.

"Giants should know their place," Nidhogg said. "No, I will not help you. I do not care if you all kill one another." The dragon turned to walk back into the shadows.

"You do care about power though, don't you?" Mordred said. "You care about Mammon out there masquerading as a dragon. You care about him going around showing everyone how powerful he is, how he alone is the dragon to fear."

Mammon's war cry could be heard in the distance, and Nidhogg stopped walking and looked up at the sky behind him. Mordred noticed Nidhogg's expression change to one of anger as he looked over toward the other dragon. When he looked back at the group, the anger was gone, but Mordred knew he had the dragon now.

"I do not enjoy seeing him," Nidhogg said. "Let's say I agree to help you. What will you give me?"

"What do you want?" Kase asked.

Nidhogg turned back to the group. "I want freedom," he said. "When this is done, and Mammon lies dead at my feet, I want to be free of this place. The prisoners are gone. They will die today, and then there will be nothing left for me to feed upon. So I want to be free."

"We can arrange that," Irkalla said. "Anything else?"

Nidhogg tried, unsuccessfully, to hide his surprise.

"Gold, perhaps?" Dralas asked.

"Dragons don't need your shiny baubles," Nidhogg snapped. "We require power. That is all. I will remain in the cavern here. I like my home, but there will be no runes holding me here, no agreement with Hel to stay where I am. Both have been tried over the centuries, and I cared for neither. You will let me feast upon Mammon's corpse."

"Deal," Mordred said, not really sure what else they were ever going to do with a dead dragon.

"It will sustain me . . ." Nidhogg paused. "Wait, did you say 'deal'?"

"Yes," Mordred said. "It's all yours."

"You kill it, you bought it," Remy said.

"Ah," Nidhogg said, clearly not expecting to have had his demands met so willingly.

"Anything else?" Tarron asked. "A cow every month, for example?"

"A cow would be nice," Nidhogg said, no longer in control of the conversation and struggling to figure out where he'd been outplayed.

"Okay," Mordred said. "You go kill Mammon, and not only do you keep his corpse, but no more prisoners, and you get a cow every month."

Nidhogg lowered his head toward Mordred. "You're not just playing games, are you?"

Mordred shook his head. "Nope. All yours. Enjoy both Mammon's carcass and our monthly bovine offering. Cows get big here, I think you'll find it a nice little deal."

Nidhogg looked between everyone in the group. "Deal," he said. His wings beat twice and he took off into the air, throwing up dust and debris all around the group. Mordred wrapped a shield of air all around them, stopping any more debris from flying around.

"That was much easier than I expected," Remy said.

"Only because Nidhogg expected us to haggle," Tarron said.

"I think Nidhogg knew someone would come to ask for his help," Mordred said. "I think he was just expecting us to fight him more on what he asked for."

"He was always someone who prided themselves on being smarter than everyone else," Irkalla said. "Even if he wasn't actually smarter than anyone else."

"We need to get to the front of the fort and help out with the battle. Those trebuchets need destroying, and I'm pretty sure they're not going to break themselves," Mordred said.

The group ran through the fortress, the sounds of battle increasing with every step until they reached the ruined gate. The battle before them was worse than Mordred had imagined. Bodies littered the ground and the smell of blood and death hung in the air. They were hundreds of feet away from the main battle, which was across the bridge on the other side of the river, but with so many fighting, the noise quickly reached them. The sounds of weapon on weapon, and weapon on flesh, were something Mordred had never gotten used to, no matter how many battles he'd played his part in.

Mordred looked over at where the two dragons fought in the air. Arrows were let loose from troops on the ground. "Dralas, make sure that nothing else bothers Nidhogg—he's going to need all his power to defeat Mammon, even if he thinks otherwise."

"Will do," Dralas said.

"I'll help out," Tarron said, and the pair ran off.

Mordred continued to watch the two dragons fight. The graceful sweeps and dives in midair looked beautiful, but were designed to inflict maximum damage.

"Mordred," Irkalla said.

"It's just, how often do you get to see two dragons fight?" Mordred said.

"Well, if we don't stop those trebuchets, it's probably going to be just the once," Irkalla told him.

Mordred turned away from the dragons and studied the three trebuchets. They were on the same side of the river as Mordred and his people, which made getting to them easier. Unfortunately, large groups of soldiers protected each of them. One of the walls of Niflhel was almost destroyed, and blood elves poured into the wounded city like cockroaches.

"Irkalla, Remy, go destroy the trebuchet on the left," Mordred said. "Kase, you're with me. We'll all meet at the one in the middle and then all three will be done."

"They're pretty big," Remy said.

One of the trebuchets threw a piece of stone that Mordred guessed to be the size of a Range Rover. "Then hurry," he said.

"Let's go fuck their shit right up," Irkalla said.

Mordred turned to Remy. "She's been hanging around with you too much."

Remy wiped away a mock tear. "I'm so proud to see her all grown up and swearing like a sailor on shore leave."

Mordred watched Remy and Irkalla run off toward their target before turning to Kase. "That's ours," he said, pointing to the trebuchet furthest from where they stood. It was near the edge of a large forest whose black-trunked trees stretched high into the air. But more importantly, it was surrounded by tall, red-and-gray grass in which they could hide.

"Let's go," Kase said, and took off at a sprint toward the trees.

Kase was considerably faster than Mordred and reached the trees well before he did. She beckoned him over to where she hid. Mordred joined her, and together they moved at a slow crouch through the tall grass.

Kase sniffed the air. "Blood elves, something else too. Can't quite figure out what it is. I think they have some elves stationed in the woods. I'm going to go see who I can remove."

"Be careful," Mordred whispered.

Kase rolled her eyes and moved through the tall grass, dropping pieces of her armor as she went until she transformed into her wolf-beast form. She was larger, but the dark fur of the beast gave her more camouflage than she'd had with just the armor.

When Kase vanished into the shadows of the forest, Mordred continued on through the grass. At some point they were going to have to confront whoever was guarding the trebuchet, but thinning the ranks of the enemy was never a bad idea.

Mordred stopped when a blood elf walked past and halted only a few feet from where Mordred was hidden. He slowly wrapped invisible tendrils of air around the blood elf's legs and then pulled it into the grass. He plunged a silver dagger into its throat a second later. One elf down, countless more to go.

The trebuchet fired another huge slab of rock, and Mordred had to fight his every instinct to run out and kill everyone with his magic. He knew he could use his pure magic to destroy the trebuchet, but releasing it now meant he would likely be weaker if, and, or when a dragon or Abaddon decided to enter the fight.

Four blood elf commanders dragged a huge block of stone toward the trebuchet. Mordred sighed; he knew the walls wouldn't take too many more hits. One part down was bad enough, but if it started to happen over and over, the city would quickly be overrun.

Mordred darted from cover, throwing a spear of ice into the chest of the nearest blood elf. He ducked under a blade swipe, slicing up with a blade of his own made of air. The blood elf dodged back, but Mordred extended the blade, catching him under the chin and piercing his skull. Mordred spun around the injured blood elf and drove his silver sword into its spine, killing the creature before turning to the four blood elf commanders. Kase burst from her hiding place, tackling several blood elves that were nearby.

"Just me and you," Mordred said, noticing the runes on two of the commanders' armor. "And two of you are wearing rune-scribed armor, so that's clearly awesome, and in no way a giant pain in the arse." He hit the closest blood elf commander in the chest with a blast of air that lifted the commander off his feet and flung him over the large piece of blood-colored stone.

The three other commanders walked away from the stone, drawing weapons, each of them smiling at the thought of what they were going to do to Mordred. Mordred smiled too, and winked at the nearest commander, who paused, looking surprised.

Mordred sprinted toward the surprised commander, avoiding an ax swipe from one of the others, and drove his sword toward his target's chest. But the commander regained his composure, parried the strike and aimed a kick at Mordred's chest that forced him to dart away, toward the two other commanders.

They took the opportunity to attack, and Mordred avoided the sword of one commander, but the ax of the other hit him in the chest. The runes on his leather armor ignited from the impact, stopping the blade from piercing him, but even so, it still hurt.

Mordred danced back from the three commanders, driving his sword into the skull of the prone commander he'd thrown over the stone earlier.

"I'm going about this all wrong," Mordred said, more to himself than anything else. He sheathed his sword and removed two sets of spiked, silver knuckles from his pocket. "Never was much of a swords-man." He put the knuckles on, tapping them against each other, and rolled his shoulders.

The closest commander charged Mordred, who easily avoided the thrust of the sword and punched him in the jaw, taking off a large chunk of it in the process. Another punch to the side of the temple knocked him to the floor where he lay, unmoving.

"Yeah, this is better," Mordred said.

The two remaining commanders glanced at one another and then charged Mordred as one. Mordred avoided the blades with hastily created shields of air and ice and kicked out the knee of one elf, but took a hit to his back as he did.

He used the momentum of the blow to roll away from the two elves and got back to his feet a short distance away as ice began to cover the trebuchet.

"I think Kase is screwing up your plan," Mordred said without taking his eyes off the two commanders.

He removed one of the two silver knuckles, and pushed out a fog of air that curled around the two blood elf commanders as they began to walk toward him. By the time they both realized what he was doing, it was too late. Mordred froze the fog in place and turned the sheet of ice into dozens of sharp ice spears that tore through the protection runes on their armor. They flashed and vanished as Mordred rushed forward, drawing his sword and cutting through the torso of the first blood elf before, spinning on his heel, he punched the second with a fist covered in dense air. The air exploded into thousands of ice shards upon impact, almost tearing the blood elf's head clean from his shoulders.

A large piece of the trebuchet landed near Mordred, and he turned to see Kase tearing apart the frozen weapon.

"Kase," Mordred shouted in warning, pouring ice into a ball of air, making it crack and hiss as it spun faster and faster, until it was the size of a basketball. Kase moved away from the trebuchet, and Mordred tossed it into the giant mass of ice and wood and clicked his fingers. The ball exploded, tearing the trebuchet apart in a shower of ice.

"Nice trick," Kase said, her dark fur matted with blood that wasn't hers. "Looks like Remy and Irkalla finished."

Mordred watched the furthest trebuchet explode, sending at least one blood elf commander high into the air, before it tumbled back down to earth.

Mordred walked toward the third trebuchet and noticed Elizabeth. She saw Mordred, jumped on a horse and rode off toward Nastrond.

"Kase, help Remy and Irkalla deal with that trebuchet. I'll go get Elizabeth."

"Be careful," Kase said, running off toward the last trebuchet.

Mordred knew he couldn't keep up with a horse at full run, but he used his air magic to increase his speed and agility. His lungs burned from running as fast as he could toward the fortress. He was not about to let Elizabeth escape.

By the time he reached the fortress and stepped inside, Elizabeth was long gone, but her horse was still in the main courtyard.

"They didn't need me," Kase said from behind Mordred, causing him to jump slightly.

He turned to her and smiled. "You did that on purpose. Go around to the rear of the fortress, I'll go through the prison complex; hopefully we'll flush her out."

Kase ran off to the side of the courtyard, vanishing from view as she moved around the large prison building.

Mordred walked up to the prison entrance and pushed open the door. One of the prisoners who had escaped earlier had decided to return. He turned to Mordred and, with a scream, rushed him, moving faster than Mordred had anticipated. He hit Mordred hard enough to fling him back into the courtyard; only a shield of air saved him from a painful landing.

The prisoner had long, gray hair, a matching beard, and wore nothing except a loincloth. His body was a mass of scars and dirt, and his frame was just wiry muscle that didn't look like it could contain the strength it did.

The prisoner ran through Mordred's blast of air like it wasn't even there, picked him up, and threw him again as if he weighed nothing at all. Mordred twisted in the air and landed on his feet some distance from the prisoner, who bared his dirty teeth and howled.

He sprinted toward Mordred, who drew his sword, trying to catch his attacker with it, but he simply swatted the blade out of Mordred's grasp, sending it cartwheeling across the courtyard, before punching Mordred in the ribs. He felt them break as he was thrown against the nearest wall.

Getting back to his feet, Mordred avoided another punch, which destroyed the part of the wall where his head had once been, and tried to duck away, but the prisoner grabbed his arm. Pain shot through his body and he screamed in agony as the blood magic that was so prevalent in the prisoners went to work. He dropped to his knees, the sounds of the prisoner's laughter blocked out by the pain that rushed through his body.

As his vision began to darken, he managed to grab the silver knuckles from his pocket and hurriedly slip them on. He turned and hit the prisoner in the kidney with everything he had. The prisoner released Mordred's arm and scurried away, howling in agony.

The pain in Mordred's arm began to subside, but it still felt numb, and his ribs still burned, even as his magic set to work healing them. He put the other knuckles on and got back to his feet.

The prisoner ran toward Mordred and tried to claw at his face. Mordred punched the prisoner's elbow, shattering the bone, then punched his sternum, sending him to the ground.

"Should have walked away," Mordred said as the prisoner clawed at his own chest in an effort to get at the broken bones there, his fractured arm already healed from the earlier punch.

Mordred punched him in the side of the head, knocking him back to the ground. He tried to move, so Mordred punched him again, over and over, tearing muscle and breaking bones until he was unrecognizable, his breathing wet and unpleasant.

Mordred's hands were covered in blood as he drove a blade of air into the prisoner's chest, pinning him there while he retrieved his sword. When Mordred returned, the prisoner's face was already healing. Mordred decapitated the creature with one swipe before stepping over the body and walking into the prison.

Anger radiated from every pore of his body. He had not wanted to kill any of the prisoners. They hadn't asked for what had become of them, just like he hadn't asked to be tortured and turned into a weapon of evil. He had wanted to give them the chance to die honorably in battle against an enemy who had been a part of what created them.

Elizabeth stood at the doors to the rear of the prison and smiled as Mordred walked toward her. Fog poured out of her hands, swirling around Mordred, who combined his air and water magics together and continued walking in her direction.

"Is this meant to be something special?" Mordred asked.

"My fog will make you sick," Elizabeth said with an evil grin.

Mordred took a deep breath. "It's not working."

The look of surprise on Elizabeth's face was almost worth everything he'd had to do to get here. "How?" she asked, running at the door, flinging it open, and running out into the courtyard.

"My magic," Mordred said, following her as she backed toward the dragon's cave, her gaze never leaving him. Mordred circled her, until he stood in the mouth of the dragon's cave, with Elizabeth's back facing the rear doors of the prison. "Combining water and air lets me breathe in any conditions. You would have been better off just using bad language."

Elizabeth stood firm, her hands balled into fists. "You won't kill me," she said, utterly sure of herself. "You couldn't look at Layla the same way knowing you'd murdered her mother."

"You're not her mother," Mordred said. "You're a charlatan, a bad copy who got the outside bit right, but can't hide the evil beneath the skin. But you're right, I'm not going to kill you."

Elizabeth's smile grew. "I knew it—you care for Layla. It's a weakness."

Mordred shook his head. "Not a weakness, never a weakness to care. But I'm not going to kill you, because she is."

Mordred pointed behind Elizabeth, who turned just as Kase plunged a blade of silver into her chest. "Eat shit and die," Kase said, then she stepped around Elizabeth, who died before she hit the floor.

"You okay?" Mordred asked. He looked down at Elizabeth's corpse and felt bad for Layla. He hoped she would be able to deal with what he and Kase had had to do.

"It needed doing," Kase said, placing a hand on Mordred's shoulder. "For Layla, it needed doing."

Mordred looked away from Elizabeth, and knew that Kase was right. "Agreed, now let's go win this war."

24

LAYLA CASSIDY

Before the team left, they found the two remaining Fates. They were drugged, but alive, in a small room with rune-adorned walls just outside the main cavern. They helped all three Fates out of the tree and joined the rest of the team waiting below.

"Where's Nabu?" Harry asked as they left the interior of the tree.

Layla looked at the ground and shook her head, pulling Harry into a hug for comfort. "I'm so sorry," she whispered.

"He saved my life," Hades said, looking more like the man that Layla had known for the last two years. "But at the cost of his own."

"How many did you lose?" Lucifer asked.

The saber-tooth panther padded over to Layla and rubbed her head against Layla's leg. Layla smiled. She was glad that her feline friend hadn't been seriously hurt.

"Three of the dwarves," Diana said, pointing over to the remaining dwarves, who had carried their kin toward the realm gate.

The bodies of the blood elves and giants would be dealt with at a later time, if anyone bothered to deal with them at all. Layla wondered if they'd be left to fertilize the tree.

"We need to get back to Helheim," Chloe said. "There's still a war to win."

Everyone started moving back toward the realm gate that would take them from the Yggdrasil tree back to Helheim, with the saber-tooth panther carrying two of the Fates. Grace walked beside them, looking worried.

"They'll be fine," Hades said. "We get out of here and remove the drugs from their system, and they'll be back to normal. It's the same stuff she pumped into my body. Some kind of blood elf commander blood concoction."

They reached the realm gate, and Zamek activated it as Layla gave her condolences to the dwarves. They thanked her, but appeared to be more interested in letting out their grief by hitting something they didn't like. The dwarves went through the gate with Layla and the panther taking up the rear.

"Thank you for what you did for me and my family," Grace said to her.

"They will be fine," Layla said.

Grace nodded. "I know. The drugs affected each of us differently. As the Fate of the present, the dose I got wore off quicker than the dose my mother and daughter received."

"I didn't know you were Cassandra's daughter, and that your own child was a Fate."

"It's an exceptionally long story, and one that I am not fond of remembering, no offense."

"None taken," Layla said.

"What is your panther's name?" Grace asked before they all stepped through the gate.

"You know," Layla said as they arrived in the temple, "that's something everyone keeps asking me. And I really have no idea what to call her. I get the feeling she has her own view on what she'd like to be called, so I guess I just have to come up with something she likes."

"Shadow?" Grace asked. The saber-tooth cat shook her head.

"Yeah, apparently not," Grace said, scratching the cat behind the ears as they reached the boats, where the sound of battle could once again be heard in the distance. They launched the boats and headed toward the fight.

"Not worried about saving some energy for Mammon?" Zamek asked as Lucifer used air magic to speed up their progression.

"No," Lucifer said. "I know what will be there waiting for me. I can spare some magic."

Layla looked at the stretched-out panther. "Tego. How about that for a name?"

"What does it mean?" Chloe asked.

"It's Latin," Layla said. "Servius was a Roman, so I know the language, and it feels like it fits."

"What does it mean?" one of the dwarves asked.

"Protect, cover, defend, shield," Layla said. "She defended us back there, and it wasn't the first time. I think it fits." The saber-tooth panther looked up as Layla sat beside her. "What do you think? Tego?"

The cat licked her hand and placed its massive head in her lap.

"I think she likes it," Lucifer said as land came into view.

As they drew closer, the clash of weapons and thunder of voices were louder than anything Layla had ever heard. A mass of people fought just outside the city walls and on the rubble where it had been brought down. A huge block of stone flew through the air and smashed into one of the still-upright walls, which began to crack and fall apart. Layla couldn't figure out where the object had come from.

"Trebuchets," Diana said. "Three of them. Two of them."

"Wait, what?"

"Someone is breaking them," Diana said. "I assume Mordred is involved."

"What makes you say that?" Zamek asked, coming up from the cabin. "The Fates are resting. I managed to scrub off the rune marks that someone had put on them, and which were keeping them asleep—it wasn't just the drugs. The mark on Grace wasn't completed before she escaped, or woke up. Either way, they'll remain below until this is done. I'll have some of the dwarves stay back and defend the boats. Unfortunately, Hades has other ideas about resting."

"I do not need rest," Hades said, exiting the cabin in full black-and-gold armor. While it resembled plate, it looked considerably more maneuverable, much like Zamek's. Hades' voice was tight, hard, and Layla wondered just how much he had left in him.

"Are you okay?" Lucifer and Diana asked in unison.

"I am fine," Hades said. "I absorbed the souls of the deceased giants as we walked past. I feel much better."

"You look like shit still," Chloe said.

Hades sighed. "I feel like shit too, but I'm still not sitting this out."

"Just don't die," Diana said. "I don't want Persephone even more pissed off than she's been since you were taken."

"Or Sky," Chloe said.

"Or any of your kids," Lucifer said. "I'm not sure how much Persephone and Sky told them about your kidnapping, but I'm surprised they didn't come rushing here."

"They will stay where they are needed," Hades said. "They trusted that the people I have around me would find me. Also, I'm certain that Persephone told them to stay where they are and let her do what she needed to."

"And if we hadn't gotten to you in time?" Layla asked.

"Then things would get much worse," Hades said. "We are trying not to have open warfare spill onto the Earth realm. I do not believe that all of my children would be capable of such restraint."

Mammon flew across the battlefield, spraying dark-orange-and-green flames over the fighters.

"We need to stop him," Lucifer said.

"We will," Hades replied, and Layla believed him a hundred percent.

"How?" Chloe asked. "Not that I want to rain on anyone's parade, but how the hell do we stop one of the most powerful creatures who ever lived?"

"He won't be at full strength," Lucifer said.

"How is that not full strength?" Chloe asked, waving her arms in the direction of the dragon.

"We beat Abaddon because she was overconfident," Hades said. "Her arrogance was her undoing. It will be Mammon's too."

"Speaking of Abaddon, do we even know where she is?" Chloe asked.

"Not a clue," Zamek said. "The realm gate destination was somewhere I'd never seen before. I remember them though, so we can at least try to figure out where she might be."

"So for now, she's not a problem," Lucifer said.

The boat landed ashore and everyone piled out. "I'm going to help with the dragon," Layla said. "Which is not a sentence I ever imagined myself saying."

"If we can pierce the scales, we can kill it," Harry said. "Isn't that how dragons work?"

"Those scales are several inches thick," Lucifer said. "Our best bet is to force him to turn back to his human form. And to do that we need to hurt him. I'm coming with you."

"I don't see a lot of magic and elements being thrown around," Chloe said.

"Abaddon's forces are tightly mixed in with our fighters, and seeing as how most of the enemy appear to be wearing rune-scribed armor, it would be very difficult to throw around magic and not hit our friends," Lucifer said.

Layla, Hades, Chloe, and Lucifer all ran toward the battle. Zamek had decided to stay behind and defend the city with the other dwarves, and Harry had been told to help them whether he liked it or not.

Layla changed her metal arm into a large, spiked shield, and charged into the fray, knocking blood elves over as the others with her cut their way through the throng of enemies. Griffins flew high above, dropping down to attack the blood elves before soaring up again, but Layla saw dozens dead on the ground, most missing their wings.

Hades threw a blood elf through the air using his necromancy and the souls he'd taken to increase his strength. The blood elf landed by Tego, who bit down on its neck, killing it instantly.

Layla was knocked to the ground and Chloe blasted a blood elf commander nearby with her kinetic energy, then helped Layla back to her feet. A few seconds later, Layla pushed Chloe out of the way of a blood elf who tried to stab her in the back, and killed the elf soon after.

Layla fought her way through the seemingly endless battlefield, staying as close to the edges as possible. She took a moment to catch her breath. Her armor was covered in blood, mostly the enemy's, and she'd seen more death since returning to Helheim than she had since becoming an umbra.

Up ahead, Mammon and another dragon were locked in combat, both whirling around the sky above the battlefield, their plumes of magical breath ripping apart the earth beneath them. Dralas had grown to almost fifty feet in height, and was busy throwing anything he could find at Mammon, including huge boulders, and more than once a blood elf that wandered too close to him.

Layla reached the bridge before anyone else and ran toward three blood elves who waited for her on the other side. As she got closer, she shot three spikes out of the end of her palm. Each of the foot-long metal spikes slammed into the heads of the blood elves, and they dropped to the ground. Layla absorbed the metal back into her arm, and looked behind her as Mammon flew over, roaring pure magic flame over the bridge, almost incinerating it. Layla threw herself aside as the other dragon, who Layla assumed was Nidhogg, slammed into Mammon, dropping them both into the freezing river.

The ground shook, and mud and freezing cold water sprayed over the battlefield, almost covering those closest to the river. Layla was far enough away to avoid most of the mud, but as the fighting in the river continued, small tsunamis of water were thrown over the battlefield, drenching everything around them. One such wave knocked Layla to her knees.

Being so close, Layla could now see the wounds that covered both dragons. She wondered just how much more either of them could withstand. Layla got to her knees as Tarron appeared beside her, offering his hand.

"Seems like you're having a long day," he said, helping her up.

"It's not been brilliant," Layla replied. "Looks like most of the blood elves over here have been dealt with." The grass was now burned beyond saving and huge patches of blackened ground littered the area.

"The dragons have been indiscriminate in their use of power," Tarron said.

Irkalla and Remy ran toward them. Irkalla gave Layla a hug and Remy bumped her fist.

"Hades and the others are on the opposite side of the river," Layla said, looking over at the battle to see Vorisbo and Jomik, cut off from their allies, fighting several blood elves. One of the blood elves caught Jomik under the arm with a spear, and Layla watched in horror as he fell to the ground, her shouts of warning unheard over the din of war. Vorisbo killed the blood elf, and more swarmed them, but Hel, Sky, and others arrived and dragged Jomik away to safety.

"I hope he's okay," Layla said.

"Dwarves are made of stern stuff," Irkalla said.

Layla was about to say more when Mammon exploded out of the river, dragging Nidhogg by his neck into the air. A second later, Mammon tore Nidhogg's head clean from his body and let the corpse fall back to the earth. The impact knocked everyone off their feet as Mammon blew his pure magic around the sky in victory.

As Mammon circled above, a blast of blue pure magic punched a hole into one of his wings and he fell, spiraling, at an incredible rate and spewing his own pure magic as he went.

Layla and the others ran toward the source of the pure magic where, to Layla's delight, they found Mordred and Kase.

Mammon smashed into the ground with incredible force, his one good wing sending dust and muck in the direction of Layla and her allies.

"Looks like we get to kill another dragon," Remy said. "Lucky us."

Mordred ran toward the dragon, throwing pure magic at the creature, who turned so the magic hit his scaled side, before whipping his tail around to knock Mordred aside. He flew fifty feet before hitting the ground. He got back up just as the others attacked the dragon as one.

Pure magic, aimed directly at Layla, poured out of his mouth, and she hastily wrapped the metal from the field around her body like a shield, making sure that none of it touched her. The steel, iron, and silver that Layla had gathered turned white-hot as the magic hit it. She poured her energy into keeping the shield together, and when she no longer heard the roar of the power, she dropped the metal all around her. The shield had saved her life, and she stood in a smoldering, blackened strip of field. She dropped to her knees, needing a moment to recover after using such a huge amount of power.

Layla stared at Mammon as a griffin flew directly overhead, dropping Lucifer onto the dragon. Lucifer hit Mammon with incredible force, his pure magic exploding out all around him, driving Mammon into the dirt, just as Irkalla hit him with her necromancy energy. Mordred joined Irkalla and together they poured their power into Mammon, tearing into his flesh and causing the massive beast to cry out in pain. Layla tore metal out of the ground, turning it into dozens of sharp arrowheads, and threw them at the dragon. Most of it cascaded off the creature's scales, but some hit its soft belly. He cried out, beating his wings, as he tried to escape.

Unable to fly due to his broken wing, Mammon roared pure magic at his attackers, causing most of Layla's allies to run for cover behind the remains of trebuchets, or large rocks. Dralas grabbed Mammon by the throat and with his free hand punched him in the maw, knocking his massive head aside. Mammon leapt up at Dralas, biting the giant on the shoulder and wrapping his massive legs around Dralas's torso. Dralas headbutted him, but Mammon's serrated tail tip whipped around, piercing Dralas's back and coming out of his chest. Mammon opened his mouth to breath pure magic once again, but nothing came out, and in his rage, he flung Dralas's body across the battlefield.

Tarron rushed to his friend's aid and Layla watched in disbelief as the giant decreased in size. And from that disbelief and hurt, rage was born. She looked back at Mammon and got to her feet. She was exhausted, she had been beaten, hurt, and almost killed several times, but anger flooded her body.

"Do it," Terhal said from beside her. "Accept everything you are. Everything you can become. Accept what you are born from, accept that you are not your parents. You are your own woman. You are everything they could never be. You are power incarnate. A weapon created to rival sorcery. A weapon that is yours to wield as you see fit. Show the dragon what you are."

Layla reached out with her power, flooding the field with it. She found every scrap of metal that she could, took apart every silver weapon as the ground beneath her feet cracked open, her skin burning bright orange from the effort. She ignored it, pushed it aside.

"This is the power of the umbra," Terhal said.

With a roar of hate, rage, and hurt, she turned those thousands of pieces of metal into weapons, throwing them all at Mammon at once. The pieces merged together until a dozen ten-foot-long blades slammed into Mammon's chest and neck. Most glanced off his scales, but three went inside his flesh, causing him to scream in pain as the silver went to work.

Layla began to walk toward the dragon, using her power to push the blades further into his body, causing him to writhe in pain as her allies poured more and more of their power onto the creature.

Terhal stood in front of Layla and smiled. "It's been a pleasure," she said. "You know what to do."

Layla opened her mouth to speak, but found that she couldn't, the pressure on her body too great for her to utter even a syllable. Orange light spilled out of her eyes, and her vision changed color.

"Be seeing you," Terhal said, and vanished from view, as a flood of power entered Layla's body, causing her to cry out from the intensity of the feeling.

Layla forced herself to extend her power as she noticed several more of her allies rushing to attack the dragon. Using the blades embedded in Mammon as an anchoring point, she took control of the tiny pieces of metal that made up the internal structure of the dragon. She dropped to her knees, the power too much, the intensity almost unbearable.

Mordred unleashed every part of pure magic he had at his disposal, Lucifer following suit, while Irkalla and Kase used their own power. Diana, Tarron, Remy, and dozens more ran interference, keeping the elves at bay, but Layla blocked it all out as she pushed the silver inside the spears into Mammon's body. When she felt that her power had pushed as much of the tiny parts of metal inside Mammon's body as she could, she pulled on all of it at once.

The effect was something Layla would never forget. Mammon's entire body was ripped to shreds as thousands of pieces of metal were torn out of his body in one go, leaving nothing but pieces of flesh in their wake. For a moment, the metal hovered around Layla, before dropping over her as she stopped using the power and crumpled to her knees, her skin returning to normal, her vision no longer tinged orange.

She looked around, emotion brimming up within her, and burst into tears. She'd lost too much. More than anyone should lose. She'd fought and fought, with no hint of stopping. Tearing apart a dragon as her friends bombarded it with magical energy was more than enough to send her tipping over the edge.

Kase immediately wrapped her huge wolf beast arms around Layla and held her. Remy ran up and held Layla's hand in his own, his words lost to her as her brain tried to catch up with what she'd done.

Eventually, Kase moved away, and Layla looked up at the worried faces of her friends. "I'm fine," Layla said. "We have a war to win."

She looked over at the battle, which appeared to be nowhere near as ferocious as it had been a short time ago.

"A lot of blood elves just ran away," Mordred said. "Most jumped in the river to escape and died in the process. A few made it across, but we'll find them. I have no idea how you just did what you did."

"Dralas," Layla said, leaping to her feet. The look on Tarron's face confirmed her suspicions. She ran to Tarron, who was inconsolable at the loss of his friend, and held him.

"He died a hero," Tarron said. "Oddly enough, he'd have liked that."

"What now?" Layla asked, looking around.

"We beat Abaddon and Mammon, and stopped Helheim and Yggdrasil from falling into enemy hands," Lucifer said.

"Not to mention saving the dwarves and stopping Avalon from getting their hands on Tartarus," Mordred said.

"My mom . . . ? Elizabeth?" Layla asked.

Kase stepped forward. She had reverted to her human form, and had found some armor that fit her. "I had to. I'm sorry."

Layla hugged Kase tighter than she'd ever hugged her before. "Thank you," Layla whispered. "Thank you for making it right."

The pair of them stayed like that for some time as cheers went up from the defenders of Helheim. Layla smiled, and looked back at everyone who had helped defend a city of people.

"We're not done yet," Irkalla said.

"Yeah, I know," Layla said. "But this feels like we did something great here. Something that people will talk about for a long time."

"We defied the devils," Remy said. "And beat the odds."

"And Avalon got its first bloody nose," Tarron said.

"Let's go help these people," Layla said. "The work is far from done."

25

One Week Later

The funeral pyre blazed high into the sky of Shadow Falls, as many of those who took part in the battle of Niflhel stood around in reverent silence as Dralas's body was sent to be with his ancestors. Layla spotted Tarron across the crowd of thousands, standing the closest to his friend's body. Tarron had been quiet and withdrawn since returning to Shadow Falls and had spent all of his time preparing to leave to search for any shadow elves that might remain in the realms.

As the night came, the somber mood turned to one of celebration, and Layla found herself having far too much of the dwarven ale that Vorisbo had brought back from Nidavellir. Vorisbo, who appeared to have trouble walking in a straight line, moved over to Layla and hugged her.

"My father's body has been put to rest," she said.

"I didn't know that Jomik was your father," Layla said. "I am so sorry for what you're going through."

Zamek joined the pair, offering his condolences to Vorisbo.

"My prince," she said, bowing her head.

"No," Zamek said. "Your father was your king, and the rightful line of succession falls to you."

"While my name has already been put forward as the next in line," she said, "I am a . . . science geek. I believe that's the right term, yes?"

"Remy?" Layla asked.

"He's been most helpful in showing me the ways of the Earth realm," Vorisbo said.

"He has?" Zamek asked, sharing a surprised look with Layla.

"He was sorry to hear about my father. He wanted to take my mind off it, so he took me to Maine and showed me around the humans who live there. It helped a lot."

Layla spotted Remy talking to Irkalla, Diana, and Hades. "That bugger is full of surprises," Layla said.

"I assume you will want to take over as king," Vorisbo said to Zamek.

"Not even a little bit," Zamek said, raising his hands to show he wanted no part of it. "I was never a good prince even when I was meant to be. I would be a dreadful king. Besides, I'm needed here, and I want to see if I can figure out where the vast majority of our people went. You're smarter than most, and more than capable with an ax and fist. Your father was laid to rest two days ago, so there's a month where people can challenge you. I'll stand by your side when that happens. Although, from what I've seen, most of the dwarves who fought beside us would happily do that job too."

"You have a month with no ruler?" Layla asked.

"It's a weird tradition," Zamek said. "No one rules, no one works, no one does anything for a month, or until the last challenger appears and the elders declare the mourning period over. Whichever comes first. I never liked it when my father was king, and I'm still not a fan of it now."

"You will do fine," Layla assured Vorisbo. "And if anyone tries to say otherwise, kick their ass back in line."

Vorisbo laughed. "Thank you. For everything."

Layla hugged her and moved away, saying hello to friends and allies on her way to find Hades and Persephone, who were surrounded by griffins.

"Lorin," Layla said, bowing her head slightly. "Thank you for your aid."

"We are happy to have helped," he said. One of Lorin's wings had been badly damaged in the battle. "We've decided to stay here in Shadow Falls until this war is ended. Tartarus is inaccessible from anywhere now that Zamek has changed the realm gate destination. I think we will do more good from this realm."

"Speaking of which," Persephone said, "did Zamek find out where he sent Abaddon?"

"The realm is uncharted," Layla said. "Zamek, Vorisbo, and Harry looked through the books they'd found in Nidavellir, but they found nothing. She is somewhere no one has ever discovered. We won't have to worry about her for a while."

"That's probably for the best," Hades said. "Gives us all time to deal with one problem. I thought you'd like to know, I received word that Avalon has withdrawn its forces from the other Norse realms. Or at least has disengaged the fighting. Apparently, the loss in Helheim was enough to make them think twice about what they need to do to win. They won't quit, and we have a lot of work to do, but this part of it is done. Helheim is safe. The Yggdrasil tree is safe, even more so now that Hel has posted several garrisons of griffins all around the mountain. And, most importantly, a large number of blood elves and powerful allies to Avalon have been vanquished."

"What about the remaining blood elves?" Layla asked.

"We're hunting them down as we speak," Persephone said. "And preparing for whatever Avalon might do next. But, right now, we're going to celebrate this win. A win we all earned. And most definitely deserved."

"I agree," Layla said. "But I won't be a part of it. I'm going to go with Tarron to find his people. Not only because it feels right to help him, but also because if there are shadow elves out there, we're going to need their help. If Zamek can find the dwarves, and we can find the shadow elves, and convince them to aid us, we could take all the realms back."

"Have you told everyone?" Hades asked.

Layla nodded. "They understand. I'll be taking Tego with us; she's currently swimming in the lake and eating fish, which is her own well-deserved reward."

The rest of the night went by in a bit of a haze for Layla, as more and more people discovered her plans to leave and wanted to come talk to her. She eventually fell asleep under a large tree near the palace, and woke up to find Tego lying against her.

"Good morning to you too," Layla said to the panther, who purred slightly, got to her feet, and walked over to Tarron, who was leaning against a tree.

"I wasn't watching you sleep," Tarron said. "I promise. That's weird, and . . . well, weird is probably enough."

Layla smiled. "If your enjoyment comes from watching a grown woman drool onto her saber-tooth panther, you probably have more problems than just being a bit weird. We leaving today?"

Tarron nodded. "There are some dwarves who want to come with us. Mostly, I think, because they find the whole thing fascinating. As is Hyperion."

Layla sat bolt upright. "Say what?"

"Yeah, he found me last night and informed me that he would be joining us. I think he doesn't want to be the leader of the Titans. It's a lot of pressure, and, frankly, between Hades, Persephone, and the others here, I think he sees it as a chance to take himself away from a job he never wanted in the first place."

"Sounds a bit like you and Zamek," Layla said. "Two princes who don't want to be princes."

"I said before, I was never a prince."

"Sorry, the son of an elder," Layla said with a flourish that made Tarron smile. "I'm sorry about Dralas. I really am."

Tarron nodded. "I know. He was a good giant. There aren't many like him, and I'll miss him a great deal. I'd like to find his people and tell them the news, but I'm not sure they'd be happy to see us."

"And you want to see if you can trace the sun elves."

"Yes, there's that too. They need to pay for what they've wrought. All this death and destruction, and they had a hand in it. It needs to be stopped. And I plan on doing just that."

Layla nodded. "Well, I'll be there by your side and hopefully we'll find them sooner rather than later."

"Before we go, Harry was looking for you. He's over by the realm gate with Leonardo and Antonio. I'll see you soon."

Layla walked away and found Hyperion on the outskirts of the temple, sitting against one of the houses in Shadow Falls that had become home for many of the Titans. Hyperion and his fellow Titans had been instrumental in the defense of the realm of Helheim. Hundreds had died, but not one civilian in Niflhel had been harmed.

"We won," Hyperion said. He'd received a cut across his nose and cheek that would leave a nasty scar. "We lost a lot to achieve it, but we won."

"I'm sorry for everything you lost," Layla said. "But I'm not sorry you came to help us. I hear you want to join me and Tarron?"

"Yes, that would be nice."

She got up and offered Hyperion her fist, which he looked at in confusion.

"You bump it," Layla said.

Hyperion did as he was instructed and smiled. "I have fist bumped before," he told her. "I just never expected to be welcomed so warmly. Hades himself has declared that we are to be as free as any man, woman, and child who opposes Avalon's rule. I'm not sure the rest of the Greek pantheon will agree with him, but seeing how most of them either work for Avalon or have hidden themselves away to stay out of the war, I'm not sure I care. Even so, our new status will take some getting used to." He unslung a sword from his back and passed it to Layla. "I want you to have this."

Layla removed the white cloth that was wrapped around it, revealing a beautifully intricate sheath of purples, blues, and golds. "What's it depicting?" Layla asked, unsure of the symbols' meaning.

"It belonged to Cronus," Hyperion said. "It depicts the uniting of the Titans against a common foe. In this case, the devils."

Layla unsheathed the weapon and held it in front of her, the blade gleaming as the light from the nearby fire touched it. It was perfectly balanced. "It's stunning, thank you."

"I saw you fight Mammon. I saw what you did. You deserve this. Cronus himself would have been in awe of how you defeated that dragon."

"I didn't do it alone," she said, feeling overwhelmed by people telling her how amazing she was.

"I know. And the fact that you know and acknowledge that means that you will be a better owner of this sword than Cronus was. Use it well. When you're ready to go, I'll join you in the temple."

Layla moved on, and stopped at the temple where Harry, Leonardo, and Antonio were standing in front of the realm gate.

"Harry, you asked for me?" Layla asked, as everyone else said hello.

"I just wanted a chance to say goodbye," Harry told her, as Kase entered the temple and ran over, giving Harry a kiss.

"You're official now?" Layla asked.

Harry looked sheepish. "I guess I overreacted about Tommy wanting to kill me."

"No shit," Kase said under her breath.

Layla stayed with Harry and Kase for a few hours, before leaving the temple to get breakfast. She found Chloe and Piper—Chloe's tall, red-headed girlfriend—in the house that had been set aside for their use while they were in Solomon, and the three of them sat chatting, laughing, and enjoying their time together. For Layla, it felt like something she imagined a normal twenty-three-year-old would do. When breakfast was over, Layla went for a shower and stood under the hot water for a long time, letting the aches and pains, both physical and emotional, of the last few days melt away. When she finished, she found a new set of leather armor on the bed, with a note from Zamek telling her he wished her all the best.

Layla got dressed and made her way to the temple with her friends. There, she found Tego at the top of the stairs, lying next to a large bag. Olivia sat beside the cat stroking her behind the ears.

"I packed it," Olivia said, getting back to her feet and hugging Layla tightly. "You're going to be missed. Keep safe." She turned to Tego. "You too, you big pussycat."

Tego flicked her tail in Olivia's face, making her laugh as Zamek activated the realm gate to Helheim. The library was Layla's first destination, and she hoped to find some clues about where the elves and remaining dwarves had vanished to.

Kase and Harry hugged her, then Chloe ran over and dragged her away. "I know you're leaving," she said, taking her over to Piper, "but I need you to know something. We're engaged."

Layla made a weird noise that made Chloe laugh. Layla hugged her friend tightly, before hugging Piper. "I'm so happy for you both. Do you know when you'll be getting married?"

"Not until this is all done," Piper said in her thick Irish accent.

"So, you'll be back, right?" Chloe asked.

Layla nodded. "No realms can keep me from being there. Also, a wedding will be a nice change from all the fighting. I'll be able to wear a dress. An actual dress."

Chloe and Piper laughed. "Glad you're so keen," Piper said.

"I never thought I'd give a crap about whether or not I'd wear a dress," Layla said. "But wearing combat armor for the better part of two years really gives you an appreciation for clothing that isn't rune-scribed."

"Take care," Chloe said.

"You too," Layla told her. "You're like my sister, and it doesn't matter where I am, if you ever need me, I'll come running."

Chloe hugged Layla again, and for the first time in the years since Layla had become an umbra, since she'd been thrown into a world of violence, death, and magic, Layla had real hope for the future.

Epilogue

Mordred

Two Weeks Later. Maine.

Mordred woke up in bed to strips of sunshine passing through the blinds of the nearby window. He looked over at Hel, who slept beside him, and smiled. *Don't screw it up*, he said to himself, as he swung his legs out of bed, stood up, and stretched.

"You are the single loudest stretcher on any realm," Hel said, rubbing her eyes.

"Sorry, I was going to go get a drink," Mordred said.

"Coffee, black, one sugar," Hel said. "Also a kiss."

Mordred leaned over the bed and kissed Hel on the nose. "Morning breath sucks."

Hel playfully punched him in the stomach. "Get me my damn coffee."

Mordred kissed her again and left the bedroom, going downstairs. Half a dozen buildings made up the hotel complex in the middle of the woods not too far from the town of Stratford, Maine, where Mordred and Hel had been staying for the last few days. Diana, Irkalla, and

Remy had all taken rooms too. Hades had practically ordered them to get some rest, although Mordred found the joke on them considering Persephone had dragged Hades away from Shadow Falls to one of the buildings across from where Mordred stood.

Each of the buildings had one bedroom and bathroom upstairs, and a small kitchen and lounge downstairs. There was a large TV facing a gray couch that Mordred was pretty sure had been made about fifty years earlier than anything else in the house. He switched it on as he filled the kettle with water and picked out two mugs from the cupboard. He retrieved the coffee from the freezer and spooned some of it into the French press.

Someone knocked on the door and Mordred opened it to see Irkalla, Remy, Diana, Chloe, and Piper, all of whom looked somewhat concerned.

"Umm, what?" Mordred asked.

"Are you watching the news?" Remy asked as Hel walked downstairs wearing a purple robe.

"What news?" Hel asked. "We've literally just woken up."

Remy darted into the building and took the TV remote from the couch, turning over the channel showing a cartoon that Mordred couldn't identify to the news. Remy turned it up.

"Our top story this morning," a male TV reporter said, "is the explosion in the town of Clockwork, Oregon. It appears to have happened just outside of the town limits, atop Mount Hood. The devastation we're seeing from our aerial pictures is incredible."

"Any chance that Avalon have started to go after civilian populations as a way to get back at us?" Irkalla asked.

"It feels like an Avalon move," Remy said.

Mordred had stopped listening to anyone and was watching the news with complete attention. "Someone go wake up Persephone and Hades."

Piper ran off as the others watched the footage from the news helicopter showing a partially destroyed mountaintop. The forest all around the crater—easy to see even from a distance—was ablaze.

"You want to tell us what's going on?" Hel asked.

Mordred shook his head. "Wait until Hades and Persephone get here."

It didn't take them long. Hades had sprinted across the courtyard between the buildings with Persephone close on his heels. Everyone piled into the small living area.

Hades clapped. "About damn time."

"'And I looked, and behold a pale horse: and his name that sat on him was Death, and Hell followed with him'," Mordred said.

Everyone turned to Mordred.

"You changing your video-game quotes for Bible ones?" Remy asked. "Because I kind of prefer Mario."

Mordred shook his head. "Just felt appropriate."

"What is going on?" Hel asked.

Mordred looked up at her. "I can't say right now, but I will, I promise."

Hel opened her mouth to argue, and closed it again, nodding slightly. "Okay, I trust you."

"It's finally happening," Hades said. "Sky needs to see this."

Persephone looked between Mordred and Hades. "This is something big, isn't it?"

Both men nodded. "This is where Avalon will wish they'd never started anything," Mordred said. "This is where we take the war right back to them."

"From this?" Hel asked.

"You might as well tell everyone," Hades said.

"Tell us what?" Irkalla asked.

"You all have a blood curse mark on your body, except Hel and Piper, who weren't there at the time," Mordred said. "When I tell you this, that mark will vanish and you'll remember everything that you agreed to have erased."

"What the hell are you talking about?" Diana asked.

"Nate Garrett is alive," Mordred said.

Remy, Chloe, Irkalla, and Diana fell to their knees as the memories that had been taken from them flooded back.

Diana was the first to look up at Mordred. "This is real?"

Mordred nodded. "That is almost certainly Nate Garrett coming into his powers."

"Then you were right about one thing," Remy said. "The only thing that could survive something like that is death himself."

ACKNOWLEDGMENTS

So, ten books published. Ten. It feels like I should get a badge or something, like I've leveled up as an author. I never thought I'd get to this stage of my career, I just wanted to keep writing stories that people enjoy reading as much as I enjoy writing them.

First of all, thank you to my wife for just being her. She listens to my ramblings and plot ideas without complaint, and I can't begin to think of a better person to stand beside me as I write.

My three daughters always deserve a mention, not just because I love them all, but because they're a big part of the reason why I keep writing.

My parents are still some of my biggest cheerleaders, and it's still both awesome and a little weird to see all of my book covers on their living room wall.

To my friends and family. Thank you. For everything.

As always, a big thank you to my agent, Paul Lucas, for his guidance and friendship over the years.

Jenni Smith-Gaynor has edited nearly all my books over the years, and I'd like to think I've become a better writer because of all the little comments and suggestions she makes. Thank you for your help.

A massive thanks to the OWG family. You all know who you are, you're all still awesome, and each of you played a part in me ever becoming an author in the first place.

To everyone at my publisher, 47North, thanks for your support and help. There are a huge number of people who work behind the scenes to make these books possible, and each of them is awesome, but a big thank you goes out to Alex Carr, who has not only supported my books over the years, but also has been someone I'm happy to call a friend.

To all of my fans and readers of my work, thank you for enjoying my stories, for sharing them with your friends and family, and for basically just being cool people.

So, book ten is done. I guess I'd better get started on book eleven.

ABOUT THE AUTHOR

Photo © 2013 Sally Beard

Steve McHugh is the author of the popular Hellequin Chronicles. He lives in Southampton, on the south coast of England, with his wife and three young daughters. When not writing or spending time with his kids, he enjoys watching movies, reading books and comics, and playing video games.